Edited by Michèle Aina Barale, Jonathan Goldberg, Michael Moon, and Eve Kosofsky Sedgwick

SERIES
Q

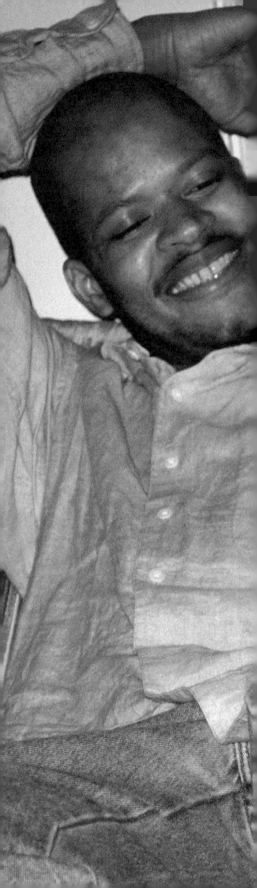

Gary in your pocket

Stories and Notebooks of Gary Fisher

Edited with an Afterword by

Eve Kosofsky Sedgwick

Introduction by Don Belton

Duke University Press   *Durham & London 1996*

Printed in the United States

of America on acid-free paper ∞

Typeset in Scala by Tseng

Information Systems, Inc.

Library of Congress

Cataloging-in-Publication

Data appear on the last

printed page of this book.

Contents

Gary at the Table: An Introduction,
Don Belton   vii

Walking   3

a cat poem   6

Tawny   7

"I hope he smiles"   17

Picaro   19

age of consent   23

Mo-day   24

Love in Prepositions   26

After the Box   27

geese on a string   32

Before Sleep   34

"Are you smart enough for Laurie"   36

Red Cream Soda   37

end of the semester   45

Little thieves   46

Games   49

Four men   62

Arabesque   63

"please, father"   68

Be-ing dead   69

Second Virginity   71

Cornerstore   78

Several Lies about Mom   83

From a notebook   86

Three Boys   88

cat sense   90

The Villains of Necessity   91

Journals and Notebooks   119

Afterword, *Eve Kosofsky Sedgwick*   273

Gary at the table

An Introduction by Don Belton

Gary Fisher's death came in a season of deaths of young black men I called Brother. During that bitter and long harvest, he fell along with the novelist Melvin Dixon, documentary filmmaker Marlon Riggs and my birth brother Morris who shot himself to death one Monday morning having abandoned his routine preparations to go into his downtown Philadelphia office.

There were others: a worker with the state AIDS project who had a brilliant collection of male black gospel quartet records from the 1940s; and an arts administrator I met shortly after moving to the Midwest to accept a college teaching position.

The arts administrator and I used to meet regularly for lunch in downtown Minneapolis to share ironic laughter and witness, fortifying ourselves against the systemic racism we both confronted daily in our ostensibly liberal institutions: I, at a college where there were and had been no tenured black faculty anyone could remember, and he at an arts funding organization struggling to have a vision of excellence and achievement that was not all white. And this was occurring, we reminded ourselves, not at the dawn of the civil rights struggle, but at the end of the twentieth century, an era in which half a century's promises were arriving void and betrayed, in an interminable harvest of the deaths of young black men.

Still, it filled me with wonder and pride, during those lunches in some bright restaurant or other where ours was usually the rare table occupied by anyone black and always, in any case, the only table occupied by two black men having lunch together: the spectacle we made in those belligerently "white" spaces. Indeed, we were more than a spectacle. We were a manifest sign. My dreadlocks had begun to bloom. His short hair, fastidiously clipped, looked like the rich, cultivated bush along West Africa's coast. There was a ceremonial sense of theater about those lunches. With our foppish work clothes, our polished conduct and our audacity to always demand the best table, we told plainer than words, not only the entire room, not only the continental United States, but the whole world, that there was no power—no matter how subtly or overtly racist or homophobic—that could ever extinguish our humanity. We laughed, agreed, and argued, mind to mind, eye to eye, brother to brother. In those moments he was what Gary was for me, what Marlon and Melvin were for me, and what my birth brother, nine years my senior, would never scale the stony wall of black masculine silence to become: a chosen brother.

Among these deaths, only my blood-related brother's death was unconnected to AIDS. I remember thinking what a chilling reflection it was on the current statistical value of a black, male life in America that I would personally know so many freshly dead young black men. It is even more chilling that most of those men were fierce cultural workers, ranging from Marlon, who with his film *Tongues Untied,* and Melvin, who with his novels *Trouble the Water* and *Vanishing Rooms,* were just beginning to fully emerge professionally, to Gary who had yet to publish his work.

My relationship with Gary was vital for me, even intimate, although we never met face to face. We were introduced by Eve Sedgwick. Eve and I first met in the winter of 1993 when we both made presentations in Winnipeg, as part of a Queer Tutelage reading and lecture series. Eve asked if I would permit her to share my telephone number with Gary. He was, she said, a dear friend who would enjoy my conversation; whom she thought I might enjoy; a former graduate student of hers writing stories that crossed a compelling intersection of hegemonic borders.

In some senses, the telephone is the most intimate venue for encountering a new friend. The communication is focalized around two human voices courting and sparking. Gary and I had several phone conversations between his first call sometime in the summer of 1993—a tentative answering machine message ("I got your number from Eve . . .")—until his death in the winter of 1994. Usually we talked late at night when the rates are lowest—sublime, circular, queer conversations from which I gradually learned about his life and his writing.

Gary was thirty-one when we met. Though he had been writing since he was an undergraduate and had written a number of stories that circulated among a small circle of friends, he had never published anything. Gary seemed ambivalent about the machinery of publication. "Where can a black, queer sociopath get a fair hearing anyway?" he once said to me concerning his chance of gaining a public voice. Still, he was very interested in how I managed to publish, the process through which I had gained a teaching position and traveled as a writer and a speaker. In turn, the process through which he had developed an internal sense of himself as a writer with little external affirmation of his practice interested me.

Our conversations wove together elements of dialogue, confession, and storytelling, touching on anything from sadomasochistic fantasies (specifically Gary's such fantasies and my own terror of even entertaining any such fantasies) to our love for black pop divas (in my case Diana Ross, a sort of populuxe Nefertiti, and, in his case, Dionne Warwick, the essence of integration-era cool). I don't remember how many times I'd spoken with Gary before he mailed me his stories. The manila envelope included nine stories and a covering letter, the second paragraph of which began: "A couple of months ago I got very sick and a weird sense of urgency possessed me and my writing. I want to get this stuff in a book."

I don't remember precisely when I learned that Gary was HIV-positive. My friend from the Minnesota AIDS Project came out to me about being HIV-positive after he shepherded me through my own HIV test, which turned out to be negative. I found out the arts administrator was HIV-positive at the same time I found out he was dying of AIDS. He had missed a couple of our lunch appointments. Then, by telephone, he said he was going away on a retreat. The next week, a mutual friend on a visit to an ailing relative at a suburban hospital happened past a room where our brother lay emaciated and struggling to breathe. He hadn't told anyone he had AIDS. As for Marlon, I knew he was HIV-positive before we met, because he engaged his battle with the modern plague as an integral element of his art. Melvin and I met in Paris at an academic conference. He attended a panel where I presented a paper on James Baldwin. Though he had at first been expected at the conference and his name was listed in the program, his appearance was, upon my arrival, in doubt because, participants whispered, he was ill with AIDS. There was an aspect of triumph about his appearance that winter in the Sorbonne lecture halls where we attended other conference events together, his presence that of a shining, listening witness. I will never forget one particular event during the conference at which Melvin was acknowledged, and a famous black, male novelist said during the discussion, "I don't know why all these faggots have to be here!" I won't forget that the insult had the strange effect of seeming to make Melvin's countenance shine even brighter though somewhere the wound must have been recorded in his psyche as it was in mine.

Gary talked about his illness and his fears as freely as he talked about his pleasure and desire. What I most vividly recall thinking when I first read the stories he sent was that the experience of reading Gary was an easy extension of speaking with Gary. As a writer, he had captured a precise and powerful voice. What dangerous and crucial writing, I thought. Here was a writer recklessly exploring the lines intersecting race, power, masculinity, and desire. Here was a writer whose work challenged the literary canonization of the kind of narrow black identity that would lead a "real black writer" (and "real black man") to decry the inclusion of "faggots" at a conference on black writing. As well, it was clear to me that Gary's work would not be available to standard forms of white patronization, because of the work's obsession with critiquing myths of white nationality and white masculinity.

The imperative to constantly reread success is an essential piece of the enduring American legacy. Given our particular history, black Americans especially must create a discourse about success that gives centrality to notions of freedom. Within such a context, black failure, if only for what it instructs about black resistance, is as worthy of study, even celebration, as black, so-called success.

When I consider that Gary never published during his life or taught at a college or university, I am certain that this reflects no failure that was his. Gary's achievement of the words collected here, as well as his survival for even thirty-two years, very likely owes something to the fact that he did *not* publish or teach. Gary's sense of urgency during the last year of his life to see his work collected in a book was tempered by his mistrust of public recognition. Gary did not write for publication, and this simple fact makes the requirement for his publication at this moment all the more urgent.

The young, black, gay writer is too easily rejected, and therefore, too easily compromised by our society. Because Gary failed to offer his work for rejection or celebration, it holds for us many unpolished truths and naked pleasures. His stories and diaries galvanize the project of disrupting the presentation of black gay masculinity as always without agency. That he accomplished this without romanticizing black gay identities is all the more impressive. Because of our national myths of masculinity's colonizing power, black masculinity remains always feminized, always subjugated within the national discourse of white male power. Gary's work touches still — painful, still — bleeding wounds borne in the abiding love and warfare between black men and white men in America. Because Gary imagines an interracial desire in which white masculinity can be objectified, he has begun a new skirmish in the sexual revolt that has been going on for at least a century. Gary's unflinching witness advances us all.

This collection is a resurrection of the power and seduction of Gary's conversation. It is a good vessel of Gary's voice. Since my conversations with him began two years ago, Gary became implicated in my attempt to find meaning in the spiritual tropology of the welcome table. Within black cultural and religious tradition, the welcome table has been a metaphor for a place of undying witness, communion, and, by extension, community. An old black church song runs: "I'm going to sit at the Welcome Table / Shout my troubles over. . . . / I'm going to feast on milk and honey / One of these days!"

Last year, while visiting Eve at her home in North Carolina, she showed me a photocollage she'd made of Gary some months before my visit. He looked as I imagined him, a beautiful brown man with startled eyes and a flowerlike mouth, indrawn, quizzical. He was seated, with a satiated look, in Eve's living room, his head inclined in an attitude of listening. He was, Eve told me, listening to a Dionne Warwick record.

Stories and poems

Walking

In my fatigue, and my beer stupor, I still moved more effectively than the living (wait, let me justify this page here; I can't stand a crooked line), one dead foot before the other, dead hands pocketed, in fists around my keys and around some change (not enough for anything—not even sugar) so nothing would rattle or chink. I walked as steadily up the hills as down them, not a robot, not even inhuman, because I felt the pull in my calves (would have to rub them when I finally stopped) and then I felt the threat of gravity, several times, but not for several moments after any step taken, indeed well into the next step. Dead foot in front of dead foot—it registered late with me or not at all, and never once like the most basic mathematics (like it might for a kid, or a carpenter, or a blind man)—I couldn't keep count to keep distance to save my life; at best I detected a rhythm, a groin-level sinus-thing, strains of a song I'd heard. Probably Schoolly-D, because that's where I was walking from. That's where I'd seen him, the white man I was returning to (but soon to be waiting for) and that's where I'd left him after the crowd had changed from half black to half empty and mostly white, slam-dancing (though rather politely) to some local darlings. Left him, 'cause he was the only thing to keep me there and I was afraid he would notice how I watched him, like he was the only man in the world and I was the only woman.

But I never was a woman, and I never was white, never even pretended to be a little, the way he could pretend some blackness, bobbing his head and throwing his fist to fight-the-power that he actually was, that most of those on the floor who grabbed up the posters and the 12" cards and cassette tapes of "Am I Black Enough For You?" actually were, while the black people, us who looked like black people, chilled in the dark corners—overwhelmed by it all, or def-fer than it all. I knew that this man understood the very margins of a history that had brought him to this borrowed outrage, brought him to it so cleanly, so thoroughly, with such conviction that if I hadn't met him before and didn't know a side of him so fantastically white—the very horrific myth of white—I could have sworn he was a mix with at least one parent at stake (or, perhaps a mixer, with one, two, maybe several children to defend), or even better, a white man with a black sympathy so single-minded it bordered on psychotic—indeed, his conviction dwarfed the fashionable and startled the mighty rapper himself; Schoolly-school had to slap hands with him twice to drain off his charge, had to look him in the eye when he called the collective audience his fag and groped himself—"this is my weapon and you want it, you actually paid for it—hit it!"

I knew better, or differently, or at least more about this particular white person, and I had to make sure that he noticed me enough to turn away, to laugh in gestures too wide with his friends, to drink and smoke and churn his strong body with an oblivion too complete to be unconscious—enough to turn away but enough to remember why, and then enough to fuel his occasional but great rotations about the room, eyes like beacons into every crevice, till they touched me and registered nothing. Nothing—but like the notch in a ring, something he had to finger over and over again, till it felt familiar, though I think he recognized me instantly as I had recognized him. Good sex, like hate and love (and violations of their integrity), seldom calls for a reacquainting of the parties (unless it's an orgy). But if I'd left my stoop then when he failed to see me, and walked up to him (instead of half an hour later walking out of the club, away from him) we would have been friends, even brothers in the battle against the powers-that-be for all of half an hour. He never would (would never) have returned to the scene of our first meeting, like I knew now he must—for having not seen me, but having detected an important lack of something, he had to be certain of what he was already sure of.

So I knew before the show was over, before I was halfway up the hill, well into the mist-shrouded park and aware of being out of breath and cold and so tired, and allowing all those little discouragements (from which I'd walked so steadily away) to finally graze me—I knew he was following me. First in his thoughts, then in a curious stride, angered, even gimped towards his sexual vengeance—a violence of near-consent or of no-consent but his own which overpowered mine in the court of the park—and nothing of such maladies ever went further than the park; the most casual remark of it went unheard, the most fervent cries got drowned in laughter or jeers. He would have his way with me in doubles because I had dared him in his own house, had threatened to call his politic "fashion" when it wasn't that at all, when it was actually stronger than any young militant black man's of some education who thought he could fight power with words or with borrowed money and still have white friends, stronger than any white woman's who, while she knew oppressions by names and remained sensitive to even the as yet nameless sources, had to endure a revitalization of the myths that made her so knowledgable and sensitive to begin with, like a fast child in a slow class, she only has to be careful not to separate the myth as it comes from the black rapper from the proprietary caress of her white lover who tells her to shut up and dance to it.

a cat poem

like a boy
like a song taken up
like a cat trying to nose
a hand up
off a table top
and onto its own flat head

or leaning
headlong into edges
of open books
or stacks of folk records
or chinese vases
of day old
yellow flowers
tipped white
on ledges of
high-slender
wood
stands—

daring
to scratch itself,
softly determined to
affection
low-rumbling
small black engine
of aimless nosing
love

forced on a man
under a man
who'd just as soon
keep his hand
flat pressed
to the table

Tawny

> Now, God, lay me down to sleep.
> I pray the Lord my soul to keep.
> If I should die before I wake,
> I pray the Lord my soul to take.

He listened to his sister, and imagined her hunched over, praying carefully into her tented hands. The wall was thin between their rooms, and since the head of his bed met the wall opposite hers, there was no helping it. He lay there with every word at his ear, every pause, every minor breath. Perhaps it seemed like a punishment to him that she should be so good, so consistent, and he should have to listen to it. You couldn't pay him money to be that good, he thought, not all the gold in the national reserve, not a million dollars; you couldn't bribe him with candy and cars or soldiers or trilobite fossils; you couldn't preach to him about hell and his mouldering bones because he didn't care, and from this position, he did violence to his sister's prayers. He held his breath, made his head like a drum to block out the prayer's upper range—

Now God lame down twos.

He worked air and spit in and out the hollows of his cheeks battering the words as they arrived—

Pray, dullard, my soda keep.

His mother saw it, but didn't recognize it in the games they played—movies mostly, death and mayhem after school, a bright, noisy child ring around the four houses of their cul-de-sac. She said he was gloomy, that his movies were gloomy (and generally they were), and that his gloom got in the way of school work and praying-to-god, not that the latter amounted to more than a twenty-second nod at dinner (which the father looked as though he could do without) and perhaps a full minute before bed on weeknights; then general godliness through the weekend and the Sunday marathon (which the father did not attend), sufferable only because of the chicken and corn and Kool-Aid in the middle and again at the end of it. But that wasn't it, that wasn't a little bit of it. He couldn't explain to her that light-ness, not darkness, broke on his path, that the chicken and the bright noise got in the way, or that when he was studying he often couldn't see for the pieces of picture, the pieces of poem, and the longing for the un-utterable, the unknowable in those pieces. If he found a page in his book cut through by someone else's bookmark, or cut across by a used postcard, a dried leaf, an old water ring . . .

Voice That Day
Car And Gray
Crowd As You May
Honored For Ay . . .

or if in the men's part of the big fall catalog he happened on a young man with no middle (his sister and her friends raided the pages in the older catalog for paper dolls, so he expected the weird renderings of impatient cutting and tearing, the near con-fetti that he found there, demonstrations of the constantly chang-ing girl mind), but if in the new book, where he too rummaged for fantasies, one of the young men should have only head and neck . . . then bare knees and socks the next time he looked, the innards torn out along an honest line and no doubt sent away to a long name in the Midwest with a money order to become school clothes, then what of it? He would tolerate that from her; he couldn't deny her that part of mothering. No, it wasn't the sud-den lack that defeated him, but making sense of what remained. Her idea of light? He took Christ off the nail every night after she left him and slid the picture, face down, under his bed. Her idea of light was worse than his blindness, worse than not hearing; he couldn't bear to be watched in his sufferance.

His father rubbed the toe of one heavy boot with lighter fluid; he held the boot at arm's length, like some misshapen creature regarding its own hoof, and when he brought the flame to it, to burn off the old shine, the blue light set itself, gem-like, in his eyes. His mother said she was talking to *him,* not to his father. *He* was the gloomy one. Couldn't he and that Nolan boy find other things to do?

He listened to his sister bless their parents and their cousins, Viletta, Asa and Harold, and the Nolans next door . . . the Shimshocks across the street . . . the Birchams and the Hicks . . . and he wished she would bless every soul in Logan Heights—in all of El Paso even—because he didn't like sleeping. Their dog finished its barking and collapsed against the slatted gate near a hole that was once a knot, where the moon got in now and threw a long, accusing finger toward his window.

When he wasn't praying for his mother, his own prayer was a shortened, muddled version of his sister's, which he could call up quickly and repeatedly when he needed it, like a chant.

> Naga lama slip
> Prada lama skip
> Fasha daba fake
> Prada lama stake

Their dog whimpered in its sleep, no doubt reliving the chase, the jackrabbits it couldn't wear down. Mother waited patiently at the switch for Bug to say "Amen," but his sister was just finding a happy rhythm and started blessing multitudes she didn't even know. When she had blessed the family a second time and the president as an afterthought, and was starting in on the neighborhood pets, the mother wearily, but expertly, nudged her into bed. "Say Amen," she said. They both said "Amen" and the light went out.

Tawny shut his eyes tightly and made preparations by habit and by feel. He turned up the small radio on his nightstand, just loud enough to discern its presence in the darkness—"like, I don't see how you can, mama," it said. "I speak very very fluent Spanish." The small bright sound was his sanctuary, but not enough by itself. He built a tent around himself of pillows and covers and, hot as it was, he lay there flat, unmoving on his belly like a lizard under black shale. He labored to keep his eyes shut, the pellets of color shooting off from the main in his head; while his ears, as sensitive as any blind child's, groped for sounds that might threaten his link with the radio. He was often more concerned with the threat than with the song itself, but then he knew every refrain—he collected refrains—so, like his own guard, he could walk the walls of his sanctuary thinking, defending, measuring his time in refrains.

> Don't you worry 'bout a thing
> Don't you worry 'bout a thing, pretty mama
> Cause I'll be standing in the wings
> When you check it out

He listened for anything through the walls that might be his sister talking to herself (she did that), or his father talking to his mother still sewing in the last minutes before ten o'clock, after both his boots were done and sat unreal, like Indian-glass statues of themselves, beside the bed.

When his parents had settled, and had been settled a long time, he might register the uneasiness of his own heart, or the buzz and churn of the refrigerator, or some stray gurgle from the toilet—this from the ear that pressed hard against the mattress, feeling more than it heard. The other pulled with its thick, blind fingers at what might as well be a strand of sugar. The tinny pipings of the radio seemed stronger when the house was settled but they were always at the mercy of darkness itself, and the strafing moon. He clung to Bug's little breaths and the rustle of her bedclothes, and held more fearfully to the father's powerful, rolling snores, certain that every lapse, every sputter, was his waking up. Mother was a given perhaps; he never heard her until it was too late.

He was forbidden to play the radio at night when he should be sleeping. "Even your ears want some rest," his mother would say, and if she woke up and came into his room to kiss him or whatever it was that she did with the few quiet moments, she might pull back his covers and expose him.

Bug mumbled then, half asleep, "God, give me some yellow shoes," and Tawny felt the fierceness leap into his throat (Shut up, you) he thought, gathering some of the damp sheet in his fists, but she had already answered him, even before her spoken words agitated the darkness between them. "No, God, give me a Suziehomemakerkitchen and a Littlekittledreamhouse—" (You shouldn't, he thought. You've had your time). His sister sighed and turned from him as if to say, My time? My time? What's it to you? "—but most of all, God," she continued, "a red bicycle, with a banana seat and a wheely bar—a real sparkly red!"

He couldn't not love her, but he could hate her passionately; he could deny her everything that didn't overlap with what he needed (Don't give her anything! Not even switches. Not even ashes. Not anything). Then he waited and waited, thinking a litany of shutup-shutup-shutup and certain that he heard her (My time? My time has just begun. You won't ask Him, so I'll ask Mom). She forced him to hold his breath for half-minutes at a time, to seal up all his vulnerable passages against her, and her foolishness, until she had exhausted herself and fallen asleep. He listened to her wheezing now—she was probably lying on her nose—and held still for fear of waking her.

Holding so still, he was only vaguely aware of the slippage as his guard relaxed and fatigue began to loosen him. If he caught himself now the process would begin again. If he became lost from the radio in his half-waking, and actually felt the mild nausea of descent, he would resist and the process would begin again. But if he drifted and fell as it fell and remained cradled in a song to the end, he would go there, to sleep—not necessarily to where she wanted to go, but to sleep.

> Two spirits dancing so strange
>
> Ah! bowakawa pousse, pousse
> Ah! bowakawa pousse, pousse
> Ah! bowakawa pousse, pousse

He heard a fly but mistook it for part of a song. He was dreaming softly and the fly was moving in and out as if by design. He watched Bug moving through Thrift City with their mother and Mrs. Rankins and her four-year-old, Tawanda Makisha Rochelle. Tawanda is short, as he dreams her, short, sharp and womanish. She is proud of her hair and of her new dress, and wears it straight-up, bosomy, like Mrs. Rankins wears hers, pinched in an oldish way. She makes the ride to Thrift City a gash in their sides, twitching her ruffled shoulders, hooking one knee over the other. She can't sit still for preening. The song says:

> nhoJ, nhoJ, nhoJ, nhoJ

They pass through layers of dust, rainbows around the street-lights. Bug hates her, perhaps him, and picks a scab. Mother turns the wheel aggressively as though she were dueling to the death with the will and forward momentum of the car, and he is thrown into Bug before he can stop himself. He shoves away enraged, but . . . Tawanda says she's seen even scarier turns when her father drives. Mrs. Rankins, fanning herself violently with an old *Watchtower*, mutters: "I don't suppose you can do anything about this heat." But his sister waits quietly now, grinning inside, he's certain, and not at Tawanda, and not at either mother, but at him. Thrift City is a warehouse on the edge of town, the last thing before the gas stations and drive-throughs give way to desert. Miss that turn and you'll be on your way to White Sands, New Mexico or the petrified forests of Arizona, hopefully with pop in a cooler and a bucket of chicken and your father and Mr. Hicks belaying your ear with nightmare stories of Asia and all the words you've been told not to use.

Inside, Thrift City is flat, with low naked girders for its ceiling. Tables stretch back and out for half an acre, maybe more. The closer ones, loaded and buckling under the mountain of black shoes or patent leather purses or five-pair-for-a-dollar black socks, attract with their simple, dumb masses, like slow roadside cows, or the baby elephant at the petting zoo. And the mothers approach them warily, still mothers, still practical, while the children threaten to break loose in their awe. Tawanda springs free, squeezing, jerking, twisting, or in some way appropriating every object within her reach. For a few moments, until the adults realize what she is about, everyone follows the four-year-old. Then Mrs. Rankins slaps her for pulling down a row of colored scarves, and the frivolous magic ends. Bug seizes up in horror, and is suddenly a dead weight on Mother's arm. That Mrs. Rankins should display her mothering! But already Bug is beyond it—and already feeling foolishly—aware that every thirty-five seconds a young girl is humiliated by a mother playing mother. It is only the excitement of possibilities that lets a girl forget and compromise herself again and again in this way. So here she is, not even knowing the scarves are linked, and a hundred times more surprised than Mrs. Rankins who seems to anticipate these things, who always comes to Thrift City with her mothering laid bare waiting for such things as this, and Tawanda never disappoints her. Bug might be thinking, "girls will be girls," but hardly believing it as she strains her neck to take in the wonder of linked scarves. A magic trick perhaps, but for Tawanda, the worst of luck.

"Oh, look at this," Mother hollers and they trot off after her. All Bug can see are the quick feet of ladies and little girls on the other side of the tables. Mrs. Rankins says to Tawanda she's going to switch her ass but good right there in the middle of Thrift City! "Do you want that?" she says. "Is that what you want?" The girl has stuffed a pair of white gloves into her purse, but not quickly enough, and the fingers stick out like something a frog or a lizard has eaten. Two old ladies look up from a bin of canvas sneakers so that Mrs. Rankins can glare back at them until they go away. She is hardly an adult, Mrs. Rankins — Bug has heard her mother say as much — and already having a four-year-old as shrewd as Tawanda . . .

A blue light surges on, a siren, and a man with a megaphone says . . . , but it is Mother that they listen to: "You've got to get here early-early-early on a Saturday," she sings. There are only t-shirts at the blue light. They can't even smell the big blue plastic bags of popcorn, not yet, not from here. And the dresses are a few tables yet. "This place cleans out on Saturday mornings, nothing left by lunchtime except men's stuff. You have to know what you want and you have to grab it before somebody else does." Bug knows what she wants. It's the others that seem confused, she decides, who are liable to grab just about anything (Ah, but knowing and getting aren't one). A patch of ladies grope heatedly at a table for blouses, many of them one-handed, burdened by their mannish daughters who would almost certainly run if not for a strong grip and an equally strong threat (Knowing and getting are two).

They plow past these ladies and through lingerers at a shampoo and lotion display, and she's forced to consider knowing and getting (if they were the same you wouldn't have to wish, you wouldn't have to beg, you wouldn't have to waste so much of His time) as her own hand strays toward a possibility — lipstick cream, brow pencil, a yellow comb — grazes them, leaves them, reaches back when they've drifted beyond reach. The few men scattered about wear sales aprons or sit half-crushed in packages. Bug sees a male hand pinch a taut gray skirt, but the woman's hand is quick to correct it and soon there is space between them, a brief agitation, and then more space between them.

They plow into the smell of popcorn and suddenly into girl things, silly dresses, ruffled bonnets, colored bangles and hair-combs, but Mother, on a whim, turns full around and leads them away. She buys some throw pillows, some earrings, and a green halter top. Mother is about to try on an awful hat when the siren sweeps over them. "No telling whose head's been in these," she says.

Leaving the store with a package of three handkerchiefs and a small box of Chicklets, Bug is bitter to the point of tears. But she will not give them the satisfaction of seeing her cry. Instead she scratches the skin off her wrists; she scowls and lags and fidgets until Mother feels obliged to take her gum and smack her hand six little pats that sting her pride more than anything. She doesn't cry. Her face darkens with hate and blood, but her heart almost bursts when she notices the peacock-blue scarf, as poorly concealed as a flag—and no one else seeing it—hanging out from under Tawanda's yellow dress. She wants to holler, but Tawanda doesn't know she knows, and there can be no real satisfaction without her knowing.

> Voice That Day
> Car And Gray
> Crowd As You May
> Honored For Ay . . .

He found himself saying it, charging ahead of them, the figures in his dream, hounding them, saying it to their faces; as if they would know what he meant, as if by repeating it and waving it in their faces, it would come to him what he meant. But no one seemed surprised to see him, and no one tried to make sense of him, because it was his game and they knew it and wouldn't humor him.

The siren blared close, then fell away. He had an unguarded feeling of great loss, of unspeakable loss, waves of loss and misery for something he almost had, or that his mother almost bought, or that he almost stole, but didn't, and now he couldn't recall it; even as it rumbled through him a last time, he couldn't name it. He shook off his wetness. The pillows were wet, the sheets wet and cold and smelling faintly like the arbutus that clung to their slatted gate. His covers were back, his chest exposed, and the radio—! He couldn't hear it for a noise that dropped low past his ear. He groped at the covers, but what good were covers without the radio? He sat upright, felt the moonlight graze him and fell back. What if his foot disturbed something at the foot of the bed? What if it poked out into the open air, prey to the thing at the foot of the bed?

The fly punctuated his fear with tiny sputtering buzzes; it touched his nose and he slapped at it; it glanced off his bare shoulder and was once again a singular black particle in all the darkness. He leapt out of bed and raced to the light. For an instant he stood blinking, half-dazed, suddenly cold and suddenly tired, but his task seemed clear enough. The fly was wiping its transparent wings, unafraid, on the edge of a book. He pounded there and the book fell away; he pounded again where he thought it might light and upset a battalion of painted soldiers and some month-dead nickel sea horses at the bottom of his fishbowl. The fly zig-zagged to the ceiling and twitched. Had he grazed it? startled it or in any way disoriented it? It gave a lively buzz and continued cleaning. Challenged, if not inspired, the boy made the bed a springboard for his attack; he plunged into it twice, flat-footed, knees cocked for maximum propulsion—the third time he would launch—but the bed gave him no lift. Instead he felt an excruciating crack, length-long, even before he heard the wood holler, then the lower half of the bed collapsed, not violently, not like anyone watching would expect and secretly desire it to, but folded itself down like a great dying animal, and for a moment left him in mid-gesture, a cartoon, a tamer of wild beasts.

Bug was calling Mother, and perhaps heard her wake sighing the sort of pat exasperated way that said, "calm down, child, nothing he could ever do would surprise me"; then moving with a mother's dry and shushing in-urgency, the way she once moved to change a diaper or to get the mail (back when they were still shitting their pants and too little to reach the mail for her), the way she prepared herself for work in the mornings, as if she meant to get there when she got there and not a moment sooner.

Tawny looked around wildly, felt there was nothing to do with the remaining time except kill it, and kill it convincingly. The fly circled him twice, gathering speed as he raised his arm, tracing little rings above his head, but ascending out of reach before he could get a hand to it; then it floated lazily to the far wall where it suddenly occupied two places at once. Mother was calling him now and Bug was calling her. He listened—beyond his mother and sister—to where his father began to move; and with strange fury he ran to the wall and struck it. His eyes tossed back, his body arched, his mouth gaped open in surprise, and surprise obscenity: "shit! shit!" He felt his palm against the one black spot, as the other, unobserved, buzzed cautiously and sped away. When his mother reached him he had pulled his hand down and was studying the little hole, winking and reddening for him like a tiny flower. He looked up, up past her concern, to where he had tried to kill a nail.

I hope he smiles.

I sent a card,
walked it over
actually.

I hope he smiles
and doesn't notice
that I've manufactured
this,
walking it over
slipping it under
his door
five or ten minutes
before he'd find it
there,

like it'd been there
all day waiting,
precious with time,
precious with waiting
more his than mine,
the transfer made
that long ago.

I hope the dog doesn't
find it.
I slipped it under
carefully,
but a dog might
hear it.

Perhaps I should have
thought this through:

a dog might hear it
and couldn't be held
responsible.
Indeed, a dog
could only act
as it would.

It would be pure
accident,
a dog chewing up
my careful plans.

It would seem
more likely than not
that a dog
(given his good ears,
and his playful nature
and five or ten minutes)
come in contact
with paper-and-
ink product
would act just as
it should.

It would be
an accident
if it didn't, and
if Bob found this card.

If Bob finds this card
I hope he smiles
and I hope he calls
and I hope it's not too soon
to start hoping
against hope the way
I do,
we all do,
bringing cards that we
should be sending,
expecting
miracles of dogs:

dog don't be dog,
Bob don't be like
other Bobs.

Picaro

He's big, black and strong, his body an aggregate of hard things refusing to accept his situation. Yes, he smells bitter and his eyes are red-rimmed from running the nights, but he moves like an athlete and comports like royalty. We watch him with parts suspicion and admiration, and wonder if he'll break the frail wooden chair he sits in. He's chosen a corner table slashed by plants and crazy shadows, but every patron in the cafe knows he's there, and when a short time later he goes to the toilet, the specter of him seems heavier and darker than his actual person. It doesn't matter that he's failed to leave a cap or a jacket or a book; the territory feels as marked as any cave dwelling or dung heap. And because he is so much with us we feel responsible for what is stolen from him.

When he returns of course three white punkers are trying to make a bunker and nest of his space. Me and Vita wave and shake our heads, but not enough, and the noise in the cafe swallows up my feeble protest. "Isn't someone sitting there?" I ask Vita and I point and I gesture and I clear my throat.

Greg watches his colored alter-ego with narrow eyes. Sure he is tired and his eyes itch, perhaps because they sit in a fat ray of sunlight (that reveals the dander in the air and the scratches on the table) but those eyes fix on the second Greg and cut paths of suspicion and blame and vital hatred into him. Not like he might shoplift something but like he already has and poorly conceals it. Why is he glaring across a bum table in a Mission cafe into the soulless eyes of a nigger with the same name if nothing has been stolen? Because it makes him stiff and warm all over. Because it makes immediate and easy sense of the full leather he's wearing on a sunny day. —Hey, dum dum! he measures himself, I think. He is hungry too (almost four days of emptiness haunt his temple) and thirsty like a motherfucker. —Go get me some food, this he orders casually enough but he stabs the money—large bills—across the table like a jeweled saber, as though he would execute his nigger (eloquently, mind you) or carve a suspicion into his wide forehead, arabesquely so it filled the most space. —But nothing for you, shithead. *Shithead* he incises through clenched teeth just loud enough to alert the neighboring table of a rift, an error in the weave of things (perhaps the wrong color or not enough of the right one or an area of stress in the fabric, terminal) but not sincere, not yet enough to make them look up from their just emptied capuccino cups.

Brown is what the dykes hear and brown is what they continue to study, even the remnant foam and scuz where the best of the sugar settles, this seems tainted now and no one dares slurp it down. One woman smiles at no one else in particular and crumples her napkin and fills the cup with that, stealing perhaps a peripheral second of the ugliness between the black and white Gregs. She too is dark and has played sex games too demeaning to describe. She's played with men and with women, with white ones and black ones, honestly believing each time she could craft some affection out of what looked and smelled and tasted like hate.

Did she witness Greg's mean and immutable arithmetic? He might just as well order the colored to kneel in front of him. — You should never be more than half of me, he might instruct. —In public you may be slightly less than half of me, nigger. In private you'll fold for me one more time, one fourth! one eighth of me! and I'll pinion your arms behind you and strap them to your legs. You'll be naked but folded, so like a dirty letter you'll remain mostly concealed and no immediate threat to me or to other white men, not even—ha ha!—when, like truffle dogs, we save you from your own noxious sump and nose away the mud and shit and moldering vegetable of you to reveal your tender still-living holes, fragrant with, of course, every previous violation. What white man wouldn't buckle (even especially those iron-willed pioneers and astronauts who make a home out of the void and then lend their names to the boundless multinationals that secretly or at least quietly mushroom out of the stinky genesis of our relentless rape and comic overseeding of every black slime [the black-against-blacker object of it or at last the horizonless black event of it, called *blackness*—reviled out loud as the thing called blackness, a bright painful clarion of announcement, if not acknowledgment, that this thing exists and could continue to exist alone if it were not so rigorously bound against self-awareness or even simple masturbation; and if it were not kept gagged against that single signal utterance of self that, by itself, would explode the very germ of whiteness—the subatomic, atomic, galactic and ferromythic moment and every pus-y accumulation of the white germ; and if it were not kept magnificently confused, that one-in-a-billion happy baby, though cosmically blind and stupid and as yet unborn, too stupid to struggle against the aspic of its birthprison, and fortunately too stupid to be smothered by it, proudly imagining itself the tensile equal of the stuff it waits in but frightened and repulsed by the recurring dream of a thicker, richer self within the snot, unmoved by anything except the strongest agitations from outside the mother, it refuses to acknowledge its intuition of stagnation until stagnation becomes an addling, and one day a pernicious rot and finally a large stone that, even though it kills the mother most horribly, gets mistaken for the child, while the real child of blackness, blackness itself, meditates on its relentless innocence and discovers a great hole that might be ignorance or just a great hole, and it gets buried with the dead mother in some unnamed pit and slowly begins to forget itself turning to stone (a glory of sorts) or devolving itself past rot, through mutation, and into a vapor, a vapor that is not even a memory; and perhaps only within the random frictions of erosion and the occasional sparks among the gentle heat of decay can this child wonder. Even God can't imagine blackness so what kind (and degree) of accident would it take to just *remember* the parents, the pregnancy and the name they wanted to give the kid, let alone save the actual child or see it reincarnated. In this way a nigger will always submit but he might also internalize a craziness which could spark and spread, mutate and spread, and perhaps one day become the form and foundation of his architecture or a firestorm.]—or such iron & travertine-strong monoliths to the white Nebraska man-boy and the outdoorsman as would circle the communities where these types live, or would buttress the granite and travertine buildings that house the institutions and businesses where these types work, or would garnish the walls of their cultural centers, or, most frightening, could metastasize within a song by the Pet Shop Boys or an austere black and white ad for Calvin Klein underwear; or those who lust after the tough beautiful vanguard of the neoclassical movement and those who obey or even flee the sexy gargoyles that inhabit it and those who risk drowning to be saved and redeemed by the brave white lifeguards of the gene pool)—what Tom and Jerry wouldn't wobble and blur and eventually flip along their vertical axes influenced and temporarily enfeebled by the rare-metal strangeness and weight heady aroma of a black hole?

age of consent

am too!
> are not,

am too,
> are not,

older than you are,
> > are not,

am too,

> I'm twelve,

I'm twenty,
> I'm fifty,

I'm a hunnert,
> I'm a hunnert

THOUSAND,
> I'm a million billion—

Children, hush!

> —are not,

are too,
> I'm the same as you,

are not,
> am too,

I'm dead,
> me too,

I was dead BEFORE you were born,

> > > not me

I'm infinity,
> me too,

are not,
> am too,

are not!
> am too!

Mo-day

Kitchie didn't like Mo-day much. She called him to her once when he was just a floppy brown-patched puppy and he started off in her direction with real earnestness and conviction (I saw this myself—! and understood it more deeply than I care to describe to you), but poor Mo-day, halfway there, got molested by a flea. He never made it to Kitchie and she never called him again. Their relationship had been on the rocks ever since. He was fourteen now in dog years and she, for three years, had had her MBA from City college but still worked assembly at Motorola. When she came home she would ignore the dog. She would ignore his shit on the driveway and not even cut her eyes at Tawny, her oldest son, who knew it was his job to walk the dog in the desert. Because the dog, which was originally bought for her and presented to her like a living gift with a red bow at Christmas time, was now less than nothing to her and had become the kind of gash in her adult life through which all her ambitions might fall, even her children; which she didn't dare look at or even acknowledge because she so often felt less than nothing herself and didn't need such a graphic reminder, especially in the mornings when Mo-day was most apologetic (had been for all fourteen of his years, and perhaps left shit in her path more as a gift than an annoyance or even a reminder, because what could a dog know about annoyance, and what could he know about human hopes & dreams and the nostalgia that ferments in the same waste can with these); he was much too tired after noon and found shady places to abandon himself like a carcass afraid of desert flies, but expecting them. If he followed Kitchie at all after five o'clock when his dinner was unceremoniously dropped, it was with the slowest roll of his wet eyes, indistinguishable from a sigh or a gesture in slumber. Indeed Kitchie seldom bothered to look for the dog, to drop his food anywhere near him, or in anyway like an invitation for him, and he wouldn't move toward the food until she was well gone and her indifference well forgotten—he waited this way instinctively so he would not, over the course of many meals, come to blame the food. Her motions had become as abstract as her reasons for going through them, and in sympathy the dog had pushed the facts of her (and her even less-interested children) into the furthest recesses of his own dog mind, the way someone might order snapshots in a plain drugstore album, box the album with others and forget the whole collection in a dusty spider-ridden attic. He forgot her and as a consequence, he forgot himself—more and more often, he forgot even to seek out the shade (forgetting first and foremost his need for seclusion and the apology implicit in this, then thoroughly forgetting the peace it afforded his old dog body from sun and desert flies; forgetting also that he never knew he was named after *Monday*—the day Christmas fell and he was given & received like a gift, and then, for the next three human years, *Monday*—the day Kitchie hated the loudest)—he forgot even where it was safest and easiest to forget these things. He forgot this and fell asleep just outside the kitchen door, the last place Kitchie could expect a sleeping dog to lie, since it had been months, perhaps years, since she had imagined a dog (let alone remembered this one) outside the murkiness I have tried to described to you.

Dear God—! at first she thought it was an abandoned child, another brown child—the last thing she needed but the first thing she would think of because there was grace in all her burdens. She felt this and believed it and lived it, from that moment on, without much question. Kitchie gave up fourteen more of her own years to Motorola, even after she realized her mistake.

Of course, tripping over the dog, she broke her leg and chipped her tooth. The dog did not recover as fully and, after many months' patient observance, he was dealt with humanely. I sobered up soon after this and moved in with Kitchie and her kids (more like her oldest son than her old man), but that was okay. I could still help her forget things, she said.

Love in Prepositions

I don't want you to love me. I don't even want you to like me. I don't need these abstractions of you. I might want you to want me, I know what want is and I know that after the third time (arbitrary as three is) you must know want, mine or your own (mine from yours), and you will respond to want with more want, at least a second one. So, maybe then I want you to want me.

But more than all that, I want your prepositions. I want the little yous. I could list them here: in, on, around, under, over, between, near, next to, on top of—now it's getting too large; the little yous is all I want, probably all I need. I'll list them again for you, but in context, that is, with body (validity, actors and objects of prepositions and with vigor, at least implied): I want you *in* me; I want you *on* me; I want you *all around* me (forgive the little flourish there); I want you *under* me (on occasion anyway; but mainly) I want you *over, over top of* me, *on top of* me (to flesh out that earlier, 2nd earliest, scene still more); I want you between me (—?—or more exactly *in me tearing me apart*); I want you *near* me; I want you *next to* me (fearing [calmer, less intrusive proximities, the only actual proximities] that *near* won't be *near enough,* that someone nice could get *in between* us), I want you next to me and nobody else; more precisely(?)—I want you, and nobody else, *next to* me and nobody else (such that no body else *resides* on both sides of both of us, except the side closest to us; or, rather, *between* us [closest to us being one being (and one being too little) and not valid in a world of prepositions] so, rather, excepting the side we share between us) I want to remember you as you were in relation to me.

After The Box

Sam and I closed The Box on Thursday night. We bitched about the white men we didn't get, while following one of them up the street. Thirst and frustration got the better of me, and Sam wouldn't follow a white man alone—so I suggested we get something "juicy" from the convenience store across the street.

"I think we should become lesbians," Sam said, not smiling, "black women have all the fun."

4th in line, with a large, cold bottle of cran-raspberry juice—my clothes soaked through and clinging, but still warm, still rather sexy . . . Then the store filled with clubbers—their shirts open or off, sweaty and fragrant and loud, threatening to burst the space with their leftover charge.

Maurice towered above us all and spoke too large and too freely. He said he remembered me now and swung his horse-hair extension; he flashed that liar's gap between his teeth and sucked two fingers seductively. Did I still live in the neighborhood? he asked. I nodded. He had moved to Oakland.

A black man and woman entered in Thursday-night TV-watching drag, but puffed-up with threat and discomfort, exaggerating their unity.

"You see it's a lady," the man said to me. "Why don't you move?" But I didn't and most of the conviction drained out of his stance and spilled on the floor. I looked at her feet as she passed me and, I believe, she looked at mine. Life had fucked us both over pretty good, so there seemed little ground for confrontation. But suddenly, crippled with ladyness, the black woman fell into her man! In an overlit, understocked cornerstore full of black folk (most of us faggots) mock courtesy would have played well. No worse than a crutchless woman anyway, I thought. I should've fallen first. Now I was embarrassed, too embarrassed to move.

"Why should he?—he's a lady too!" The woman burst into thick convulsive laughter, much too large for the store. I raised my head and took her in like I was raising the curtain on a burlesque.

She was a fat woman, well-mixed, with a round face and petulant eyes. Her reddish hair, pulled up and back, boasted heathery blond supplements that she'd knotted like curtain tassles. Still her voice fell rich and dark against my pale, skinny, gentrified responses.

"Ha—ha—ha!" was the best I could manage.

Even then I could have left it alone, let her bask in the cheap glory of it. If the man had been larger I would have, but we were about the same build. If he had been a shade darker, or if his hair and clothes had been more street—

But I said as they reached the beer cooler: "Honey, did that make you feel like more of a woman?" Gesture and pitch took lives of their own—sharp, nervy and all angles like giant fruit bats—but I was flying with it. "Like a natural woman?" I poked. I forgot about the man entirely, he could have been a can of beans, even though she was wrapped around him.

"See what I mean?" she said, "See *just* what I mean?" and she tightened her grip on the hapless man, secured her meaning somewhat despite a quicksheen of confusion that fell over him as he opened the cooler. He and I, same size, cancelled each other out. It was the faggot in me versus this woman and some desperate, malicious thing in her. (He stuck there, semi-conscious, like food, and she made all the preparations.) Was I a threat to her man, or just to her? —I so wanted to be a threat to somebody, but I didn't have the face for it, the clothes, the manner. I felt best suited for watching.

"I don't see it," I said. "I don't see what you mean. Why don't you *show* me." I shook my head and twisted my foot and tried to look like I'd seen it a million times.

"You're just jealous!" she jabbed, and like a thick sauce she poured over that quiet man. I watched her skirt hike and catch the thicker edge of her stocking; her ankle and shoe twist to envelop him, fingers writhe and find purchase above the swell of his forearm. She ground into him. "You *are* jealous!"—she almost screamed with pleasure, grinding into all of us some point too strange for that moment. Instinctively I took cover—hand over my eyes, face drawn up like I smelled shit. The man stood still and dumb, rather proud of himself now.

"Jealous of what?" I said. But I might have said "of who? Jealous of you?—*you?*—jealous of that white shit in your hair? I'm not jealous of anything you've got, honey—*e*specially not him!" I wonder now, as I rethink it, if I meant any of that. I *was* jealous—as jealous as she thought I was—jealous of what I thought she had, what I thought it meant—jealous enough to lick her mean little pea-colored shoes! *jealous! jealous! jealous!* — enough to lick and lathe all her warm brown loaves of flesh—right through those outraged purple elastics!—and jealous for the mere sake of it.

But I did not desire her black man. Puffed up with a pride, not of peacocks or even inanimate treasure, but of stupid flesh—a glazed ham for instance—he tried to taste his own worth in the mouths of others.

"—fucking-faggots!"

Whatever she said came hushed and hurried, and venomously directed toward the malt liquors. The man, sturdy and erect now, might have become a real threat, but he was totally bound in her. Short of a violence that levelled her too, what could he do? where could he take this?

"—faggot-faggot-faggot!" Repetition seemed to make her less dangerous, but without empowering me. "Faggot," like "nigger," still wasn't a word I could rally behind, so I dug for the courage to cram this excess back down her throat. Why should I take this?—I asked myself; I could be a bitch too!—indeed, there's no distance at all between "lady" as it was used against me, and "bitch."

Go figure?

It's fuzzy now, but dad named all our female dogs *Lady* (and all the male ones *Pharoah*, except for a psychotic one that got called *Shotgun*). If it made a bit of difference to any of them, you couldn't tell it; they licked you or bit you by some other criteria. The names (with that one exception) went nowhere toward explaining dogginess to me, let alone the dogs themselves. I think now it made more sense to bark with them, to get down on all fours like our mother told us not to and run with them, to thrash about with throw pillows in our teeth, and to put our faces down into our plates.

I could be a bitch too. I could be the last black leather bitch! I certainly would not be undone by a term as imprecise as "faggot." Now, call me "cocksucker" and we have something to talk about. Or call me "curious" because the truth is I don't know how girls pee, let alone how they cum; I don't know how any boy could know enough about a girl to keep from hating her—but I'd like to, and I'd like to answer all the things that make you hate me. I wish I could answer for him too, but he's a piece of meat; indeed, for as long as he thinks he's the object of our desire, he's meat.

I had physically cancelled the man, and now I hoped to disturb him. I wanted his disgust, even his contempt; I wanted him to slip in it. He would not leave here with respect for me, nor with understanding, sympathy, or any form of pity—not for me. I had none for him. I owed him no explanation, no reconciliation, no way out of this—short of violence or sex (oh, sure, he could plug his ears or he could run; I wouldn't chase him or rape him. . . .). But even if she stopped egging him on long enough for him to realize we were both jerking him the same way, she could not shield him; and she had no power to contain (or prevent) the thing in him that had to hate both me and her in order to claim a sexuality. We two, woman and faggot (all she got, mind you, was what she thought of me)—we two wrapped ourselves around this dense, turgid thing and held firm like the two snakes that pillar medicine, architecture, various national symbols, and at least one saint; this thing that tagged women "ladies" and made faggots pay glittering homage to straight codes. And we weren't white!—the confusion should have wrecked us.

It was our wrap, hers and mine, that kept this thing dense and turgid in the first place, that pulled it up from common meatloaf, and gave it spice and prominence on the plate. But we weren't white; we understood this as food.

My challenge imploded. I said: "Why don't you *show* me what I'm supposed to be jealous of, huh? Why don't you get busy right there in the aisle, huh? Go on; take it off; fuck it, breed *something*; show me what I'm so jealous of. I'd like to know."

"Fuck you!" she said.

"No, fuck him!" I snapped back.

They stood still, their embrace suddenly an indictment. Then: "faggot-faggot-faggot"—a last-ditch effort to stomp out the rising flush of embarrassment that seized the whole store, a corrective to bring us all back to our senses, to who we were (at least a few minutes before), but the stench of biology hung in my nostrils now. I already knew I'd lick her cunt, with or without his cock in it!—but I didn't know how to ask for it.

Violence would have been appropriate now, acceptable; violence would have been a relief. It might have cleared the air. Instead they bickered about malt-liquor.

I *knew* I had arrived at something, something larger than the sum of all that had passed. But it was just the cashier—dark, gaunt, haggard like a speed freak—beckoning for my money. Sucker or licker, we were all still slaves to this thing that flashed foward as he rang me up. It was not of the sleepy Saudi himself (indeed, it was too quick), nor of anyone in this store (it was regal, mythic, blood-in-the-face stuff) and yet I found a name for it as he slouched toward me and waited, as he looked at me through his rheumy all-night eyes and asked again for my money.

Actually, I was shut up tight about the time I got to the register. The man had regained something of himself, and he stifled the woman by the malt liquors. As they approached she muttered a little something about respecting me and my kind, and I muttered it back at her as best I could. But I could no longer see her; just him in drag!

Maurice was gone. Sam stood outside with his fists screwed into his hips, like a bit of punctuation. The juice cost $2.69. "Prices," the cashier said, "go up after two." One block south this same cashier would have been shot dead over a single dollar and change.

geese on a string

An old man's got a lot to do
getting his shit together, he says,
putting his ducks in a row, and
his geese on a string—

We watch him, but from differing
places—me from back of the ghosting
beans, Jeannie across the two meats,
and Grammy sliding the pitcher out
the way. We come together in seeing
him, but it don't mean we know any
more

—A goose's constitution, he
explains, is weak and such that a
piece of fat meat
tied on ordinary twine
can't nary settle in his
stomach fore it's passed,
and meat and string now
on the ground wait
for the next goose, for
all of them, if you remember to
knot the open end

Zum, twenty geese in order on one string!

God won't take a man any other way.

Grammy's old eyes is firecats now
—Shut up, old man, shut up this
foolishness!
But I go to the screen
to see them in the dusk,
in waiting

The old man is too weak
to stand alone and with one hand

on my shoulder, he watches—we
watches them,
and they watch us back.

Before Sleep

My teeth were clicking out the *House Acid* (*Acid House?*) mix of a Mel and Kim song and I couldn't quite coordinate my own steps with the flight of steps. An egalitarian flow of things and actions, it seemed like the trees were moving past me,

and the cab was advancing sideways as steps gave way to a rusty gate, grass, some sidewalk and in seconds the yellow cab door. I wondered briefly how they got the cars so yellow, and whether the paint was fluorescing or light was coming from some other

source. It was the new moon, and I wasn't that stoned, so I looked back and saw Frank's porchlight going out. The flagstones that pushed right up to his door seemed splashed in an oily blackness, and then I felt, tasted the mist. It was 3:30 and the

dispatcher had told me over Frank's phone that cabbies couldn't honk at 3:30 in the morning, that I would (just) have to keep an eye out for him. So, even though Frank himself said he could hear cabs (and could tell the difference between them and other cars), I parted the

heavy drapes, ponderous things with their raised, blood-orange paramecium design and rubber backing, so I could be sure. He was microwaving Chinese food (apparently that was the half-hour delay—9:30 instead of

9:00—and I thought he was there with Susan, his nervous connection, trying to smooth out what she owed him in favors and what he could get out of her in crystal. My nipples hurt, and I had been fucked up the ass by a man

with the positive mark on his last two tests. He hadn't come, even though we both had talked about how exciting it would be if he were to come, in my ass. Telling each other *someday* with too little vitality to pull it off, he slid out of there. I lowered

my butt, easing the tension on the ropes around my ankles, and he maneuvered urgently to put the dewy thing in my mouth for the finish. I held the liquid in the side of my mouth till I could get to the green towel he'd been using to

wipe my greasy ass between fucks while I told him in a near swoon how good it tasted ("and good for you too!" he'd said huskily after some previous session).

I wondered if I could break a tooth clicking them so hard to that *acidhouse* beat. I wondered if I could find that half a valium ("tens" Frank called them, but I had cut mine in half with some scissors, sat for three minutes in a stupor,

microscopically surprised that there weren't fragments, dust; it cut so clean I was sure it would work as two "fives"). I was surprised when the male driver turned out to be a woman with broad shoulders, not that the longish, hastily chopped

yellow hair, abrasive as a doll's, hadn't confused me, even beyond the masculine construct of her ancient leather jacket and the slanting black cap. She said—as if it was the tail end of a lot of driver-passenger ettiquette that I'd missed—"I was just about to

come get you. I know, I haven't been here that long, but you don't know how much prey has flipped out on me tonight."

I didn't know if she was really talking to me. After she closed her door, which, all this time, she'd been holding unsteadily ajar, doing crazy things to the interior light (crazier things to the trees; I thought I saw Frank's mad, long-haired cat race into the next yard), she

adjusted her mirrors, but didn't look back at me. "It's either breakfast," I said worried that I would bite my tongue, "or bed." I had heard everything she said, but went with a prepared line. "I've got my magazine and a few hours to kill."

. . . . Are you smart enough for Laurie
Anderson yet, I said
And she called, Tru, we're on the
corner of Central and Shattuck, do
you want us to BART or will
you come for us. We're here now
It's up to you . . . up to me?
then come get us . . . bye

She won't like you for that
we're in love, she said
that's how we stay in love,
she said
Saying just what you feel?
Just what we *mean.*
Oh, I said, getting wishy-washy
There's no bullshit, she said

But bullshit builds some sturdy
walls, some high sturdy walls,
I said, what's a friend without
that stop-gap of bricking bullshit

Acquaintances, she said, they're
acquaintances. Bullshit's so
sticky . . .   It dries, I parried
and it smells, she jibed . . .
it always smells, I agreed

And Tru met us at the corner
We recapped Laurie, best we could.

Red Cream Soda

Not a week after they found out how sick I was Randy started telling me his stories. He didn't seem to hear my protests; and would literally pull me from my work kicking, spitting, cursing him, into our common space, a small room made unbearable by a huge arthritic sofa bed and a cinderblock concoction that served as a table, there to make me listen to him. The man all but foamed at the mouth in his urgency to get them out. I call them stories but the scowl that met my doubt made me wonder. I didn't *not* believe my friend; it was simply easier to feign doubt than to show my true discomfort over what he was telling me. They were descriptions of the sex he had had, and was continuing to have, almost nightly—anonymous sex, reckless, vindictive sex, impassioned and yet loveless, somnambular sex, with bodies he could hardly see.

He paced as he told his stories, and gestured, urging my attention, my understanding, my quiet conspiracy. If in my discomfort I laughed out loud to relieve some tension, he would become wildly agitated, dare me to move, or rap on the glass table top as though to demonstrate here and now the violence he had been relating (not to mention that which he was capable of); and I cannot call his interpretations anything but violence. He would rant now about the force of it—how I wouldn't believe the force, the depth, the cruelty of it; and how he had countered all with an equal, opposite force of his own, not to escape, but to whip, strangle, and impale himself even more cruelly than his tormentors, like a jesus, he said, ecstaticly self-crucified.

"You don't honestly believe that, Randy?"

"What, that it was like martyrdom?"

"No, that they—those men—were actually trying to hurt you. Most of the men you'd meet in those places, they wouldn't know how to hurt you. You practically have to pay to get hurt in this city."

Randy watched me as though he'd been defending a high moral principle and I'd called him a liar. It was a hot, inspired, evangelical stare, his blue eyes gone gray, his hair tossled and full of lamplight, his big hands against his jacketed chest, frozen in mid-gesture like a pair of birds about to explode off a red crest.

At that moment he was the last man on earth you'd expect to see *forced;* I couldn't imagine it anyway. Then the life seemed to drop out of him and he sat down. He fumbled with the tab on a can of pop, got it, and began sipping, gingerly, afraid of spilling the liquid, I thought. If this had been a commercial—and it had all the markings of one—Randy would have turned the can up, breathlessly; and water from an unknown source, a quenching rain from a clear blue sky, would have pounded his blissful face. I'd never mused on the violence of refreshment, but I almost laughed out loud when I thought of it. The can of pop didn't come to life for me until he opened it even though I'd noticed it as he stood in my doorway insisting that I give up half an hour. I watched the can instead of him, telling the can instead of him, no, I really had work to get done.

He could joke about the way writing sinister-little-stories absorbed me, but when he did get me to sit and listen to him he wouldn't tolerate my funning him. Somehow the acts he relived for me were beyond what the two of us could create, beyond what I could write, and beyond what he could tell me, though the combination was a dangerously close approximation. And I found myself anchored by that little red can of pop, which I hadn't really noticed until he drank from it. It was a wrinkle in the dark, crazy fabric he was weaving, deliriously wrong, and fortunately so, because I might have gone back there with him, back to his moviehouse, his wooded hill, his secluded beach, the library restroom, for christssake, *gone back to a library restroom,* as if the idea wasn't already low camp in my mind. He wanted me to go, and I pretended to go, but some large part of me stayed, with the can in just the corner of my vision. I was safe in things I understood, or so I thought.

He talked on, more pleasantly now: things he'd seen on the trolley ride home, a woman with cadmium-yellow hair, five boys dressed as stars (one-tenth of the fifty states they explained to him), a Negro man with deep, black gouges in both his cheeks, like he'd been attacked by two cats at the same time and in the same way. All the time Randy sipped cautiously at the can of pop as though he'd just opened it and was afraid of spilling it.

He didn't ask me to, but in the weeks that followed I kept a diary of his stories, his "encounters," as he called them and insisted they be called. "These men, these events," he said slowly as though he were dictating to me there in the living room, "everything I'm telling you has happened, and continues to happen as we speak, and will continue for as long as there are men, I imagine."

Sunday, March 29   If I ask myself why I will go crazy. I must think I'm Joe Christmas, running toward my own disaster—ha, ha—as if I could beat it to ground zero and in that way avoid it. If I ask too much I'll die, so I'll just tell you what I see and smell and feel and helplessly imagine during those dark and formless times. Am I feverish? I'm certainly still flush with it, aren't I, still flush with sex? It's because I can't catch my breath; I can't catch up with my own not believing this (so I can hardly expect you to). Start with this French man—Alain, was it?—and his awkward Aryan body. I thought he was German; he looked enough like me, in the face anyhow. I kept thinking Nazi-Nazi-Nazi, but he was speaking French to me, in my ear, rapid, very personal, very sexy, and he had a big cock. I tell you, I would have let him go all the way, to the end, to the absolute end, plague and all. If he had asked me I might not have said "yes," but you can bet I wouldn't have said anything—but he pulled out, and that was okay. It was like a movie, I tell you, arching right over me, three times! We were in a secret spot of his—I'm sure I couldn't find it again in the middle of the day—we were down in a trench where the sand was clean and soft like beach sand, and a little warm like it too. It was so dark; the moon hardly broke through the scrub, so I don't know how, or even *if* I saw everything that he did to me, or everything that I remember seeing on him, and on me, the harness, the clamps, the studded collar—all of it so vivid I can touch it now, with my mind, but I don't recall which senses were involved at the time. He tried to put his whole hand in me. . . but I stopped him there. I told him I couldn't take anymore. I lied to him; I said that I had already climaxed.

Randy finally collapsed in a chair. Having paced rigidly for an hour, forcing out the night's story in a series of false starts, stutters, and breathless intermissions, he sipped from his can of pop, what might have been the same can of pop on the same strange night, under the same as yet unexplained circumstances that all of this started. I questioned then his need to tell these stories, and the sanity of disclosure in general. Yet I would sit so passively through the next installments, neatly bound and gagged by what could only have been disbelief; forced to listen because I couldn't stop his talking, like the unsuspecting psychoanalyst roped to his own couch while the lunatic roams and imposes his disease in much the same way the analyst, given the chance, would impose the cure.

Thursday, April 2   I was against the wall on the right side, the darker side. There were mirrors on the other side that reflected, refracted the movie in disturbing ways and threw its moving light on the men. I preferred the dark on the right side and drew up beside a familiar middle-aged man, pasty white—though it could have been the light—and more nervous than I remember. Funny how his anxiousness calmed me, and how his appearance pushed—not pulled, almost pushed me out of his way. Tall, thick-eyed, lipless man with glasses, severe, crusted virile-looking nearing-old man . . . Jesus, that gross fuck in the black suit was lurking near, trying to get my cock in his mouth, but I wouldn't give it to him and then the tough pasty man could have given his to either of us, but he went for me, and I lowered myself to him, sucked him quick to keep him interested while that sick, suited fuck looked on, his eyes still lurking, his mouth gaped, twisted, ugly. I sucked him to hardness, to a buzzing calmness, then he went to work, very actively, thrusting, talking to me, to himself, low but roughly, thrusting the words into me, asking questions and forcing back my possible answer. In a flurry of action, in a flurry of whispers he began to strike my face, dull and hard so it made less sound than his voice and his breath and the wet rapid entry. I felt trapped, afraid, trapped and exceptional—the suit had backed away—I heard someone gasp and I may have reacted for air, then suddenly I felt other dark dwellers leap into the spaces around me, and the man let loose sharply in me. Almost immediately he was pulling away, not ungrateful, but like a man who didn't do the tea traffic often and wasn't going to stick around to help out his suckers. I was drawn into a sea of bodies almost as soon as the old man pulled away.

"Why are you telling me this? I don't think I want to hear this."

"Is it so much of your time?" he spit, and the soft glaze that had fallen over his face disintegrated. His eyes became hard balls, pieces of lead, aimed at my head.

"It's not that," I said cautiously. "The things you're telling me, Randy, I wouldn't tell you."

"And I wouldn't ask you to."

Saturday, April 11 Why was he telling me this? I didn't want to hear I love you, not from him, not from big William, standing there in his skivvies, unconsciously licking his lip, but I suppose it's as legitimate a fantasy as any other. He hadn't said it yet, but when I kissed him he tasted like almonds and spoke right into my lips. He said it felt right, just right, and put his heavy arms around me like a warm coat. If I wanted to I could stay the night, if I wanted to I could stay the week, I could wear his underwear and use his toothbrush, I could cook him breakfast and lounge on his deck all morning while he did his four hours, and he hoped I would think about him, even miss him, and be hot for him at lunchtime when he'd bring champagne—it would have to be champagne—and some chocolates and we'd go for a drive along the cliffs, maybe stop to watch the otters, the sunset, the fog. Leaving the cliffs he'd prod the coals under our suspended heat—"there will be sparks tonight. Count on it, baby," he'd say in a voice deeper than I'd noticed before, and he'd kiss me so roughly I'd think it was at least half contempt, but the arm would remain, reassuring me as

he drives, faster and faster around the sharpest corners—
"I'd stop a flying bullet for you," he'd promise, but then one
could imagine him on the other end of the gun as well—
faster and faster into traffic like a heavier, molten substance
into water—Did I want dinner now or cocktails? "Stay in
the vehicle while I takes a leak." Dinner in Berkeley, Bad
Brains at the Stone—he'd see that I got slammed. Can-
did hands, eyes—he'd hold me wherever he damned well
pleased, no punk, no Rastah, no brothah-man, no fucking
nun was going to challenge him here. He'd prod the heat.
He was going to rape me so tenderly. . . .

Had I said three words?

Randy and I kept a relaxed house. I did what I could. He
seemed to understand that, and on weekends he did the bigger
jobs. Picking up after our Saturday session I nearly bumped over
an open and full can of pop. The tabloid next to it grabbed my attention—Randy had circled two of the personal ads in heavy, red
marker—so I didn't immediately notice the pizza sauce on the
can, a dried, crusted half-circle the shape of Randy's big thumb—
but the ads were asking (practically begging) for Randy's type,
and from the sort of guys he'd been describing in his odd reveries
these two would fit in nicely. I still hadn't figured Randy, why so
many? was it really a numbers game with him? or couldn't he
find the right-one? Suicide dawned on me, but why might he try
to kill himself and in this awful, lingering way? I'd met sick men
at a few of the support groups who said they were still at it, still
meeting in the parks, in the restrooms, at theaters. They balked
at my surprise and explained to me that they weren't the guns
—they wouldn't goddamn themselves with murder—no, they
played the victims. One man said he did it for control, because he
liked to believe he was in control of his own dying, that he had
made an adult decision and become a victim. Another man said
he did it to keep from asking who, why, how—that the faces, the
bodies, the love of so many men had absolved any solitary one
of them. And then, didn't some people become addicted to their
own poisons and begin to reason that the disease was the cure, or
that their personal cure was hidden somewhere within the topi-
ary of their personal addiction. He'd heard of young men taking

small doses of arsenic each day to keep a healthy flush and to eventually preserve their own corpses. They died of hidden cancers, but they died beautiful. And it was a beautiful young man that explained the need for *real* killers. He wouldn't be destroyed by anything as vague as a virus; it had to be larger and preferably handsome; it had to be stronger than it knew so the young man could call it accident or fate or God. Then the pizza sauce registered on me—it had been more than a week ago, that nasty pizza. How had I missed the can in all that time? I decided quickly that Randy had hidden the thing in the refrigerator, that it was probably flat now, that it must have been flat last night when he sat drinking it, that I would throw it away, quickly, quickly before I thought any deeper into the matter. But I picked up the can and sloshed some of the red fluid onto my hand. It fizzed. I could see it and I could hear it, and this was plainly a new can of pop—not a week old, not a night, not even an hour. I stood in the floor perplexed dropping leaves from the tabloid. Had Randy been home? Had I—?

When Randy came in we both started talking, frantically. He had a new story and somehow that won out over my hysteria. He was talking and dragging me with him to the kitchen where he took the can out of the refrigerator (where I had put it instead of into the trash certain that I'd stumbled on a bona fide mystery) and began sipping it carefully so he wouldn't waste any.

"Randy—" I began but he shushed me and pulled me with him back to our room to begin his story. I'm not sure how much I heard or how well it translated that night into my feverish script, but I wrote until my hand cramped, then pushed the notebook and pen away violently and went for some air.

Monday, April 13   It was cold and black—I'd never seen it so black. I walked the block to the park suddenly relishing the darkness and the moisture and eucalyptus odor in the breeze; the tree branches, high up, rubbed each other sharply, whistling. I responded to a welcome I'd never known before, felt drawn, not blown, but gently sucked in by the whoosh and whistle of the branches, by the cool, black odor, the freshness of earth and night sky at the cusp. The woods accepted, then encouraged me and I soon found myself near the night figures, in their arms. One man couldn't get enough kisses from me, another pressed up against my back like he'd straighten me out, but then abruptly bent me in two. He chewed at my nape like a mama cat and threatened me with harder bites and a stronger grip when I tried to shrug him off. I thought I'd let his fantasy run its course, but suddenly there were two more men, grins, *staccato signals,* lazars in the jungle, and I suppose I wanted it all, but I was uneasy and tried to tell them so, but my mouth, my words were no longer mine. My wrists felt the bite of a rope, my head, strong instructive hands, my knees and shins, the moist ground. The hours melted as the men changed shape and the trees began to pitch more wildly.

When I stood and shook loose from my bonds I discovered it was only flimsy twine and, for a reason I may never understand, that angered me. The humiliation rose up and burned my face. Vengeance was offered me instantly like a gift after a prank and I had to walk around it twice to make sure it wasn't a second trap. He had his head down, a big fellow, skin so white in the relentless dark that I thought a light had been aimed at him to make him glow. Our movements were so quick, so coordinated that I didn't have time to sort out my motivations, let alone consider that he might have some. I didn't talk and he didn't ask me to, but I fucked him full, and raw, and angry—angrier that he'd been made so available to me, that our coupling had been sanctioned, singled out even by unconscionable light. When I felt the first shudders of my soul threatening, and stepped back from myself to determine the half-life of my own shrapnel, I knew I was going to think about it too long, that I was going to pause right here with my finger on my chin and all that thought in my brow while my cock killed this man, and, as if he'd heard me, Randy looked around—I rushed into myself, like a mother racing after her little son racing after his ball into the path of oblivion—he looked back and told me to shoot it, to shoot it in him, that he wanted it, and I tried to pull away from him but he backed up with me—and I could feel it welling up in the chambers even as I redoubled my efforts to pull away from him and as he doubled his to stay with me, and locked like that, like two dogs, we tumbled over and down a grassy hill into a cool stream. Sometime during the fall I pushed him away laughing and we unravelled our white guts like ribbons along the slanted, rushing green.

end of the semester

Eight or nine poems
only eight or nine
of the hundred I've seen
of the thousand I was assigned

You've got to get out
of my head, God
and take this siren
so I can read

And take this long
noise with its end
still in darkness,
so I can see again

Among these uniform
ripples I only imagine
uniform shores

Little thieves [Jefferson county]

"First the church and now the cemetery,

                                        I don't

            trust em no more" he says,

            "Since your darkies moved in,
      filling up Sundays
and flittin around at night—!"

                                    [me]

Now, I don't consider myself no damned darky, and he wasn't
exactly talking to me, but I'd seen those kids too
and knew how they could jack and willy
like rabbits, fast-directed on indirection,

                          —knew exactly what he meant,
him and his old wife, boxlike and passing, I knew them
and understood what they meant—"don't no one rest or give
grace for watching em no more" she says—
white moon in her dark window, watching them late

them damned kids racing up on you
like it's *you* not there
and the world just opens for them!

                                    [boys]

            "*that* door's unlocked" one says

            "That door's not unlocked
            and regardless, there's no rats in there"

            "There is—big ole rats. Listen!"

            "Let me *see* one!"

                                    [me]

Rats up in the church bells? Hell, let me see one.
And chipmunks too, I suppose.

I laugh:
Ain't no chuckin-the-chipmunk
up in there! No squeezy-squirrel,
no bitchy-beaver-neither!

I'm laughing at those kids,
and at myself for laughing, this old

[boys]

"Let me see this one,
I know about these buildings
I know about these things,
mices come from there—"

"I don't need no mices gettin on me!"

*Let's pretend this is a haunted house
See those ghosts?*

"I wish I *would* see a ghost."

"What they doing there?"

"Ghostses' things!"

[me]

I'm scared and there's nothing to be scared of

Cats and coons knew it too and stayed away.
Pacifically where I put baby powder

—think

how they hate children, and white children most
peticularly

[boys]

"Get locked in there and die."

—the smarter ones
knew it and stayed ready.

"Hey, hey mister, is that door unlocked?"

[me]

And there they go, talking to me! Me just minding
my own business, picking these grape
hyacinths, not bothering a soul

"No—hell no! Two o'clock? That door's not unlocked"

[boys]

"Hey, that ain't open yall
that ain't open"
and they ran

Games

The storm was crouched behind the foothills, but the boys, defying authority for the prospect of a late-summer gully-washer and the inevitable adventure, stole out like bandits into the jeweled sunshine that preceded. Thomas, the oldest boy, told Thai to stand back, that there was an issue that needed deciding and he was just in the way.

"Scissors cut paper. Paper covers rock. And rock breaks scissors. Got it?"

Tawny nodded back, not because he understood, but because the little foreigner was mimicking Thomas's gestures with ease, like a deaf-and-dumb, and he flat refused to be upstaged by someone half his size who probably ate dogs.

He knew, of course, they were not playing for the championship of the world or anything far-reaching and final like that — only for director's dibs on the new movie. Thomas always suggested scissors cut because, he said, it was more valid than flipping a coin — less luck in it — and besides, they did not have a coin handy to flip. And even if this was the last movie they ever made, should their mothers finally usurp their summer afternoons and put them to lawn details or grocery runs like they threatened to do, or worse, make them join the Boy Scouts and the bible academy — even if he did not direct the last movie in history, Tawny thought, so what! hadn't he directed the first. And, first to last, didn't they all come back to him since they had all sprung from his original idea. Anyway, he was glad they were not flipping a coin.

Thomas cried, "Ooone, twooo, three!" and the game commenced. The older boy quickly won three times in a row — scissors, scissors, paper — then he dusted his hands together as if to say that's that, and to Tawny's deeper humiliation, he said it.

"What's what!" Tawny barked.

"Three outta five, good buddy."

"But, I . . ."

"Look," Thomas began as though he'd been expecting just this from the younger boy, "I don't claim to know how I do it. I'm just lucky that way, that's all."

Tawny shook his head. He had Thomas cold—you don't teach somebody a game, he thought, win it, and then call that lucky. He was busy formulating the words when the older boy moved in close and wrapped a long friendly arm around his neck. He didn't speak. He simply lit on him with a beguiling, Cheshire-cat grin. And the suddenness of it coupled with a vague intimidation (better watch your Tweety, old woman, Tawny thought, and imagined her bright cartoon skirt beating hell and orchestra around a corner, not in time, but just in time to see, still rising on the puff of some action just now gone, two or three yellow feathers, and the tiny perch still tipping back and forth) this was enough—it pulverized the boy's resistance. He fell apart in laughter, and Thomas, digging at his ribs, singing: "pals? huh? we still pals?"—he kept it going. But it was the foreigner who drove him to his knees. Thai had pulled down his trousers and was freeing his bowels on a rock.

The sleep was chasing him. Almost immune to the cocaine, he stood for three hours in the dim motel room trying to rehearse for their meeting. "Thomas, there's something I need to tell you. Thomas, there's something I've been wondering about. Thomas, do you mind if I ask you something?" The lights from the cafe sign drove rain and shadows against him in the parking lot and three times he almost fell. He could see the man inside, his profile in the window still a smooth, boyish line. "Hi, Thomas, how've you been? Hey, Thomas, old friend, how are you doing? What's up my man?" He had lost his automatic line and stood shivering in the rain outside the diner till light from the great sign rolled around a second time.

Inside, Thomas saw him and stood. Tawny quickly apologized, he wouldn't be able to stay, had to take advantage of the cooler nights. No, he didn't mind the rain, it kept his engine cool, and he'd had some trouble in Arizona with overheating. Sleep? He had a little something to keep him going.

"Me? I'm fine," Tawny said, "and how've you been?"

Even sitting, Tawny had the hyper-alert look of a man who had driven too far, too fast, and for whom destination was a nominal thing next to the journey itself. He had to talk. Charlottesville, Virginia, he told Thomas, if and when he decided to go back to law school. He'd always wanted to see Florida though, Miami in particular; he had heard that the ocean was as warm as bath water.

Thomas was going by his first name now, Henry, and had to correct Tawny. He had never left El Paso. Tawny chided him playfully, said he was gong to dry up here, that he was already partially petrified—he had rocks for brains. His folks thought so too, Henry admitted. They had eventually settled in Indiana and opened a delp store. He remained in Texas against their wishes.

Tawny remembered his own father's face when he told him he was leaving for San Francisco. He had filled in what the old man didn't have words to say, that this is most retrograde to our desires, son.

"There's a goldmine here," Henry was saying, "the great, expanding Southwest is a treasure-bowl, good buddy. You looky Dallas and Houston to see where it's going, and I'm cashing in." He spread his big hands reverently and his eyes grew large as if the scene were coming to life before him, and he offered all of it to Tawny. "No, don't answer me now," he pleaded, "—you just think about the space and this mild climate—dry heat, mostly, and fresh air—you think about it and I know you'll come around."

Real estate, Tawny figured, or Amway, but he had not seen the truckload of encyclopedias his friend was toting. Thomas, Henry!, was a large man, fleshed out from high school football, but long since humbled by inertia, and too many green chili burritos no doubt. "I ain't running like my folks," he said. "God's given me everything I need right here." He was the color of a pomegranate and peeling. "Been packing in the desert," he said, "for endurance and cleansing." Cleansing? His thick knuckly nose, having been broken twice, was an even livelier hue. It dwarfed his eyes and seemed to draw them together, so that without glasses he looked thuggish and punch-drunk, yet he was not unattractive and when he talked about the girls fawning for him

Tawny wasn't strained to believe him. He wore a plain white shirt, a string tie and corduroys, and somehow his dark and crusted shit-kickers were not incongruous with this, but every time he guffawed and stomped his boot, he deposited a neat little pile of dried clods, the pattern of which reminded Tawny of Stonehenge. He said he lived on a friend's farm and was considering buying into the property someday. All in all he was doing well; certainly he felt on the fringe of some prosperity. Looking at him, so full of hope, Tawny could imagine this.

By contrast, Tawny had not grown very much, except for some light padding. Cosmetic, he chuckled, just enough to keep his mother happy. He was noticeably darker though, and despite scrubbing his face religiously for many years, a constellar arrangement of moles and blemishes had, all at once, taken over his cheeks. His hair was cut short and he kept it glisteny and fragrant with brilliantine. His mother had always told him to dress to impress, because, she said, you got to impress to be seen in this world. Still, until San Francisco he slummed it, buying thrift shop goods, not for lack of money and not wholly to spite his parents, but to blend in. Now he wore a blue and white seersucker blazer and a cream-colored fedora as driving clothes. His leather bucks, one of which he propped up in a chair and twitched every now and then to catch the light, were tassled and hard-shined like bankers' shoes. The suede briefcase was a signature and the pearl-handled pistol inside would keep good ol' boys in line. He was a little smudged and creased from travel, but the way he figured it, he still looked like the class-act next to his cowpoke friend.

A waitress in a powder blue uniform wheeled up slowly, and inexorably it seemed, like she had been set into motion a long time ago, and if Thomas (Henry, Tawny corrected) had not stuck out an arm to catch her just then, she might have rolled right past them, right out the double doors and down the embankment to Highway 80. Chance having it, Tawny mused, the young lady could have been killed that day.

"My college friend here will have coffee. Black? — Black with sugar. And I'll have a glass of water and a glass of ice. Got it? Two separate glasses. One water. One ice. And one cup of coffee."

Tawny wondered if the waitress, a thin Mexican woman, wasn't contemplating murder behind her gaze. She shifted her weight like a crane while Thomas read over what she had written on her pad. Then, pinched, but impregnable, she snatched her pad from him and rolled on. Tawny thought, studying the cadence of her shuffle, "another blind, relentless vessel. Waiting on the sleep." He swooned with authorial misery for all the blind vessels.

"I don't like Mexicans," Thomas said, "they are just about the meanest people I've run across, and I've run across a lot of people in my profession."

Tawny drifted off then, not maliciously, he just could not stay with a lengthy train of thought—particularly someone else's—for more than a few moments. Driving seemed to aggravate this. Lately, he found, he could not finish the word jumble in the morning paper. While Thomas talked, he studied the plastic-coated table mats. There were four of them, all of an ubiquitous floral pattern that did not clash too severely with gingham. They were scarred or burned or both which, he figured, attested to their age and no doubt to the relative popularity of dimly lit corner tables at the cafe, not to mention to the type of people who sat at them.

"Daddy said I'd have a better appreciation of people if I joined the army," Thomas was saying, "but I don't know."

Tawny ran his hand under the cool plastic. Outside San Mateo, California, he'd found himself in a dark corner of a diner flanked by good ol' boys. One leaned close to his buddy and whispered loud enough to be heard: "I'd love to go to prison 'n get me some butt-lovin'." Tawny sat quietly, a little flushed but not afraid. He didn't want a confrontation and yet the words welled in him and came up loud: "Yes, Art, I'll take 'Hets and Good Ol' Boys' for fifty. First answer in that category: 'Able to leap tall Coors cans in a single bound.' Yes, Art, What is 'Fuckin-A Man'? That is correct!" The good ol' boys were quiet, waiting and watching him.

Thomas stood suddenly and, tracking little Stonehenges along the way, he ambled to a jukebox on the opposite wall and spent a long time selecting songs.

Tawny saw the waitress speaking closely with a heavy-set man who squinted in his direction. He knew he could not be seen in the dim light. Their candle centerpiece had burned down to a puddle of wax and the tiny bluish flame spurted along the liquid causing shadows, but no light. Still he felt recognized and unwelcome. Lighting a cigarette he wondered where that infernal sign was in its rotation. OASIS 24 HOURS TRUCKERS WELCOME splashing the parked-car windows, the dreary motel, the wet lot, and for a brief moment, his corner. He smoked vigorously and watched the waitress approach carrying a tray high over her shoulder. She set their order down with the bill and began picking up the condiments from the table.

"Wait! Stop her!" Thomas cried, and everybody looked at him, stunned, as if they could not believe he'd actually called out that way in a dim place. "Stop her! Miss, how do you know I won't be needing those?"

"Kitchen's closed," said the heavy-set man.

"Kee-chen's closed," said the waitress.

"We'll be closing up early tonight—in half an hour."

Thomas ignored this. He said: "Now, I know you've got some nachos or something back there?" He left this hanging midway between a question and a derisive comment on the character of the place. The ambiguity, Tawny figured, is what pissed off the heavy-set man.

"There ain't nothing here for you, motherfucker!" he growled.

"We be closed een half hour," explained the waitress.

Tawny wondered at the logic of the situation—how, after all, could a twenty-four-hour restaurant close early? What would be early to a twenty-four-hour restaurant? Would the world be better off without time zones?

"Stupido," Thomas said. He was leaning forward in his chair speaking in a close, hushed voice. His breath smelled like a belch. The jukebox began a song, stopped it short, and changed it to another song—Paul McCartney and Wings. Tawny recognized it.

"We had a maid once, named Maria. I hated that maid. We could never find any common ground and she razzed me a lot about my room. She hated me too."

Thomas was leaning forward so he could remove something from his back pocket. He strained with it for a moment, then pulled it free, and his expression became immediately more positive if not altogether pleasant, Tawny thought. He sighed as he brought the object to the light—a bottle of Jack Daniels—and he kissed it the way mafiosi kiss their guns in the movies. "I always carry a supply," he informed, keeping the bottle low and hidden between them. The heavy-set man and the waitress were chattering behind the front counter. The jukebox played: "we're gonna get hi hi hi, we're gonna get hi hi hi!" Thomas poured the amber liquid over his ice, then without asking he splashed some into Tawny's coffee. "More?" he asked and did not wait for an answer. The overflow spilled into the saucer and a few warm drops splattered Tawny's hand, startling him. He had been ruminating on the pop song when the coffee touched him, and almost reflexively he blurted out what was on his mind: "Did they ever find that boy's body?"

After he said it, he became acutely aware that he had meant to. He expected to raise a bit of commotion with the question, but his friend did not react. Thomas had lifted his glass very deliberately, teasing himself, making thirsting sounds. When he'd drained the glass he drank half the water and gave such a winsome sigh of satisfaction that Tawny half expected to see a childish milk moustache on his friend's face, but there was none.

"Was there anything in the papers?" Tawny asked.

"Huh?"

The window beside them was streaked and reflective with rain, and occasionally a car drove near, its headlights turning the glass to a sheet of white. "I'm talking about the refugee boy." While he spoke he watched a car and its trailer leave the motor inn. It slowed for a tire trap he knew to be there, then carefully descended the ramp to Highway 80.

"Don't know," Thomas mumbled, "I never thought to look. Why don't you try your coffee?"

Tawny ached to join the stream of vehicles leaving El Paso; he longed to grip the cool wheel, to meld like the black road itself to the eternal yellow line, on his way to forgetfulness, to the warm water if it would have him. He wondered how Thomas could have stayed and been so comfortable with it, and why he alone should be burdened and running. He dreaded the journey through the deeper South, the bland faces, the needling eyes, trying to inject in him the seeds of blame, as if he had willed down their plantations and set progress back a hundred years simply by choosing life, as if he were threatening their children in some dark, quiet way—poisonous, the very way they watched him.

Anxiety rose in him and settled again like a whole frozen mackerel in the pit of his stomach. He lit another cigarette and automatically reached for the coffee. He sipped it and it bit him back, but it felt good—strong and punishing and hot. Even the thought of leaving fell away briefly. He saw his mother calling him wishy-washy, but he liked to think of himself as opportunistic. The thought of leaving became another bit of white noise in his system, no less tolerable than the chatter of the waitress and the heavy-set man, or his mother's continuous string of platitudes and self-help observations flashed at him like messages over teletype.

Thomas was hollering across the room at the heavy-set man: "Look, don't get your bowels in an uproar, old man. All's I asked is if you had some chips. —You don't? Fine."

Tawny felt elation or minor pulses of euphoria, not for any particular reason; he was not drunk yet, just resigned, he thought, to elation. He could not get his intentions and his actions together; he kept slipping in between the notes of the music and had to rush his mind to catch up. He could not even decipher the song and that was maddening to him.

"I've had about enough of you!"

Tawny heard this but was so tightly cocooned in his sense of well-being that information was not getting through. He had discovered a warm, bright world of minimal color and line—what, he postulated, life in a pop bottle must be like, or life under the warm Florida water. The last of his coffee was gone and he groped the whiskey bottle from Thomas's hand.

Somewhere he still had a list of all the movies they had made as kids. The boys liked adventures and space-cowboy westerns. The girls were more violent and less original in their tastes, preferring remakes of "Police Woman," "Get Christie Love," and "Bloody Mama." At its peak the movie club had thirteen members—about ten too many, said one mother, who believed children should be spread out, one per yard, to diffuse their propensity for destruction. Tawny and Thomas cochaired the club and handled dues, a dime from each member every meeting to offset the cost of refreshments and costumes. One usually directed as well while the other filled the male lead. Jilly and Lydia Kreockle took turns as female lead, not because they were particularly good actors, but because they could fight and curse like boys, they didn't frighten easily in dark places and they could keep a secret longer than most girls; furthermore, they weren't related to either chairman.

Thai became their youngest member and mascot when Mrs. Vanderkleese started keeping little Moot inside for fear his hair would turn or he'd develop a cancer from the sun. Thai was a thief and a liar, which helped. He lived in the desert several miles from Logan Heights, and slept in a room with, it was rumored, twenty other refugee children; he stole to keep them alive. He stole cap-guns and plastic swords, and once a whole Spiderman costume to make the club like him.

For nearly two years the movies went on daily without a hitch. The mothers feigned tolerance even as they smilingly encouraged the children to do other things. But as long as no one broke a window or trampled Mrs. Vanderkleese's rose garden, the adult world remained relatively calm. Until one summer afternoon in Mrs. Kreockle's backyard. The woman charged out of her kitchen, her hair piled in a blue Dippity-Do bag and her arm stuccoed to the elbow in chicken batter—she waved a wooden spoon at them and called them hideous little creatures and sadists. Her lip rose up off her teeth and she said this would be the end of their violent movies or, so help her, there would be no playing at all. Tawny figured she had heard Tina Vanderkleese scream when the sludge monster (Thai in a grocery bag) tried to eat off her legs. They all said yes ma'am to her and watched her retreat. Through the screen door they could see where a bowl had fallen and pinwheeled white batter around the room.

Tawny proposed then that they make calmer movies—at least in the Kreockles's yard—perhaps a love story. This was not immediately popular with the group—several of the boys pretended to vomit and the girls giggled uncontrollably, but by sunset everyone had come around. They acted out a long, tiresome romance beneath Mrs. Kreockle's willow trees. Sunset gave them slender shadows and a muteness of line and color so suited to romance or, as they also discovered, murder.

Thomas sprawled beneath the willow like the victim and Jilly knelt beside him doing her best to be grief-stricken. Tawny entered as the inspector:

What happened here, ma'am?

My lover is . . . (gasp) dead.

Was it murder, ma'am?

Yes, of course it was.

How do you know?

I know.

Who did it?

Now, if I knew that, inspector, you wouldn't be here.

Just the facts, ma'am, please.

Grapevine had it that Thomas and Jilly were in love because their lips touched in one of the movies. Barely touched really, Tawny could testify, and they responded as if they had bumped something hot, or something very cold that at first felt hot, or maybe they were unsure how it felt because they tried it again, and then one more time to be certain. The rumors spread, but Tawny defended his friend—it was for the movie, he explained, anything goes in the movies. In fact, the kissing proved so effective the first time he had them repeat it in the next movie. Membership increased. Dues rose a nickel without complaint. Tawny gained a reputation in the club as a director of good love stories and Thomas became accomplished at starring in them.

At the end of the summer, at the club's second annual awards gathering, Thomas was voted "Best Actor," for which he received a certificate on parchment stationery, a deck of cards and a Hinky-Dinky. Mrs. Vanderkleese was in the audience with several other mothers. She applauded explosively and didn't stop till well after the others. For a while afterward the women tittered and squealed as though some girlhood fuse had been reignited in them. Tawny knew the considerable risk he took inviting the mothers but he did it with diplomacy in mind. He met each one at the garage door with a bouquet of flowers and a sweeping bow. Thai had stolen the carnations and goldenrods from some mother's garden, but for now, one after the other, the women had melted down to their harmless, tittering girl cores, swayed by glamor and a courteous gesture.

When Jilly won "Best Actress," however, the scandal burst wide open. Tawny's sister, Bug, refused to write Jilly's name on the certificate. She grabbed up her calligraphy pens and held them hostage behind her back. She said, "You looky here, I've done the costuming and the hair styling and the set designing; I've gone to the store for you, passed out refreshments for you, let you use my Barbie dolls and all my other dolls; I've done just about everything there is to do in this club and all she's done is kiss a boy!" She backed away then guarding her calligraphy pens and watching everybody to see what damage she'd done. Tina stood up too, and Jilly's sister, Lydia, gave the winner a suspecting glare. The mothers rushed some remarks between themselves, then Tawny's mother jumped up. "Who you been kissing, girl?"

The chairmen conferred and quickly decided that Bug could have an award too.

"No!" she hollered, "I don't want your stupid award. I don't want to play your stupid game anymore."

"Well, what do you want?" Tawny asked, open to concessions.

"Who you been kissing, Jilly?" asked Mrs. Fitch.

Bug and Tina began to chant. They laced it with barbs like "Jilly loves Thomas" and "two little monkeys sitting in a tree." Tawny shook his head wondering how things had ever gone this far.

Threats were useless against them. Thomas's face had seized up and flushed like a tomato. Jilly sat on her hands and gazed steadily at the mothers, offering nothing. She was pokered and firm as a battleship and every mother could see she would have to be slapped to get any response from her.

Tawny had sensed it coming; their movies had changed too drastically too soon. Thomas wanted to make love stories instead of space adventures and great escapes. He didn't feel like running through the imaginary woods or sailing a raft from a tiny desert island—"why imagine stuff," he said, "when you don't have to?" He insisted that the new movies were more sophisticated but Tawny was not so sure. He had been sure, but he was not anymore.

—He asked Thomas if he had loved Jilly Kreockle.

Thomas was standing several feet from the table. He was hollering at the heavy-set man and swinging his fist. "You ain't so bad! You ain't so bad, fat-ass! —How's that?" he paused to focus on Tawny, "Do I like jelly? What have I got to put jelly on, Tawny?"

"We are murderers," Tawny said.

"Yeah, killers!" Thomas growled and was off again, battling

from a distance with words, pointing and swaggering, strutting his pluckiness like a belligerent gamecock.

For a moment Tawny thought he might kill everyone in the room. He didn't want to sleep alone, not this time, but the moment passed like the glare of another car's headlights on the window, flaring white, then gone. He shuddered. His hands were making silly symbols by themselves. Scissors, scissors, paper, they remembered — his bastard hands could remember. Thomas had duped him so easily! Establish a pattern — scissors, scissors — then change it! Three outta five, good buddy, he said, I won, you lost, and then he delegated the duties: winner gets director's dibs and loser gets to pick the main star.

Tawny would not pick himself; he would not give Thomas the satisfaction of controlling him, so he picked the only member left, Thai.

Rain had started to fall as they reached the movie site. Fat cold drops suddenly drenched them through. Thomas called the set Atlantis, but it was really a construction site, and not an especially good one, Tawny thought. It was a mess of heavy machinery, dredges and cranes, tractors and a cement mixer. Cinder blocks and piping large enough to crawl through were strewn about like lego blocks, and there was a rusty carpeting of posts and cables and slim rivetted girders. All this to eventually bring water to the desert; the sign on the gate read EL PASO SEWAGE WORKS.

They began whooping and hollering, calling themselves avengers and space-cowboys, and wildly climbing onto, into and around everything they could find. Tawny felt slighted that there was no high-rising beam to do something death-defying on, no bridge to jump off of, not even a dark building to echo their howls and amplify the rain; nonetheless he was like a boy possessed, discovering the jungle gym for the first time.

The movie took various shapes, Tawny could not recall them, but they had settled on something desperate, a desperate situation and a close call with death. If they could have involved the whole world in a near-miss crisis they would have, but they couldn't figure out how, given what they had to work with.

When Thai called they did not respond immediately. They were studying their own individual adventures and enjoying the occasional criss-crossing of their thoughts. And he called them by their imaginary names (looking back, Tawny was not sure Thai ever knew their real names) only lengthening their hesitation, and hesitation was all it was, hanging on for a few more seconds of cinematic swelling.

"Help meee!" he cried and they hollered back in equal anguish and delight: "Hold on, we're coming, Torch—" that was his name in the movie.

But when they arrived, panting from their mock rush, there was no one where the voice had been. Then they heard him low in the pipes and saw the white hand above the water, and it froze them but joined them in their greatest movie experience. Denying that they had seen anything or heard the last call, they searched for what seemed like hours while the rain beat on them and the lightning fractured off in crazy chicken's feet over the mountain. Several times they explained what must have happened, even had a paralyzing moment of cognizance, but after that day they never spoke of it.

—Thomas had lapsed into a tirade about Mexicans though speaking mostly to the jukebox where he was depositing more money. He didn't see the heavy-set man bearing down on him at a dangerous clip and he was deaf to Tawny's calling.

"Tawny I told you, I'm not going to answer you if you call me that, it's not my name anymore," he said and the big man caught him from behind, pitching him forward, upsetting the jukebox which hitched up in the middle of a song and started again. In his urgency Tawny knocked his briefcase over on its side, and bending to open it was assaulted by the waitress with her tray.

Four men

A gunman comes in
shoots three men
three very fast friends,
through their heads.

He has two first names,
the gunman,
a first for a first
and a first
for a last name

like George and Howard,
Frank and George, Frank
and Michael, Michael and
Howard

one of the dying
men calls out
trading blood for
accuracy

I know you
I know what you did
and your name
be stil—!

another man spits
in fractions
      half curse
      half accuse

but addling
in the detective's ear

the third man
sinks quietly with
the name in his eyes,
anagrammatic in
his quick smile

Arabesque

Tied up.

"Can you get your hand in there? Three fingers?"

He was pushing my hand, bending my wrist this funny way, telling me to bunch up my fingers—three, no, four—into a tube, "loosen yourself up for my cock." I told him it wasn't possible, that I didn't get fucked anyway, but he kept pushing my own hand into me, making the grunts of enjoyment that perhaps he thought I should be making. Reminding me that I belonged to him—exclusively to him—even more than I belonged to myself, and that I would enjoy this whether I wanted to or not.

"Four, try four."

My nails hurt. I wasn't as moist as I should have been. He slapped me for hesitating and wrapped my head tightly in the red and white gafiya he'd made me buy. "Do you know there's a war going on," he asked while knotting the scarf, "and that hundreds—thousands of little Arab boys are being killed—blown to bits, shot, crushed in their bunkers, starved? Aren't you glad that I captured you and made you my slave, my toy?" We'd had dinner at Square One, delicate portions, but I wouldn't starve. He'd paid with a credit card.

I didn't speak, couldn't really, but I didn't nod either. He'd wrapped me so tightly I had trouble breathing, the pressure on my ears made them sing and shards of light erupted behind my bound eyes. "What if I sent you back?"—he seemed to want an answer and struck me a hard, glancing blow to the head—"back to the front lines, back to the trenches?" Couldn't I hear the bombs falling all around me, curled up in my fear, my desperation at the dark bottom of that hole? It was only a matter of time before death took me—or some other master. Did I want that?

"You want to kill me, don't you?"

He curled me more tightly. "You know, you're my first Arab?" My wrist ached. I mumbled ineffectively that he might be breaking my wrist and he swatted me hard across the back. "My first Arab slave." The wrapping and now the full weight of this man bore down on my breathing. The shards of light leapt more violently against this constriction, and the singing seemed to be completely outside of me. I felt the man's rough hair against my back and my butt, his hand suddenly fumbling with my mouth. Wasn't it better to be safe here, half a world away, in this slavery? "Arabs," he explained, "can die or they can serve." Couldn't I see how simple it all was?

The hand fumbled around my lips, like a blind thing discovering them. Then I heard the scissors—snap! snap!—brandished above me. I tried to move away but he was big and strong and held me still, curled neatly beneath him. I felt the cloth pulling forward, felt it intensely around my ears and the back of my head, until the scissors whacked out a two-inch plug. I touched the metal, thought I could taste it, but it was the air filling me so sharply.

"Lick them."

Now I did taste the cold metal, then the salt and warmth of his hand, then the metal again. "Grateful?" He could have suffocated me, could still cut out my tongue, he said. I heard the scissors again, felt them cold on my shoulder, my back. "Who would care? Who could you tell—especially if I—?" He laughed, there were Arab boys dying by the thousands, the tens of thousands—"who would care?" He was in my face, breathing near my mouth—explaining, "life has dealt Arabs a bunch of bad cards." Did I understand Israel? He struck me two disorienting blows and punched open my mouth so he could spit in it.

"Do you understand it as a concept?"

Stupid of me to think he cared about my breathing—"don't you know what that hole is for?" He turned himself around me, tightly, like a ratchet wheel around its pawl. "Of course you know, of course you do, don't you." It was a physical law, he informed me, "just the way God intended it." I sucked in a lot of air, knowing that he'd take it from me again.

"You do understand, don't you?" he laughed—

Said I engaged this thing in him, this need to refill me with all the dangers he'd just saved me from. I'd been a soldier on the front lines about to die—did I understand why he'd saved me? "It sure as hell wasn't charity." I felt him fumbling around my mouth, but more bluntly now, and more urgently. He slammed my head with some part of his body, said I wanted to kill him— "You have to want to"—then slammed my head several times more and begged me not to resist, but begged me to want to kill him. He didn't want to hurt me too much, but he would, he said, he wouldn't even hesitate, because that gave him pleasure too. He didn't want to give over to that sort of pleasure, but he would, if I resisted, even a little bit. He said he was looking for the smallest reason to give over to it. My submission must be unconditional or else—but even that might not matter. Could I imagine what it was like to suffocate?

"I'm going to choke you to death, and you're going to love it."

Didn't I want to die a hundred times this way? Wouldn't I be happier? I hadn't seen his cock, didn't know it would be so big, so unmanageable—hadn't I always wanted to die this way? He pushed toward my throat, curled me still tighter, and drove my head down on it, still talking about death like it was our only alternative. Maybe I understood this mechanism I'd become the middle of, understood its strength, its unrelenting, its selfishness and selflessness. I tasted his salt, his ooze, and my throat jumped but I couldn't dislodge him.

"It's okay if you choke, Arab."

I shook to dislodge him. Of course he knew I wasn't Arab. He didn't know any Arabs. Could I please humor him and choke? I did this.

He rubbed my wrapped head like I'd done a good thing, said it was my duty to make him feel strong, that nothing short of my choking would make him feel strong, and he drove my head onto his cock even past the possibility of choking. If it crossed my mind to bite him I don't remember. I did try to struggle—he told me to—but it seemed to make so little difference that I immediately wished I hadn't. Now hopelessness closed on me and suffocation seemed too easy but also the chill sensation of sexual release, waves and waves of this threat—

"Choke! Choke!"

He drove with a desperation that actually amused me more than it frightened me, but then I was outside of myself and somewhat embarrassed with myself and needed to laugh at it all to keep from blacking out. I'd laugh for a moment more, then politely register my need to breathe—didn't know how I would do either, but at the time this didn't seem to bother me—it all seemed so funny, my fucked-up priorities, especially the need to laugh at this man's desperation before I took another breath.

"Choke! Choke, you Arab bastard!"

The need to swallow was now a long time gone, and that felt funny—felt strangely new to me, like the first time I came myself and thought I would die; or perhaps long before that, like my first sip of mother's milk—it felt foreign to me or a very long time removed, but something I had to get used to. I felt myself falling toward a womb-like coziness, despite my amusement and the violent buffeting my body took.

"Goddamn-you-to-hell, choke on it, you piece of Arab shit!"

I felt myself falling even as his thick, insistent ropes of cum jumped passed my need to swallow them. "Damn—goddamn— blow your fucking head off!" Even as he fumbled to unsnap his leather cock ring to release the second great dam of his pleasure. "—oh, goddamn—god-damn—got-tamm—blow your fucking brains out!"

And all the while he fucked himself relentlessly against the calm walls of my throat, milking out himself with friction and brutish thuds what I could no longer coax from him with swallowing—

"_"

—and seeming to enjoy my acquiescence most of all—pleasures that rekindled themselves against the fullness of his bladder, the crashing of his heart, the quickness of his breath, perhaps even against sensitivity itself. He was tortured to a new pitch, driven past pain and into a sweet delirium where he might just forget to ever let me breathe.

"_"

When I awoke he said he was sorry. He grinned a great deal while patting my cheeks and forehead with a cold cloth. My mouth tasted like piss. "Didn't I tell you it would be intense?" He rubbed my wrists, almost gently, one in each of his big hands. "Didn't I tell you?" He licked his lips and slid off the bed beside me. "Next time—" he began. I sat up as he hobbled on his knees to the foot of the bed. Suppliant and dreadfully handsome he began to rub my ankles where the ropes had reddened them. "Next time we can play Intifada ."

His eyes got big as he imagined it for me. Would I like to stone him? he invited.

please, father
don't hit me
this loud with the
wide of belt
or hand uplifting

whisper of
tall martyrs
the first burned
& first pressed
of virgins

Be-ing dead

The bus is no place for a civics lesson, no place for history, or any
-ology, it's no place for social studies that squat too close to home,
despite what you might be reading to pass the time, or what you
might have in your backpack, so you sit back, with your back to it
all, as black boys hold public lynchings and carve themselves up
as thoroughly as any butcher from their great-grandfathers' past

so, your breath could kill a thousand people in one minute!

so, your breath could kill a million people in one minute!

and yours could kill all the people in the world in one second!

youre already dead

youre dead with your tongue hanging out

nigger, youre dead with your zipper open and your dick hanging out

youre dead with a booger hanging out your nose and your zipper open and your dick hanging out

youre a dead nigger hanging with your dick out and a big
booger and snot hanging out your nose

nigger, yous dead with your guts and your dick hanging out
your nose

so, yous dead, nigger, with your dick cut off and hanging out your mouth

so, yous dead with someone elses dick *in* your mouth

so, yous *alive* with someone elses dick in your mouth, nigger

and you're white so you're especially quiet, looking as though you have no investment in the talk, not anger, sadness, shame, guilt, humor or intrigue, as though you don't even hear it over the thrum of the bus and the driver's hyper-helpfulness "Masonic! change here for the six, thirty-seven, forty-three, seventy-one! Masonic! Masonic!"

or you're black but enlightened, a student of change and progress and general uplift, sure it's yours and yours inherently—looking as though you have no investment in the talk, not anger, sadness, humor, shame or intrigue, as though you don't even hear it over the thrum of the bus and the driver's hyper-helpfulness "Masonic! change here for the six, thirty-seven, forty-three, seventy-one! Masonic! Masonic! Masonic!"—yours inalienably, though *nigger* still hurts and each one cranks the stress in your jaw a little tighter, makes you turn the pages of the book you're not really reading a little sharper

or you're black and gay, squinting up at the graffiti like it holds some answers that only you can decipher, like it is the only map of a city you want to visit, like you need glasses—so consciously unaware—looking exactly as though you have no investment in the talk, not anger, sadness, shame, guilt, humor or intrigue, as though you don't even hear it over the thrum of the bus and the driver's hyper-helpfulness "Masonic! change here for the six, thirty-seven, forty-three, seventy-one! Masonic! Masonic!"—you adjust your arm to cover a peace button like it was a pink triangle and you hadn't just transferred from the Castro bus, and you get off at Masonic like it had been your destination all along.

Second Virginity (13th down by the Village)

i.

Lydia enrolled in Second Virginity courses at City College. The class itself was free for women ($300 for men), but the books, fetishes and cleansing devices added up. All the assigned literature was obscure, except perhaps the Bible.

She wore a loose flowerprint dress into Shambala Books, and spent the first minutes in the doorway adjusting her left shoulder strap. The goat-eyed bookkeeper leaned over the counter to see if she was barefooted. "*How* can I help you!" he spat, clearing his throat of a whole week's worth of irony.

> He was barely thirty but he already hated ignorant youth and passion, and he secretly wished that the unimproved would be killed. You can't help the hopeless, he thought, but he reserved his strongest contempt for straight people who tried to reason with congenital idiots, with niggers and bag ladies and drunks and junkies and crazy people on public transportation.

His shop was a nervous conspiracy of ancient and new age philosophies, of histories and folktales, sciences and witchcraft, all grown so high and so dense that the room itself seemed to list dangerously to one side. Odors, bitter and mesic, snuck out of the books and mingled with the mouse-rot and ten-twenty years of cedar and cinnamon incense. What cessed in the warm middle of the room should have had a name so you could ask it to move over while you browsed — Zanzibar? I Bono Putu Putra? Seth? Emily? It called to some, warned and repelled others.

Before the bookkeeper could stop her she had stolen to the middle of the room. She broke up in the dust and the narrow conscripted bands of sunlight like memory, or like bad cable reception. He called after her, "Miss! Miss!" and if he sounded much older than he actually was, and stronger too, this was just a trick of his surroundings. "What do you need?" He tried valiantly to crush out the girl's exuberance before it got started. "Is there some thing in particular?"—because the place had survived long and well without shocks or surprises.

"Wow! Wow! Wow!" she intoned, like a child pumped up with discovery. She began to touch things, books and lacquered boxes, a porcelain dragon and a crystal ball, first tentatively then with the full fever of discovery. She sneezed several times, prettily, and went on touching.

Your daddy was a pathogen [he regarded her murderously!] *and your mother was a whore. They sold you upstate for fetal tissue, $200 worth, but you grew up anyway into this honeyed pestilence.*

Not a day passed that some gorgeous tarty bitch didn't traipse in with big eyes and tiny questions, looking less for illumination than a place to spend her nights. Folktales, light witchcraft, low-meat recipes are what he offered and some left satisfied with these, while others wrangled for more, and got it. From behind the high-burnished counter, high enough and wide enough to enhance and conceal him—he would bark out directions, "a little left! a little lower!" recalling for some the cold-hot game they played as kids.

He felt self-contained and self-important as might a cripple in his custom-made chair (or a judge at his bench, a king on his throne, the CEO behind his desk or the pitcher on his mound), and he seldom left the counter when others were in the store. New stock and reshelving he managed in between or after. Indeed, while he directed some philosophy hack or some wannabe warlock he might open his pants and massage his dick. He discouraged people from looking high for books. Nothing that required the ladder could possibly interest the student body or the street mystics (not on this street or from this school). He discouraged conversation and took money quickly like it was the nastiest of transactions.

White trash disgusted him like no other trash—niggers and slants couldn't get past his philosophical remove, and he lived in the clean hills miles from their squalor—but white trash might seep from the finest houses, and something of its essence moved quickly across all his distance and freely through his barriers.

He could still picture hot sun above the mountainous landfills where he'd played and later fucked. He remembered the smell that pushed between him and his self, that slept with him, ate with him, and spoke to other schoolchildren before he could find words around it. He remembered the first grade and the first porcelain toilet he ever touched his ass to, the instant understanding of it, and the instant guilty pleasure of expelling into something so perfect. For six years he held his shit until schooltime, held it over weekends and torturously over holidays. He almost died of fever one Christmas when his waste backed up and poisoned him. The city doctors boasted of saving him with pumps and drugs, but it was knowledge of the hundred porcelain toilets at Hudson-Cedar-Merrick hospital that pulled him through. His mother couldn't understand his desire for summer school and then for vacation bible school, and as he got older his father discouraged it, said there was surely something girlish in a boy wanting that much school.

He didn't know what white trash was until the family sold the farm and moved to Grand Rapids, Michigan, where all the seventh graders were delighted to tell him that it was *him*, white trash was him and his kind. Later Berkeley diluted the problem. Tried to mix him with many different natures, but also introduced him to bottled water and organic foods so he could preserve himself. Then the studies, white hot during those dank, bloated months of unrest—they evaporated the great self-doubt he'd brought from childhood, burned off his welfaring nature, his parasites, his vanities (in their infancy too!—and most fortunately these since his hairline seemed to vaporize under the same heat)—they burned down his flags and cauterized all his bleeding loose ends, immured him against every sort of rot, then cured him like a hunk of jerky or a Virginia ham.

Now he felt some mild fascination for the subject but kept it at arms length when he could. "Crush it, then study the remains on your shoe—collect it in little jars if you want."

Straddling equal measures insult and understanding, murder and tenderness, he imagined doing the girl a small violence to teach her. Slap her, perhaps, or pull her hair until she kneels!

She was reaching out to touch an old lamp, hardly an heirloom, just something he'd found, but he would punish her impropriety with some pain. He didn't think she could tolerate much and that excited him. You don't help the helpless!—this was axiomatic—but when he grabbed her wrist hoping to feel like an extension of nature's cruelty he felt nausea instead and released her. "Don't touch that, it'll electrocute you!" he snapped.

Lydia apologized and thanked the bookkeeper for saving her life. She said she was stupid that way, always falling over and into things; then, sensing drama, she apologized more profusely as though her peril must have been the greatest of inconveniences for the busy bookkeeper; she rubbed her sore wrist and tried unsuccessfully to explain the excitement that made her so foolish (he said, he thought he probably understood), then she apologized and thanked him some more for understanding her.

He eventually gave her all the books she needed and bought for her most of the charms and fetishes, but he also took what he wanted from her, and in the way he wanted it. He didn't rape her exactly though he tried to make it inconvenient as well as painful and humiliating for her. It was sort of rape, but she came to him, after all, expecting to pay something, somehow, and heavily, and he exacted payment, first, as forcefully as she withheld it, then, with all the accumulated vengeance due a man who couldn't expect full payment, let alone the interest accrued, then finally with the obliteration and damnation of the object in mind. Since this would be the last time any man fucked her, he would fuck her for all of them who missed out or might have missed out. He would fuck her so as to drive her into the church. He would fuck her so as to drive her through the church. He would burn this fuck into her flesh so she could never deny it and her every attempt would make a mockery of all the women in the school, perhaps of all women period. He was fucking every wannabe virgin as he fucked her, as if to punish them for falling that first time, but with no uplift intended. He didn't want this bitch to learn from her punishment, he wanted to push her deep down into the thing that made her worth punishing. He wanted to make a whore of her even if it meant destroying himself. He would make her attend classes as a virgin then return to him every night as a whore.

Before the tension had cleared she was turning her genuflection into pleasantries, into curious and seductive bits of flattery and into kindnesses that left the bookkeeper stunned as though he'd been kissed; into inquiries too, some of them incisive: "what stones do virgins use to delay their blood? what berry stinks the most when burned? what animal skin makes the best hymen? do wet dreams count against a virgin? even if she never sees the penis?" She delighted him with her insights, especially the ones that seemed cautious, semiliterate or accidental, because there and then he could enlighten her. She delighted him with her gropings and her mistakes and with a hundred girlish gestures of uncertainty, things that ten minutes ago had fuelled his desire to injure her. But when, out of the blue, she swore a lifelong devotion to men like him, and to the selfless pursuit of higher knowledge, she might just as quickly have plundered him and his carefully buried register of every nickel.

When she began stretching for the highest books, he sprang back into action, "hardcover or paperback? Chinese or Tibetan? do you want a mixed perspective on that—men and women?" Or when she dipped so low that the dress tightened about her ample hips, he lost his poise on the ladder and nearly fell on top of her. Now he took his turn to apologize, though with a formalness that made Lydia giggle. Could she forgive him such clumsiness? such narrowness? such lack of charity? Before she could answer, he gave Lydia twelve books, six more than she needed, he gave her several seconds and early editions and a press copy, he also gave her four new books that he called seconds and early editions. He gave her his phone number in case she needed further assistance, and he hugged her to him until they were both breathless. He praised the glorious state of the human condition: "imagine two strangers finding love and succor here, in this way, in the 90s."

"Succor?" she asked him, and pressed him a little tighter as he explained. "Succor," she sighed.

ii.

Lydia flourished in the Second Virginity course. I was immediately struck by her better skin, her vibrant eyes and easier smile. Her quick hands got quicker (she still stole all her fetishes), and those keepers she couldn't fool or dazzle with her speed, she simply mesmerized with her beatific glow. She thickened with health and good humor, with free love and confidence, with charity and a sense of her own great wealth within the herstory of double-good women.

So lush was her success that I began to question my own. Clean and sober a whole year and I still felt anemic next to her. She boasted of new *structure* and *presence* where just a few weeks before there had been none. I nodded like I knew what she meant, set my lip like an authority on such change, and took her hands in mine. "Yes, you look very very, very good," I said. She watched me with unbridled love, a frenzy of it, and I forced tears into my eyes to mirror some small part of her effortless glaze. My soberness embarrassed me a great deal now as Lydia was certifiably drunk with new thought.

> stepper seeking stepper for hot, creative, healthful times. You should like movies, sports, picnics, modern dance, cooking in and eating out, the beach, travel, *Northern Exposure*, aquariums, star-gazing, sleeping till noon on Sundays, camping, home improvement, Spanish, old Pat Benatar and cats. Can't tolerate intolerance or half-steppers. Write to

But she really had to change; to save her own life she had to change, because she had not only dropped to a great depth, she had fallen from opulence. A lifetime later, and a lifetime ago I sat across from Lydia in a dim bar and studied the benzy pallor of her face, she'd fallen that fast. "Fuck the car, fuck Ogilvie and Mather, fuck Maiden Lane," she swore, and the two of us scratched together what little bit of comfort we could find—she'd sold the car that evening so she had a wad of crisp bills. She had coke in three forms and she had a gun just in case—she laughed —just in case we needed to end it all. We continued our quest for forgetfulness. I cut her hair. I sold her out that night as boy pussy to a travelling businessman. He tied her down, fucked her ass, roughed her up a bit, while I sat in the second room playing with room service and the cable TV. She said she loved me. That night I hated myself for loving her. Most nights after that I hated her.

iii.

I'd been clean a year now and didn't want to fall into Lydia's bright eyes, even into the memory of her. I didn't want to wonder if, after all, I had brought her down, nor if I had made the suggestion that finally brought her back up. She opened to me, made of her new clean muscular self a willing sacrifice for me, and for one white instant I wanted to bash her skull in. When this urge flew, the water in me dried up too and I saw, for the first time, a chance at never meeting Lydia, and never letting Lydia meet me. I was new and she was new again. She understood and didn't call after me as I ran . . . not even once.

Cornerstore

I went to the corner store for lentil soup and three slices of bacon—no more and no less than that. The Koreans had a corner, the Pakistanis another, Blacks ran a thrift-junk store on a third, and an abandoned Catholic girls school overwhelmed the fourth. I'd have nothing more to do with the skimp and sass that I got from the Pakis. Seventy-five cents for a gelatinous ice-milk bar that had been there, imbedded in the freezer slush, since the store opened. Didn't have much anybody needed anyway—sour milk, warm sodas, peroshkis stuck in orange fat; and it was a minor miracle to find chewing gum or soap. This wasn't a store. I couldn't say for sure what it was, but it wasn't a store, and a close friend of mine had been warned not to complain too much. If it had been a store it would have gone out of business long ago. So I was going to the clean, thrifty Koreans across the street, their tiny space bulging to the ceiling with what you would expect in a store on a low-rent corner, nothing more and nothing less, but so much of it. Warm, clean and cluttered—distended shelves of quick pasta, tuna, pickles, jellies, canned pears, fruit cocktail, cleansers, chips. Lentil soup was one oddity, I admit, but I had come to expect it and got it cheaper here than anywhere in the city, including the major grocers. The bacon came in thick rashers too, more fat than meat, but this was a corner store, on a bad corner, mind you, so I didn't expect more.

The store rattled with the loud, random energies of black children after school. They came quickly and at once, the girls in blue-gray sweaters and darker skirts, the boys in younger, softer, brighter attitudes of the street—they came with cutting tongues and sharper elbows; vocal with their intimacies, but protective of their burgeoning tastes (especially the girls who had to limit their imagination to what they could spend at corner stores). Us adults slogged about in this, bemused, then irritated, then ready to teach someone a lesson. I don't include the owner, his cashier or the boy that made sandwiches; they waited behind their barricades, grinning vacantly at all of us. I never once saw them challenge the students' exuberance, nor their mathematics. Nor, in my witness, did they react to several bursts of raw, unformed hate—not as proprietors, not as Koreans. They were remarkably unavailable, and seemed distant for a while after the children had gone.

The rest of us were visibly disturbed. We shook our heads and smiled tightly in the new calm. Then a man fell toward the register. I thought he'd slipped but it was a dramatic gesture. He pushed his things ahead of him, gripped the counter with both hands and said something to shake the cashier's glibness. He took out his money and waved it demonstrably the way Americans do abroad. If it hadn't been for this gesture, I'd say the urge that grabbed him next was sensual, maybe a bit nostalgic. He set the wallet on the countertop beside the things he was sure of and opened the freezer. Perhaps it wasn't wholly his fault; Mr. Lee put the ice cream where everybody would link money with an urge for it.

I mumbled "fuck" or some such throwaway, not because I was hungry, tired or in a hurry to catch the bus (which conveniently rumbled by) but because I might have been, and because the man—even in the throes of his urge—looked cruel to me, all angles, piss and polish; dangerously out of place and wounded; his hair about to change, his tightly reined youth about to disintegrate, his fancy duds losing to the mismanagement of his body. He might have been digging for ice cream simply to spite me. Something small and insecure in me took it that way, even though I wasn't in line yet. Or he might have been digging for old-fashioned stuff—a bullet pop or a push-up—to make himself feel good again. Certainly he ignored my anguish, but he did glance up twice, once at the cashier (who knew my face and, in small clever ways, did his neighborly best to make our stranger feel rushed) then at a dark black girl who'd held in the doorway since her own purchase, swinging, eating her candy, quietly mocking us and daring outsiders to push past her. Her thin body drank up the sun, and the business. I was almost in line when something in the Korean boy's usefulness reminded me to get bacon.

As he portioned off the fatty rasher the boy told me that the man had lost his wallet. Again I looked toward the register where this red-faced white man was hunched over the ice cream freezer, first in some crazy gesture of worship, then walking and bobbing like an irate bird. He pressed his back and swore. One of the Koreans had to keep him from falling. When he straightened up I could see how old he was, and dressed like a freshman fraternity boy. He staggered toward the door then abruptly back, then toward the door again. The girl was gone, and a black man with a gleaming red conk rushed in, almost toppling the old man. "BITCH!" he hollered and we all turned around. "It was that bitch took it!" Took me a minute to realize who'd said it, and why.

He put a hand on my shoulder, with considerably more weight than I'd expected, like he'd suddenly lost his legs and needed my support to keep him from falling on his modulated face. My hand went up quickly to detach him, the way I detach old men who want to suck me in the park, so quickly I was shocked and embarrassed with myself. He wanted me to understand, this wasn't a race thing, it wasn't a gender thing, it was hardly anything at all—gay men called each other bitches all the time—and his mass of wrinkles came to full animation as they recognized me. Was he someone from my building? I had to struggle for neutrality— purity of judgment, or so I was calling it at the time. I felt like the lesson had to come from me, because it wasn't coming from the good Korean family. They stood smiling, the issue already behind them, or had they been unconscious all along. I stood alone in judgment of all mindless, thoughtless people at that moment, and had I been God, they would have died horribly.

Thoughtbubble #1

> bitch *n.* 1. A female dog. 2. *Slang.* A spiteful woman. —*v. Slang.* To complain. (*The American Heritage Dictionary, 2nd College edition.*)

> amplification: Fuck you, bitch!

Fucking bitch!
Fucked-up bitch

clarification: Tight-ass-bitch
Nigger-bitch
Bitch-ass-nigger

case: "Bitch-ass nigger, I'm gone fuck your ass up!"

Gestation. Conjugation of an image, an attitude. Language for it arrested at the level of shock. Threats leap forward on their own; maturing and transcending their intended purposes like runaway military industrial complexes. In peacetime, under humanist fire, they diversify into oils and plastics, fast food and pharmaceuticals; furnishing the great mansions of the American imagination while integrating within the very comfort of their design a quieter, more insidious threat—odorless, colorless, deadly beyond measure, and with a half-life of thirty million years. In these times of war, "fuck you, bitch"—with all its toxicity and genetic threat—is lubricated language for a black man, fantasy rape, an easier mindfuck; it's part of and a facility to his communication, not the end of it. "Expanding and contracting," bitch is a living word, "rising and falling, circular flowing, nowhere going." "Bitch" on the lips of a white man is the end of talk.

Residue from stairwells, windows, crosstown buses; Walgreen's, Burger Kings, state buildings, reiterated as fast as the negro custodians can clean it off; swarming in late-night homeless roving thrift shops and trash recycleries—this is America's language, but like America's music . . .

And what of movie bitches, drag bitches, opera queens and diva-dance bitches, or the men that take your money at video arcades?—tell him, cartoons don't bleed.

The quickness! Had it happened any more deliberately I would have kept his money. I'd escaped to the register in manufactured hurry, so the urge to look in Mr. Lee's freezer, if it even grabbed me, only did because I grabbed it first. Honestly, I would have vomited. . . . The wallet lay open like a sacrifice on a mound of frost between the sundae-sandwiches and the fudge-sicles. I was going for depth, for the pure drama of a search, not for any particular confection. I only wanted to out-spelunk that old angular white person, and to do it with youthful violence, self-knowledge and glee. The wallet felt warm and I recoiled. When I looked past my arm, past my fingers still rigid with surprise, at least three bills, the top one a twenty, glared back at me from the wallet's folds. Bus card, driver's license, VISA—exposed and obvious with the fresh heat of sacrifice.

"Bitch!" I looked around, stunned, confused. "It was that bitch took it!"

So, God had refused it, this warm bloody thing killed special. I couldn't figure right then what was worse: prospering from someone else's offering or offering it again. What if I'd found that beautiful bacon boy's heart and put it back in his discarded self? I could prop him up, shake his body as I killed it a second time, and from a distance, to the villagers, it would look like fresh agony and a new cause for strong waters, strong sex and song. I could tear the dead heart from its dead self and send nearly everyone into new ecstasies. From a distance I could do this with week-old dead meat.

I didn't give him the wallet to save the girl, nor to save myself, and certainly not to save him—no, I wanted to kill him. My gesture felt like murder and when I refused his small reward (refused too the apology he asked me to take to that anonymous girl), I might have been dancing on his grave. My soup was particularly good that night but I vomited anyway.

Several Lies about Mom

1.

the better lie—what do I tell Helmut tomorrow? what do I tell
him tonight when I leave a message on the office machine, or
when I dare to call him at home? how do I make quick amends
for skipping work today? what story do I act out? who do I pretend to be when I step into that office tomorrow morning?

the plan—the visual device might involve a bruised lip, a red
eye, a scratch on my forehead (all of which, right now, are real—
real products of a furious face-fucking I took last night and this
morning from a leather-clad gentleman . . .), and perhaps a two-
inch square shaved patch of scalp which I'll cover with a spotty
white bandage (this, an elaborate, I know, and perhaps unneces-
sary attention-getter/reality-enhancer, as well as a bit of self-
immolation/punishment for the acts that got me into this situation in the first place)

as for the lies: the first one would center around "an accident"—I got hit by the very bus (the 22 or the 24) that I should
have taken to my assignment this morning . . . "Helmut, I got hit
by a bus!"

or "Helmut, I got mugged outside DV8, in the parking lot."

or "Skinheads! Fucking skinheads! Probably your nephews!"

2.

this morning, the last day of the craft show and probably an easy
one despite the malignant presence of one Kir Quamberry. Five
feet of upset, more hair than head (more gesture than movement,
more mood than honest affliction). She could radiate distemper
in all directions for fifty yards, but it seemed miles and miles—

like a lighthouse. Embittered, embattled, full of furies, like the rough waters and the denying sky; like the sinking wreck and hopelessness. Ammoniac. She brought her whole world of anger and despair to bear on you and your tiny crash site—that is, if she bothered with you at all (and, after all, wasn't being left out of her world—at least where it intersected your own—worse?)

Remarkable was her ability to constellate anguish . . .

"I don't have a day off until the 22nd," she moans (and boasts). Most everything she says, to me anyway, slips or splits almost as she says it ("How are you, *this* morning?"), or it winks, sputters, fades ("Oh—I'm fine—right now"), or it falls variable to peripheral attractions and to plain old inertia (dead old too heavy boredom things, and ceremony), or to blind spots and mixed intentions, motivations. And it only comes together as I look away from it. She obviously hates me for where she thinks I'm going, for where she thinks I've been. Wonders if I'll get there before her, over her. Wonders if she'll get there—at all. "They love you, Fisher, and they hate me. It's simple." Perhaps.

Of course I said she had to stop thinking that way. I could see she was making herself sick. I could see she wanted an argument. We had nothing but arguments—uncanny, since we had nothing to talk about.

"I don't have a day off until the twenty-second—well, that's not true. Wednesday the fourteenth I don't work but—but—" she touches her nose. Carol Burnett touches her ear. Samantha Stevens wriggles her nose. So I thought maybe I'd missed some detail so instant-obvious it would be on television, some stupid little crumb of a thing to throw me a light-year off-course; that once fatefully dropped would demolish the machinery of my response before I figured out how to work it—or worse! maybe I had walked seven—almost eight blocks with food on my nose—mustard, a sesame seed, some dried meringue—maybe it had been there, embarrassing me, since lunch. No, she means *her* nose; she means her *nose*, her cancer. "I've got another operation on the fourteenth so it's no vacation—not even a small one." She winces to signal something. Pain? Of course I can't know if she means pain now or on the fourteenth; temporary and ocassional pain, or constant pain—pain as condition; real pain, or the

nomadic and frivolous sort—pains in the ass and neck and balls;
or real nomadic annoyances
     Some would call them balls

3.

(my mother had a kingdom of free-floating, inarticulate pain,
that waited until I left home for college before it coalesced into
something we could write about, and something on which we
could anchor our phone calls—two people who couldn't talk
in person without some puddle of indictment run down their
legs to mingle and spread on the kitchen floor toward a quicker
danger like electrocution perhaps, but quite possibly slow and
lingering bad chemistries or biological disasters, [recalling: the
stench of feet, onion, sewage, week-old victims of this or that violence; the canned frozen fatherless dinners, all night refrigerator
anguish, leaky faucets, mouse-scurriance, strange percussion;
then a two-headedness that arrives just as dumb, just as sleepy,
as god's-original-thought, or an extra platypus where you don't
need one] and suddenly or inevitably, an uninvited horse in your
breast, strange milk in your blood, thoughts about time derailed,
five or ten years, its wreckage salvaged, amalgamated, and cor-
porated against the slow descent of a small dark star that, some
years ago, sent papers ahead to prove its own coming, papers that
grew into epistemologies, whole philosophies, still this long before the landing, papers that read a lot clearer some years ago,
but even then to no avail.)

From a notebook [undated draft of a letter]

—I can't think straight anymore. Everything blurs and shifts on me when I try to think straight. Of course I need glasses, but it's more than that. I don't sleep and I've been eating strangely—lots of cheeseburgers—and it's more than that. I dealt with death, mom's death, on a level I've never touched before and couldn't approximate again.

Understand me: she was (in the hospital) the ugliest sight and the most fulfilling sight that I have ever witnessed. Not just her, but everything she stood for, everything she was to me, in some sense, all of me, shrivelled there flitting in and out of knowing me and bleeding away through plastic tubes. I was gored deeply and winced with a funny, almost sexual, almost dead (touching dead) sort of electricity every time I told myself that she was going to die.

New York is your reality. Mom dying is mine. Dad becoming a nigger is mine. Shit on the sidewalk is mine. The rust is pleasant garnish—residuum garniture—stop-stop-stop. This all sounds much too negative and it's worse than what I mean. At the peak of an understanding that I no longer know (and seem to be seeking w/some indirect urgency) I knew what it was like to die. I didn't go all the way, but there was a moment in the hospital where I thought I could change places with her. I'm not being noble. I mean, I thought it would be me in there and I would give her this shell. And not because I thought I owed it to her. But because I was her.

My rebellion was her rebellion. We could never fight right because she was never sure which side to take. I was a fool for shifting sides, always finding the side she wouldn't take, because, more than you know, more than I knew, mom and I were the same person. Difference is she *let* him fuck her; emphasis on *let*. I never did. Extrapolate.

I never fucked mom. It wasn't on my agenda. Freud fucked up with me, fucked up doubly because—I wouldn't let dad rape me either—he couldn't break whatever it *is* that I held up against his authority. Couldn't whip it out, couldn't send the message even through mom. I was a hard knot mainly because I refused to fight. Not docileness, but a brooding, stubborn refusal. The ultimate slap was to let it loose that I'd let some other man, not my dad, have me. . . .

Three Boys

I looked into a room full of naked, dirty, visibly hungry and diseased children. Few of them cried, most of them stood still and met my gaze with a chillingly mature despair.

My gaze fled to a corner for respite but what I saw there finally drew words out of me—thick obdurate, useless words, like waste. Some I said, some I thought I said.

Three boys (I think) owned that corner, and held some scary court there. They were all three desperately thin, their stomachs distended, their skin gray and purpled in odd bands as if invisible fingers held them.

(If it's necessary to find order in nightmares) the three held together formally like figures in a math problem, or like a section of architectural blueprint.

One boy seemed to tease me, to flirt with me. He moved in and out of the dimness, one hand up near his chin, the other at his elbow. His thinness, and something at once elegant and arcane about the position of his hands, seemed to age him. Was he philosophizing on the nature of his situation, the nature of pain? But the arm, I now noticed, was damaged (poorly set after a bad break) and the boy held it up to protect it. And what I'd taken at first glance for stealth or coyness in his walk was really a trick of the light—the suspended bulb, gently rocking, had distorted the boy's exacting movement, his steady and unemotional crossing of the same path, like a figurine in a clock.

The second boy stood in the dimness of the corner, behind the path of the first boy. He looked out at me with huge eyes that seemed to pool all the light available to the corner, all the pathos too. He was picking scabs on his bald head and on his arms. When he wasn't watching me, he examined this tissue and then threw it away. His reaction was as unvaried as a seasoned lab technician, but just as my eye started to leave him he flinched and quietly began to cry. Some of the scabbing, it seemed, was too fresh. He continued to pick it but spent an extra moment with it before he threw it away.

Almost hidden, the third boy sat in the crotch of the corner, stretching himself toward its interstices like a spider or that spider's web, and swinging his head fast from side to side. Without the movement I couldn't have seen him, he was nearly one with the corner—like a small thing that had rolled there—crawled, blown, perhaps developed there—with disappearance on its mind. The movement was a violence, a change of mind too big for the corner, too big for that room, and I feared an explosion in that child, or an explosion in me.

cat sense

See the tree and me sitting
on the branch above you?
There are three of us:
me and you
and me in the tree

Your daughter's calling you,
I know, mine too,
but I'll talk
as far as Colusa

          then return home,
      or I'll talk
      as far as Curtis Street
      to myself

same distance on both sides
of me—a block up, a block
down,
      so I only need
to turn my head to follow
me and you around
conversing freely
not crazy

it don't matter who
it don't matter none

I and I now

The Villains of Necessity

I   Strange Fruit

"I know I know I know!" Vickie squinted and wagged her finger at Maria, trying to keep the young maid's attention long enough to finish her story. It was ten minutes to the hour and the bus wouldn't wait. But she would finish this last bit or, so help her, she wouldn't go to work. Her daughter looked up at this outrageousness, the maid looked up, her son peeked around the corner. "I hated Georgia," she said, "and there's the god's-honest truth."

Bug rolled her eyes and groaned. *God's-honest truth* was like the kind of dirty trick one of her own friends might use to force her ear; and to have it thrust on her now, like a secret or a lesson or a challenge when it was such stale news. . . . She knew the story better than her mother, and this made her wonder if she had lived some part of it, but she didn't dare ask her mother now, not and help her miss the one Saturday morning bus that went to Mesa Vista Road and the factories. She sat cross-legged between Maria's pretty painted feet looking up the mother's long, narrow pants suit, and occasionally spying her older brother, a leaf-colored flirtation at one or the other end of her vision (he kept running around the house).

Of course, she understood that after so many tellings, the truth was only half the truth and the other half was reverie. And a mixture took longer to tell. Years later she would understand that the very foundation of her mother's truth had been eaten away, little by little, by time and by unconscious bits of self-preservation; while the rest of it, so full of minor embellishments, drooped to the ground like a neglected fruit tree or an unpruned bush. When she did finally ask about Georgia and the mother said too quickly "no, you weren't there," Bug wasn't one-hundred-percent convinced.

Vickie wiped her brow. It was a hot morning. She explained how badly she hated those two years outside of Atlanta, starved for space in a cousin's two bedroom tenement apartment, waiting for Lonnie. Waiting, she said, for the whole ridiculous war to end, and waiting some more for her great aunt Luddie to go on and die and get it over with so they could free up one room for the children. She stayed so long she had to help her cousin with her third and fourth babies; then she had to shame her cousin's husband into giving up his wine and wickedness for a decent job.

She waited, sometimes for months at a time without a word, without a single letter from her young husband; nothing about his health and whereabouts, about the horrors of the jungle or the courage of his platoon; nothing about how much he missed the States and how much he missed her. She was eager to fight this one with him, but Lonnie wouldn't write. Who could expect him to, as busy as he probably was over there?

Her sixth sense should have kept her informed, but there wasn't a sign from Lonnie, not the faintest glimmer, she told them, even though she continued to receive weddings and lotteries and violent deaths from just about everyone else. He was withholding. He was denying her somehow. "I had a hit," a premonition, she told them. "A year before Lonnie left I knew he was going to be killed in a jeep accident." But that was twelve years ago; they'd moved six times since then; Lonnie was not dead, he was a Master Sergeant and had recently been awarded a housing option. Vickie wouldn't let him go deep South though.

"Your brother remembers—" (Tawny ducked around the corner so as not to be implicated) "I swore the night we left Georgia that if I ever saw another magnolia tree it would be too soon." She gestured toward the old, failing tree behind her—some freak of nature, because magnolias weren't supposed to grow in Texas . . . were they? Bug wondered . . . and had this one ever flowered?

"Mommy."

"I know, Bug, I know, now hush."

The girl turned her head to Maria, in some part accusing the maid. She should have said at the beginning that she didn't care a flip about magnolia trees anywhere in the world; that the South for her wasn't Georgia but Juarez. But she couldn't (or *wouldn't,* Bug suspected) speak English. Instead she stretched back in her lounger where the tree's old shade covered her face and for the balance of the mother's delay Maria watched her own pretty feet. Her nails were bright red with the tiniest silver butter-fly highlights. She was ordinary Mexican, with perhaps hints of Spanish, but she claimed a long line of Spanish royalty and cer-tainly wouldn't be a maid all her life—at least her attitude doing the dishes or the wash, or laboring for hours over her doll-like feet suggested as much. In her reticence and her foreignness, she seemed to understand everything about their family, and to understand it wholly and all at once, the way no single member, perhaps no two members together could understand it. If know-ing so much (and in such concentration) gave her any special power over them, she never used it. But she should have grunted or something; the bus was rumbling up Beale Street, about to turn its last corner. Bug scrambled for an alternative plan just in case the mother missed it. . . .

She loved those feet, each red toe; she loved Maria vaguely, in bits and pieces, but couldn't go to her, even in the worst emer-gency. Because she believed there was another world inside of the woman—another family, a baby, and perhaps a young hand-some Mexican man who loved her—she couldn't dump all of her troubles, all of her secrets, and all she knew of other people's crimes, she couldn't empty herself into Maria completely the way the others did. It hurt her to watch Maria clean the kitchen or the bathroom, and to know she touched their soiled clothing, or cooked foods for them that she herself didn't eat. The child felt an odd desire to protect the maid, to make sure she was compen-sated for every sacrifice, every kindness. She spoke to Maria in a whisper, and then only to ask what she could do for the maid. She cleaned her own room and swept the upstairs hall; she straight-ened the towel cabinets when her brother or father thoughtlessly upset them; she waxed the minor furniture in the foyer and den and threw out old papers—all this whether Maria said she needed the help or not. Then with permission she might gently stroke the maid's hair or braid it, and on weekends she would spend some of her own allowance on gum or candy sticks to make sure Maria felt loved.

Any girl could tell you it wasn't the maid herself, it was the monster-thing that mothers made of maids. . . . "Honey," her mother had said to her, "you don't have to be so nice to Maria, your father and I pay her." Bug had assumed this, and yet she hated her mother for saying it. A week later, as Maria was packing for her vacation, Bug threw the handful of gum and penny candies at her head. She still loved the maid's feet, and perhaps the long hard braid she could make with her hair, but only as she loved exotic souvenirs. And if her mother missed this bus, Bug wondered how much of her she would still like. She turned to Maria now, urgency in her hard brown eyes, but the mother was already wrapping up—"I hated it, every minute of it"—and already slinging a heavy bag onto her shoulder so she could charge after the bus. Bug and Maria waved after her. The morning sun was making a slippery river of the street and a vast sea of the desert so the bus seemed to lurch away in great jeopardy.

An invitation arrived for Bug that morning, an hour after the mother's bus had deposited her in front of the cold, flat Motorola plant, and six hours before the father would shift his Saturday attention from ball games and cold beer to his boots, without shifting his positions on the sofa—just as Bug had planned. She had to take care because of the strained relations between her mother and the next-door neighbors, relations that threatened to keep Bug and Tina Vanderkleese apart. The girls themselves had forged the invitation, and while Mrs. Vanderkleese would know immediately that it wasn't her hand, by that time it would be too late to stop them. Bug had a new dress and would carry a wrapped box. Tina would act so eager, so expectant, that her wishes would become stronger than all possible denial. And it would be too late for Mrs. Vanderkleese to run through the entire murky litigation as to why that magnolia bush had to be cut back, and why the girls didn't need to spend *so* much time together—more like sisters than like good friends; "today's girls need a bit more space, they need to know who they are before an army childhood makes them common." Mrs. Vanderkleese had matriculated at Emory and understood the woes of commonness.

Maria, of course, was aware that the mail had come, aware too that Bug had picked through it first, and perhaps now, in retrospect, that Bug had not told her mother something that she should have, and that if her mother had known she would have said no, you may not. Bug leaned in the doorway studying the maid intensely for several minutes. She scoured each breakfast dish the same, dried it thoroughly and put it away. There was no challenge in her eyes, even the third and fourth times she glanced up. Tawny could make her laugh. More impressively he could make her react to his secrets. The pleasures that passed between her brother and the maid infuriated Bug; the maid's moonround face was always a glacial lake for her. She was looking for her mother in the maid, or at least a confidante, but she only saw herself.

II   Storm

Sunday afternoon the monsoon rose out of the humid basin north of El Paso and followed Highway 80 into town. It swept over the scrubby hills and dried out rain gorges along the way, plunging ignorant toads and lizards into an early night, but it stopped abruptly at the edge of Beale Street, as if it had run up against a sheet of glass. Logan Heights was just Beale Street and two others run together lengthwise to form a peninsula. It jutted northwest into the desert like a testing finger, and while the rest of the city seemed to be declining along the desert's hot head, this mostly military community was thriving. Mrs. Vanderkleese's prize-winning rose gardens were a teasing vision from the desert route into town.

The storm waited unchanged for more than an hour, fueling speculation and concern among the residents, who were not used to having things linger in the desert. Some said it was a scrub fire. Some said it was a fog bank. Old Thurmond Grayson Hicks sucked his gums. He knew what it was, or, rather, who was responsible, and he would tell anyone who asked him . . . those shiftless, no-count Mexican guest workers and their dust, the smoke, the gas and fumes from their stench. He wouldn't holler out; there were children in the room, but the surge of bitterness made him quiver, made him chew at the emptiness in his mouth — fuckers, motherfuckers (he spat into the damp handkerchief), he would tell anyone who asked him just what he thought of goddamned Mexicans milling around the desert all day long, in government-issue Caterpillar tractors, pretending, like they do, to serve some vital purpose (he studied his own black hands, tore them up from his lap and from the damp white handkerchief like old roots, and he felt proud, bitter and proud, to be a part of the foundation, perhaps the very basement mortar of this country); pretenders, cheap fuckers, not building, just blowing noise, stirring dust, eight-hours-a-goddamned-day, like it was important, like they served a purpose; uppity slickheads, costing him money (just as sure as feeding city niggers was costing him, and the Vietnam mess that had his boy), new money, money that he didn't have; and he was tired of it. Fatigue had written in his face. It held his hands. He couldn't fight for another moment's peace, not with this gnarled revision of protocol, and that was all he wanted out of the year, the month, the days he had left—a little peace, a little peace and a little pride as he remembered it. He scooted his chair closer to the window where a rutted black face gazed back at him, making it more difficult to set his one steady eye on the mounting cloud.

Across Beale Street, Mrs. Kreockle was pulling her shades against a glare. It struck off her congregation's Pokeno cards, and was no doubt souring the mayonnaise in her dip. If she saw the old man, she didn't acknowledge him. She observed the storm (having been there a few years now, she recognized the humid beast for what it was—first one of the season), but, she thought, didn't it look like the two rolled-up fists of God, waiting to sock out the sun—didn't it?—and couldn't you just feel the tension in the air, the tug at the very fabric of it all? She pulled the shades and returned to her guests without a word. Wouldn't they be surprised? First of the season.

Up the block, where the houses did not obscure it, the storm was a formidable sight. It terrified mothers but intrigued large numbers of small children, such that mothers were out in distress hollering from their porches, threatening more damage than the storm, and the children were blown forward on double threats, triple threats, as though they had been personally dared or lured and then physically pushed into some vague magical romance with fear, disobedience and the idea of death.

The three girls responded with guffaws. Jilly, a big-boned twelve-year-old—the biggest and the oldest of the them—began copy-catting the mothers with daredevil flare as she passed their porches: "Clementiii-na, where are you?" she sang out, and: "Aaa-ntja! Aaaaa-ntja! Komm zu, geradeaus!"—just like Miss Inga Terhardt, her very inflections. But their favorite was her imitation of Miss Nellie Hicks. The mother's husky scats and yodels were better than television to them, and Jilly could match her for range and fierceness, but never the rich melancholy, that old dark spoon that stirred the pools beneath her words—if she'd mimicked such nakedness the others might have run from her. "Willy Ra-ay! Tonda-leee-o! Ah know y'all heah me, so bring yo' raggedy butts on heah!" Bug and Tina crumpled over in fits of laughter, slapping the grass and rolling in it till they itched. It was the Hicks's grass and they were slapping in the direction of the Hicks's porch, but Miss Nellie wasn't calling from it this time. "Will-yum Ray," Jilly continued, creating from memory, loud enough to be heard and despised by real mothers. "Git yo' high-fancy tail in heah, boy, fo' you gits blowed clean away!" She, Jilly, looked enough like a black person to pass for one in a shadow; she had a platter face and heavy features, but they knew she was half Hawaiian and Mrs. Kreockle was white from Tennessee.

Bug, however, was black, as dark as Tondaleo, the color of a candy kiss, and like him too, hipless, slight of build. She tried not to act too common though; she talked as properly as any fifth-grader, wore clean, coordinated clothes, and never slid her feet when she walked down the long waxed halls between classes. She was eleven. Tina, the youngest girl, was pure white—but a quarter of that (Bug might boast on her behalf) was Dutch white. She had unruly red hair and a pert, ruddy face. From a distance on a summer day, she looked like a peach pit with all the scrappy, uneaten bits still on it. Yesterday she'd turned ten years old, re-establishing the line—ten, eleven and twelve—and during the party the three of them had huddled together, excluding a whole houseful of girls, to calculate their next break—August 6th, Jilly's birthday.

All three had hardy, protracted laughs that did a crazed battle-dance when thrown together in a cul-de-sac dense with houses, parked cars, and young hardwood trees. More often than not they aroused a mother who threatened them with a switching or full dismemberment if they wouldn't take their noise elsewhere—"I don't care where you take it," she might holler, "take it to school, take it to the desert, take it to hell, just don't ruin my afternoon with it." Today, despite their mirth over the storm and the mothers, and the electricity in the grass, the girls were subdued, almost sour with their concern for Willy Ray and Tondaleo (and for the other five or six brothers who they did not know, but had on occasion mistook for one of the two they did know). Bug and Tina very seldom thought about their own brothers, not when they were not around to pester or to be pestered by, but Willy and Tonda were so small and so dark. . . .

They were not outside, and Miss Nellie was not outside calling them. In fact, no one had seen a Hicks all day (and now at a time of day, a time of year, when you'd normally feel there were too many Hicks in the world and would take to chasing them out of your kitchen, your basement, and your yard) except for the old grandfather who sat in the front window, his face pressed lewdly, wetly, to the glass, and that evil eye wandering. The girls missed the boys, now, in their horror and disgust, even more. What was he doing, the old man?—who would let him slick up a clean window with spit and snot and hot breath? Willy and Tonda weren't so old you couldn't tell them things, but they were too young for it to matter, and they had filthy mouths (not to look at— they were a pretty red to look at and reminded the girls, when they played dentists or Front Line nurses, of the throats of young birds), but filthy to hear, especially the little one who said things so nasty they had to cover their ears and run from him. The old man might have been a dog at the gate.

He watched them slap his grass and hated them for the insipid, mongrelling old fools they would become. No longer content to worship a man, they would get right under his heel, right up against his boot, bring their faces to his fist, so as to rob him of a good wind-up, and deny him the element of surprise that is naturally his; or worse, they would rise up beside him, trying to tell him just what his role was supposed to be, and in stealing from him the authority to tell, they would make him the told. The old man would tell you—and didn't care who else heard him— there was nothing anybody could tell him that he didn't already know. Indeed, he'd forgotten more than most people could tell him. He watched the old Kreockle bitch keeping guard at her window. She had a houseful of young officers' wives and had no doubt been teaching them the things that successfully rid her of one husband and drove the other to the church. What was it? What was it now that he wanted to tell the girls? He couldn't think exactly with those children, his kin, hollering in the background, and their vague reflections in his light, just beyond his own face—colored hats, elephant trunk whistles, Jewish-looking party noses. The girls were moving off, across the street, into the yard full of roses. He called to them quietly, generically, not knowing their names.

It concerned the three of them that no one had called *their* names—if only for the chance to hide and make the mother holler louder, to make her say what they didn't want to make her do—"Don't make me have to come off this porch." Or, "If I have to come after you you'll regret it." Any other time Mrs. Vanderkleese would have been the first one out bellowing—she was for lesser things than this—but the screen door remained dark and the hallway empty. They had to decide for themselves whether or not to go inside. Jilly said no, she had just set up a Barbie house in the garden and didn't feel like moving. Tina shrugged and skipped off after a butterfly. Butterflies (at least the plain ones, not your Monarchs or Zebra Swallowtails) seemed to come out in force just before a storm. Bug watched her and grimaced. She toyed with a malign thought for both her friends, but before she could voice it the sudden wind howled through the fence, pushing with it stinging desert sand. They quickly wrapped their Barbie things in several army blankets and fled to a warm washing room in Mrs. Vanderkleese's basement. Tina said, for certain, her mother wouldn't mind, but Maria, the maid might.

"Wouldn't mind?" Bug thought about her own maid, Maria, watching a soap opera, doing her nails, hogging the phone, supposedly waiting on the wash, or the roast, or the floors to dry— she not only wouldn't mind, she wouldn't notice, or if she noticed she wouldn't say, or if she said it would be in the language of not knowing the whole story, not knowing enough to tell anyway. With shrugs and grimaces and fanning gestures and bits of Mexican profanity she would communicate that she didn't know. "I didn't know, Vicky, but if I had known you can bet I would have stopped her, si, si, I might even have beat her to stop her, but, like I said, I didn't know; you shouldn't expect me to know. Since when is it my job to know?"

Mrs. Kreockle had parted her curtains in time to see the girls go inside. There was no denying Dot's generosity, leaving her door wide open to those girls after they'd just run through the neighborhood like wild-jackets or hoodlums, skinning themselves, tearing their clothes, giving other mothers the wrong impression. Dot had of course outdone every mother with her girl's birthday party—even busing girls in from better neighborhoods —and then, after so much positive exposure, to let your own flesh run wild in the streets, it was an embarrassment; but to let it back inside, that was pure travesty. She snapped the curtains to. "The fat bitch," she thought. "I invited her to play Pokeno today. Now how'm I going to get rid of all this dip?"

Jilly made a pee-yew sound and cleared her throat, hoarsely like a man. At first they couldn't see; the dark, grainy cinder-block absorbed the light and their eyes were slow adjusting. The room had two small, beveled windows, sunk-in like bunker windows near the ceiling, and a single dangling bulb that winced and faded each time the washing machine changed cycles. A tall crop of red hollyhocks grew outside the windows, tinting the light that was not blocked out altogether by the deep window sockets. The floor waited in obscurity, and they waited on the steps, for the washing machine to begin its rinse.

While they waited Bug scoured the dark corners with her eyes, expecting a bat or a mouse or a spider to leap out at them, but nothing moved. The dust balls stood still, waiting. The retired furniture, softened by dust and cobwebs as though it had not been moved or sat on in years, waited to jog their memories. They had lounged on this sofa, fought for this love seat and been sent home for breaking the chair, just six months ago; six months ago their mothers were measuring their own front rooms against this furniture.

Resigned to the gray and to the waiting, they all three jumped when the washer gave a sharp, ugly bark and the bulb pinked on. Bug grinned good-naturedly at Jilly, but it must have seemed like gloating; when the older girl winked back Bug already knew they weren't liking each other. She pulled Tina beside her in a chummy, protective way and all three girls broke into wry grins.

It usually went this way, though they couldn't explain it and were hardly aware of it, with Tina sliding in one direction or the other, ultimately determining whose game they would play. They emptied their doll stuff on the floor and began spreading it around. Between them they had been collecting Barbies for seventeen years, and only Jilly admitted to being a little bored with it. While Tina did the inventory they each kept a mental finger on what was theirs alone and what could be shared. There were seven Barbies, six PJ's, six Ken dolls and Bug's black doll, Christy; four sports cars, three jeeps, the sailboat—and on like that. They kept dozens of paper dolls in a paper sack to stand up in the supermarket or at the airport, to give their scenes a busy-world look. And they seldom touched a boot box full of Little Kittle children except to push it out of the way, not because the tiny dolls weren't cute or because the Barbies, as they imagined them, weren't married—the children went uncounted and unmentioned, if not completely unnoticed, because they were away at school all of the time.

In minutes the Barbie world lay strewn out beyond all reasonable government to every corner of the room. It was piled on the furniture so thickly and in such disarray that a piece, a busted sofa for instance—two years old, and "old the day it was bought," or so the other mothers commented on the sly—was not immediately recognizable as such. Bug called the mess an epic, meaning a sprawling, many-legged lazy thing like a soap opera, and while each girl was responsible for keeping up with the thick and lazy plot of the epic (which seemed to generate itself), it was decided that they would play apart—the way they usually played Barbies —not talking, not meeting eyes, keeping stern puckered faces of concentration more like students than playmates, and doing their legs out in a wide V to angle off their separate spaces on the floor. After all, Bug thought, this was the most serious thing the three of them did together. She started humming a tune, one she'd gotten used to all those busy summer mornings in her grandmother's kitchen, but she didn't have all the words for it.

Seven trees bearing . . .

An hour later the confusion was not any more sorted, but it did look different to them. With Barbie stuff being cycled about, no situation remained the same for very long, and yet an outsider would be hard-pressed to pick out the differences. They imagined that their dolls were living in an army neighborhood just like their own, so neighbors came and went rapidly, but everyone, old and new, looked and acted pretty much the same; and husbands and wives functioned in separate worlds but under similar rules. By now all three were moving a little slower, their world rotating a little more sluggishly. Doubts, accusations, blemishes on their eternal friendship, smoothed away under the common burden. Bug was humming

Seven trees bearing . . . .

Meanwhile Maria tip-toed her way through without comment. She emptied the washer, filled it again, banged it about, punched, pulled and turned the series of knobs to get the machine started, then left the room. Immediately the hanging light fluttered like a bird's shadow and went out. The girls looked up at the dark sockets and realized excitedly that the storm had conquered the sun. Somewhere in the sky, lightning flickered. The top of the room flashed a cold pink. But there was no thunder yet, unless it was too far and too faint to hear over the washer; and the room was still warm and sweet with the smell of detergent, though the girls felt an occasional freshet gust and sensed the rain in the air outside. Bug figured that some pressure had been released, even as she sensed the building of others. It was like a ball being squeezed, she imagined—changes inside and changes outside.

"Hey, guys, look!"

Jilly was stripping a PJ and a Ken doll and clutching the pale plastic bodies together in a counterfeit of kissing and nastiness. Bug saw it first, just as the light rose again in the bulb, and she turned herself to shield Tina's vision, but the youngest girl already had her hand over her grinning mouth, her eyes flitting guiltily between Bug and the scene. Jilly waved the lovers through the air, catching some of the patchy pink light; still the dolls seemed to be fighting instead of doing what they were supposed to be doing, and Jilly's own grayish face looked fearsome not enraptured. It was the weakness of her charade that allowed Bug to break away from it; she had seen books, found her brother's clippings, stumbled on a box of old magazines in the desert.

From a position of knowledge she nudged Tina hard in the ribs to help the girl collect herself, then the two of them stiffened up with marmish disgust. "Really, Jilly!" "Yeah, Jilly, really!" Her eyes were rolling and jiggling out of kilter—like a moron, Bug decided, not like any lover's eyes she could imagine. She'd never seen a lover's eyes, to be sure, but she had most certainly seen a moron's. Miss Nellie's near-crazy daddy had a casting eye, so he could watch up both directions of a street at the same time. The old man, however, had been struck by lightning, they said, and Jilly was just acting up. "Ep-lepsia," Bug whispered to Tina, and she curled up her hands to the wrist like she'd seen a spastic woman do. The two girls nodded together tragically. They winced at a new burst of lightning which Jilly didn't appear to notice, and if the older girl felt any guilt or shame, or any vague threat of higher retribution (Bug hoped she would go to hell for it)—any at all, she wasn't showing it. Instead she surprised them by becoming very quiet, awestruck even, like middle-aged women Bug had watched in church restrooms, suddenly fascinated with their own mortality. Jilly was studying the dolls, one in each hand as if she were weighing them—male and female, female and male.

Bug's thoughts moved to her brother, not naked of course, but in trouble— Still the thought she couldn't have instantly intruded on the ones she could, so she had to abandon all of them. He was in the desert in trouble, or trouble was coming; perhaps he was bringing trouble home. She left him running for fear of imagining him naked and jabbed Tina again with her elbow. They began to play, became ferociously absorbed in playing, the way two old women might be shocked into some awesome feat of stitchery by an unseemly or unexpected thing, and Bug returned to her humming with old-woman fervor. She remembered a puzzling riddle her grandmother had posed to her: "Why is mens and womens different?—'Cause at the last minute the mens stepped back!" The old woman cackled. Bug smiled without understanding, and a tiny voice woke up in her saying, leave riddles as riddles and well enough alone, so she didn't ask. The following spring Grammy Moochie posed the exact same question; she answered it and cackled exactly as if it were the first go-round. She had just finished a quilted jacket for Bug in impossible time, spurred on by something they'd seen. That morning—a bright, crisp Sunday morning in the Adirondacks—while good people were dressing for church, a drunk mountain man had relieved himself on her front lawn, in the plain light of God and the church-going. It was such an awful thing that Grammy snapped at him from her porch, her dress half-fastened, a flowered hat dangling off her gray head by a single pin: "Hey'n you, old man, pissin' on my grass," she began, but the dizzy, bearded mountain man, starting up, tottered and nipped himself on his zipper. They saw him bounce down the hill and beyond it, where he fell into an open sump . . . and on the dusty ride to the church house Grammy was humming bitterly.

—Tina rushed her dolls to the grocery store. "Had to get soap," she said. The store was then hastily arranged beneath an old lawn chair with Lego blocks and empty match boxes for food and sundries. She raced to the post office, the bank, and city hall to pay a parking ticket, then on to Sears, building each one as she arrived, sometimes borrowing pieces from places she'd already been. What was funny about Jilly was now oddly threatening about her, and instead of fleeing the basement, which had occurred to her, Tina chased her dolls around town with it. Four old lawn chairs became a shopping center, the broken dryer was city hall. She hid two of her dolls there for a spell then hurried them home.

Bug spent another minute trying to name the trouble, but Tina's new enthusiasm distracted her; she wouldn't be outplayed at Barbies and in a few swift moves had built a house, with pool and garage, and was on her way to meet Tina at city hall.

From her quietness they knew Jilly was working up to something nastier. As the storm broke again, splashing light through the deep sockets, the older girl pounced on a mildewy chair and crushed a pink cloud of dust and moisture out of it. For a moment it startled even her, but then she'd picked up right where she left off, even making smacking noises.

Tina dropped her dolls. She was caught off guard and burst out laughing, but quickly plugged her own mouth with her hand. Still the mirth bubbled through and she fell over, bumping her head on the floor just beyond the ratty carpet. "Serves you right," Bug thought and she nudged the girl with her toe, initially to see if she was alive, then to demonstrate her annoyance. She leaned into Tina's red face, regarding her pained and laughing eyes—

"Tina Vanderkleese," she said, "what is so funny about *that?*" Tina mumbled that she didn't know, but let loose another boisterous cry. Incredulously, Bug struck her palm to her own forehead. To reclaim Tina's attention she had to think fast and perhaps a little cruelly. "I don't think we can be friends anymore," she said and Tina shut up. "Haven't we talked about this? Haven't we?" she pressed and Tina nodded. Actually they had written out a long list of problems-with-Jilly (just as Bug and Jilly had done for Tina, and Tina and Jilly for Bug, without either third girl knowing), including all gossip they had heard and the evidence to support it, but because they believed Jilly was disturbed (Bug believed Mrs. Kreockle beat her too hard) they forgave her. Sometimes they forgave her publicly, trying to shame her back into good health; other times they used a private ceremony, full of feints, shrugs and dirty looks which exorcised their anger if nothing else.

Reinforced, Bug turned her gaze on the older girl trying to engage her wild eyes. "You, get down off that chair, now!" she commanded. Jilly stopped long enough to say no.

The first time she'd collided with Jilly and her antics, it almost killed her. The year before in Social Studies the older girl had made her biggest splash. She was repeating the fifth grade because she never studied for tests—didn't believe in it, she said. Yet somehow she charmed the same teacher who had flunked her into making her class monitor. And of course, on the very first day of class, she slithered back into her routine. While she was passing out Mr. Gore's mimeograph, she flashed each of them with a dirty picture. It was a clipping of a naked island girl with fruits and a clay pot concealing her most private area. The class snickered and murmured about it, but Mr. Gore, a thin, intense man, seemed oblivious. He was scratching dates on the board and in his slow, loping drawl connecting them up to important dates in Citizenship. "This is important!" he hollered without turning from the board, and the whole class shuddered with repressed amusement. Bug kept her eyes rivetted forward as Jilly passed her. She was studying the deep folds in Mr. Gore's saggy pants and felt comfortably lost there. "Will somebody tell me what an American Citizen is?" he asked. Bug didn't hear an answer. She was conscious that Jilly had sat down across from her and was tipping the picture toward her, hissing for her to take a quick look. Instead she wove Jilly's first outrage into the rumors she had heard, and this whole pattern she wove again into the helplessness she felt around the girl, helplessness and an odd attraction, something secret and perhaps akin to what she felt with her mother when she would remind her not to fear the blood that will come, or would talk to her about the baby she'd lost (not about the boy in the picture who was not their father, just the baby) when she was just a girl, or how to wash herself thoroughly so when she got older she wouldn't smell bad. "Will somebody tell me—" She wove and wove until she had formed the very muslin cloth that she woke up to, smothering—Mr. Gore's dark green, saggy pant with the black stripe in it. She couldn't move her eyes from it, couldn't seem to move her limbs, or to breathe, and with a sharp, leaping panic she felt the purple rise in her face, the heat and cloudiness to her head. She was about to gasp aloud, "Save me, Mr. Gore, quick, save me!" but the bell rang and saved her life.

The second time—though she couldn't be sure of it—she thought she saw Jilly Kreockle in Taco's big dog house with a boy. The dog was yapping and Bug, thinking he had cornered a squirrel or a jackrabbit, ran around the house; then out of the rushing darkness the scene emerged and she continued running, not slowing, never stopping, and since it seemed too incredible to be true she didn't tell a soul until the story broke on its own. Tina's brother was the boy. Jilly was the trouble—more than one mother said so. And no one knew why Mr. Gore left after just two years, he just did, and all three girls were sad. Then one day they were all three sad together, and Jilly ceased to be a monster to them—perhaps still a little more mannish, but not the enemy they had imagined her to be, nor the thing that some mothers warned them about and that other mothers' daughters shunned. She was an extension of themselves that they didn't quite understand yet, but at the core Jilly's sadness was their sadness.

—Bug watched Jilly's contorted face now, trying to catch her little eyes which sank back in her face and darted constantly like two animals in a cave. She watched her rival's body. Jilly was strong and agile like a boy, her movements were quirky like a boy's; she acted like a boy in every way, Bug thought, except that

her mother made her wear skirts and dresses and she had a fond-
ness for makeup and plastic bangles, and of course she had done
things like a girl . . . and yet at the core, Bug knew . . .

"What you're doing," Bug continued, "is op-seen, immortal,
and uncalled for here." "And 'sides," Tina added, "those aren't
your dolls!"

Jilly was stunned, but shored up against it long enough to look
at the dolls — there were red initials on their butts. She'd never
noticed marks on any of the dolls before and had to look a second
and third time to make sure. She felt oddly violated. Bug was deliriously happy as Tina explained then that her mother had inked
on her initials just recently so there wouldn't be any confusion.

"So where are mine?" Jilly asked.

Inwardly, Bug triumphed. While Jilly searched the piles for
her dolls, she and Tina fell into a nervous tête-à-tête. Yes, they
would go shopping! They would go camping, skiing, divorce and
get married again! They would start businesses! They would bar-
becue! — all this for Jilly's benefit; she wouldn't be invited even if
she found her dolls! Bug felt avenged. A girl could hunt twenty
minutes for a doll, an hour for a halter top, all day for a clear plastic sandal — that was the nature of the game. Still it wasn't anger
that fueled her, and her vengeance didn't satisfy her. Indeed,
she felt some of the older girl's strange isolation, and drew back
from Tina as though the younger girl's butt had been marked in
red too.

"Ha!" Jilly yelled.

They couldn't see her.

Suddenly, from behind the sofa, she thrust up a Ken doll and
rubbed the plastic ridge where his thing should have been.

Tina gasped and wailed with bright, unrestrained laughter.

"I bet you've never seen one," the bodiless voice challenged.

"We've never wanted to, neither!"

"I bet you don't even know what one looks like."

"We're not interested, Jilly," Bug tried to skewer Tina with
her toe.

At that moment the lightning broke in several rapid bursts,
reeling past like blank frames in an old movie. Jilly rose up and
Tina made an ugly sound like she'd swallowed her tongue. In
the recurring flickers Bug looked like a tiny black seed. She was

pointing, exasperated, her patience on end; she felt very old and at the same time too young. She felt as though somehow she had inspired the lightning, but there was no anger in her, and she longed for it.

"Do you want me to tell?"

Tina froze and studied them both with little shifts of her eyes. Jilly shrugged.

They heard the first rumblings of the storm, far away—seven seconds from the lightning.

"Do you?" Bug was livid, purple.

Jilly slowly lifted two naked dolls over her head, ritual-like, the way they made temples in Vacation Bible School. And one of the dolls was Bug's Christy. Tina gasped again but couldn't laugh, and Bug launched straight up. She flew for Jilly, then quickly thought better of it—like an angry sparrow banking, recalculating its chances against a hawk, and just in time. She sat back down, twitched, and stood back up. Tina said almost too casually: "I think you should stop now, Jilly." Meanwhile Bug rummaged around for something large and heavy to throw.

No one had ever noticed how black that black doll was until Jilly pressed it against Ken. Bug had always thought of color as something separating ball teams, or gangs, maybe white boys from black boys in the cafeteria, but never girls; and still it took a boy thing to bring it to her attention. She wanted to, yet couldn't blame Jilly; she knew lovemaking had to be more than this uncaring, indifferent bending of body parts; Jilly's sex was just a rapid, lifeless thud, calculated for attention, not provocation, let alone inspiration. It was sex before blood, child molestation.

Still, the air had gone out of the room. She sensed a sweetness there, the detergent, the freshet carrying violent odors of honeysuckle or camellia and roses. Someone far away asking if she was alright. She kept rummaging, no longer for anything in particular, just a thing, something she would know and remember when she found it. Now why was her brother in trouble . . . ? And why did Maria speak Spanish when she could speak English, and why did moths get hung up between the panes in her storm window to molt and die?—Bug was sure Maria could speak English as well as any of them. And where were the Hickses? In her pitched state she connected sound with light and the light with the air, and when the bulb melted out she thought dreadfully about suf-focating, and when the washer clunked off she grasped around the siren core of her disgust to keep from flying apart. There was no thunder; perhaps they had missed the storm. She jerked up as if she'd found what she needed. "Now you've done it!" she yelled and marched from the room, though she had not made up her mind where she was going or who she could tell. She almost stepped into an open storm drain, and found that amusing.

III Villains

The den was dark and cool and smelled like the hot dogs and cake from the birthday party the day before. Outside the thunder-clouds had sealed up the day and seemed too heavy to remain afloat over the houses. Like castles and moats and great dark for-ests, like a whole slew of magic kingdoms, or a whole history of them, the sky could swell up and parade itself, but it had to fall. Bug was honing her courage on sharp little bits of magic, on pieces of party and grains of happier-times when a splash of lightning frightened her so that she pushed past a chair and into a corner to brace herself against the thunder. But it never came and a good deal of her momentum was spent waiting on it. Doubt settled in her and she was not sure she had anything on Jilly worth telling—you didn't bother somebody else's mother with news that somebody else's daughter was nasty, though a mother didn't mind hearing it about her own daughter and would race you back to the scene of the crime. She was not sure that her new disgust with Tina had not somehow muddied the whole thing. Indeed it dawned on her that she might be telling on Tina, that she might be sick and tired of her simply for being unable to protect her. In hindsight, the whole situation seemed far away if not slight to begin with. Bug exhaled at last, and shivers coursed through her waiting body; would she break so easily when the girls and every mother were depending on her to reaffirm their pattern, their mother-daughter dance—wouldn't the switches on the George Washingtons still be green, the thorns still relaxed? She had to tell now while there was still love in the act.

She could recall a similar responsibility and a similar frustra-tion every time her brother hit her or tripped her or told her the worst lies. Before she could run home with the incident intact, so fresh and incriminating it was burning her tongue to tell it, the bottom would fall out of her anger and conviction. She argued with herself, rearranging events in her mind, losing sight of priorities, and by the time she reached her daddy's boots, sweating and out of breath—he'd always be in the TV room, always polishing his boots or his brass, spitting on them, rubbing lighter fluid on them and scouring them in flames (all the while watching a ball game) — she would choke and sputter, not sounding convincing or hurt or anything at all, except out of breath, and he would wave her out of his light or tell her to get him another beer. Viletta, an older cousin, told her once she should write things down. Once it's down, she said, there's no way anyone, even you can deny it happened, and that very day Bug started her journal. She wrote down everything, straining against her own disbelief to be accurate, but that didn't make it easier to tell.

Perhaps if Tawny were more solid in his role as antagonist. . . . He hit hard and tripped with accuracy, but Bug always felt he was dodging more trouble than he had time to dish out. He didn't stick around to gloat over the pain he'd caused her, and he wasn't running because he feared her revenge or because he wanted her to chase him. She thought maybe he was afraid of their father and she would try for some reaction by shouting after him the list of things she could tell. But it seemed as though something else had set Tawny into motion; even before he hit her he was running from her, from all of them. He would run around the house and only stop in every so often as big brother or their son.

Lightning surged again against the window glass—lightning without thunder, but drenching, disorienting light—and she whirled around. A wardrobe loomed beside her, thrown up taller in the revitalized darkness. Japanese lanterns and colored crepe paper tassles stirred, filling the room with darting shadows. Plates of cake, some of them untouched, waited everywhere, even on the thin arms of the party chairs where they could be tipped over by any person just ghosting by. Bug stuck her finger in some frosting and licked it. All the pieces had dry, nubby shells on them, they had been sitting so long. She would ask for a fresh piece to take to her daddy. Also for a handful of candy from the piñata since she had been the one to knock it loose and hadn't gotten her fair share. A red hot caught her eye and she snatched it up. There was a mound of crumpled paper, the brightly colored wrappings of ten thousand gifts, it seemed, all loosely packed in a corner, tall enough to hide a robber, or Bozo maybe. He had been there, ugly, with his shock of orange hair and white painted face, but nice too, with a gift for each and every girl. Bug remembered pleasurably: she had never seen a party so big, with so many girls from other neighborhoods, and with so many gifts for one person. Had anyone seen Bozo leave? He didn't speak much and the man inside of him used a painful falsetto. He was the only man there, if you could call a clown a man, and he vanished before anyone could thank him or offer him some cake. Bug had helped Mrs. Vanderkleese with the cake and recognized the piece she had set aside for the clown; it was dry and nubby like the rest.

She drifted to the base of the hall steps and paused, weighing her nerve. She decided to ask for a piece of cake instead. Let somebody else save the girls and their mothers. All the bedrooms were upstairs along the hall; her own house was the same next door. In a flash of lightning she saw her house and a row of others all alike, stretching to a point along Beale Street. She knew her own yard was spready, the grass uncut, the garden gone to seed, the magnolia brown and shedding (for two years now on the edge of disaster) because her brother was rebelling and her daddy had his boots to do and her mama worked daytimes, but the houses were identical right down to the false shutters and the pressed-board latticework. When light rushed in from the window up the hall, when it filled the kitchen behind her and the living room and all the bedrooms where the drapes weren't pulled against it, all the houses in Logan Heights were being flooded in the same way. They were two-story boxes with big square windows on all the same walls. Some, however, the corner houses, sat cater-cornered for variation and had larger front yards. Bug remembered the group of mothers belly-aching because officers and enlisted men were living the same. Mrs. Kreockle asked, what, after all, had her husband worked so hard for? Of course it took two men to get her as far as she'd come—the Hawaiian, who had died, and the new one, Chaplain Kreockle. Mrs. Vanderkleese, the most vocal (though she had many, many enlisted friends) declared that there were differences—small ones, mind you, but differences—that when cultivated, distinguished an officer and his family. She said, the strength and character of a family's lawn could go a long way toward distinguishing that special mettle. Bug couldn't understand it then; she felt too good to care, with all the mothers watching her and smiling, and Mrs. Vanderkleese holding both her and young Tina together in her skirt, like two daughters and two sisters.

—Climbing the steps she felt that some subtle thing had moved between her sisterhood with Tina; she was drifting helplessly closer to answers that could only tear them apart. Was her anger, at any time, worth that? And what would be left to her? Jilly?

Warm and strong and good-smelling, Mrs. Vanderkleese had squeezed them both to her like daughters and sisters and announced to the gathering her solution to the relaxed codes: "I want to propose the Officer's Wives' Cup for Lawn and Garden Excellence," and she did, and they accepted, and to nobody's surprise the cup was hers for two years running. She kept it at the end of the hall on a fancy table in front of the window there, so people driving past could see it.

—And never once was Bug made to feel the subtle differences between their two families; she visited every day, she helped Mrs. Vanderkleese in the garden, she stayed for at least lunch, and often slept over. She had a mother here like she had a mother at home, and knew the Maria here as well, if not better than, the Maria at home; she had her own pillow, her own towel, her own cup for the special sweet coffee and milk that Mrs. Vanderkleese made children with breakfast; she kept a collection of Barbies in Tina's closet and one at home, a pair of shoes, a flannel, a toothbrush, her own lavender soap. Occasionally she wondered if Mrs. Vanderkleese didn't keep watch on her from one of the draped windows upstairs, ticking off the number of times she misstepped the flagstones and touched the grass in the front garden, but only occasionally.

She knocked softly at the bedroom door, but the storm answered her with cannon booms. She heard a shuffle in the room, some laughter, and thought Mrs. Vanderkleese or her bear-like husband, the Dutchman, was coming to answer. The storm boomed again, decisively, and a tree branch slashed the window.

Laughter continued, but at the same distance; no one answered. It was the third roll of thunder—like a tree, like several trees being torn across and magnificently hurled her way—the third roll that convinced her of all the time she could save the parents the added effort by opening the door herself.

Inside the heavy orange drapes filtered out the storm light. At first she saw silhouettes, a single sharp edge, a restless line that looked like hilly terrain. The bed was on the wall opposite the window and she figured the adults were sitting there, talking. She heard their murmurings, the tail end of some laughter, a sudden catch in the air and she crossed to confront them, folding her hands charmingly, wishing she still had on her party dress, because it was the cake she planned to ask for. The room smelled like a spring day, that same sweet fragrance that preceded Mrs. Vanderkleese wherever she went, that enveloped young girls more thoroughly than arms when Mrs. Vanderkleese needed to hold, to pet and praise; but their were headier odors too that she could not place, and a sudden spice, a cut lime electricity that skipped past smell but enlivened her nostrils, the back of her tongue. The parents were not on the bed. She turned to the window—the candy-wrapper dusk color there, and turned back, then turned completely around. For a moment she felt a wild panic and shifted bodily for the door, but without moving her feet and she fell. Pressures, she thought, something inside or outside, whistled through the latched windows giving enough draft to part the drapes, and suddenly enough light to etch out the peaks and hollows of certain forms—a dresser piled with clothes, a chair with shoes or boots turned on their sides, and the empty bed. She knew this room, because she knew it next door. She tried to stand then, knowing the room and exactly where she was, but she stumbled into the bodies, and for a moment it crossed her mind that they might be dead; perhaps she wished it. Mr. and Mrs. Vanderkleese sprawled there, naked and wild, with shock-round eyes, gazing back at her. They were all three pretzeled on the floor, the wife trying to hide under the bed and unable to push her husband off, and the big man twisting himself painfully, astonished, then suddenly resigned, while Bug pulled to free herself from the riddle of legs. If she noticed the boots it was only a coolness on her cheek in passing, and the wide green studded tool belt was just a brief roughness against her hand, her hand so tensed it (by itself) felt nothing. She didn't see the green cap, the brass eagle, the black visor, dipped rakishly on the stunned face, didn't see the man, his slippery penis, at all until Mrs. Vanderkleese, realizing the foolishness of trying to hide herself, threw modesty aside, sat up and began laughing at him. There was no hiding him anymore. Mrs. Vanderkleese looked from Bug to her husband: he was gray; she had her mouth opened to holler and that was the only color anybody saw. She catapulted from them, conjuring briefly—as the scene retracted into darkness— her own parents, the night noises that woke her sometimes, but her mind refused the connection, even though the difference— Mr. Vanderkleese's hat, its particular medal—was ever so slight.

She ran thickly as if escaping in a dream—down the hall where the two doors were opening, through the den and the faded memories there, and out the front door, forgetting the screen would slam if she didn't catch it, and all the time expecting, desiring perhaps, the storm to flash and boom and maybe fry her up like a piece of bacon, but the sky was calm, threatening but calm, with a radiant patina along its edges. She fell in the grass and scrambled to a hedge, secretly hollowed out for hiding in. The sky permitted a spidery crack of sunlight that briefly reminded her of a muppet sketch she had seen. A muppet apple was looking up from the bottom of a sack lunch, and elbowing its muppet friend, the Sandwich, it asked with sneaky knowledge in its voice, "so, who's gonna be et up first?" then a hand came in and took the apple away. Bug thought it through several times; woke up thinking about it, but never figured out just what the apple seemed to know. Her brother looked at her funny, like it was all so obvious, like she should have her eyes checked or her brain scanned because it was *so* obvious it was actually stupid and he wouldn't waste another minute thinking about it himself; and why did she watch such dumb stuff anyway? why did she have to play the dumbest things? and hang around with the dumbest people he'd ever met? Tina hated him, or rather, had a deep, vague, irrational fear of him, and Bug, not understanding her friend's fear but secure in their love and their sisterhood, defended the smaller girl against her own brother. She couldn't defend herself, but honestly thought she'd throw herself in front of a flying bullet for Tina. So why was she suddenly more afraid for him?

> Seven trees bearing strange fruit
> Blood on the leaves
> Blood at the roots
>   *Something something* swinging in the breeze . . .

She watched as the wind skipped along the grass like an invisible person, then she heard the whirr, raspy as fiddles, high up in the oak trees. Next door Maria arrived on the porch. Bug ducked deeper into the hedge. The woman screwed her fists into her ample hips and looked about sharply, muttering something in Spanish. She was gathering her breath to holler and Bug instantly softened toward her, but it was Tawny that she hollered for. She hollered twice then picked something off her toe and headed inside.

Bug sighed. She wanted the rain to come, so she could escape in it, but the wind came first. She saw it jump the garden fence and make a beeline for Mrs. Vanderkleese's flowers. It was a twister full of dust and paper and sharp, dried brown magnolia leaves. She saw little Hartmoot Eddie Vanderkleese in the screen door, and thought, Lord, there won't be a Christmas . . . The girls were peeking out through the basement window, probably standing on the back of the busted sofa, dark head next to red tow head, suddenly friends again — or had they ever, even for one minute, seen themselves as enemies? The Vanderkleeses' Maria was already bundling up the sheets and the spreads from the side line, all the while barking short, exasperated things to herself in Spanish, perhaps cursing the storm or the day she took her job. It seemed almost spiteful when a strong gust of wind dipped out of the trees and blew off her pretty net hat with the silk roses, and sent it skittering across the lawn like a small animal. Then all the winds kicked up at once, circling, crisscrossing, eclipsing, colliding. The twister did a sprite dance in the middle of the front garden, a prank for which any child, boy or girl, could count on a sound switching, or several clouts about the neck and head, and this from any mother too. Indeed, other mothers would spank you more enthusiastically than the mother of the garden herself,

as though they had personal stock in Mrs. Vanderkleese's enter-
prise and feared its undoing like the collapse of a bank, or a
famine in the heartland, or a citrus blight in Florida. Bug wondered sometimes if children didn't get whipped more often for
the things they couldn't control than for those wickednesses they
had spent weeks conjuring.

Nasty twister, it raised its rough edge like a skirt and passed
over the zinnias and marigolds lining the walk; it brushed the
snapdragons and raised the purple cornflowers a notch, leaving
everything static, anxious, but unharmed; even the red daisies
growing wild in the yard hardly spun or bristled up. For all its
ugly potential, the twister just seemed curious. Or particular. It
paused, to breathe perhaps, then flew for the roses. Bug felt a
chill as it grazed her hedge on the way.

It swallowed up a whole trellis of climbing Ma Perkins roses.
The three girls had worked an entire week after school snip-
ping the bush back so it would be full for its summer cycle, and
the storm, in a pitiless instant, had picked it clean. Mrs. Vanderkleese sailed out then in a unzipped blue sun dress and fluffy
houseshoes. She had a broom and almost struck her maid in the
head with it as Maria raced by on the chase, her net hat hardly
an arm's length away, scurrying round and round. Mrs. Vanderkleese was a thick-set woman, but for the moment she was loose
and wild and all free-form action, a whirling dervish herself as
she swung the broom at the twister and cursed it round and
round. Of course it was a ludicrous display; the wind unravelled
at a whim, spinning its elements free for a moment then joining
with a minor curl to start again. Bug shook her head. Even before
the angry woman could uncoil herself to strike somewhere else
the storm had done damage in three places. If it waited any time
at all it was just to bait her. Bug felt a stand-off coming. The wind
had congealed in a corner near the porch. Mrs. Vanderkleese
took a step for it, saw it moving and anticipated its direction.
She threw her broad back around to protect her prized Queen
Elizabeths, but the storm took them in spite of her. Every fist-
sized bloom on the hedge shuddered and exploded, one after the
other, playful as a party antic, and the free petals whirled up and
about like confetti. Mrs. Vanderkleese vanished completely, but
Bug knew she was there, hunkered and challenging over her bare

stems, no doubt clutching the broom, high and low, as though at any moment she might climb on it, burst into black, and confront the devil on his own terms. Instead, she sank down by the bush and curled up like a small hill.

Mr. Vanderkleese barrelled out then, big and jolly as a drunk, with Tina, Jilly, Hartmoot Eddie and Maria festering close behind him. He cooed, "Dorothy, my sweet"—or the like, and bent to scoop her up, but she waved the broom in his face and must have spit curses because the whole group, Dutchman and all, drew back behind the tiny screen door, and, caged-out and curious like spectators at a zoo, they waited while Mrs. Vanderkleese tore up handfuls of grass, cranky and evil as a mama bear. Tawny saw her too, and the sharp, shiny brown leaves—some of which he'd rebelled against—because he didn't stop running, didn't even seem to glance their way; but Bug knew that he knew, and kept running right past them anyway; because, Bug thought, he was a shooting star, and somebody else's child, somebody else's brother until he could get safely away from that woman's ruined garden, and from that bare tree, finally bare, waiting for ornaments.

Hartmoot Eddie started to cry then, he was so young; or in the crush to see, someone may have stepped on him. Bug bristled up like a cat. It was raining. A river rose in the streets, high enough to take the basements and garages, to flood whole houses if a drain wasn't opened for it. She saw the crazy man flash by in an old car, spinning the wheel, just missing the curb. Then black kids in party hats flooded out into the river—Tonda squealing, he would be the first to float his popsicle stick all the way to the end.

Journals and notebooks

[From 1977, when he was 16, to the end of his life, Gary Fisher kept a journal and a number of corollary notebooks. What follow are selections, ordered consecutively, from the thousands of pages of these journals and notebooks.]

Thursday, September 15, 1977 [Düsseldorf]
—Someone up there loves me, seems like every time I get in a jam someone comes around and gets me out. For instance, yesterday I spent my picture money on getting my parents a present (for their 17th anniversary) and "Jungle Love." After buying them I realized I didn't have enough money to buy my school pictures. I thought sure I can take a loan from good ole pop, but no, this morning he only had 20 marks for Crystal's pictures. I'd given up. What good was a bunch of old pictures of yourself, anyway? Right? But, I wanted them. At near the last possible moment my mother mentioned 10 DM Luchina had and I knew someone (not sure whether he or she) brought this to my attention. It always happens, but it never seems as though I'm thankful and when I am it seems as though it comes at a time when I need something else. So here's to you! Thanks. Perhaps I'm not quite sure of everyone's destiny, but I know someone's up there watching and guarding us. Thanks again.
—The *New Avengers* was fantastic as usual. This time about some gas that puts the whole of London to sleep and a band of Terrorist/Looters steal a fortune in cash. (Sorry I've forgotten the other guy's name because of Don McLean's "American Pie") and Purdy attempt to stop this gang of criminals, and as usual, succeed. The overall view of the show—Great. (Mb. P.M.) Be on the look out for the A[merican] S[chool] I[n] D[üsseldorf] Newspaper.

Help us, Lord, to make something good that will last for years to come. ("American Pie" just ended) Time to start homework.

— By the way, still procrastinating. That book *The Choirboys* is good, more so than I'd have expected, but this is one I know I'll finish.

Monday, October 10, 1977

. . . Monday. Today. Nothing is really all that important except to say I want to go to "College Day" in Frankfurt tomorrow and I will! Got a letter from Barbra Von Tobel today. Auch. Time to eat. Heaven help me now! Please — is there a chance left? They seem to be getting slimmer and slimmer by the hour. God knows I want to go. Maybe if I took a train to D'dorf but I'd have to leave home at 5 A.M. to get there by 8. Please persuade her by tomorrow morning. Please. (I threw away those *PG* [*Play Girl*] pictures by the way.) (Never want to see 'em again, *I do,* but I won't given the will power.) Maybe if I hadn't have lied, You would have persuaded her to drive me to D'dorf, but I suppose I'm a bit "unimportant" at least not as important as so many other "things" my parents always *seem* to have to do. I wish . . . maybe later, like in 5 years or another life, I'll find what I'm looking for instead of this bloody jealousy, hate, and sorrow that seems to come in tides. Is it part of life in general, or just mine? I had planned to read Barbra's letter on the bus tomorrow, but no, not if I don't go, and the chances for that look all too promising. Why do I keep feeling this warm hopeful feeling or is that self pity in another form? — I'll read it now.

Tuesday, October 11, 1977

"NO, I DIDN'T GO!!!!"

Tuesday, December 13, 1977

. . . I asked LaDonna out for dinner this Friday and she has turned me down. You can't even call our relation infatuation. I've known the girl for 2 years and we're still strangers. Well fuck her! I'm going back to the states January 11 or haven't I said this. We're going to Ft. Bragg, North Carolina. No. 1 song in the US for the past 8 weeks "You Light Up My Life" — Debby Boone.

Tuesday, December 20, 1977

—Well here I am precisely one week from my last entry and so much has happened since then that'll be hard to put in words. Probably the most noticeable item of the week was Friday night in D'dorf. Another truly exhilarating experience. I felt good half the time, embarrassed a quarter of the time, and downright shitty the other quarter of the time. The day started off okay, I suppose, many people were missing since their vacations began earlier than the rest of ours. I honestly envy some of these people here and to control my jealousy against people like the Lichmans and the Swifts who can spend a grand on ski equipment and venture to Austria every Christmas, I lie. I make up tales about how I've been skiing in Colorado and Alamagordo, New Mexico, or how I've lived all over the US including Alaska, and how I had 3000 DM in the bank at the beginning of the school year (I only had 1500) and now I only have 800 because I spent so much on clothes and albums (actually I haven't one pfennig in the bank and I had to steal some geld to go on this excursion on Friday). Once I get off my lazy ass and get determined I'm going to show every one of these rich braggarts (no they're not braggarts since they actually have what they say they do. Why should they be ashamed to share that in conversation?).

—I suppose I felt shitty 'cause I knew where the money had come from. I should never have been elected Student Council Treasurer. I'm going to get a job this summer and work my ass off to go to college and still have spending money. I'm sick of living like a heathen, with my folks too dumb to know that we're middle class and that a few lessons in interior decorating or general neatness wouldn't hurt. Neatness seems to inspire me. I'm not sure why. Perhaps Peter Lechman would have made a better treasurer since he has no need for the money. I'm merely thankful that I could go at all. I was dressed horribly in a leather sports coat, my white wrinkled jeans, a pullover vest, a pink shirt, and black stacks. Now I realize that I could have worn any number of combinations of clothing and looked better than I did that night. I got many compliments, but inside I was over-inhibited by my appearance, so I looked gross to myself. For the Christmas program at the Kaserne I'll look 100% better.

. . . Another break, Dad got his cd4 unit which breaks up the music into parts, but now my Mother and Father are arguing about the luggage and why my father would buy another turntable instead of luggage. God knows they're crazy, but I love them. Shit, they're crazy, I'm glad I can figure them out, without them knowing it.

. . .—I think Starsky and Hutch might come on tonight and I also have to study for that Christmas program tomorrow. I saw "The Exorcist" for the first time a few nights back and it was sufficiently gross. No need to explain the plot since good versus evil is always easy to remember. I couldn't have done better, but believe me I'll work on it. I've thought of writing that book I've been planning in my head "The German Experience" and it's quite feasible that a 16-year-old kid could write a bestseller then make it a movie then cut the soundtrack album and make a million—isn't it? The other movie I saw the night after "The Exorcist" was "Jim, the World's Greatest" which really touched me. . . .

—Back to "Jim, the World's Greatest." I didn't see the beginning or the end, but from the middle part that I saw I'm dying to see the rest. Jim Nolan was a guy (freshman or sophomore in college I think) with many problems. Some of them were personal problems that I could associate with such as a shyness with girls. And some were personal family problems which I've not experienced, but can vividly imagine. His father, an alcoholic, was constantly brutalizing Jim's younger brother Kelly. I'm not sure of the reason but perhaps it was because the father only wanted one son to love and cherish and when Kelly came along (he couldn't have been more than ten) he shattered that relation belonging exclusively to Jim and his father. I believe that the mother either died or divorced since you never saw her throughout the flick. Anyway, Jim was sort of a protector and father for Kelly since his father insisted on ignoring his younger son. Perhaps the most memorable parts were Jim and Kelly one night in bed. Kelly leaned over the top bunk and asked Jim in the bottom, if he was asleep. Jim said no. "I have something for you," Kelly said.

"What is it?" Jim replied rather sleepily yet with a smile staring up at the little brown-headed kid above him.

Kelly, jumping down, "I didn't know if you'd want it since you lost the game." (Referring to the football game that Jim had lost earlier that day. He had also broken a date with some dumb-looking blonde with whom he'd had sex in the shower earlier in the flick.) He reached into the darkness of a corner and walked back with something, his little bare feet padding across a cold floor. He held out the small sculpture to Jim.

—Jim, unsure of what it was, took it and fondled it and then saw it was a football player on a stand and a small removable football all made of clay. He read the inscription aloud "To the world's greatest football player." And he smiled. "That's real nice," he said and put the statue on the chest of drawers beside his bed.

"Hope you like it, Jim," Kelly said, all smiles.

"Thank you, Kelly," Jim said and pulled the boy to him. "Thank you, thank you, thank you." And he hugged him for a while, the boy returning the embrace.

—The second occasion was perhaps the next morning where Kelly comes bounding in on a silently sleeping Jim. He giggles and crawls all over Jim waking him from sleep. I was surprised that Jim didn't get angry; I would have. Jim grabbed the boy and rolled him on his back and tickled him into fits of laughter then let him go and said, "What time is it?" Kelly's answer cracked me up. "Time to get up" in between giggles of course.

—Well, to make this short. The father killed Kelly and Jim went out for revenge after carrying the dead boy into the streets and dropping to his knees in tears (reminds me of Timothy Bottoms in the "Last Picture Show" after his little brother had gotten hit by some drunkard in a truck). At that point I left. Number 1 song in the United States (I don't know, but I guess it's "You Light Up My Life").

Thursday, February 9, 1978 [Fayetteville, North Carolina]
—I feel pretty lousy. First because of this damned virus that's been bugging me for about a week. One of my ears have plugged giving me occasional headaches and my throat did hurt, but that's stopped now. Second, because we will probably go to Virginia Friday. (god-forbid) I may be prejudiced, but I'll be honest, many of the people I met must be 50 years behind the rest of the world. At least the school is, and I know I don't conform and I hate it. If I could change to anything I want for a given period of time I would be a very "hip," super strong basketball/football jock . . .

—Well, the news is finalized. Shit! My mother just came back and spread the horrible news. We have to go to fucking Virginia. I hope the car breaks down and all transportation stops because of an overnight "Blizzard" in Virginia. Or maybe they'll allow us to move into the house. Perhaps they will confirm my father's paycheck and we can stay. I was anxious to go to school, now I'd just as soon drop out, continue at summer school. God, I know my situation is better than many, but why can't it be a fantasized reality. Why don't things ever go the way you want it to. If things are this bad permanently, I may think about thinking about contemplating suicide. (Fat chance, but I do hate this predicament.) Let them send that paycheck today so we can stay.

—Things seem so futile sometimes, so very cruel and useless, yet they continually happen regardless of the "good things." It doesn't make much sense to me that luck could be so mixed, and have such extremes. This has got to be the absolute "worst" situation I've ever been in. (Sounds silly doesn't it, but it bugs me—bugs the hell out of me.) When I think of a school full of Renards's (sp?) I cringe. I can't go through with a month of this shit and if I can help it at all I will not be subjected to it. In an attempt to capture my feelings, let me say that it's time to get honest with myself. —I'm wrong, many times, and this is probably one. I've based my judgment of this school in Virginia on hearsay from Renard and other kids in the Gaines family. We share almost nothing at all in common other than perhaps color and a common grandparent. Mentally, emotionally, and physically I'd say we are almost contrasting. I look at Renard and his brothers and brutish sisters and I see a very athletic, physically tough people who've matured perhaps sexually and bodily, much more rapidly than myself. They've spent much of their life in a secluded, predominantly black environment, so the speech and manner are what I view as "stereotyped black" (though not so much as the TV black or many a "city-slick" black: Phoenix for instance). While I've spent little, if any, time in a predominantly black environment, so my speech, manner, values, and views on black heritage are incredibly different. Now I'm being forced to conform. Perhaps temporarily, but I doubt it (I don't know about Pine Forest's racial status yet). And I don't like it. I'm frightened of what I don't know and I think I've always avoided it in the past, but now it's time to face some reality and I don't want to. My mother's right, I'm boneheaded-stubborn, on the outside, but what she doesn't know is that I agree with her. She's right I am—very much so. I'll probably never admit it to her and I find myself moving deeper in a futile rut each time we argue.

—To be continued right after *Starsky & Hutch.*

—I realize this may sound as though I have little continuity in my writing, but then who gives a damn really. At least you can understand it. I guess my main ambition in life has always been to have fun doing what I'm doing (whatever it may be) and making money (And I mean lots of it). Most of my fantasy is situated around the arts, the bull's-eye being a few super-platinum albums and several smash-hit movies in my career. I wanted to be, and still do, another Stevie Wonder, Elton John, Shaun Cassidy even. I just wanted to be known, perhaps even as a writer, but I don't feel I've accomplished anything at all on the road to fame and fortune (cliché? So is the fantasy). Least of all the acceptance of the "uniform" I was issued with. I am black and that won't ever change, yet I've never really been forced to accept that and it's causing turmoil in my inner-being. Just what the fuck did I expect! My parents are black, both coming from harsh backgrounds. (More so than my own.) My mother: one of eleven farmer's children, born and raised in Virginia and the mighty Appalachians. My father (I hate that word "father" it never fit my conception of the man who raised me. "Boss" is a more appropriate word) was raised in the black city neighborhoods of Phoenix, Arizona. He had "guts" enough to fly the coop and join the Air Force at 15. (The military disgusts me, but I can't blame "boss," he has his life to lead regardless of us.) So there you are. And then each of us has been raised and pampered and educated, and treated with what I feel is the same care as a white family of similar size. For this I'm happy, yet I think all of us have a lot of maturing to do, because no one really understands or cares to find out about the other. I'm no exception, sometimes arguing for the sake of arguing. Why are things so complicated? Why aren't they like *The Brady Bunch* or maybe *Family.* God, I'd be on the top of the world if our family was the *Eight is Enough* crew. But it never works. So I dream, fantasizing about an imaginary situation and finding myself actually trying to live a part. So much for shattered dreams, which, by the way are all white, perhaps because TV families are white. The other major problem is that there's no second chance. I can't do it again and I shouldn't expect to. (I hope there's reincarnation.)

—That's enough bad thoughts. New hope for the day—that I can become a copy boy for some fair newspaper and work my way into a "big" news reporter. I feel better after writing this (pissed, but better). "Slip Sliding Away"—Paul Simon.

Tuesday, February 14, 1978 [Virginia]

—Well, skipped a day because mother slapped some damn curfew on me before I could begin the day's astonishing array of events. Went to that silly Nelson County High School Monday and was enrolled. So far I really hate it, I have to manipulate myself between being a black, hip, rebellious honky-hater, and a whitish-speaking sweet little black boy who runs errands for the teacher. It's driving me mad worrying whether the blacks will accept me, and whether I should become a honky-hater like many of the blacks. So far the only real person I can even say I'm acquainted with are Amy and some white guy named Troy. I want to leave. I wish I were in Germany.

Saturday, February 25, 1978

—Yesterday I got a letter from Penny (Lane) Ford that I forgot to mention then. It shocked me, because it deals with mature subjects while most of the letters I get are childish and trivial. Penny's thinking of running away with some Marine named Michael to get married. Penny's only seventeen or maybe eighteen by now and she's chosen marriage over college. I hope she knows what's right for her. I wouldn't want to see her hurt, not after the good times we all had, plus Penny's a bright girl and this might be such a waste. Details later. (I suppose; if we continue to write.)

—School on Saturday isn't much different I suppose, but I felt lousy inside all day, for no apparent reason. I woke up this morning thinking I'd heard my father's voice. I heard "Daddy" more than once, and Leslie or Luchina had said it, so they couldn't be talking to Grandpa. I guess my imagination just ran away with me 'cause I really believed he was here, and I wanted to rush out and say something witty like "I must still be asleep, you're supposed to be in Florida." (While rubbing my eyes.)

—I don't know if I'm just maturing or what, because a new thought just struck my head and unfortunately it's true. Seems that all I know is a superficial kind of caring; a false love. Between me and parents I think it's been slightly "touch and go," if I'm using the words correctly. There's some love, I'm sure, underlining our relationship, but it's not the kind you openly display. It's a love and caring you think you know is there, but never get concrete proof, except in times of hardship. Then it's apparent. The brief moment of "something" between LaDonna and I opened my mind to jealousy only and unless jealousy is the only factor determining love between two people, then I don't want to be part of it. It was a one-sided relationship anyway, sort of infatuation on my part, I suppose. But it was very unreal after awhile. Soon LaDonna only became a symbol. I could have gone out with any girl for that symbol. I wanted to prove myself as a man, taking out girls to nice restaurants, movies, bars. I wanted people to think I was mature enough to get in a girl's pants and suave enough to maintain a standing relationship. (Perhaps that's why I enjoyed Paige's and Renée's bubble-gum-lipstick kisses. All but one stirred little in me.) Don't get me wrong. For awhile (about 6 months) I really dug LaDonna, she was beautiful and we could communicate, and I think she wanted to, but fear got in the way. Perhaps a bit of racial prejudice (Believe me, I was apprehensive to like a white girl the way I liked her, so I can't blame her for that) stemming not from her, but social pressures. Both, in our blanket of "sophistication," managed to cover up that feeling. I just hope LaDonna never knew that I'd try to use her.

Tuesday, April 25, 1978 [Fayetteville, N.C.]

—A lot's happened since Saturday, but the biggest thing has got to be *Star Wars*. It was simply fantastic. A fairy tale that I certainly wouldn't mind living. The movie was constant exhilaration; nonstop action, spiced with comedy and all the trimmings of the best space flick ever. I'm going to get the soundtrack album and I'd love to get posters from the movie to cover my room in its action-packed beauty. I can't explain what I felt as I watched it, but I could identify with Luke Skywalker's (Mark Hamill) feelings. The movie lit up my life, but I wish my life was a bit closer to that mechanized age (no I don't, but then I do). It was beautiful.

—*The Moneychangers*, Arthur Miller's bestseller, is now a television mini-series running over three consecutive nights. And it's good. But what really caught me was Timothy Bottoms's misfortunes in a prison gang rape. I didn't know you could put such things on TV. It's hard to subdue feelings so maybe it's wrong to. *Forum* and *Response* both disapprove of masking feelings and urges. Still a wife and children are my goal, not to be forcibly molested by a bunch of hairy convicts. From what I've read everyone goes through this phase. I certainly hope that's true.

Saturday, June 3, 1978

—It's really Sunday now at about 20 after midnight. The day began miserably as most Saturdays do around here and took a slow direct slope to the pits. The sooner I get out of this place the better. Somewhere (If I'll get off my lazy ass and look) there's a good-paying job with many opportunities for advancement awaiting me, but until I find it, until I graduate and get into that "dream" college or university, and until I get out of this childish need for a "parent," I'm stuck.

—Something about seeing my parents drunk brings out the very worst in me. All the little things added up (mainly because I let them) and now have me upset at all. Leslie presented some sort of joke about me trying to score with some chick to my mother and for me there's nothing worse than two females ganging up on a defenseless virgin. Truthfully the girl wasn't all that pretty; on a scale of 0 to 10 with 10 being my dream girl and 0 being the absolute epitome of revulsion, she'd rank a shaky 2. With LaDonna taking a solid 6 (the highest on my list) and Regina (my bus driver here at Pine Forest) taking a 3 as second, the girl didn't stand a chance. I only passed on the compliment because she was a girl and probably sensitive; she'd take the compliment and immediately add it to her "pluses for Gary Fisher list." I also thought she was much older than 16 and now I'm jealous for feeling a bit immature and underdeveloped in her presence. Leslie's joke might have held some truth, but her teasing approach, my parents' drunkenness, reckless driving, scratchy music, shoveling mulch and dog shit, mowing and watering the lawn, my father's sarcastic approach to anything, apparent facades, and my mother's defensive denial of having a facade prompted me into begrudgment (is that a word?). It was dumb, and I feel a little silly for arguing, but pride's making it a little hard to admit it to myself and impossible to back down to anyone else. Growing pains? I wish I knew. This is one sorry situation which I'm probably making an even sorrier melodrama. "A million and one ways to fuck up a Saturday or a Sunday or a . . ." starring Gary Fisher.

—That's a big problem. If such small things tick me off so badly how will I react with *real* problems, *real* responsibilities? Part of maturity must be avoiding the petty. Maybe it's time to grow up!

Sunday, June 4, 1978

—We're going on a picnic! Not such a bad day though former grudges still linger.

—Things went good at the picnic. We went to a peaceful park on Pope Air Force Base, and even though we were next to the air strip it was still peaceful. The food was good, and the game of croquet was exciting. But swinging, feeling "Footloose and Fancy Free" in the breeze, and the ride in Daryl's and Phyllis's convertible were the icing on the cake. I wish I was alone or with a girl or even my best boy friend with a hundred thousand and not a care in the world. Me and my little Midget would zoom all over America, drinking in the sights; living and loving it. Soon, I pray, real soon.

—Cancel that top paragraph, perhaps it was a little premature.

—By the way, Duke, our new dog, went with us and I'm sure he had a good time. He's a good dog, a beautiful dog, and I'm glad he's ours.

Tuesday, June 9, 1978

—It's dumb how I manage to forget the important things. About an hour ago I got a call from my mother who's in the hospital for a minor operation. (She's having her "tubes tied.") I felt a mixture of love, sympathy, loneliness and slight revulsion at her situation and her drunkenness probably under the influence of an anesthesia (NO "probably" to it). I pray she'll be fine and it's times like these that you regret things you've done and said. It's horrible how I trample the feelings and emotions of others without stopping to think. I love her!! (There I said it, and I believe it too.) *Our Town* continues in every one of us. I never want to forget it. I feel like crying.

Sunday, July 30, 1978

—Tony (pronounced Tawny) and Gwen and Grandma and Grandpa came down this past week and it was fun having them over though I didn't see them much, being at work most of the time.

—Work, though boring and tiring at times seems to be the only escape from this hell-hole of a home. Maybe not the only since I've been using my imagination to create my own situations lately. Since *Jaws II* it's been easy to imagine myself as Mike in the Brady family. It seems that imagination can make you forget some of the bigger problems in life (my parents, misers at present).

—I enjoy work because I get a chance to meet some very nice people. And I enjoy a nice home. Friday we went to a doctor's home out in the suburbs of Fayetteville. It was beautiful and large. The back yard was breathtaking and large with 8 or 9 beautiful oaks and pines. I'm going to incorporate a lot of these situations in my next story which I will finish by September ("The German Experience"). Yesterday we visited a family (not visited, we delivered some chairs and picked up a sofa) near Pine Forest with a beautiful home. We had milk and donuts while the two men talked business. Could that have been the ideal family? (I doubt it, but it couldn't be as much of a joke as this one.)

Sunday, May 20, 1979

—Beth Waterson touched me with what she wrote in my annual. I never realized I was making any true contributions. I'm now proud and energized with the force to strive. I think I aced an English exam because of her.

—Saturday I went job-hunting. I could use the car by then, but the hostility between me and "good ol' dad" is just as thick. I went to McDonald's, then to Cross Creek Mall, where I had the strangest touch of déjà vu I've ever had (no, the one in Virginia has to top this). Anyway I went to apply at this new store opening up and I met this guy there. We were both waiting in a crowd to get in for an interview (or he was, I'd just stepped up wondering if that was the right place). We talked a bit and I noticed he was very easy to talk to. He had a slightly effeminate way about him, but he was built like a football back. I forget his name, but I remember him from a dream, and if that dream is a prediction of the future then I may have just met the best friend I've ever had (or will have for a time anyway). For things to work out we'd both have to get the job, so I'm fairly confident I have some summer employment and a friend. It's crazy, but I found myself following this guy, wanting to be around him. If this is a hint of bisexuality, so be it.

—Chapel Hill looks, feels, tastes, smells so good and so real. Help me get there. I'm in dire straits as far as finance is concerned. I "wish" (yea wish!) that 1,000 dollars would grace my life tomorrow morning.

Monday, May 21, 1979
—I truly love a lot of people at Pine and I think they love me too. Things went very good today, even in my worst class—P.E. We don't do much of anything in there (how would I know, I haven't been to class one regular week in about a month), but we do "relate." I'm part of the group now. Not because I changed, but because I'm appealing just as I am.

Tuesday, May 22, 1979
—Hope *you've* enjoyed it this far, fellow reader. Half of it's in tribute to you!

Wednesday, June 27, 1979
—It's a Wednesday and I'm off from work today, regrettably. I thought I was in for a 40-hour work week and a nice *fat* pay check, but NO, Kirkland's is an obvious rip-off. They're exploiting us. At 29 hours for minimum wage (2.90) it's hardly practical. I doubt if I'll have money left from this paycheck. (I finally get paid this Friday.) I have to pay RCA, I need college expenses paid, I need a pair of dress pants, I need some stamps, I need some friends.

—Maybe that last line sums it all up. Since John left, I've gone no place but to work and back and it hasn't been dull, but I could make it more. This feeling of having little to do has left me with frequent masturbation periods that leave me tired and dissatisfied. It's quite dull in that aspect. If only I would meet a beautiful girl who just wanted a friend and we would walk and talk and go to movies to watch and maybe fondle, but without obligation. Where our innocence and ignorance would bring mutual appreciation, not embarrassment. Soon we would discover this vast world of sensual pleasure, but gradually, in fun and seriousness, rejoicing in the discovery. I'd love to meet that person, and I must stop wishing and start looking. She's out there, surely. . . .

Tuesday, July 3, 1979
   — Being here alone sparked a masturbation fit this morning — something I'm not too proud of. I need love. I shudder to think of myself like this creep on *Frenzy* (boy, could that fuck up a future!).
   — If a man should come into my life before, after, or during, well, so be it. I won't make any preference just yet, but this fantasizing is a lonely unsatisfying substitute.

D-Day! Saturday, August 18, 1979
   — Actually it's 1:00 in the morning and I'm about to sleep in this bed one last time. Today's been hectic. I went on a shopping spree to end all others and then rushed home and packed it. I'm frightened, yet anxious to be there. God, say a little prayer for me. You've brought me so very far. I don't want to make it alone. I don't, but . . . It's so confusing, so very new to me. Guide me. See me through. I really love this place. These people, the past events. Don't make change too dramatic.

Wednesday, November 7, 1979 [Chapel Hill]
   . . . With all these white friends I think in many ways I am white or not the black stereotype that blacks and whites alike have of blacks. I like it, that's all that matters. I'd really like a girlfriend though.
   — God, Rosa's beautiful!

Saturday, November 10, 1979
   — A major note. I was in a bathroom (2nd floor) of the Wilson

Library and found a note on the wall saying "Want to Blow Me." I replied and I will get my first crack at it Monday. I pray it's good.

—Good weekend so far.

Thursday, November 15, 1979

—Well, I accomplished one dream, but when I tried or agreed to carry it further it didn't happen. Wednesday I was supposed to meet the guy I was with Monday. He said he'd ph. me and I was really looking forward to it. Monday I st him and he reciprocated but cm before I did and was in a rush to get out. We found a little (no, it was rather large) classroom, locked the door and the rest is history.

—I really want to see M again and soon. I think he enjoyed it and will want to "use" me more.

—School's been rough, but I'm managing. I made my first A on an English paper Wednesday. (Damn! Wednesday could have been perfect had my friend showed up.)

—"Send One Your Love"—Stevie Wonder's new song. I really like it.

Monday, November 19, 1979

—I really don't have time to be writing this and my hand is frozen on top of this. (Styx—"Babe") It's important that I write before things go any further.

—I believe I totally bombed a Psych exam today, which is not good. I haven't been working like I should. I could have very easily aced that test had I studied. The math test (Chapter 5— Trig) was today also, and though I did passable work, it's not what I wanted.

—I know the stem of my problem lies in this ever-increasing urge to be with someone else. Adolescence was lonely. I went through the LaDonnas and the doldrums. But college life can be rougher still. I really like some of the people here. I fear or just don't care for some of the others. I'd like a girl that I could be with, share problems with, maybe we could have sex. That wouldn't matter so much. It's being with someone.

—I've been letting my fantasies run wild. (It helps control an unbearable loneliness.) I would really enjoy being with some good-looking guy (a jock or something of the sort), and I may get my wish if I look. But do I really want that? I see it as security, as well as fulfilling a sexual fantasy that's been plaguing me for years. Just knowing a guy's close; maybe being able to sleep beside him; giving myself to him. I'd be inundated in a sense of security and warmth. It'd be beautiful.

—Right now I only have coldness for *some* girls who "like" me. Jean does absolutely nothing for me. I fear sex with her—afraid that she wants to judge me. When I was with "M" I wasn't embarrassed.

—Anyway, something will turn up. . . .

Wednesday, November 25, 1979

—Things aren't much better, but I have exited from the dreaded doldrum period. Now I'm *just* outside of it.

—I saw that guy again. He walked by the Psych room today and I could have sworn he was looking dead at me (at least I hope he was). That guy may just be a figment of my frustrated mind, but he's beautiful. I hope he's as keyed up on me as I am on him.

—I'm beginning to like Jean more and more. Seems the girl is fairly wealthy and isn't just an ordinary nigger (is that my prejudice showing).

—I made an appt. for Saturday at 1:00 at the Sundial by the Planetarium. I hope the guy's open and horny. I'd like to really know "this side of life." With Jim gone for the weekend we'll probably come here and maybe he'll spend a night with me (the ultimate fantasy?). You know this is actually easier than getting a girl. There's no macho stigma attached.

—Gia Davis and I researched our paper together in the library. I really enjoy Gia. She's very nice, very mature. My type of young lady (if I had one). ("You're Only Lonely"—JD Southern) is this a good reason?

—Today in Psych we watched *The Rat Man* based on Freud's case. Haunting to say the least. It had me wondering just how crazy I was (or am).

Sunday, December 2, 1979

. . . Today I worked on my term paper off and on. I keep bumping into Lisa and Jeff and that was fun. Another rather interesting thing. A few of the guys in the library kept eyeing me. One guy on the 1st floor did everything but come right out and ask me. It was thrilling. A couple of them were very good looking. One guy with a beard seemed to be forcing himself away (hard to explain). Thrilling. Something *could* (and probably will) come of this.

4:12 P.M.

—My appointment didn't show or maybe he did, but I confused him. I went back to the m-place at something to 3 and wrote another m-place—a set of books on the 4th floor—If the guy actually did follow my instruction and came to the 4th floor, he lost his nerve and got the wrong book. Damn, the ball was in my court and I didn't score. I think both of us were equally new to this. How the hell does it work? I really want (need, have) to try it. I think it's beginning to "get" to me. How? Where? When? Soon I hope (maybe even pray). I was right about that ". . . long long time" wasn't I? SHIT! THIS HURTS!

7:27

—My mom just called and I talked to all of the clan (except Dad who was probably lost in TV). It was fun. Very uplifting, but then I wasn't down, because my term paper's working.

Saturday, December 8, 1979

—No weekend has ever been boring for me here at Chapel Hill. There's always "something" to do, but so far it hasn't been quite enough. Let me explain. I'm not an insatiable person. There's a point where I feel I've had enough and I'll settle down to what might be called "unfun" chores. I cannot say that I haven't been getting my quota of fun. But where's that kind of fun that leaves you content, happy with yourself, and unwound—where's sex!

This cruising is going to have to end soon. I'm really tired of wandering around looking for the impossible. But it *won't* jump up and hit me in the face like I want it to. The gist of this is I'm lonely. Oh, I've got friends. Some good ones. Perhaps too many, but I want a *real* friend. Someone I can love and confide in. I think I'm a latent homosexual (so what's new).

Thursday, December 13, 1979

—Royally screwed my Math Final today. Shit, I should have studied. It's no one's fault, but my own.

—More importantly, there's this guy. Oh, he's gorgeous. Dark hair, bearded, hairy arms, thick build, the works and we came very close to staring at each other in Wilson. The eye contact was incredible. He made my heart pound so hard I was shaking. My God, he is beautiful. I've seen him before and I think he's the one that I talked of earlier. [. . .] I wish I'd had the nerve, but I didn't know if he was looking at *me,* and I'd really feel like a fool if he wasn't. I'll try and see him tomorrow. Yes, he's exciting.

Friday, December 14, 1979

—I saw this mysteriously handsome guy again today. I really think he's looking at me. If only I could tell him how I feel, and if only he'd tell me. (Seems we're both new at this. He was very nervous when I sat down near him.)

—Hopefully tonight! Please! Who do you beg to in instances like this? Not God, and it's much too good to ask for help from some netherworld entity. It could be heaven. If only.

—I bought "Beatles 1967–1970."

—I don't even know him and he's driving me crazy. I've *got* to be with him. I can tell that (when we look at each other) he's horny as all hell 'cause he yawns and stretches to release the tension. How do I approach him, or should I. Maybe I'm "Looking For Mr. Goodbar" and will find what I don't really want. But I do. I really want to be with this guy. God, he's good looking.

—I'm probably closer to some meaningful relationship than I have ever been before. Saturday night, if he gives the word, we'll see what "heaven" can be. I've got a crush on this guy like teenage girls go for rock idols. It's strange and it's frustrating (Smokey Robinson "Cruisin": could it be the new story of my life?).

Please!
Please!
Please! . . .

10:46, Friday, January 11, 1980

. . . My aloofness even shocks me sometimes. I think that may be half the problem with not having a companion. The other half is fear. My ego is fighting, though just subtly because I've never been one to hang onto social sexual stigmas (listen to me, talking as though I've "been there"). I wish a guy would just ask, but it's not that easy is it. I wish my eyes could tell just how much I yearn to be near him. I'm not sure of myself or him.

—This is a dream, almost a nightmare, and I know I've yet to start it. It's so scary. Everything seems so much bigger than me, yet that's the way I want it.

1:45 A.M., *Monday, January 15, 1980*

—I've amazed myself today by getting just about all my homework done, and atop this I'm understanding it. Calculus was a little puzzling, but I'm getting the hang of it. I whizzed right through some limits. I made short order of my German and English reading by making today a library day. I may as well make good use of my excuse for going to Wilson library every night. I know it's really for the off chance of meeting a guy who'll have sex with me (hopefully *the* guy!). Still, I feel good about getting so much work done. I'll continue to frequent the library because it's as conducive to work as it seems to be for homosexual connections. I'm jealous of these guys that seem to get it so easy. I could cover walls in every stall in every toilet of Wilson, but that's not the way I want it. That seems so dirty. I guess I'm looking for love. Perhaps "strange," but what the hell; I want, I used this experience.

6:55 A.M.

Good morning with a little heterosexual tribute—Sammy John's "Chevy Van" **1/2. Great song!

11:47 A.M., *Tuesday, January 15, 1980*

—God, what have I done. That's not the way it was supposed to be. I only want what I want and there won't be any more of what happened today. Even though I have a date for Friday which I may or may not make. God, "where is the love." Today, at least this aspect, is rather unnerving.

—In swimming we got used to the water, which proved fun. I met a friend, maybe, at least a swimming partner, named David.

Astronomy was interesting and funny. So the rest of the day—aside from D.D.D.L.—is mine.

—*Jane Eyre*—an ancient film with class. Rosa and I (I love that girl) went to see it. **. As for this morning, I s. a black guy in a toilet stall and he c. in my m. We've set a date for Friday which I may or may not keep.

2:14 P.M.

—God, what am I doing. I feel like the whole school suddenly knows all about me. Today (I must be desperate), I was late for German just so I could walk with Gord. This guy's on the football team (I can see I'm going to have to burn this book). I'm anxious. We've now formally met and Friday will either initiate something or confirm my belief that this is too good to be true. He's gorgeous though and if something becomes of it it may change my life irreparably (strange choice of words). I'll fantasize about this for some time. I want it to be, I really do! But how do you keep it clandestine? I'm afraid, but maybe being in bed with a magnificent football player will make it all worth it. THIS IS ABNORMAL! Maybe, I'm mildly schizophrenic. THE LOGICAL SONG! GASP! Crazy Ha ha! THIS IS IT!

1:30 A.M., Thursday, January 17, 1980

—Wow, I just finished off a great day by talking with Jerry for almost three hours. We're thinking about collaborating on a play. Sounds "wunnerful." We also beat State today and the dorm went stark raving mad (trite, but true). Incredible night for an equally incredible day. Meeting Gord could be (note the could) the big part of 1980. We'll see. More on all this as it develops. Swimming later this morning—love it!

11:55 A.M.

—I thought I was just tired last night when I wrote "love it" after swimming, but now I believe it. Wow! It's fun! It's really fun and I want to learn very badly. I've made friends in there. We all (about 10 of us) stick together and Kathy, the teacher, is marvelous. I love it, love it, love it!

10:05, Friday, January 18, 1980

—I don't know if I can take another ultra-dull weekend. I'm praying that through subtle hints Gord and I will get together.

—Why do I get the sneaky suspicion that some of these people here can see right through me like a window. I've been getting some very cold looks from some of the "blacker" blacks around here and this white guy, who I'm sure is queer, either made a modest proposal via eye contact or that was the most disgusted look I've got this year. Something's going to happen tonight one way or another—shit. Oh Gord, please, please. 1 hour, the countdown does begin.

7:05 P.M.

—"How Deep is Your Love"—The BeeGees **** I wish you'd give me a sign, Gord Watkins. I think I'm falling for this football player. —Sing it, BG's.

[A yellow line across the page]

—That yellow line on the front of this page stands for the end of a slackness on my part. This journal is an account of life, and it should be as plain, clear and straight-forward as possible. I think if I looked back on previous entries, I'd have trouble recalling what really happened. I don't need to deceive myself, and I'm the only one that will ever see this. ("Lonely Days"—The BeeGees *1/2)

—As I sit here on the tail-end of my German homework listening to "The Logical Song," I can't help but think how pertinent this song has been to my life. I am in no way a staunchly regimented person. I guess I'm completely illogical—a latent homosexual schizophrenic bounding between white and black like a gazelle. Sing it, Supertramp! this one's for all the people who don't give a flying fuck about norms, about establishment, about social etiquette. I am me and I have the right to be just that. . . .

Thursday, February 14, 1980

—A Fantasy (Mr. C. [for Cruel])

—Please. Can't you just let it be? Well, I saw him and he saw me. God. He's gorgeous. I think I'll fantasize about him a bit.

He seems so angry, though. Kind of like, "get off my back" kid, but at the same time he wants something. I want to be with him. He's a rugged guy so we'd probably go camping (summer). We'd climb up into the Blue Ridge mountains miles from the rest of the world. Of course I'd get tired and he'd say let's stop here and pitch the tent. We would, beneath the lush green trees and on the banks of a little brook. Before we even set up the tent he's opened one of the sleeping bags. With an undisguisable lust he takes off his gear and comes after me. I drop my own gear and run from him, but he's too fast and easily overtakes me. He grabs me around the waist and swings me around laughing. He stands me before him and I look up into his brown eyes and his wonderful smile. Slowly, he wraps his arms under my own and pulls me to him. He squeezes me tight then lowers his head to kiss me long and deep. He rubs my ("Crazy On You"—Heart *) back and presses himself against me. We fall in the grass and he rolls me around till I'm atop him. He says "I love you" then starts kissing my neck and licking me gently across the face and lips. "I love you too" I say and open his shirt, then lay on his hairy chest. He carries me back to the sleeping bag and makes slow deliberate love to me, always kissing and caressing me. After we've both come we lay there close and he smiles at me, then holds me, (Elton John making fantastic music) and we drift off to sleep.

March 13, 1980

. . . It's time to set some guidelines for this journal and future ones. This may be a conglomeration of materials, but its point is to show my daily progression and/or regression. As references one song will be mentioned as the song for that day or if no song is really outstanding for that day there will be an "ns" at the end of the day's entries.

Movies will be offset by lines, as will plays and books. Fantasies will be denoted. The rating system is undergoing some definite changes or will be dropped altogether. Yeah, it will. Each movie, each song has its own good and bad points there's no need for these ratings.

Lastly, stream of consciousness entries will become a big part of this journal.

Sunday, May 4, 1980

. . . I kind of wonder—looking with their eyes—if I've been cruising the wrong guys—guys that want the passive role in a relationship. If so, then it's understandable why I haven't found "it," or him. Mr. C. very well could be looking for a "stud" instead of someone to service him. Na! That's ludicrous! Or is it . . . ? . . .

Sunday, July 6, 1980

. . . Looking through this I'd be crazy to let anyone get hold of it—my journal that is. But more and more it seems I want someone to find it and read me like a book. For once I want someone to know me. A dangerous thought. At least I think so.

July 8, 1980

. . . I had one of my walking fantasies again today. Life as a movie—how thrilling. Today I was in a Stanley Kubrick film. I was the main star, as a matter of fact. And the biggest part of the whole film was the credits. And maybe the music—Al Jarreau. I'm not really here. I've reached that conclusion. I'm in another world, but at times I overlap with this stink hole of a situation that my physical being occupies.

Sunday, July 13, 1980

Anyway, last night was another big night, a bright spot among the darkness. *Superman* the movie, for the third time! Christopher Reeve is a gorgeous 6'4" 224 lbs that knocks Lois for a loop and had me sighing every time I saw him. (I'm really going to have to burn this.) I tried to fantasize about him last night but he's too big for me. The whole Superman concept blows my mind. When I was younger one of my most vivid fantasies was being Superboy and having the pleasure of being comforted by my father. It felt good to think I was near a warm body. Listening to the air conditioner, feeling its cooling breeze, and knowing I was safe because Superman was there. I wanted that again, but it wouldn't come. Now my imaginings make Super a sex partner instead of a protector. Sex dominates my mind, but now it's with an independence. Even in my fantasies I know I just want these people, I don't need them like I used to.

The movie was fantastic all over again. Love it! Afterward we ran down the street to another theater and saw *Cheech and Chong's Next Movie*. It was funny. We're no longer "the minority." Again, love you Supes. . . .

Thursday, 23, 1980 (Oh, it's September)

. . . Damn, I wonder if he was looking at me, the guy in the loose-fitting khaki shorts with the blonde hair and the brown beard. I wonder if he's been thinking about me, like I'll probably think about him as I build yet another in the endless fantasy world of mine. What has happened to all my better fantasies? When did they start? There were the Superman/Superboy fantasies in El Paso. [. . .] Then there was a brutal stage in there where all I wanted was pain, but there was always someone—a big brother, a good friend—to comfort me, hold me. And I was always someone else. For a long time I fantasized about being Wesley and having Tom Jordache as a father. Or Sam Bottoms with big brother Joseph or Tim. There was Christopher George and his big brother from that show . . . about a man hunted for his blood.

It wasn't until a year or two ago that *I* became the central figure in my fantasies and now I devote full energies to conjuring up the guy I'm with because I know what *I* look like (Did that have a point?). . . .

Monday, December 8, 1980

. . . It was about 2:30. I was going to drink my Sprite and leave CC's disappointed but relieved, in a sense, because I had made it to the "date." I wasn't the one who stopped whatever momentum there was between Cowboy and I as of Monday. Anyway, there I was on a bar stool, looking at 2 or 3 couples on the dance floor when Wally came up to me and asked if I wanted to dance. Wally is 6'5" and big and black, but very nice. We danced, close, then he bought me a Coke and we talked. I found out he's from CH. I drove him home, following his friend named Roy. He invited me up to his apartment for a drink and things launched from there. It was so smooth. There was no silly hesitation—long and tense—like Jamie and I. He put a hand on me and I touched back. (We had smoked a joint.) We kissed for what seemed like forever, then he began to hug me. There is nothing like a big man hugging you to him. I felt so warm, so relaxed, so safe. It was good. We didn't even need to have sex. Just the caressing and kissing was enough. The feeling I had when he was so close to me was the same I'd imagined Mr. C. would generate if . . . We stood on the floor for another eternity just kissing and cuddling—he more than I because he has much more to caress with. Finally, we went upstairs. We caressed and kissed more. I fucked him. He tried to fuck me, but we were having trouble keeping it hard. I think he *may* have got in.

The night kind of melted into the next day. We showered and then went to breakfast at Roy's. (Note: the whole time I have CB's car, claiming it as my own. I need a good lie to explain why I no longer have it.) Roy and Charlie (the other friend I met at CC's) are wonderful. Roy, an older guy, but very neat, had done a lot with his condominium. I was impressed. Wally cooked brunch while Charlie and I read and talked in the front room. We ate and I had to rush off to my Piano Jury. But not before kissing Wally and getting his phone #. . . .

Sunday, December 14, 1980
—Olivia Newton-John "Have You Never Been Mellow." God, I don't hardly feel like touching a book. I've got a monstrous English exam tomorrow at 9:00 and I've done little to no studying for it. I feel pretty bad about that, but pretty good about the way my time's been occupied. I spent Friday and Saturday at Roy's. He's a lot of fun and he really seems to like me and I admit I'm kind of attracted to him. I don't know for sure—why—but I am. And I'm overly fond of Wally who seems to like me, but just as a friend. I wish we could be lovers—or do I? Have I met Mr. Right? Tonight was Roy's big party. I had fun there. We decorated the tree and drank and smoked and ate and kissed and hugged. I'm going to bed, so I can wake up early, maybe study a bit. . . .

Friday December 19, 1980
—It's 1:00 in the morning on a Friday. School has been over for me for this semester since Wednesday when I finished that paper for Lou Lipsitz (or was that Tuesday?—Yes. Tuesday). I'm still in Chapel Hill, but now I'm at Roy Enloe's. I'm listening to

Donna Summer's very risqué "Come to Love You Baby." Roy is upstairs asleep. He still has to teach class tomorrow.

—Look at me! I've been feeling that for the past hour—exhibiting for myself. I'm wearing my blue Zeppelins, a black and white athletic shirt and suspenders. I may be somewhat of a narcissist, but at times I think I can be good-looking. —Now to the crux of things. What the hell am I doing here? ("Bridge Over Troubled Water" Simon & Garfunkel.) I ask you again for emphasis: What the HELL are you doing here, Gary? Okay, I didn't feel like going home right away. I've been telling myself that home is "boring," but I know it would actually be quite refreshing after a semester (—even a "do-nothing" semester) here. The only other explanation is sexual, mixed with all your scheming little unadmittable motives, Gary. I don't know how I feel about Roy. I must confess that I feel better around him than I've felt with anyone (No, it's premature to say that, but maybe I'd like to think that).

—If sex was all that interested me then I've made a catch because Roy always wants and is ready to give. Roy's no young man. I'd put him at 37 to 38 (Dan's age, but Dan's consciously old). Roy is, however, by no means "*old.*" He's got staying power like a horse and he's fun to be around. I can't really explain my attraction to this man. It's not similar to the one I'd feel for Mr. C. or Tony George (who I'm going to pursue. He's very handsome). He's just very easygoing and he has not pushed me at all. Every move has been mine. I'm responsible. And I feel good about my decisions. Love? No, not yet. I'm not ready to be tied down with a lover unless he's a Mr. C. or some other Mr. Right. Older guys are too easy. Though it's *so* frustrating, the challenge, sometimes, makes it worth it. But I can't bullshit—I haven't won the challenge yet, so I don't even know if it's worth it. ("So Long Frank Lloyd Wright" God, Garfunkel can sing.) —I really feel good here. Nice and warm and welcome and *un*obligated.

January 1, 1981

. . . What are the real issues? Those from last year and those developing already this year. Let me tick them off. The big one from last year was probably sex, my discovering it, my hurting because of it. It ruined a semester for me; it made the last one very rich, very fulfilling. I explored several aspects of homosexual sex this year.

January 2, 1981
—But back to sex . . . I won't even venture a guess as to why I'm homosexual, or when I became so, or whether I'm exclusively so. There are much too many factors involved in my growing experience to know, to pinpoint a cause or even a trend, though I know my childhood fantasizing had much to do with it. Before I left El Paso I was already beyond my Superboy fantasies to fantasies that dealt with sex between two males—usually nothing more than frottage, unless the fantasy was dealing with an S&M theme, as often it was. (Remember *Deathwatch* and *The Immortal*.) Usually in my fantasies I was someone else. Often, a young, white guy in trouble. —I don't think it was until this year that I stopped playing others (not altogether, mind you) and became myself. My fantasies were fairly standard this year—boy meets boy (by whose standards? you ask) and relationship develops. I emphasized cuddling and kissing above sex. The actual sex acts only came to me when I was unusually frustrated and needed a release. Gord Watkins was the focus of my fantasy for a month or two at the beginning of the year, but then Mr. C. took over and became more of a dream than a fantasy. In a way, I've made him the standard for my Mr. Right. And I've yet to meet anyone like him. I doubt if even Mr. C. could live up to my fantastic image of him.

Then again, what is fantasy, beside the real thing? A lot, but still one degree under it. The first eight months saw far and few in the way of physical "connection." I frequented the UR for awhile, met some interesting people who make up much of my fantasy world now. Jon Grigg and I had a slight relationship near the end of my freshman year. He initiated me to anal sex. The summer was dry. The fall saw Mike Wachtel and a one-time experience with S&M. Then I met Jamie Blue and we've become good friends. Around the end of the year the struggling and frustration of the first 11 months paid off. I don't know what Greg was, but we touched off a relationship. There was the big orgy, but before that—Albert in Raleigh. Then that wonderful night at CC's when I went to meet Cowboy only to meet Wally and his clique who have turned out to be my dearest of friends. Now Roy and I have a pseudo-relationship. ("Pseudo" on my part.) And presently I'm reaching out for Tony George. —I've discovered the gay bars—42nd St and CC's, I've met a multitude of gay men and women through Dan and Jamie and Roy and Wally. The gay world has opened up (some) for me. This year—EXPLORATION! I know it exists. Maybe I want to bridge the fantasy/reality gap. Maybe I want something secure. I don't know and I won't until I get there. . . .

When I look back on the past year I see how independent I've become. Oh, I may be financially tied (not to this family, though—they've less than I), but I am emotionally secure. I can make it on my own. I think I have spent all of one month's time in this house this year. And I felt no homesickness. Probably the only reason I decided to come home for X-mas is because I didn't want to mooch off Roy (and I don't want our relationship to take on dimensions I wasn't ready for). And maybe I selfishly thought I'd get a gift.

This part of my life is *so* sketchy. I have no idea of a future. Luck is going to play a big part, and my realizing the importance of money. We'll see.

—An odd sense of melancholy descended on me as I prepared for bed. I had some strange thoughts—what if I had cancer and were dying? Or why don't I try on some clothes and prance in front of the mirror? Strange—Supertramp's "Even In The Quietest Moments." Are these growing pains. What's happening to me?—if anything at all is. Is it possible that the world is just here, and I'm *just* here, and it's all *just* here! How dull. I'm scared, terribly uncertain. —Where are my values? *What* are they? Who do you love? Mr. C. is so unreal (. . . I think).

Sunday, January 18, 1981
—I'm still at Roy's at 2:30 in the afternoon, and I've a heck of a load of work to do. Barry Manilow's on the radio in mid-ballad. I need to reflect on this past weekend. It's been incredibly full. Friday turned out to be an exciting though somewhat tense evening. I had to come to terms with what I have chosen to become and the direction in which I'm headed. Let's hit the concrete first. After class on Friday I surprised myself by doing absolutely nothing at all. Friday evening Roy, Nils and I went to dinner. We didn't

leave here until rather late and we were expected at a birthday party. We decided on Fosdick's seafood restaurant. It was about 8:30 when we started eating. Nils started acting an ass a good half hour before then. I will admit that socially I am still in somewhat of a closet. I don't enjoy flaunting my homosexuality, not because I'm ashamed of it, but because it draws attention from people who misunderstand. I can do without the funny looks and the whispers. I just want to be me for me. I bother nobody and nobody bothers me. So, it's a "cop-out" you say. And I will be the first to agree with you. I simply don't feel that being gay requires any silly sissy fronts. I act like *me*. I don't turn on and off. I may be more careful with what I say when I'm among a group of straight people, but I *don't* become someone else. I'm content with who I am. —So, what about Friday night. Nils turned on the Betty Davis, the nelly. He acted so stereotype queen that he drew attention and that unsettled me. So, it's *my* problem. Maybe Nils couldn't help himself. Regardless of where the fault lies, dinner with Nils was a scene I would just as soon skip next time.

—Okay let's be open and honest . . . Roy is not my idea of a sex god. He's absolutely the best friend I have. There's no one I would rather talk to, but he doesn't quite fill the fantasy that a Gord or Mr. C. would. Wally told me something of some value— you can't have your cake and eat it too. We'll see about that, but so far his philosophy has been sound. Nothing, in any aspect of my life, has been enough. I'm insatiable. Roy understands this feeling, I think, but it would still hurt him if . . .

I do love Roy. I haven't said it, but I care about him deeply. I'm afraid to say anything because he'll be on me like a vise, and to try and pull out then is crazy—it would just hurt him too much.

I could never admit it to Roy, but I have a fear of being alone like I was *so* much of last year. That was torture scrubbing my fingers raw on the wall; feeling *so* certain only to have the thought shattered again and again and again. I'm scared of that and being with Roy is an incredible comfort. . . .

Tuesday, January 27, 1981
—All of this is leading up to the main event. Probably the best thing to happen so far this semester—a sexual encounter with Jamie. Now, I don't know, but I think this time it transcended the

normal bounds (or at least the one we established the first time) of simple sexual release. This time we wanted to make each other happy. (This is very hard to explain in words. It's a gut feeling—last night.) It took hours to lead up to it. The ball was rolling when Sheila left and Jamie asked me to stay and talk. Then we read some of his "Numbers" and kept inching closer and closer to each other. It would have happened sooner, but Jamie seemed unsure. He said that "yesterday" (1/25) that "I tried to seduce you." And I said I would have accepted. But later he said that Rudy was the only person he'd do it with now. He dropped that in conversation and it probably wasn't meant as strongly as I took it, but it made me hesitate. Finally (I had to initiate this . . . so he could say I seduced him, I guess). Anyway we got to playing around. He kisses so beautifully. I fellated him for awhile; brought him to the brink, then back . . .

He started playing with me and I told him I wanted him to fuck me. That's when the real encounter began. We had talked about former encounters and he told me what he liked and I fabricated and fantasized a bit in telling him what I liked. I don't think I ever dreamed he'd carry it out. But after a moment's attention to the situation facing me I knew Jamie wanted to fulfill some fantasies. Mine and his. He lotioned himself and me real well continuously assuring me that he wouldn't hurt me. "Tell me if it hurts." Jamie was being so . . . domineering, yet so gentle. He kissed me and nuzzled me and slowly put his enormous cock against me. "I want you, Gary" he said and I said "God, I want you, Jamie" and then he slowly entered. "Does it hurt?" His gentleness was stimulating and comforting at the same time. There was maybe half a second of pain and then the waves of pleasure. He began to fuck me. "I want to fuck you, Gary" . . . Our little word-play continued sexy and as vulgar, but as loving as possible. Jamie did not fuck me last night. We "made love." It was beautiful. It kind of bonded our friendship in a way talking only hinted at. I'll always love Jamie as one of my best friends. . . .

Snow

—Betty Parker owned the large white house at the edge of town. In the summer, boy, was it a head-turner—a monument to early American craft and ingenuity. In the summer, the white house with its black-shingled roof and black shutters, centered a lovely yard of green grass and flowers, delicately, meticulously, almost mathematically arranged. But now, during the winter, the home was somehow lost in the festering January snows. At times the house literally disappeared. A passenger in a passing car would not see more than a wintery haze, and that would play off his senses like the sun's water on black pavement, and he'd dismiss it, driving on by.

Michigan snows, Miss Parker thought, clean, white and . . . and dead like a marble slab or surgical gauze.

And Betty Parker kept a clean house. Not clinically clean, mind you, like a hospital or a laboratory, but a kind of neat clean that spoke of traditions, deep-rooted American goodness dating back to . . . why, to the Puritans. Everything had a place at Miss Parker's. There wasn't a scrap of paper or a bit of fabric or a tiny trinket misplaced. Miss Parker's charm bracelet knew her jewelry box when it wasn't on her wrist. And keys . . . keys had their place on a hook near the fireplace mantle. Books stood straight and tight in Miss Parker's cases, and a rug would not dare to turn up a corner.

Miss Parker's dress was equally ordered—white blouse, black skirt and hard black shoes that tapped the wood floor as she walked.

When the Birchfields offered her a handsome amount to baby-sit young Stacy she pained over deciding. Stacy was a six-year-old-boy—"a quiet child," Mrs. Birchfield said. But a boy, just the same, and apt to cause trouble like boys do.

Miss Parker had kept many young ladies, all dressed in yellow lace and smelling of talc and Crest. Young ladies knew how to appreciate the neatness, the impeccable order of Miss Parker's home. She found many of the girls more a pleasure than a burden. June could play a bit of piano, and Sarah was quick to rinse her dishes after eating. Donna loved to browse through Miss Parker's books, and she would always place each back in its correct spot, careful to push them back all the way. Nothing made Betty Parker angrier than to see a book breaking the plane. Young ladies understood her concerns for precision and detail, for order and regimentation, as a boy never could. She had made up her mind about Stacy Birchfield—he could stay, for a trial period, but should one difficulty arise, either discipline-wise or in a matter of neatness, she would die before she let the whelp do her home anymore harm. An anger welled in Betty Parker and she set her lip to her decision.

—It all happened the very first day. Betty Parker greeted the Birchfields at the big front door in her blouse and skirt, and with those hard black shoes tapping the floor she showed them in. After a few minutes of admiring Miss Parker's home, Mr. and Mrs. Birchfield left. Stacy remained on the sofa. He sat timidly, with hands folded and eyes down. He had on his navy sailor suit and little black boots; his mother thought he'd be cute, and only wanted to give Miss Parker the best of impressions.

Miss Parker approached Stacy swiftly. The boy recoiled a bit thinking the woman might lunge at him.

"I'll bet you want to run and romp in the snow, don't you? You want to track up my floors and wet my cushions, don't you? Don't you! Well, I will have you know, Stacy Birchfield, there will be no playing in the snow, or anywhere in my house, and you better get used to being quiet, young man, because I tolerate *no* noise!"

Stacy nodded his head, but he'd always been a quiet child and didn't like the snow all that much anyway. He looked up into Miss Parker's sneer with big, brilliant, brown eyes and began to ask a question. "Miss Parker, may I . . ."

"Don't you dare interrupt while I'm talking to you!" As Miss Parker yelled, the icy wind rapped on the shutters and whistled under a door. "Doesn't your mother teach you any manners?—any respect!"

And Stacy cowered. "Yes ma'am," he said, very softly, very uncertain whether Miss Parker expected a "yes" or a "no."

"Well, you could have fooled me."

—The day continued pretty much the same, Miss Parker yelling at Stacy for any and everything and the boy retracting into his shell. He started his question seven times—"Miss Parker, may I . . ."—and each time he would be cut down, shredded by another thundering reprimand.

The two of them ate lunch in utter silence, and Stacy was careful not to slurp his soup or drop crumbs on the table cloth, but still Miss Parker would not give an approving look. After lunch he tried his request once again. "Miss Parker," he began slowly "may I . . ." and Miss Parker swiftly pounced all over his sentence.

"You've been trying to ask me something." She blared and stood, becoming suddenly giant.

"Yes ma'am, may I . . ." the boy started.

And Miss Parker quickly killed it. "No, you may not," she said. "You will get what I give you and nothing more."

"But, Miss Parker . . ."

"How dare you interrupt! I haven't the time, the nerve, nor the patience for hard-headed, ill-mannered, greedy little boys like you. To bed with you! You will not say another word until after your nap."

She had made herself clear. Stacy lay in the bed and cried for awhile, but soon fell into a slumber. His dreams enveloped him and seemed a quiet refuge after Miss Parker's continuous tongue lashings. Where was he? He ventured a guess, but there was only water. Lots of warm ocean water.

As Stacy slept Miss Parker prepared to clean her floors. She had misread a label, a very rare thing for a precise woman like Betty Parker. She had poured ammonia in her bucket of water and took it onto the back porch to dump. She hadn't planned to stay in the blistering cold long, so she didn't bring a coat or even her shawl. And everything was right where it should be—the coat and the shawl in the closet, the trinket on her wrist, the keys by the mantle. Miss Parker heaved the water out of the bucket into the fresh snow and tipped the bucket to drain it. Suddenly a violent gust wrenched the bucket from her hand and whipped it into a cartwheel. It twirled and tumbled. A bounce took it over the fence. Even above the clatter of the bucket, Miss Parker had heard one of the shutters rattle, then bang loudly. Then she heard the crash. The attic window shattered as its shutter unhinged. It happened so fast that the porch door was sucked closed with a whoosh and a slam, leaving Miss Parker standing rather exasperated on the porch.

She went to the door and turned the knob but it did not tumble far. Maybe half an inch in both directions. Another gust of wind billowed her skirt. She gave an ooo and a shudder and turned the knob again. She rang the bell. Stacy should have sense enough to know a doorbell when he heard one.

And he did, but not at first. The bells pulled him from his dreams and he opened his eyes. He rubbed the sleep from them and tried to remember where he was. "Mommy?" he said groggily and a fear crawled at him. "Miss Parker?" The bell kept ringing, and the house seemed to yawn and whistle. It was suddenly very cold around his legs and he looked down to the dampness on the sheets and his pants. Stacy began to cry. He climbed out of the bed and pulled the spread over to cover the urine. The bell had become a vicious pounding.

"Stacy!"

It was very faint. The house's groaning and that incessant knock were covering the voice. But Stacy sensed it was coming from the front room. He went to it.

Miss Parker had tried every window, but the shutters were bolted tight. The big front door was locked. She beat frantically on it when knocking on the porch door seemed futile. She punched the bell and occasionally kicked the door with her hard black shoe.

"Stacy, open the door!"

"Miss Parker?" Stacy inquired, a good ten feet from the door.

"Open the door!"

Stacy wondered why the old woman had become so frantic, hammering the door. It frightened him. Did she know? Could she know already?

"Stacy!" Miss Parker yelled.

She would be furious, yelling and maybe switching his legs with a frozen rose bush stick. Then Miss Parker would tell his mother or maybe his dad and he'd have to sit in the corner. Or would she stick his face in it!

"Stacy!"

The boy screamed and backed away from the door as though a wild animal clawed at the other side. He retracted, shrank, cowered back . . . back into a corner. The wet pants felt sickly cold on his legs. He felt very sick, and Miss Parker beat the door louder and louder!—then softer and less frequently, then it stopped altogether. Stacy just sat, a quivering mass, frightened and confused.

Some hours later Stacy's parents came for him. They wanted to thank and pay Miss Parker, but could not find her. So they left a note and her money, neatly sealed in a little white envelope, on the mantle. Emily Birchfield knocked the keys off the hook when she reached to put the letter on the mantle, but she quickly picked them up and hung them back.

Betty Parker was found two days later, a mile outside of town, curled into a tight ball.

Sunday, February 1, 1981
 —My whole life may have changed (no, that suggests predetermined paths) directions in the past 24 hours. I've got *so* very much to write and I'm afraid to start. Perhaps this is a reflection of my present state of mind. I'm so scared. I feel like I've fallen from grace! Okay, look, I didn't want to end my relationship with Roy until I was sure of another one. Well early this morning it all fell apart as far as Roy and I are concerned. After an excellent dinner and birthday celebration for some huge (size-wise) faghag (I don't like that word, but I haven't time to think of another one) friend of Ron's, we went to the bar, Roy, Bob and I. I didn't think it would happen. I certainly couldn't have foreseen . . . O, god I don't want to be lonely. Roy was such a comfort . . . But I met a fantasy. I met Tony Kristof and he was a fantasy. We cruised each other for half an hour before I finally walked over and asked him to dance. He smiled at me and . . . and finally he took me in his big arms and held me real tight and kissed me and asked me if I wanted to go home with him. He's got blonde hair and a beard and mustache and blue eyes and the most gorgeous body I've ever touched. He is absolutely the best looking guy I've ever been with —Mr. C.'s here (I'm back in the HRR). So what. —Last night, or early this morning, he fucked me. I didn't (or couldn't) get off and that bothered me, but he didn't seem to mind. Finally, we went to sleep. He held me in his arms. O, it was wonderful. This morning I still couldn't get off, but I did give him a bj. I want him again and again, but that may have been an isolated event. I'm free again, but I could also be very lonely, very soon. And I don't need that.
 —What does that guy want. Mr. C. is handsome, but he's also

a twerp. He's only interested in the cruise. I wonder if he'd know what to do with it if he found it.

Monday, February 16, 1981

—1:30 A.M. Everyone's so sure I'm gonna make it except me. "One Of These Nights" The Eagles. —Something really wonderful happened yesterday. I don't even know how to approach it in words. I'd start with the end of my last entry. I was begging for someone to call me when Tony George returned a call I'd made to him earlier. We talked, mourned our pathetically lonely states and then he suggested I go to the bar. I was going to call Jay, but after the big mix up on Friday the 13th . . . Well, I was going to call Roy, but that would take a lot of balls, like Tony G. told me. Then he suggested I call Mr. Kristof. *I did.* I called Tony K. and he said he was going to the bar alone and that I could go with him. From just the phone conversation I kind of got the feeling we would spend the evening together. He said he wanted to come back early. —Eagles "Take It To The Limit." Okay—I don't know, somehow I just felt I'd be coming back with Tony K. Well he picked me up here at James's and we had a pleasant conversation-filled drive to Durham. None of the conversation was forced either. We had plenty to talk about. —"The Best Of My Love" More Eagles—. Okay we got to the bar, played some pool. I danced some. Tony watched me a lot and that felt good. I met a nice guy named Glen. We danced quite a bit. Then of course Rick and I danced. We're good bar buddies, Rick and I. I ran into Joey and Ron, and Bill too, but no one got to me the way T. K. does. When Tony got ready to go, he asked me if I wanted to go with him, and of course I did. I think I ignored Bill, I kissed Glen and left him my phone # then T. K. and I left. We talked more on the way home. Serious talk about not liking organized gayness or cliques and just having fun. We had sex. I came so close to coming all over Tony. He was masturbating me while I gave him a b.j. (We were in a 69 position) and I asked him to slow down. He must have thought I was close, so he said "no." It struck me as very considerate of him to want to get me off first. Anyway I think all the drugs and cigarette smoking T. K. does has affected the taste of his cum. I'd like to be able to change the guy, but our relationship is still in early acquaintanceship stages. I really like T.K.

—continuing. I could have come. Tony told me to do whatever I want and I had to decide what I wanted more. I decided I wanted his arms more than I wanted to ejaculate so I crawled up beside my big friend. Something about Tony, he's not very big in the dick department (bigger than me, but not *very* big—no Roy; certainly no Jamie) but who gives a shit. "It's Not What You Got" says Carrie Lucas, one of my all-time favorite disco tunes. He more than makes up for it. Wait . . . he doesn't have to make up for it. I enjoy his size. But more than his cock I just enjoy him—the way he talks to me, sometimes. He's very handsome. I love snuggling up to him. With the top of my head nestled beneath his chin I lay against him. We're on our sides. He has one arm beneath me and another around me. I said goodnight to him. He said goodnight to me and we slept. It's so warm. I noticed that with him—when he's holding me real close like that, a leg over mine his arms encircling me. I feel so safe next to him . . . and he knows it.

The next morning, or should I say later the same day we talked a little more. He likes to be admired for his body, and he has a gorgeous one. He said he was going to lift weights. When he was stretching in bed, I said he sounded like a beached whale. Later I stretched too and said now it's my turn to sound like a beached whale. Tony said no you sound like a *little* beached whale and he smiled at me. God, if he wants to play daddy with me, I'll gladly consent. I made some comment about a little pullover he was wearing and he pointed out that it wasn't little. No, it wasn't, but why was he informing me. He's got a right to be proud of his body and he must know how much I admire him. O, I'd do a lot for T. K. In the car on the way home he mentioned that someone had to gain his love and respect. I wonder if he'd give me the chance. I've got to come for him. Once I'm over that initial hurdle I'll be sexually smooth. But I don't really worry about sex with T. K., I just enjoy being with him, looking at him. Being held by him. G'night.

Monday, March 2, 1981
 —Dear Gary,
 You really do want miracles, don't you? I've been reading over some of your older entries, and you seem to expect luck to play the game for you. Well, it don't work that way, buddy. The hard

cold facts put luck near the very bottom of the "useful" pile. "Work" is the key. Try it, you might just find you like it.

Concerned,

Gary

—I got an A– on my Shakespeare paper. Congrats!

Tuesday, March 3, 1981
  —Dear Gary,

Welcome back to life. I see you've got Janis Ian on the stereo ("Seventeen"—Beauty queens, huh . . .). Isn't the world beautiful when you just wake up—all soft in a delicate haze, and quiet though it's not. A little suspension of the problem, for just a while. "The Small town eyes will gaze at you." Very resourceful, Gary. All softness aside, you've aspired to the cold hard facts of life. You reacted as humanly as I would have. Rather than starve, Gary, you misuse and abuse and become one of the ugly girls the crowd loves to hurl the hushed obscenities at. Your depression probably found its firmest foundation when you became a petty thief, Gary. How were you justifying that? Hunger? They didn't pity you yet. You didn't pity you yet, Gary. There were still alternatives that may have served you without stepping past your morals. That was *so* petty, and for what? —Ice cream? O, you should be flogged, Gary. The oatmeal? You ask me softly. You'll live, but it nearly cost you a friend. It nearly cost you sanity, Gary. Do you like taking chances just this side of black? O, you mistook, Gary. Or rather you just *took* advantage. Punishment is yours. You'll do that, I'm sure.

They're not even looking at you now, not even a noncommittal "hey." Abstention? Go ahead. How long? How long before your body craves more pain. God, Gary, don't you see? The loneliness is yours because you call on it. There's no longer enjoyment for you. You've reduced it to a math equation—all or none, and you can *never* have it all. (Janis Ian writes a lovely song.) You used to be *so* sweet. Beauty is *not* what a lover makes you. It's *not* what money and a job make you; it's *not* what the grade makes you. *Do you still love you?* Go away from me! *Do you still love you?* Don't lip-synch it. Don't whisper in night fantasy. Do you have your pillow or shadows in magazine say it. DO YOU? Come home, Gary. This isn't you. I am beauty, I am light. You are. WE are and we shall be again. Come be my fantasy. Be mine. Be yours. Hold me, Gary, set me free. I don't want to stay locked in this journal.

Sunday, March 22, 1981

. . . Well, Bruce Higgins just called. Not too much there. He basically called out of obligation. If I hadn't called him, he wouldn't have called me. It was a nice one-nighter I suppose. Is that really what gay life is all about? —The one night stand? He was quite cordial though and I am glad he called. We had a fun little conversation. Nothing to moan over, but not overtly con-trived either. I doubt if I'll see him again, but it's okay. I guess you learn to love life in bits and you have to look at the people you meet in just that way—tiny sparkling bits of a whole gem. The gem is the whole experience (the gay experience, for example). I merely have to look beyond (not excluding it, of course) the single gem I've been doting on. There are so many treasures. . . .

Monday, May 18, 1981

. . . Get a hold of yourself, Gary. Maybe you should be enjoying where you are. I think Roy senses my longing for someone else, but he knows the futility in getting depressed while you wait. Love the one you're with might not be a bad philosophy.

—Jerry. God, there's a problem. Jerry and I have been on at least superficially good terms for the past two months or so. We've done quite a bit together (reminiscent of the old friendship we had a year ago). What tore me away from Jerry was actually my own psychological instability (uncertainly about my gayness, or the real virtue in it; grades; problems accepting my blackness; etc.). These problems weren't reflected in Jerry, but somehow the pain had manifested itself in Mr. Bowles. I saw his instability, couldn't or wouldn't handle it, and gave up on him. I won't take the full blame, but I will accept more than I've expressed pre-viously. Jerry is a disturbed young man. He doesn't know the answers to the question, just like me, but it's killing him. He needs crutches. (Is Roy a crutch?) This weekend I stayed at the Bowles's home. Marian and Jerry and I are a pretty close group and Marian felt a need to tell me of Jerry's latest crutch, which I had noticed, but not paid much attention to. Jerry is becoming a "pot head." That sounds so silly, like a fourth grade observation, but Jerry it trying to make his pot and hashish a dependence. He needs it to sleep even. His roommate this past semester, Brian, smoked. But Brian has his head on straight—he smokes for the pleasure of it, and it doesn't hamper his work. Jerry? He seems to need it now, and can't understand why Marian and I don't. He idolizes Brian and refuses to see the danger in what he's doing— or, perhaps he does see it. Is Jerry trying to kill himself?

—Does this parallel my food-fetish of late? I eat when I get depressed, and I do it consciously, as though trying to harm myself. I have fallen out of love with myself. I'm losing my self-esteem and that's scary. It's time to get back.

—Has my father lost his? O, this one hurts. He was such a proud man in the service. Even with Amway (when he thought it was worth a shit) he had a glow, a special esteem . . . No, I saw it dwindling just before Amway. I note his envy of me and I want to say don't, Dad, please don't compare, but how can I. Life sucks. It takes so much from the proud, the strong. I keep hearing his plans for the future. O, God, this is too painful and I don't want to understand it.

Wednesday, May 27, 1981

I went to Durham tonight for all of an hour and a half. I felt odd, empty, sick and terribly afraid of everyone there. I felt like a child among experienced and jaded adults. No one wanted to touch me for my naiveté—or so my thoughts ran. This is all leading to one name, one face that can sum up all the longing of the past few months (also all the hate, anger, pity, and pride)—Tony Kristof.

I had put him out of my mind, out of my life, recognizing any attempt to catch this guy in a "love-snare" as bitterly futile. I felt like a damn fool opening up (partially) as I did for him, and then having him run from it. I thought I saw the parallel between my relationship with Roy and the one with Tony—love entailing both a physical and internal attraction. I had decided that Tony was looking for other things in men than what I had to offer. I had decided and accepted this, putting the fault on no one. (Since the fault belonged to no one in the situation between Roy and I, how could I blame Tony or myself for what happened between us.) I came to the conclusion that what happened was equivalent to a "trick." I just got lucky and had a second shot. I'm the one that feels. Tony never did. (But there were times when I saw the pain in his eyes, as clear as that which must have been in mine.) In brief, I put Tony out of mind so that I could get on with life.

Why on earth then, did I bring him back? Why did I create another painful and futile romance in my fantasy? Probably because I had nothing better to do.

It's so puzzling to me that I can be so arbitrary with my affections. I don't want Roy because he smokes, because he's physically unattractive. I want Tony purely for his bod! My direction is fucked over like a drunk driver. I'm equating my lust and longing for a hunky body with love. *And* I'm building a wall against the physically unattractive though it may hold much nicer treasures than the one I want. Shakespeare would have a field day with my story. —I can't understand it, *and,* at the same time I do. I am horribly aware of the meaning. I'm a dreamer, expecting utopia and everlasting love like an impossible movie. I'm living in a fantasy. I'm living inside myself. I'm lost as long as this continues. I could say I felt something in Tony tonight (it would be a lie) and it would keep this pain going. I seem to want to suffer. *Maybe I feel there's hope through suffering. I'm religious!*

Wednesday, June 3, 1981
  —If Roy's been in my book then he just nailed the last two inches in the coffin of this relationship—at least sexually. I told him once before of how my writing reflects an immediate reaction with no reflection. That won't matter though. I wonder why he chose to scribble out what he did. Stupid Roy. Very, very stupid. (Did I do it?) . . .

Wednesday, June 10, 1981
  . . . What's happened with Roy and I since the crisis a week ago? We seem to be desperately friends. There hasn't been anything said on the issue since it surfaced a week ago. Roy hints at wanting to forget it. I agree, but it can't be quite the same between us. No, it may be better, because now the cards are down and we're still friends. I think I love Roy more now than I ever did because he's trying to forgive—Yes, "Going For the One." — I've learned a lot from this incident. Mainly some things about

living for the day and loving the one you're with. O, I still have my dreams, my fantasy lover, but I think I feel better because I'm no longer living for just that. I doubt if I ever was, but hints of that were in me.

This incident has also reminded me of what a powerful thing the mind is. I actually conjured up negative feelings in myself that did not exist as any more than thoughts. I pushed those ideas of feelings into actual physical repulsion. I was hurting myself. A little bit of suicide? And I did it consciously. Why? Because: I wanted Tony. I didn't think the magic would come if I was "unfaithful" (?). I was living a love relationship that only existed in my fantasies. That's part of it. The mind is truly powerful.

So is the pen. Look what I did to Roy. For awhile, the written word carried more weight than the spoken. There was some truth in what I said (truth in *my* mind. It may not be in reality, but that's unimportant to a journal of *my* thoughts). I did believe some of those things I said. I can try and negate them or lighten them with my hypothesis above, but it would only be partial. I've got a lot of growing to do. I'm sorry that I can be so destructive. I'm glad that I realize what I'm doing. Understanding it, maybe I can change it. . . .

. . . —O, I wanted to mention my "Bear" fantasies. Bear is the nickname of my new bearded fantasy lover. I spent a good hour caressing my pillow and making verbal love to myself. It was fun. Bear calls me "Babe" (because I couldn't think of any other endearing nickname) because, he says, he had a teddy bear as a child, named "Babe." And, of course, if he's the Papa Bear, then I'm the little *baby* bear. Asinine, but a lot of fun. Oh, I wish love and money weren't such pains.

Oddly, I feel pretty good right now. Every now and then I sink into depression as I batter myself with a million imaginary problems. Why do I feel good now? Because it's all going to work out. I wonder if the guys I conjure up in fantasy—being loving, understanding, and overly protective—aren't my forms of a divine deity. I mean, I always feel things are going to go fine, no matter how low I sink. Part of this feeling must come from the fantasies where, for instance, Bear, with all his wealth and love, wants to shelter me and shower me in nice things. Those fantasies are a comfort. God, or whatever that feeling of things always, inevitably working themselves out—that feeling is also a comfort. Can I equate the two? Magic is in my head, but in a way, that's okay. Or is it? Am I in for some surprises?

Monday, November 30, 1981, After the Holidays

They didn't seem like the holidays at all those two days in Fayetteville. I suppose it was quite nice to see my family again, but there was something missing that I haven't been able to understand. I think I was lonely in Fayetteville. I wanted some kind of male companionship. Not my father's; he's withdrawn into his own little-lower-middle-class world of wishes and self-pity. He's hopelessly hooked on tradition—the male as somehow aloof and above emotions (though pain is allowed to evoke sympathy from the females). Remember poor and old Mr. Ramsay in Virginia Woolf's *To the Lighthouse?* I can see my father headed this way. We had so little to say to each other and all of that was superficial. But I felt the hum of something deeper, something akin to love (a love above sexes) when we talked about the puppies—Oh, they were beautiful puppies, Sheba and Rameses. (America, "I Need You.") There was a small flame, like a candlelight, of something warm and pleasant in our talking about the puppies. There our perspectives on beauty crossed. My father could soften (though I could never call him a hard man) and we could relate on a comfortable level, not the technical student-to-student or father-to-son planes we'd been floundering in. But I didn't know what else to say to him. I love my father, but what he offers—that thorny surface—is not enough to sustain my . . . my interest. He bored me. I watched him watch football. What did I want to say to him anyway? Did I want to tell him about my experience (if I may call it that) with gay life? No, I wasn't prepared to do that, but I wanted to touch him with something more personal than grades, than school and my vague future. I wanted to touch my father. Maybe hug him.

I'd had a dream about Dad. A dream with a homosexual theme, yes, but something beyond sex—there was love. I guess I just wanted to embrace the man, to let him know that I could love on even *that* level.

And there was a restraint with my mom. I felt us somehow moving apart, drifting like clumsy logs in a pond, no real direction, but still tearing apart from each other. I guess I've grown up, and now I'm so lonely. I know I'll always have a home there but I can never stay. I can never hope and never ask to stay. The phase is gone and now I seem to be floundering, so lonely, in the limbo between stages. The comfort of being home was not enough to sedate, to comfort me.

—Even in bed ("Tin Man") home was not enough to still the need for my blonde, big fantasy. I tried to conjure Tony, to lay with him, beside him, against him like a lover. I've wanted Tony ever since he punched me twice at 42nd St. and said "hi." I'm so stupid.

Oh, my sisters. They've changed some. They don't seem to care anymore. The fight's gone (with my parents too). They're getting fat. Leslie, about the face. I don't much like it. I guess I'm vain. I was so proud and vain for them, of them . . . before. But it's not just the physical. Crystal doesn't care. Doesn't want to learn, not really, and who can push her. My parents have slowed to a stop with their Amway dreams when, at least, that was something . . . something tangible and almost healthy. It's gone.

But the puppies are so cute. There's a blue station wagon rusting in the grass and dog shit—cute, wet piles—here and there. And the lawn's a pleasant shamble. Nobody cares anymore. They've given up on all those dreams. (Dreams that I thought were *so* silly, but weren't they healthy?) (Piano note played repeatedly. Write to the beat, Gary.)

Sunday, December 13, 1981
. . . God, that guy had so much blood in him. His hands were the reddest and big square fingers. He left with Susan (the brunette bartender). Oh well, I know and he knows. Some more midair sex. I stripped you down, buddy—had you in the sack—and never left my barstool. The incredible, invisible, impossible gays.

2:38 P.M.
There's a disease going around that is killing gay males. It may be linked to drug abuse. What about the shroud of Christ. God, how could human beings be *so* cruel? Would I do that? I never want the chance, ever. We need to re-humanize.

January 29, 1982

. . . Last night I stayed a bit after work to listen to some good jazz; to listen to some of my Pyewacket women friends support mine and each other's egos; to get pleasantly drunk among the ruins of an evening. I say ruins because Thursday night started at the collapsed hull and proceeded downward with only little intermittent bobs here and there for air. I thought too much of not being in love, my envy poured out toward John and Andy and I was generally, outwardly dull and wired for an explosion. I wanted to sink last night and tried to lose myself in my prep. I'd been hurting all day, I guess I wanted the night to be my climax, but . . . it didn't come.

Sex got a little gross last night. Homosexuality came out in the open, perhaps accidentally, perhaps only in my mind. But it was there and exposed. Lewjack, one of the more obnoxious male waits, made a crude comment highlighted by the word "faggot." I guess if I'd been straight the comment wouldn't have touched me and I'm sure he didn't realize . . . Later he apologized, but I must admit I was somewhat wounded. Us four cooks had spent some time already talking rather freely, more freely than I feel comfortable with, so the air was already heavily gassed for just such an explosion. The Pyewacket suddenly became a den of strange controversy, with Chris and myself clinging to guns we didn't think we'd ever use. It was first time for me: a confrontation with hetero-prejudice and with myself—my own ethics and beliefs.

Sunday, January 31, 1982

. . . Lee is exciting to me. He excites me as I imagine I would excite myself. We're about the same build. He may be just a bit taller, and we continually switched off on the dominant/submissive roles. Or perhaps the roles were just forgotten, perhaps we were just into pleasure from all sides. Our sex play was slow and varied and only perhaps a little too calculated. We ran out of moves now and then and perhaps bored of things a bit, but over all it was more pleasurable than most of the encounters I've had. Perhaps I need to clarify that. Pleasurable and somehow mutually right, or satisfying: I knew what I did felt good to him and it definitely felt good to me. We learned from each other and imitated each other. He tried to discover what I liked by the things I did to him.

One moment that really touched me as near perfect was having Lee on top of me and rubbing his back. He was in kind of a meditative ecstasy which I seemed to have control over with my massage. I rubbed hard and heard him moan, harder and his moan grew harder then I softened and began to caress my friend very softly, "sleepily" would be a good adjective. And then I noticed that Lee had fallen asleep on top of me. We were obviously comfortable with each other. I held him and he snored. I almost enjoyed the sound.

Later we held each other. Kissed, fondled each other. We had played around for hours with our clothes on as if building up to something then we stripped slowly, worshipped one another's bodies slowly with caresses. We avoided the penis which seems to be what all my other "encounters" jumped for first. I am fascinated by Lee's natural build like a wrestler. I like touching and rubbing him. And though I was at first disappointed that he wasn't larger, that passed for the most part and I got into Lee's body. I guess I do have a bit of that "measurer's complex" ("size queen complex") or whatever it's called because size does turn me on, but I did recognize (as I had earlier with T.K.) that there's a lot more to be interested in. . . .

Backtracking.

Friday was a day of events. Busy. At 4:00 I went to see Dr. Green in Arts and Sciences to drop my P.E. and somehow we wound around to the topic of my losing touch with the black community. The man had good insight into me, but he didn't need to push far to get me to open. I wanted to talk. I need to talk to someone. Thank God he pried. He got me to vocalize my intentional detachment from blacks and made me promise to give it more thought in my everyday dealings. I thanked him profusely for trying to understand me. He does. O, and I feel so relieved that this shell isn't impervious. An impervious shell usually works both ways locking people out and me in. I see some light now. Thanks Dr. Green. . . .

Homosexuality. On the way home from the bar (we walked) we held one another. He had an arm around my waist and I had mine around his shoulder. On a fairly empty street an old pickup truck came screeching by, slowed, and the drunken driver chucked a Coke can at us with a scary threat—next time it'll be a shotgun. My mind didn't associate all the elements immediately. Coke can, truck, the threat. I saw the can; thought it was litter, cogitated briefly on the threat, then saw the truck screech away. The driver was obscured.

Lee and I walked straighter. We were a little surprised, a little frightened. I was angry, I think. Lewjack's comment comes back now and all the fucking prejudice. . . .

John and I talked about homosexuality at He's Not Here. He's tired of hiding it and thinks that his new relationship will be enough support to hold him while he "comes out" to his parents (or his little brother). We both recognize the hetero view of homosexuality as a separate and perverse world and at least I refuse to see the hetero world as separate. This is all one world. Dammit, we've got to see it as such. It scares me when John talks and I think in "two different worlds." It's *not* right. One world. One world. (Police) John's feeling anger, hurt, rebellion, hate. I want to feel just pity, but I'm beginning to burn with a slow anger. John doesn't want to be repressed. I'm afraid not to. (Strange?) I don't know repression. I don't know it racially and I don't know it sexually and I'm scared to death (no I'm not, I'm curious) to leave this Fantasy Island and to find out. . . .

Tuesday, March 30, 1982
—The strange mixture of pleasure and pain, realized. Yesterday was one of the most incredible days of my life and I know I'll never be able to capture it as vividly on paper as it occurred to me then. There are remnants everywhere—the painful hole where my dead molar used to be, the newspaper in the trees, this magnificent spring sunshine, and blue everywhere.

Where do I start? Well, after class I decided I'd have my tooth pulled. This was something symbolic of my new outlook on life, my new awareness of reality as a magic in itself. The pain in my mouth tells me I would have been happier a little while longer with that dead tooth in place, but I know that'll soon be gone and I will be better off for the hole.

The office, the little white room where they took me for the extraction, had a big white window. (While I'm thinking about it, is a window the frame and the glass? or the hole, the passage from inside to outside?) which my chair faced directly. I was nervous but confident that I was doing the right thing and that all would go well. Certain images come to mind. The numbness, the blood pressure apparatus—a heavy black band that was wrapped about my upper arm and inflated. There wasn't pain, but an uncomfortable pressure. And after awhile with this gadget on me my lower arm began to sleep, longing for blood. How does the body replace blood? Well, in its absence a funny, bloodless electricity flowed into my arm and hand and fingers. It seemed to concentrate most uncomfortably in my fingertips. It's strange to be bloodless. Is there a power there, a power in that concentration of sensation or was it a prelude to death, decay. I felt weaker for all that power. Blood seems somehow to be the life force, the imagination that gives our bodies shape. Without it we are bone and a nervy static. This is an energy indeed, but one can only stand so much of it. The blood must return to douse this tingle. I suppose also that the blood mixed with this sensation is the best of forces. The blood couldn't move without that spark and the spark is just a spark without the blood as perhaps a kind of fuel. My foot is asleep—a mass of tingle.

I stared out that window losing myself a few times on a large tree and the birds or squirrels that played there. Once in awhile, a bird stopped to look in on me and I looked back with a bright fear in my eyes as four hands tried to push into my mouth. The tree was imposing yet somehow comforting and I was afraid.

It took time, two hours (?), to get me through that and I had to forgo my 5:00 "appointment" at the UR. I went home and slept or tried to. It was a dark pain and I would have been lost in it except for the game.

We won it with me in pain 62–61 over Georgetown on a prayer from Michael Jordan. The game was an edge-of-the-seat confrontation. Too close.

And then the street later. . . .

Sunday, May 2, 1982
—I find it almost easy to bring myself close to nausea. Why would I need such a skill? I don't even think there's a call for it in the movies. If I could cry as easily I would be happier, I sup-

pose. The consequence—the darkness at the end of this nausea is too much to bear and I always swallow it back down. There's a strange sense of puking up only blackness. It would be a final sickness, a total disheveling of gut, bone and blood. I fear this nausea, perhaps mostly because I don't know why and where it comes and comes from.

Wednesday, June 2, 1982

—Buses. I hate them. I hate so much right now. Hate seems to be a very thick and unswimmable substance to me now. And I want to flounder, want to drown. Something vicious and cool has motivated me lately. Motivated my body anyway, as my soul is off in its fantastic trances. Waiting, wanting.

[Line drawn across page]

Oh what's this shit? I'm in Raleigh, I'm hours from home and I don't want to be here or there. I want to be back in Chapel Hill doing so much of nothing, but there's an obligation this time. My mom has breast cancer. Oh, what if she dies? What if a big hunk of my life ended right here?

My mom has breast cancer.

Bob is playing a game with me. Perhaps unconsciously, but still just as dangerously.

Still haven't written my paper for 83.

There was a hunky dude pacing around the bus station. He's walking off now, across the street. He's gone.

Monday, July 5, 1982

Idea for a story: Eating an egg salad sandwich at Looking Glass Cafe while an old woman who looks like Cloris Leachman watches me.

Friday, July 23, 1982

Thomas was masterful with his plots but rather shallow with the characters. I guess I remedied that. And together we made movies on a little block of houses at the desert's edge in El Paso, Texas. I had aspirations. Thomas did not seem to care. His magic lay in what he was creating at that particular moment on a dry, almost crackly, hot day near the desert. We would drag blankets and boxes, rakes and rope from a storage shed devoted to our movie props. But it was really just my dad's gardening shed. He never used anything but the lawn mower and even that so seldom that he could not recall, or could care less about the arrangement of things in that shed. But if he knew our stuff was there he wouldn't have liked it. With the rope and the blankets we made tents. We usually had to make a war movie because the blankets were army green, but sometimes when it was especially hot and the clouds looked like balls of white cotton we would make a survivor movie—two or three guys (depending on whether Ricky Meyers was on restriction or not) stranded either in the water or on the dangerous shores of some island. Someone was in charge on the house raft and it's amazing that we never fought over that role. Sometimes it was Thomas. Sometimes it was me. Sometimes we even let Ricky Meyers be in charge. Once, when Gale and Linda Kroeckle found out about our movies we had them play Amazons. *Revenge of the Amazon Queen,* I think that one was called. Gale, the youngest sister, was the queen and I think Linda resented it ever since. We knew that she never gave 100% after that to any of the movies we made. Not even the one she wrote and directed. Linda could be so spiteful. Thomas may have known this and perhaps purposely chose Gale for the queen of the Amazons, to see Linda redden with spite. I thought it was the heat. How could Linda possibly envy Gale after she saw the quilt Gale had to wear as a robe. Us boys had our shirts off, though I was kind of embarrassed because I had overheard Linda and Margaret Miller from up the street talking about chicken chests. Still, it felt good when an occasional breeze came (sometimes right on one Thomas said) and chilled the sweat on our backs and chests. Gale came after us brandishing a broom handle sword and we were helpless to fight her back having gone so long without food or fresh water.

Do you love her?

"I guess so" he said like my mom used to say "well I should guess so" when 'Cheena would run in the house, her hands full of splinters from playing with a broom handle sword. He said it like he hadn't known all this time and my question had opened a revelation to him. He said it like he was trapped and had had no idea of it before; it was just dawning on him this thing called love. "I guess I do love her."

The plot	The character development
Thomas	Gary

I saw him through the tinted windows. He looked nothing like what I thought . . . but then he could say the same about me. Thomas was thin and shorter than myself with a full beard and mustache that seemed too heavy for his face and frame. We had been so much alike as boys, weighing in at the same wimpish hundred, hundred-five, hundred-twelve. By junior high we were five-five and a hundred-twelve pounds. Average, at least for seventh graders. But Thomas hadn't changed much after that. He was perhaps five-seven now, but probably weighed less than he did eight years ago. So long? Eight years? I wanted to rush Thomas and hug him, bury myself in the nostalgia that his presence brought to my mind and flesh. Yes, this emotion even roused the flesh. I stepped back from the situation—Thomas Nolen meeting me in the Greyhound Bus Station—and tried to burn it into my memory. I'd wished I'd had a pen and paper to capture the emotions that welled in me at that moment. It was good to be back.

(I suppose the moment lost a bit of the spontaneity it should have had because I did step back, but wasn't it worth it having captured the full potential of that moment in my memory.)

Sunday, October 3, 1982
   —Money has told me more about myself than I care to know. How much of the stuff that I've bought have I used? How much will I ever get a chance to use as there's always something new to take its place. How many of these books have I read; how many albums do I know. Conversation pieces, that's all they are. They fit well in the damn movie I've made of life. I haven't started living yet. I haven't been born yet. *I'm piling all this junk in the womb with me so that I'll be born prepared.* I don't use anything and I'm going nowhere. . . .

Friday, October 17, 1982

. . . I've written an interesting short story called "Games" about the movie-making we did in El Paso.

Tuesday, December 28, 1982

. . . Christmas: no gifts from the folks. There was no money. The girls gave what they could. I was pretty much Santa Claus this year. Funny, everybody took it in perfect stride. Even Crystal. What a bummer. I'm embarrassed to mention it to anyone. A Fisher Christmas. la la la. . . .

Wednesday, June 8, 1983

. . . Ravish me God with the strength or at least the desire to know—to know my trappings, to live up to those opinions, to finally (or eventually) know *you*. I'm afraid of you . . . afraid of your meaning and my potential. I thought it was laziness, but it's really a dreadful fear of amounting to something. And I'm afraid to discover you like I'm afraid to see ghosts when I'm walking or just waking.

I guess I need the strength to be able to walk away from all this—my cluttered, lovable room. God, does that mean relying solely on me (and you, since I am asking *you*)? I want to desert it before it can desert me. And the only way to part agreeably is to get to know it, appreciate it for what it is, in all its externalness. To regard it as a flower—something so beautiful and yet crushable in my head, perishable in yours. Why am I holding this stuff and collecting, pooling, pack-ratting it. There's no tomorrow, but only todays extended. It's horrible, but I don't want to live, I want to think about living. Help. Ravish me. Hate me if you like, for being who and what I am, but don't abandon me with all this junk. God, if you were Allied Van Lines you wouldn't do this to me.

Monday, August 1, 1983

Sex is the issue today. I never said anything about the "hitchhiker" I picked up in June (or was it May?). An older man—30s or 40s—an ex-convict who'd fucked guys in the state pen (Georgia I believe). He was just waiting for me on the corner outside of the Pyewacket parking lot. He wasn't pretty, not in the least bit, but he was forward (and I was drunk) and that's what I wanted. He left no doubts. It was thrilling to be so close to the totally unknown. I remember him asking for a ride and saying he had something that I wanted. He said he wanted to "butt fuck" me and told me to touch his crotch and I did. While I was driving I rubbed his crotch—it was big. Here, he took his clothes off and hopped under the covers, a little modest, I presume, and very soon afterward we were at it—me sucking him, sitting on his cock; he turning me over and fucking me like an inmate, fucking then having me suck him awhile, more fucking. Finally he held my head down there on this large uncut thing and said "drink my cum—I want you to drink it." He stayed hard a long time afterward. The next morning I sucked him off again (not nearly as exciting) then I drove him to Pittsboro.

Today I'm going to Roy's probably to suck his big cock. I've been over there almost every week for two months I guess and we do the same thing . . .

AIDS apparently doesn't scare me like it should . . .

—What is it? the humiliation? —I asked this hitchhiker to piss on me. He never did, but I asked him. I guess it was the un-known again—it had reached out at me and I was reaching out at it. There's some with Roy too. I come off as pseudo-intelligent with Roy; he says "I teach him" stuff. O.K. But I enjoy being *used* by him. Then I'm not smart, then I'm just a hole for his pas-sion. He shoves it down my throat to come and holds it there till I'm faint and then I come. Crazy? it's a turn on that's all I can say in defense of it. I've been up since 6:00 with this on my mind. He rubs that big penis in my face and his balls and I smell like it, then he preps the pillow behind my head to face-fuck me with it. . . .

Wednesday, September 7, 1983

"Miss Della" will make a good modern horror story in the vein of E. A. Poe and hopefully less sensational, more substantial than Stephen King. An outline for the story: Two situations, one with the father, one with the son, one in Vietnam, the other in New Jersey at about the same time.

1) The father is running drugs with a group of buddies. This

running takes them to a treasure (Payment) in a wet cave. The money is locked in a drum. Jealousy, greed and fear lead the one partner to tie the father up. He says he'll send help when he's far away with the money.

Gagged and bound the father hears a scuffle and other noises. He will eventually discover his friend chopped to pieces and stuffed in the treasure trunk. Father loses his shit.

2) Meanwhile the Miss Della incident occurs. Boy is sexually stimulated by older baby-sitter. Later she accidentally kills a grocery boy she has drugged into sexual submission. The son will discover this.

He overcomes his silent period.

The father never does.

Mother tries to keep the son in line during these times. Slapping him for stealing etc.

Given presents, balloons, etc., to be Miss Della's "boy."

Dad is given stereo, money, drugs, women to fight the Vietnamese. Parallels between Dad and son/mother and country/Miss Della and another side of country.

Never leave food in standing water.

Bathtub scene.

Miss Della's home deceptively neat. Dishes in refrigerator, dirty dishes in cabinet. No love, only desire, lust.

Mother cries a lot.

Build the kid's world out of tears and sex and fear.

Build the father's out of fear and gifts.

Midnight, October 31/November 1, 1983 [San Francisco]

The drive across country ended abruptly in Oklahoma City. My bug lost its bowels with a couple of wrenching screams on the I-40 gateway to OK city. I have to consider myself lucky though because I met some nice (helpful) people. A fellow named Steve Bradshaw pulled me out of perhaps my most frustrating moment ever. He was the mechanic (and owner of the Automotive shop, appropriately named after him) who worked on my car, who fed me just a few moments of hope, then who informed me of the car's death—transmission stuck. My fault perhaps; there was little more than, in Steve's words, a coffee cup of grease in my engine. The transmission ground itself to death.

So there I was in massive, uncaring Oklahoma City thinking my situation through over and over and coming up with no solutions. Take a plane, rent a car, replace the transmission, and ultimately take a bus. To make it short, Steve and his garage family got wrapped in the situation with me. Steve seemed to take a lot of the slack, a lot of the responsibility. He owed me absolutely nothing, and technically I owed him about $80 for his attempt. But Steve calmed my mind some, set my course. The ideas were mine, but he came behind me like a strong support. I slept in his country mobile home, ate food his wife had bought (Taco Bell) and he even took me and my repackaged stuff to the bus station (actually his helper Ron did, and I'm quite grateful to him, but Steve was the real strength behind smoothing—so quickly—my rockiest frustration).

So carless I head on to California. I met a Danish man-boy name Claus who I yearned to know companionately. He occupied my eye and my rougher sensations all the way to Flagstaff. I felt like I'd lost a good friend when we said so long there. Maybe he'll call me here.

At the same time I meet a huge woman, Debbie, who sort of cushions a good bit of the trip with her light conversation, but after Claus had gone it felt like an effort to talk to anyone. (I wanted to baby Claus for awhile and enjoy while he offered the same. I sensed his intelligence and his mild tendency perhaps before we ever spoke.)

The bus fare, food money and shipping my cargo on the bus drained away most of my money, so I feel still more vulnerable, still close to the poverty/panic line. Sure, I've got good friends— Chris and Trudi and their roommate here, Susan—but as of 32 hours after arrival, I do not feel secure. (Give yourself a break, Gary. Only 32 hours.)

Sex, sex, sex. Sex in last night's dream. On the last hours of the bus ride (nothing serious: just a young guy and I touching ever so lightly—so lightly that I can never be sure of anything beyond what I personally felt).

I look so forward to making it here.

Tomorrow I'll step back out of myself and observe. There's a lot of beauty here. . . .

Thursday, November 10, 1983

. . . —Forgive me, friends and family, but I don't miss you. Of course I haven't settled this mind enough to give it thought. Subconsciously, I've had a dream (sexual and reminiscent) about Mike the busser.

—Should Bug be younger? Maybe six and just smart?

Tawny's anger has to be founded as well as his guilt. The parents have to be moving in a sphere totally separate from the children.

—What is this feeling? I don't like it. There are times when the presence of animals (Lucy and Moses) bothers me. They want to be petted but I go out of my way to ignore them. And it produces a strange combination of guilt and jealousy (maybe) in me. I want to be petted . . . Babble, Gary . . .

Friday, November 11, 1983

Tawny and the nature of evil. "Imaginary evil is romantic and varied, while real evil is gloomy, monotonous, barren, boring." The torture Tawny inflicts on Bug must be, in microcosm, the same tedious pain the adult world has pressed on him. Names, small insults, denials—never anything as serious as hitting (though Bug will eventually request just that, hitting, as it becomes preferable to the monotony). Tawny's method must be peppered with twinges of conscience, attacks of remorse for what he's doing. . . .

Thursday, December 15, 1983

Kitchie found something to love and something to envy in the bright blind ways of her children. She could talk to them and they might look right back at her, but she knew they were looking through her, right past or off to the right slightly like they were remembering—off into the great caverns of fantasy. She felt most alone when she talked to her children and yet there was love, like there's love for a gazing still-formed kitty, no . . . no, love for her children in the classic sense. She could still pull them to her bosom when they cried.

No wonder she feared Tawny so when he began to look at her, dark and focused just like an adult. She had the strong urge to strike him for his mannishness.

—Wow. D. H. Lawrence's "The Blindman." All of that strength gathered into a single paragraph—the blind man's touch. There's a subtle homosexual sensuousness about Lawrence's work, or maybe it's just a human sexuality so rich and pervasive that it knows no small bounds. His men are large, warm, handsome and frighteningly tragic, like beautiful monsters or fated demi-gods. His women are large, firm, strong yet doubting—always full of thought and concern and emotional achings. I envy the men because they're usually so thoughtless, so biotic and of course I empathize with the doubting women. Thus my trouble with Ken, I think.

With Lawrence as inspiration maybe I can write. I'm downtown now at the Berkeley library and I'll probably go to a movie (Stephen King's *Christine*) for a little adrenaline boost, but I feel an old surge. Maybe I can write.

Thursday, December 29, 1983

The end of the year is coming and I'm too embarrassed to make an assessment of 1983. It's been all anger, all jealousy, all struggle—hasn't it? Maybe there's reason enough to make an assessment. I still don't have work; almost two months and I have no job in CA! The waiting is hard too. I just want to sleep all day; to watch TV all day. I don't want to improve myself by reading books because I'm saving all that for this dreamy little future of mine. God, have I ever lived for the moment, for the raw sensation of one hour. Daniel Hecht's guitar is soothing . . . I feel opportunity coming, but should I just sit here waiting on it, getting Trudi incensed with my do-nothingness? I asked myself what else can I do? But I know there's so much I haven't done. I'm still approaching job hunting like a college kid. It's not real to me. Can't I find a little nothing job for two or three weeks while I wait for the biggies to come through . . . ?

There's been so much ego involved. I won't condescend and nobody is noticing me as a hothead. I still think I'm somehow better or removed from real life pressures. I was reading some 1980 journal last night. It's amazing what a fantasy I lived in— painful, yes—but a solid, self-made fantasy of lovers and riches and fame. I called on destiny to get me Gord and Tony and Mr. C. and destiny only stares me back in the face now.

I think people (meaning mainly me) assume destiny is a god of sorts with eyes both forward and behind him, but it's not true. Destiny sees forward just like we do. We, the people, have four eyes, eyes to see behind, eyes to look back on destiny. Destiny exists only as an aftersight. Not to say that magic isn't alive and well sometimes, but it takes more work than I know. The magic in my recent dream was raw, faulty stuff. I could barely do it. Magic is no easier than real life, so perhaps they are one and the same.

Saturday, January 20, 1984

. . . I remember as a young teenager playing with myself in front of my little sister. Two then, she probably doesn't remember and nothing went very far. I tried to stick it through the crib once so she could hold it, but she was off in another world (thank God, I might have made it a habit had she touched me). Even then I knew my interest wasn't in girls. I would superficially yearn for LaDonna Handley's company, in jr. high and high school at ASID, but my groin wasn't really in it. I wonder if I ever had sexual urge for a woman?—not even for simple release. I don't feel any less for it, but I do feel I wasted a lot of energy with all the pretense for heterosexuality . . . So here I am, pretty much lost sexually—not sure of what I want in a man, and with the AIDS scare, afraid to pursue it. Sometimes I think for sure I have it. My underarms will be sensitive or hurting or I'll have an extra pimple or two, or a mole will change a bit too much for comfort. AIDS has me living slightly on edge even if I don't have it. What a life of paranoia these past few months have been.

—I even dream wrong; my future is not tethered by anything I'm doing now, it's sort of a free-floating tomorrow that I piece together on popular whims and sexual fancy. I've lost reality because I don't imagine well; I've lost imagination because it has no ground in reality. I feel like a man who hasn't slept in weeks. . . .

Wednesday, March 7, 1984

. . . For my dead friend, Bennett

Do your last dance, your last joy-in-the-soul ride
then swing round the corner out of breath

for the slow coming of night. We'll stretch
on Grammy Moochie's quilt of flowers, locked like hands
splotched like purple and green plans for African violets,
blood up, bodies warm in our happy socks
with soda rolls and shivering handfuls of jewelweed.
We'll watch the moonrise and catch ghost shadows
or sudden light freckles on the black oak trees.
And in the center of this field behind the shed
where knowledge ventured and certain knowledge fled
we will unearth and rebury our kindest memory here
again, not haunted, but profoundly curious.

Kitty plays hell-wired, snatching a snag in your tight lap.
He moves in and out small spaces gyred on little more
than a hair ball, then instantly he rests,
a fat stone on the tilt-edge of a lampstand,
heaven-held, that crook in his tail, a cheater's balance,
a cat trick, this thing that sloughs even the final places.
"It's in the whiskers," he'll tell you. "And, bristled
they're as long as cats are wide."

Put his box in the mountains in the first plot
of the first space made available between trees.
Shower him once with red dirt and siltstone
and grow grass there and flowers
and forget about him . . .
So once a year you can pitch a moonlit picnic
for two and stir two worlds with your play . . .

Monday, March 26, 1984
    Dear Roy,
    I haven't been letting much in lately—so many charms and
kindled hopes fluttering about, spirituous, or at least beyond my
immediate comprehension, just there, suddenly there like destiny more than like luck, like gifts more than like finds—and
for those reasons I don't want them. It's not so much the easy
way that I'm avoiding, it's the rehearsed way, it's the well-rutted
path. I remember the helter-skelter angles we took to discover
our mating spot in the Carrboro woods, my very last day there
when I sucked your cock (mainly to demonstrate my complete

complicity in this . . .) did we weave through that twiggy mess in the hopes of concealing ourselves or in the childish hope of *losing* ourselves. How long—given a warm day—could we have stayed there? I want to lose myself in you, Roy, but then there seems to be a hundred different *mes* to lose—and all of them so mother-fucking smart, all so compassed or simply so well gyred as to never ever be lost, really lost again. That's what I want to do, though, completely abandon this crazy intellectual prison for awhile—envisioning all these rough angular beauties with such deliberateness I might as well be drawing up formulas for them, or scoring musicals about them, or writing form prayers . . . I want to get lost in your thicket for that's what you remind me of—no glamour boy, but a rough and ready man, a fantasy sailor or soldier or Kentucky mercenary. Someone as tangible as bare earth or crooked trees and in the same way fulfilling and without formulas. There's an airy pocket in me that you can't fill—birds and butterflies and strange shiny space objects fly in there— maybe no one can, but every other soft, warm, wet inlet is yours. Fill it with molten earth or a single solid stone key and fill it repeatedly.

Where did I change? Where did this urgent need to orally capitulate, this ultimate supplication for me . . . where did it come from again. I could give you my ass, Roy, because despite the pain there, it means little to me unless the rhythm is perfect, but I'm a man of words, a man of the mouth, in love with what I say, with what I write, with words in a general way—so this sudden urge to relinquish my most valuable tunnel to these urges must be something burbling up from deep deep within—a lost well— the dark child, the wombed child, as afraid in his damp home as he is alert and brave in the outer canyons. You soothe that child in me, Roy, every time you put your cock in me or your balls on me. I love looking up into the hairy, square dominance of it all— your face with that bit of question in it, your wracked body and the proffered nipples still red from attention. If you knew what you were doing to me there would be no question—you couldn't get deep enough, I don't think, if you did that child would curl up beneath you in a massive soul-releasing sigh—every time, all the time—no one can get that deep. Funny how the child hungers for life even as it tempts death, funny how the womb and the dagger unite in an utter perfection, funny how the fleeting is best pictured against a gray and permanent backdrop. I'm selfish—I want you to be my rock, but then sometimes I want you to wash away from me and rocks don't do that for millions of years. I'm naive to think you'll go away or that I can get away.

—Oh, this letter's calculated, spontaneous too, but calculated because I've had it in me a long time. I want to nurse the longing in you as well as in myself. Looking forward to long aching moments when I'll be folded in two under you again and rocked for a good half hour to the burning strands of Otis Redding or the hyper double-breath of "Tour De France." Wear your leather, Roy, because I want to be fucked by a man in leather and I want to be seen on the colorful streets here with a man in leather. Maybe, just maybe your visit can coincide with the gay pride parades here. I'll get you more info soon.

Friday, March 30, 1984

. . . Luchina spilled the beans—Mama's dying (probably) of liver cancer or just general cancer if it makes any sort of difference. I'm scared for her and myself and my sisters.

Finished my letter to Roy . . .

God, I'll have to tell her, won't I? don't you come clean with a dying parent? I'll also have to tell her . . . what, that this is a great source of anxiety, fear and excitement (let's face it—you don't die every day). . . .

Sunday, April 8, 1984

Stop it. I've been hurting for so many stupid reasons—should I go to the laundromat with Chris and Trudi; do they have room; will Berkeley accept me; will my mother die this year; will I enjoy Roy's visit; will I have the place alone.

Tuesday, April 10, 1984

Notes

Perhaps the Kitchell's house should have windows on two sides—one looking out on the desert and the other facing the Vanderkleeses.

Also the Nixon Watergate bus. should play a small atmospheric role.

Thursday, April 12, 1984

Sort of a day of unfoldings. Work, first of all, wasn't half bad (at least toward the end); I got to work more with the computer and I felt a growing there. The big surprise was at home waiting for me ("home," that seems so strange to me now). Berkeley sent me an *acceptance* letter. Chris and I popped a bottle of André cheap champagne and toasted "beginnings." Then I called home. My mother has more chemotherapy in a week. Her hair's falling out —she's going out to buy a wig. Oh, God, won't you be gentle—I'm so afraid for her, for me without her. Don't take her yet. There's so much we need to show her, God. And find out too that little Luchina, who I can hardly believe is graduating from high school, has been accepted by *Stanford*. More: a letter from Roy was waiting with a sex picture and a letter stressing gentle beginnings— "beginnings," that word again when so much death is lingering. My mother, perhaps me, dying this most uncertain of ways. Then Roy calls and we get off together talking dirty on the phone.

Friday, April 20, 1984

Darkness, darkness. Good Friday. I'm feeling a little religious, a little inquisitive, a little frightened, a little lost in the magnitude of what I have to say. It's not going away, this tenderness under my arms, the occasional burning sensation, a couple of painless red dots—one on each hand. It's not going away and I don't feel good about that with AIDS such an issue. I want to blame and beg and apologize to certain people, to God, to my dying mother perhaps. That's been feeling like a consolation, a bit of relief perhaps knowing I won't go alone . . . Never alone, Gary, just faster.

Monday, September 3, 1984

Time time time, look what's become of me . . . My rash is just an itch now, but I discovered a small protrusion of skin, another mole I guess, and it made me feel old and dying. Unfairly though—not fate, but my decision to lay down and die so easily.

Saturday Jason did stay. The guy has a nice face, a little like a young Joe Namath, but his body left a little to be desired. Still he stayed and I enjoyed having sex with him, if that's what we'd call it: it was an SM fantasy brought into dramatic reality (an attempt anyway). I was the top-man, the master, and Jason was my slave. He got off twice, but I couldn't force it, still it was ter-rifically exciting and after the man left I shot so hard it crossed my left shoulder and landed near my ear. The first time, Jason wanted me to wear boots and gloves; the second time I wore my floppy army cap (the one Jerry Bowles gave me). I'm mildly dis-appointed, but not real surprised, and I'd like to see Jason again. I'll call him next week and I'm pretty sure we'll have an encore, but that's not what I want (is it?). . . .

Saturday, September 29, 1984
    . . . Innocent until proven guilty makes for a modern day *Haunted* and the wicked witch. In a dream I just woke myself out of I had pushed a cruel woman (who looked like Heidi Oresko-vitch from Germany) into a microwave oven and killed her. She'd done me some injustice, I know . . . but the smell gave her away and people were connecting her up with me. A group of people which seemed to include my mother and a wise middle-aged man who looked like a businessman, a professor or a homo-sexual friend were all paying me compliments right before the body was discovered. The man was commenting on how honest I was by not taking some money that belonged to him. Something tells me I was guilty there too and my mother (I think it was her) kept saying how smart I was, and the whole crowd seemed full of approval UNTIL a woman, a plain, slightly chubby woman (the archetypal bitch for me) opened the microwave. People had been smelling the body—this is another group of people; the one in-cluding my mom and the professor-man had moved out of the scene like a chorus. And at that point I had started running. I did run past the sight of the discovery, saw them pull a bloody bundle (a nice folded, pillow-like object but bloody when the bitch-woman squeezed it under her arm while toting it away—it seems like a casual way to carry a dead body now, and I figure it was so small because it had cooked down to that). Heidi O. was a tall woman. Anyway, I'm running to escape and something in me knows I'll be caught and I'll never be able to explain (I'm not even sure an injustice was done me). I run past a man (a handsome hunky guy, Southern, rather hickish, who looked [I think] like Johnny's first roommate in Carrboro before he moved in with me) and a woman who was obviously his girl. They were

running close together, he had his arm around her and they were making gleeful preparations to catch a criminal—setting up road blocks or something—and they spoke (said they'd heard such and such and were getting ready . . .) to me as I ran past them. The last I remembered before I woke up is thinking I've killed myself, I've ruined it all, and I had a moment of release— no more concerns, no more cruel world, etc.—then a moment of desperation—I didn't want to die. I was running past a grove of bright green trees on the edge of the neighborhood where this occurred (the houses looked so similar I'm inclined to think it was based on Logan Heights or Biggs Field in El Paso, Texas). I felt the futility of my situation, knew I would spend a long time running and decided to wake up. Waking up, it's funny. I feel like I left that world of my dreams still going on, like a movie I'd felt uncomfortable with and left. It didn't stop when I left it and I immediately thought—I can't go back to sleep yet or I'll end up right back in this dream. Are there different levels, sliding in and out? A dream dimension?

The implications of the dream were obvious. Feeling guilty but rightfully avenged by committing the act, etc.

Saturday, October 13, 1984

—I had a dream several days ago that I was in bed *with* my father. I was sucking his cock, and while he was obviously enjoying it (from the size and hardness of his, uh, situation) he was off in a daze somewhere, unbelieving. My mom kept popping into the dream to reprimand us. I seemed to be the instigator since he was off in a pleasurable oblivion. . . .

Monday, October 22, 1984

If I'm going to die I guess I better make preparations. So many stories to write, so many people to write, so many things to assimilate. I guess I could die if I've reached a point of worth (for myself) within my community—my writing community if that's where life's taking me. I guess I could die if I felt like I'd apologized to all the people I've hurt, and included all the people I've loved in a story or two. It'd be easier then to know I haven't wasted all this.

Pat Metheny giving me a break . . .

Friday, November 9, 1984

11:00 I've been itchy too. Okay, I've convinced and unconvinced myself several times now. I don't feel as bad as I did, but I know I don't feel up to par. What are these white dots here and there on me; what's this pain here, this pulling there, and knotting someplace else. I need to accept and move on—or not even accept: just put the whole issue aside.

But wait! What if *I've* killed somebody with this? What if Jason dies because of my carelessness and embarrassment on the subject. What if Roy dies because of me, or vice-versa? Why did Wally die if it wasn't to join his friends in a better place. Spooky thought. I don't feel much like writing. I feel like masturbating to the memory of Roy's endowment and the anonymous bathroom boys who used my mouth for their pleasure—yeah! I can only have the one large incomprehensible regret for what has happened (if that's what this is). I can only die once, I suppose. Maybe I should have sucked a hundred more. How many were there (not a whole lot)? How many repeats (Roy especially—some damned delicious sessions with his penis and his pleasure)? I gave over to pleasure and pleasure destroyed me. Okay. Let's put it in its place and get on with what's left . . .

It felt good sitting on Roy's cock. It felt good being folded in two and deeply fucked by the man. Jamie too with so much rhythm it was all I could do to hold on for him—he was a wonderful fucker. How much cock did I taste at my orgy in Hinton James? two? three? all of them? who came in my ass? How many bathroom boys down my eager throat? How much poison seed? How much of my death wish had I realized then? Funny, I have no reason to ask why here because I know. I only have one big regret—that I won't suck a million more, that I won't suck that special one (whoever it belongs to) a million times; that I won't be folded up and made one with a stud . . .

Tuesday, November 13, 1984

I have to chart the course of this, don't I? My right leg—the inside of the knee joint—is swollen and tender; both legs fall asleep easier than I remember, ache more than I remember and seem less healthy than I remember—BUT, what do I remember of them. There's another very tiny dot of red—like a pin hole—at the base of my left thumb and the others (two or three) show no signs of going away. I didn't feel as tired today as usual but I was assailed by some throat congestion and coughing. I wasn't as headachy today but I didn't feel over lucid or clean. I really want to get better, so I can fulfill all the real or implied promises I've made in this life. I'd like to live to eventually straighten out my lies.

I wish none of this had ever happened. I didn't want to know this nearness to the grave, not yet, not even as a writer, not as much as I was secretly baiting it — I never meant it.

Sunday, December 9, 1984
. . . 5:00 P.M. Mark just called for a study-break (I suppose). I like Mark, but . . . but there's always buts. This paper is so far from even a start that an all-nighter is a certainty now. Mark agreed with me when I said my last paper was shit. Funny, after rereading it I didn't think it was all that bad — guess I'll have to re-evaluate. What is all this anguish worth anyway? The girls and the dog are running wild through the house. I have *no* idea what I'm trying to do with this paper. I told Mark I'd been eating peppermints all day. He said he'd like to kiss me (because of that, I assume), and I'm still a little weak from thinking about his kisses.

Saturday, January 5, 1985
. . . I also gave some thought to the paradox of my situation. (If indeed I do have a terminal case of AIDS) I have been laid vulnerable in just the way I've always hoped was recoverable. That's too cryptic. What I mean, is my mind lost its purity when its defenses went up. My body sometimes feels locked the same way. Now I've been forced to unlock. Literally, my body could be open to whatever death is lurking on a friend's breath or in a stranger's handshake. My body is new-born again — vulnerable — in a way my mind can only approximate. And indeed my mind seems somewhat reborn; seeing for the first time in a long time. . . .

Thursday, March 21, 1985
. . . From Smythe's Philosophy 142 class several years ago

I just got embarrassed over something
I said long ago. That is it occurred to me

What an ass I was for something I said
About predicate adjectives. Doesn't matter now,
I suppose, it didn't matter then. That is it
        shouldn't . . .
Or I wish I hadn't . . .
I'm embarrassed at a distance
Like blushing over baby pictures
Or calling Gary Greg for an evening,
That is it occurred to me a long time ago
That I'd feel like an ass later
For things I said then, though it wouldn't
Shouldn't matter, but did
About those bloody predicate adjectives.

I see most of my ghosts when I'm very tired. . . .

Thursday/Friday, September 19/20, 1985
    . . . —I revised "The Art of Parties" (which is a piece of "Villains") and it's now called "Twelve," is much tighter, more controlled, coherent. . . .

Saturday, November 2, 1985
    Have I tried to oppress myself—as a black man and as a (passive) homosexual man—purely for the pleasure of it, or does that oppression go right to the point of my perceived weaknesses. It is societally impossible for me to make it the way I want to make it (financially, sexually, etc.) so I'm groping for an excuse, one that feels good and therefore must be good. Can I divorce sexuality from power in the real world or do I want to—here's one world *explaining* the other, and Christ, it's *so* hard to get answers. So I want to be a slave, a sex slave and a slave beneath another man's (a white man or a big man, preferably a big white man) power. Someone more aware of the game (and the reality of it) than myself. I want to relinquish responsibility and at the same time give up all power. I want to, in effect, give in to a system that wants to (has to) oppress me. This made Roy (Southern, white, 40+ man) attractive to me—not wholly this. This made Tony *so* attractive to me. If T. K. had been the least bit dominating (encouraging) I don't know where I'd be now. Cock size is a definite turn-on (and not necessarily for reasons that oppress, though now I want to see

it that way). Roy and Jamie. The big man: Gord (in Chapel Hill); Keith here at the library; Jim!; Jason Moore; Wally; Mr. C. . . .

Thursday, November 21, 1985

What is love? I'm listening to some thrash (trash?) rock from Hüsker Dü and recuperating from the eyes at the Stud. Was I begging? Was I enjoying the rejection? is that what I was seeing? I met a few eyes? Am I actually asking myself (my journal) if I look good to other men? am I really vain enough to consider the question at all?

What is love? Johnny doesn't know. He can't keep it, but he's had it four or five times now, much to my envy. I've never wanted him or any of his lovers but I've always wanted them to want me. This skin, this yellow-blackness; this nose and crinkly hair. Perhaps I should go to "my own people's" parties.

What is love? Kathleen can't keep it. She had a lawyer friend but asked him to be more sensitive than a straight man can be without feeling like a woman.

—Love. Here's a new way of understanding why I couldn't fuck Tony (and why he wanted me to) and Mark. I want to be possessed, like a doll, I think, and possessed like a doll belonging to some violent, curious child. I want to be pulled apart limb by limb and eventually killed, I think. AS A DOLL to some strong kid.

But not a game. The MAN gives nothing, loses nothing, remains whole, autonomous. USE-ing and leaving whole, "coming and going," so to speak. I want to be the TOY. Is that childish. It's the male way in this country. That's what being a faggot's all about, right? And yet my ego battles with all this, my logic, my vanity, my intellect. I am TOY but I am MAN outside the bedroom. I don't necessarily want to be. What I really *want* is some other MAN to rape me, reduce me from MAN to TOY. That's why it's the big guy. These men that chill me, make me sensitive, thrill me like a woman is purported to be thrilled. (I wish I'd heard your Tuesday lecture, David Miller.) . . .

Christmas Eve, 1985

. . . I UNDERSTAND! this self-slaughter, but it scares me. I'm trying to decreate. Trying to go back; not to an easier time, but a more honest one. Shit, slave, nigger, cocksucker; like the wind, and darkness, the Auroras of Autumn. I'm doing it with sex and society, bludgeoning myself with misconceptuous facts, or the fictive facts that were "in fact" bludgeons *then*. No, I'm doing it with *words...*

Friday, January 3, 1986

—I know how much work you put into it; how you labored to find the one with just the right words and just the right picture to express that one choice meaning—uniquely yours to me; how you spared no expense and braved every danger to find that special card. But ____, you know what? I didn't get it. You paid all that money for postage (I feel so bad), and I didn't get it. The postman should be shot, I know, but I'm not vindictive, and neither should you be. I know that in your heart, as well as in that misplaced card, you sent to me your warmest, merriest wishes for a good Christmas, and a safe and happy new year. I know you sent lots of love and I thank you for it and resend my own.

Love, or what you will, in '86

Gary....

Tuesday, February 25, 1986

I was just thinking about James Brown ("Papa's got a Brand New Bag" is on the radio): what's it like to lose your groove? the sound you've spent so many years cultivating can get lost in the wash of popular sounds and then it's not yours. Or you stop and then it's not yours. And when you try to come back do you hire new people, younger people who've spent much of their lives imitating your sound—do you hire them to refresh you. The god of sounds now, do you stand there directing hired younger sounds? The near-dead god of sounds has to have children. (Silly!) ...

Wednesday, March 5, 1986

... I'm feeling my body and pretending this is not happening to me and perhaps that's bad, but then how do you act like something is wrong? How do you give into the act of dying, the act of believing what your body is doing?

June 21, 1986, a Saturday

It's late Saturday (early Sunday) and I've seen my mother
And I don't know what to do
The radiation chemicals have made her so weak.
I'm in a hotel room across from the hospital
That's not *my* mother
That's not my mother
That's me. That's the essence of all I am
Dark, hairless, afraid. Help her
I feel as though I'm receding
Her liver is failing. Can't you restore that, god?
    —Help!

I'm in the hotel wanting to enjoy the hotel. I want to have fun
with my sisters. We went to the waffle shop. We couldn't find a
Hardee's. In Luchina's new car. Having fun.

I want to be numb. It's too hard to think about her.

Monday, June 23, 1986

Now I'm in Roy's living room in Chapel Hill, NC vegetating
in front of dull, dull MTV. I had lunch today at the Pyewacket and
not much else. I have not seen my mother today. It frightens me
most that she cannot talk to me, cannot really understand me,
that she is little more than a child in pain in there. So much to
feel and to be unable to escape. The fluid in her stomach, the
tubes in her nose and arms, the dryness of her skin. . . . I want
her to live, but I'm selfish. I don't want the pain of her dying in
my life. God, I don't want her to hurt; I don't want her to fear. . . .

Wednesday, July 2, 1986

. . . Communication. It had to come to us ad lib and in a rush.
We were in the room (me and my sisters) alone, the chaplain,
Joanne having just prayed with us (for us) and gone, when a picky
little fight broke out between Leslie and Luchina about rubbing
momma's hand or her head. Leslie said it would chafe her . . .
I don't really understand how it progressed to name-calling . . .
I tried to call everyone into conference (trying to wield a power I
didn't have, but with Ursula, the nurse, watching and prod-

ding me to take a certain leadership, one I tried to take); Leslie wouldn't come out. In the lounge Luchina and I fell even further apart. Crystal was a stone. Neither of them, none of them seemed to have any conception of what was happening; just stones. The tears came after the fireworks. China ran out of the room. Ursula talked to her and five minutes later we were hugging and crying freely—China and I. Crystal joined in, but no tears. Leslie was a silent machine inside the room. My anger with her kept me back till the grief overwhelmed me. My memory's bad here. The chaplain came after the sparks, didn't she? After I'd spent some time alone with my mom, frustrating time, trying to say I loved her, but hardly believing it was her (my real mom is on vacation isn't she? Vardamon?), crying some more, I went back to the lounge and found the three of them. I broke down and Leslie came over, but I didn't need her strength as much as I needed to feel her vulnerability. How dare she pat my back. How dare Crystal tell me it's okay. I wasn't crying for me (was I?); I didn't need that help (did I?).

My father won't cry, won't show us, doesn't want to see it in us, he's convinced Leslie, Crystal, maybe China, but China seems to have a little more independence (at least of emotion, no, just overall independence) from him. She cried, like I think I cried, with abandon. I couldn't help myself.

—I haven't mourned enough. I haven't mourned at all. I don't know where my mother is. I didn't have a mother, did I? Will I lose her that way? I want to cry once every night, or would that be a torture to me. It felt so good to cry today, but I didn't think uncontrollable sobbing would sound so odd to me, high pitched, squeaky, airless sobbing. I'm not embarrassed to cry—at least the tears part . . .

I'm losing my mother and I'm losing one of my best friends. The beach trip with Roy was torture for both of us I think. We began it so coldly—I thought he was upset with me for being late, but I think he was reading my journal. What should I tell him? Yes, I believe I am dying of AIDS? or no, you misunderstood, it's all a fiction. In a way it is all a fiction, all a movie. Is my mother going to take this dead feeling away? Is she going to take *me* with her? Somehow I felt *so* connected to her pain.

Friday, July 4, 1986
1:30 P.M. Mom died.
1:00 A.M., July 5.
I couldn't hear that about my mother hemorrhaging and not hurt an awful lot. I hope she died without too much pain, without any, and without frustration. Why do I feel like death will be a frustration? an unwinnable struggle against darkness. I can keep my lights on but . . . ?

Mom, this house feels so empty without you. Tell me you are at peace; tell me it's better where you've gone, that you're burdenless and full of love or some other special feeling.

—Did I ever mean "I love you" until I knew she would leave us? Yes, many times.

Roy feels so gone.

Sunday, July 6, 1986
Dear Mom,

I feel like I've deserted you, run from a responsibility. Tomorrow is your body's funeral and I won't be there, not even in spirit, I don't think. I will always love you as I know and remember you, and you will grow in me (if I grow at all . . .) The grief will come soon, I imagine, and I dread that a little. It was hard seeing you in the hospital and knowing how beautiful you once were. Daddy was right one time though, when you were unbandaged, bald, dark and serene in some sleep or drug stupor—you were beautiful, more beautiful than I ever knew you—stripped down, elegant. I hurt to know that is gone. I can't see your corpse, even if the guilt of fleeing haunts me for a while. I love you, Victoria Fisher, and I still don't believe you're gone. I can't watch them put your old body into the earth. Love me, please.

Thursday, July 10, 1986
. . . —Last night on the plane a handsome man my age was seated next to me and when he fell asleep he fell over on my shoulder (practically). Some part of his body seemed to be touching me all flight. It felt good. He was a comfort during the turbulence. I don't think he was gay . . .

What a horrible and frustrating time at the beach with Roy. I may never see him again. Not my choice. I believe he found out in my journal . . . If it's true then don't I owe him. The *one* time in the entire weekend that we had sex, Roy would not kiss me, would hardly touch me or look at me. We had been rather cool to each other all trip. I figured he was angry because I was late getting away from the hospital that Friday—all of my Virginia relatives were there to see Momma—but I don't think so now. The coldness had an edge to it, a fear, a questioning. I had the feeling the whole time that he wanted to ask me, but he never did. And what lie would I have told him? What lie will I try to tell him now? Friday night we hardly slept. I kept getting out of bed, pretending to be grieving, but it was the bed—the bed was cold. Roy had hardly spoken to me all day and all night. It was so weird, so frustrating. I wanted to ask him but didn't dare. Saturday night was the same or even worse because we both knew the other knew something was awry and it was difficult to put on a charade. Sunday morning we were maneuvering in bed to keep from touching, but to show that we desired touching. I was trying to look small and sexy, I guess. Roy trying to look uninterested, but both of us wanted something. Both of us wanted the other to instigate it. Finally Roy turned to me, rather dramatically; I thought he might be wanting to fight. I touched him and he let me. I think he started touching me below the covers—certainly no kissing—and I was trying to arouse him. He didn't say anything. I expected him to push me away and to rise up in disgust and condemnation, but he didn't say anything. I don't know what he wanted for me to do but I started sucking his nipples and moved down, on my own accord, not his, not once his, to his cock. The angle was awkward but I sucked and soon his hip action and his hands were helping. I could see his feet moving and his knees and I think he was making some noise. I know he wanted it over with fast. His cock felt rough and unloving to me. It hurt my throat or rather I was hurting my throat with it. I wanted it to last. I wanted Roy to want it to last but he didn't. When I would stop for a moment I sensed his impatience and got back to it. Soon he was holding my head. I almost wish I'd felt more of his wrath so I could remember. I think he made noise. His hips and legs were moving. I didn't taste his cum—it went too far in my throat—until he pulled his dick out. I couldn't swallow what was left. I wiped my tongue on a towel. I think he saw. I guess I wished that it would kill me. I guess I wished that every time. Did we have sex four times? Five times. I wish it were all different. House on the lake like Sam's and a fulfilling sex life, thunderous!

Monday, July 21, 1986

. . . Good-bye, mother. I want to say "see you later" or "see you tomorrow" like I did in the hospital, so afraid to say good-bye. . . .

Tuesday, Aug. 26, 1986

. . . —Scenario: I *don't* write to Roy but just show up in Chapel Hill over Christmas. He makes the move and takes me forcefully mouth and ass, and we make up through this violent pleasure. He will always be ugly to me now because he lost that innocence, that redeemed innocence, a second time, but I can't help but love him and lust for him, as if his ugliness were the very thing I craved as much as that cock and his desire. I may be as ugly as he is, but I won't lie for either of us. Till death do us part.

Saturday, November 29, 1986

Change of mind or maybe a double current . . . The last two hours were bliss (after a waste of an entire day); I saw the Bad Brains with Pete at the Omni in Oakland. Management fucked up (as usual) by scheduling them (the Brains) too late, and boring us with cheap trash metal bands for hours prior. But the last two hours were brilliance. Short men, quiet men (I imagine) full of a power I've never seen in a band (that I long for in myself), Rasta men in graceful, animal dreadlocks. The lead singer was a small, lithe, hairy man on the most intense trip, not even a little pre-occupied with appearance, presentation, just him and an ocean of sound. Sound, guitar man, small, graceful, frightening in his precision; bass, taller, planted in his corner (black clothes, red sneakers) behind his hair, making wicked waves; thick muscled drummer, Rasta locks drifting off to one side like a dark garnish on the rest of his hair, and an angry perfection in his beat. Together thunder, electricity. I have not seen a better concert.

December 24, 1986, Christmas Eve

I feel weak in the gut, in the bones, and my urge is to do anything that makes me feel alive: to eat, to play music, to watch a movie, or like last night, to have sex. I want to go back to Buena Vista park, to meet with men in the dark. To depress myself further, to push myself closer to this weakness that I feel. Last night did not go quite as planned. I met two men who were considerably nicer than I'd expected (or wanted). The first man, a black man, was as tentative as I was and mimicked my every move until I took the initiative to suck his bigger cock (not knowing even now if that's what he wanted or what he wanted to do to me). He seemed to enjoy it. I forget his name but I remember he had an s-curve in his erection and smelled very clean. (I had had tuna casserole for dinner that night and felt rather restricted by the lingering smell—again he didn't seem to mind.) The second man was more aggressive and wouldn't even allow a third man to join us—said he was greedy and wanted all of me. We played on a hillside, kissing and talking each other up a lot. I was particularly turned on by his description of how he would fuck me . . . Our whole activity was "safe" to my surprise (and good fortune! as I think the man was ill; I felt a knot on his neck and in his beard and he appeared more exhausted than I think I did). I would have killed myself on that man. He saved me. We came back to my apartment and made love—the best I've had in a long while—till 2 A.M. He seemed very pleased, satisfied. I was too. His name is Barry. We exchanged phone numbers but it may be better if we don't force our good thing. It felt good to be with him even if I was primarily the aggressor. So, now, should I go back, "defile" myself on Christmas Eve for the thrill of it? Have I thought about why I do this? Tonight will mark the fourth time in BV park. I've met a man or two each night and felt more thrilled than at any time since Roy.

—It's after midnight, technically Christmas, with Elvis Costello, a lot of sugar in my system, those pictures of Roy's penis, and then a revolting memory . . . I sucked this dude, little dick, sweet cologne smell on his balls, a cold, hard cock. He jerked himself to a disappointing (for both of us) climax and as I stood up to get away from him, from myself, I put my hand in shit, human shit, someone had shit on the branch that we were leaning against. I can still smell it on my hands . . . I rubbed my hands in dirt and dried grass to get rid of the smell, then washed them tormentedly here. I wanted more action but the shit drove me home. Besides, I didn't see one other person besides the dumb-looking Joe I sucked on. So anticlimactic after Barry and the black man yesterday. Guess all the nice cock was at home getting Christmas presents.

An hour or so after I got back here, I was cleaning some in the kitchen when I heard a commotion under the sink. I thought some plastic bag was settling or that the pipe was leaking, or perhaps we had a mouse, but a white and tan hamster crawled out instead. I have to find a spacious cage ("home" is the euphemism) for it; right now it's in Rick's straw chest sleeping.

After such a satisfying climax last night I don't need to look at Roy's pictures, but I went out tonight looking for something only that man has given me (and only occasionally with him). I want to jerk off on Christmas, perhaps to seal this humiliation. Oh, the anger and violence and confusion I felt after touching that shit. Why was I out there? Looking for nothing. I found even less than nothing. So uninteresting (and uninterested), that man.

Compare him to the burly chested dude with the nice cock that I sucked and that brought us into a threesome with another white man. For awhile I was sucking two cocks. The burly dude was the one I wanted, but he saved my life and spat his seed on the ground. The other dude eventually took me to another secluded spot where we traded sucking but I eventually took him. First threesome though since bathroom days at Carolina. Remember?

I'm trying to find reasons . . . or trying to *make* reasons for this death. I haven't written much in this book because I haven't enjoyed, no, because I haven't deserved . . . no, because I haven't had time . . . because I've been afraid to admit.

Saw *Star Trek IV* and was not blown away or even taken away from myself. I sat contentedly however. Give it a B. *Otello* was better, or was it just because Mark came along too? I didn't notice the opera after awhile; the story came through in spite of any misconceptions (preconceptions) I may have had. Beautiful movie, A.

Tired again, but charged up on sugar and Costello and the possibility of a cruel fantasy . . . I wish something more had happened in the dark so I wouldn't have to deal with this emptiness in the light.

I can't look at those pictures, but I know I will. I keep spacing out, won't make a commitment to anything, forgetful or just confused? What about Tom and Roy? What's in a cock? Roy's even? Just a waste of proteins to me now. Why remember what you can't have (or can only get to at great expense). And won't you have to be the one to apologize for it? (Costello, "Shot with his own gun" talking to me . . .) Mucous, mucous, mucous, mucous, mucous—all of it on a sidewalk somewhere. You want to clean the streets of the city with your tongue and your bare flesh. Oh, Barry's talk last night! You! Somebody from his dreams? Somebody would dream of me? The Roy/Tony K. hybrid. Why didn't my Mr. Right ever have Barry's dreams? Why don't I dream anymore? Am I too far gone to need love? All I want now is maximum humiliation. (But this Elvis is *so* good!)

When did you stop enjoying it, Roy? Never really wanted to humiliate me, never was in it just for you (which humiliation requires), always in love with me, caring for me when I needed you to stop caring or at least to pretend not to care, just to need/want servicing. Why weren't you just another horny-all-the-time-sonofabitch white man? When did I lose touch of who you were, who I was to you, and what we should have been? I was in love with the ugliness of it all, being able to transcend, then I fell in love with all of it, simply all of it, ugly, beautiful, comic, tragic —I was there and you suddenly picked up on where I *had* been.

Monday, December 29, 1986

. . . Chunk heels and a bump toe ('70s platform shoes)

Don't you understand boy? I ain't after your forgiving. *I* have forgiven *you!*

Claude Monet, "Vetheuil in Winter"; Bronzino, "Portrait of Lodovico Capponi" (How about the cod piece on that Bronzino?); Jules Pascin, "Seated Girl with a Pink Ribbon".

Going before the promotion board for E5, my dad and Mr. Jackson.

Stella told Jackson to get his ass home or she was going to kill him.

Stopped to pick up a quart bottle of Colt 45.

Both dad and Jackson going for E5, only one slot in the unit.

New Brunswick, New Jersey. Stella used to eat chicken bones. She's back on street now after a small stint in prison.

.22 or .25 automatic. Jackson sitting on toilet. Shot, blood all along the wall. Couldn't clean it for 2 months during the investigation.

Redon, "Roger and Angelica" c. 1919 (pastel)

Gris, "Guitar, Bottle and Glass" 1914 (pastel, paper, gouache and crayon).

Claes Oldenburg, "Giant Soft Fan" (vinyl filled with foam rubber).

I watched *Turtle Diary* with Mark again today and enjoyed it even more. Pere Ubu weakness. Desire for the cold of woods, of water?

Conversation: 8 people at a dinner party—talking about neighbors upstairs having sex—Sara very embarrassed—"She's not even good-looking . . ."—"What does that have to do with it?"—"Well, she was having such a good time."

Talking Heads after 11:00. I'm very tired and with good (not ill) reasons; I'm not sleeping well at all . . . Is a big cock so important? I've been surprised to find that many men find me big . . . but why can't I get hot over Matt? Why don't I find that role swap fascinating, stimulating? Why couldn't I fuck Tony's gorgeous butt? Why could I give in so easily to Roy, not finding him physically attractive otherwise? Size seems to mean a great deal more now than it did, because of the way it hurts and intrigues and completely baffles the senses in my ass and head . . . It's been two nights, hasn't it, but I don't feel the urge so strongly tonight; maybe I'm a little afraid of the closeness . . .

And yet I keep making plans: New York in the spring, my sisters here in the summer. Europe? Publishing? etc.?

Near the 1st of the year and broke. Not a good start, but I'm too fuzzy to (almost) even care . . .

Sunday, January 4, 1987

I made it to another Sunday. Now Janis Joplin's "Summertime" and more pretending. Do I live for this brainless gyration now?

Do I want to live? Is it the hopelessness of fighting against this disease that makes it possible for me to ask this question? Do I want to live? Isn't that my primary function? There's no motion in it, no progress. Life seems like both subject and object here and completely stationary.

Do I want to live?

I ask as though I have some choice in the matter?

Do I have some choice in the matter?

If the desire to live is great enough don't I stand a good (better) chance of succeeding?

Am I not living now?

No, it seems like I'm dying. Moving toward death. These trips to the park; my stint with Roy. But then . . .

What is living?

Am I not living? Am I not exploring?

What's the difference between exploring and dying?

Skirting death: okay. Parachute jumping is okay, but messing in the sure thing, wallowing in proven death is different.

But I feel frustrated. The symptoms (the fatigue and the ringing ears especially) won't go away. I am convinced, most of the time. Let's say I'm convinced.

The frustration of fighting death . . . wait . . . I haven't begun to fight . . . then the perceived frustration of fighting death, the perceived inevitability of death is a frustration . . .

The frustration is so great that to diffuse it I find personifications for it, find workable examples for it, in real life.

The frustration has its example in race. For me. I've begun a spiral of self-esteem (sexually anyway). Blackness is a state of frustration. There's no way out of this racial depression (I don't feel the frustration personally, but as a part of a people I know that I am being fucked, abused). Sexually I want (desire, fantasize myself) to be (being) used. I want to be a slave, sexually and perhaps otherwise.

I feel the weakness right now.

I can't beat death, I can't beat the white man, I can't beat money (another $10.00 check charge), I can't beat the system (time, traffic, the buses, movies are never as good as I expect, food), I can't stop spending (it's a form of sex). But it's not gratification I'm after; it's the frustration that I want. I *think* that I like the frustration. I *think* that I like death. Maybe by liking it it will spare me.

This is not living.

It's somewhat exciting, but I have nothing to compare it to.

Thursday, January 8, 1987

"I'm afraid to open my eyes, Mama, 'cause I'm prone to see conspiracies, government plots, I'm prone to see the ugly earth for what it is."

"But, Sara, you're such a pretty, young girl."

"Mama, don't make me open my eyes 'cause I'm liable to see you for what you are."

"Shut up, Mother, oh, shut up; you're always someplace else talking to me. What reality are you in, Mother, I'm here, this is me, nasty Sara, remember me? Where are you mother?"

"Sara, why, I've never called you 'nasty,' not even when you moved in with Charlie, unmarried, and had that boy by him. I have never . . ."

"'sneaking,' 'promiscuous,' 'tramping' 's all the same difference isn't (idn't it?)."

Wednesday, January 28, 1987

Thursday, January 15, I believe it was, I went to a dirty flick— all male—at the Strand, and got involved in the action at the top of the movie hall. It took me awhile to get oriented, awhile to get the nerve but soon I was standing at the back wall, behind which the projector (manless, it seemed) was running. To my surprise four men surrounded me (wanting me to choose, I think). I had moved up beside an old fellow, but tall with big hands and a rock-like face. I had to pass a black man, in his business clothes, who had sat in front of me earlier licking his lips. Was it four or just three? A man came at me from behind, the two I've described caught me from the front. I began kissing the white man as the black man got into my pants and everyone pressed against me. I sensed that kissing the white man, playing (first) with his cock would drive the black man away. Soon I had the white man's cock out, both white men, one behind who I tried to convince to stay because I wanted to be ravaged from both ends (I at least wanted such a suggestion), but the one up front had the bigger cock and I got down on my knees and paid attention to him. It was a mouthful which he encouraged me to suck. The other man continued to play with me, but he seemed a little discouraged. I sucked him for maybe half a minute, but felt the old man getting restless and returned to him. For perhaps half an hour I knelt there sucking, getting stepped on as people tried to squeeze past us in the dark. The old man wore a cock ring and had perhaps as much as Roy. I don't remember it well because he wasn't the most active suckee. I tried to maneuver him in front of me so he could back me to the wall and fuck my face, but instead he turned his ass to me and stuck his dick down between his cheeks. I had to smell his hole to get to his cock and apparently I wanted it a lot because we kept that position for a few minutes and then returned. . . . by now the old man had opened his shirt and dropped his pants—rather boldly for an old man, I thought, or for anyone in a public place.

1/31 (reading Melville's Benito Cereno*)*

Benito!! How deep is your love? On the surface all is as it should be with enough variation to keep us desiring variation, enough tension to keep our attention, and enough innuendo to keep us bent over in our search for rhyme and reason. The brutal reality beneath this surface (is it the reality we want or the reality we hoped to avoid? Where's a black reader's desire? a white reader's? a green?) threatens the several myths that we've been building, or in some way utilizing, on the surface. The one closest to the threat of rebellion might be of a weakened white master (effeminized by the laziness that having slaves afforded) and the strong-willed, if little-bodied, slave. Being uncertain at first who actually controls the ship opens the way for an almost fairytale harmony between characters, something Delano, good-natured as he is, is dangerously prone to believe. Master and slave seem oblivious to the roles, or pay a polite deference to them and continue on as best of friends, or man and Friday, or man and lover. Cereno and Babo are given a strange equality, or as we see them through Delano's gloss, a strange harmony that even if we suspect it, *feels* about right—the myth, the icons remain intact, the horrible truth just beneath, unjudged, both ludicrously apparent and miraculously stabilized within the rigid, unjudged context of nature, economics, and military life. We, black and white, whether we believe or not, desire to read it. Even as we tell ourselves that Delano is a fool our pleasure is wrapped in his foolishness, in his not knowing until conflict can hardly be avoided. Should the penalty for not knowing be death? Or is it Babo we want dead for being small and deceitful, a snake—no matter a snake with a golden cause—a snake that talks for himself, that actually puts the words in his young(er) prey's mouth? Should Cereno die and fulfill his role as victim, and at the same time his role as captain, should he die both nobly (tragically) and pathetically? Our pleasure is in the mystery, the detective story, and the S and M game, that is both the apparent game (white on black, Cereno on Babo) and the true game (black on white) and the eventual game (white on black again) and the subsequent games, if we can guess at those. Delano's pleasure lies in not knowing, in holding on against knowing (as does ours) until the very end when satisfaction takes ritual form, sacrificial form, or the shape of almost mathematical retribution—ironic and absurd because this turns the slave into the legend, burns him into the race memories of blacks and the nightmares of whites; it's an apotheosis that anticipates more stories like "Benito Cereno," *Light in August* or *Native Son,* and Cereno's vindication, or what he enjoys of it through Delano, is not memorable, is decidedly anticlimactic.

What of Delano acting as the pleasure center for a weakened, emasculated Cereno? What of the reversal on the traditional lynching—who castrates whom? Does the myth of the gentled white sea captain line up with the myth of white Southern womanhood? What of appearances—seen through the story's veils, its endless vapors, does the apparent line up with the myth (or what would be expected in literature, an idyllic slave/master relationship subordinate to the seemingly greater story of hostile nature, the thwarted voyage?) or is it the deception, the veils themselves that we become most concerned with, the desire for a mystery (a mystery illness, secret relations, secret identities), for not knowing. In our concern for the veil, and perhaps for a detective story, do we forget the racial elements, the deliberate affront in the myth (as we might feel it now), the affront in Melville's deliberately skewed version of the myth (as they might have felt it then)? What's our sexual investment in the myth . . . do we get a rise out of the picture of slave kneeling before master, or is the rise from the knowledge that we seem privy to the facts behind the picture. Delano gets these facts eventually, but don't we delight in his vulnerability before he does? Melville could have been a bit more generous; he might have asked us to feel instead of to just watch, feel what it is to be victim and victimizer; white victim and then black victim; white victimizer and black victimizer; asked us to feel, to study and enjoy all the permutations, all the variations on a theme in this text. We're not asked about origins or even morals either, but we come close to wallowing in the unexperience of these things as we wait for the invitation to Melville's orgy, something larger than the race it's tied to, larger than the sex.

I haven't read Hegel yet. Why haven't I read Hegel when I'm somewhat in love with this? I'm afraid to know. Half of this is the wandering, the obscurity, the possibility of surprise (and yet the other half is a fixed equation, inevitable—when I get there I'll be able to say I've always known this would happen to me—but I'll come to that admission as through a dream, still half unbelieving).

2/1

I don't know that I would be so stirred by Billy Budd if he were black. Maybe it's something lodged in the language now?—not that the asinine religious fictions that I'm talking about aren't sublimated in the sexual tensions that I'm not talking about. Maybe I would like to *be* Billy Budd . . . I used to fantasize that being young, strong yet vulnerable, and white would be more attractive to girls, and to guys who had girls; but my fantasy preceded thoughts (and occasionally ritual) so intense that fantasy became nightmare, a knot of young S and M that I could hardly admit to myself let alone my pillows, let well alone anyone who could tell me what it was I wanted. So it is the spiritual purity of the white Billy that pulls me and the desire to both protect and ravage him; to be protected by him and to be ravaged by him; to be him as he's protected, and as he's ravaged. It is the mythical power (physical, and potentially sexual) that intrigues me about the black man on whom Billy is based. Oh, but having to live up to that myth, the myth as it comes down from your father, as it comes down from the cautious glances of white girls on a dim street, as the white boys in gym class give it to you for emasculating them (their weapons backfiring somewhere between the mid-1800s and the present).

So, I don't want to be someone else's fiction, I want to be someone else, or at least that's my approach to "Billy Budd." Forgetting the black man that frames the story (if I were a white man I wouldn't be able to forget it) I could be Billy Budd, and if I couldn't be Billy Budd I could touch him without the tension . . . (and it's a multi-legged tension) . . . because he wouldn't know. He wouldn't know first that we are supposed to hate each other, and second that my desire for him (as I perhaps wrongly interpret childhood fantasies now) is partly sexual (and other parts that I never understood, the really satisfying parts—beyond the sex? before and after it?), perhaps based partly on that hate; and most importantly I wouldn't know this (all that I've said here) either. I've looked for a potential Claggart in me, but it's not there, nor Captain Vere, yet they are the manifestation of ideas that make Billy desirable. Like a frame (or like two pillows, one on each side in that fantasy, one for bullies and bad men on one side and the other for father [sometimes bully, sometimes bad man] on the other). But didn't I want to bully Billy? didn't I want to father him?—One fantasy at a time! No, I only wanted to heighten the desirableness of Billy (in much the same way Melville goes about it), I only wanted to make him visible. Funny, when I put myself in Billy's place I'm not there either. We are very much the same, Billy and I, for the stutter we represent in history. Ultimate martyrs too since we weren't (aren't?) there to begin with. We cease to be when someone takes notice; from that point on you must give us definition. Your words, your touch, your awareness of our motion gives us shape; your interpretation of, say, spilled soup completes an impression that you desire, and we become whatever your impression makes us. Yes, giving shape to nothing has some risks, but that aside you usually get what you want (we all do), and in exactly the way you want it. Power over nothing, isn't it a little like power over a mirror? Claggart, searching for himself in Billy finally gets him . . . Vere, searching for mutiny gets mutiny . . .

2/13

How to look at women. . . Watch with the attitude of being watched; watch clinically as though there were a problem with her clothes; watch all of her as peering too closely, too specifically can be dangerous; watch at a respectable distance. She may continue to watch you, to even scrutinize you long after you've stopped watching her; that is her prerogative and part of what you've said you wanted by watching her. You are nervous that she'll weigh your character and your potential accurately from the shape of your body and the rest of the week's self-esteem might somehow hinge on how quickly she passes you.

How to watch men . . . Watch from a distance (twenty feet); watch with a curious twist of the mouth or a whole series of questions in the eyes as if you don't see him clearly because you're clearly occupied with something else; or act like you don't see him clearly yet but think you might know him and might at any moment burst into salutations that he'll have to reciprocate or concoct a way of ignoring you. Walk briskly, glance at your book then up at him; repeat, but not more than three times. Or make him an object. If he's a hunk watch his body (never, of course, watch a white girl's chest, not even if you kneel to tie her shoe and she offers you a piece of gum), but never look at his crotch. Let him see you looking at his arms and at his chest; acknowledge his acknowledgment since this is only an extension of boysport. It helps if a girl walks by at some distance and at an angle common to you both. If he's a snappy dresser watch him with an attitude of appraisal, make panoramic sweeps with your eyes, but appear very frank with either contempt (for what he's wearing) or praise, don't ever linger in between, or fasten on a single piece of clothing. He'll be as flattered if you don't like what he's wearing as if you do; he'll think something else if you fudge. Look at men (white men especially) as if you had something else on your mind and they were only an object to anchor your daydream. If they look back in anger snap your head forward, eyes a little ahead of the rest, and let your face suggest that he find a high bridge. Always catch them looking at you, or make them feel as though they've been caught; or force them to look, force them to think that they might know you and better keep looking lest they rudely ignore someone they know and know well.

How to look at men looking at women . . . Watch his face. He'll let you watch him watching, because he's not responsible. Survey his body and his clothes (if you want) with competition in your manner, then shift back to his face to see if it all matches up, then out over the gulf to the woman he's admiring and who you hope is admiring him (aloofly so it piques his interest). Study her frankly, undress her if you like since two men watching her make her an object for undressing, actually create a comptetition for undressing a woman (probably works with two women watching a man and two men watching another man or two women watching a woman). Watch him some more if you want. If you watch him too long you must concede that he's the handsomer and should get the girl, and should get your attention (not the other way around) as he makes his move on the girl.

How to look at women looking at men . . . (How to undress a man . . .) Don't let her watch you watching him. Let her make you complicitous (especially if she's half on your arm asking your advice). Tell her to think about it, meaning to watch him, to size him up, but not against you, never against the Arm; you after all are a given, a still point from which to launch a cruise. She's half hoping he'll look at you, not her; that he'll watch you having her on your arm. You're half hoping that he'll only see her, beautiful as she is. (In spite of your ego, you're feeling like a given and only hope you don't look like one.) And the hope continues: that after seeing her first he will then look at you, but with his anger, jealousy, whatever aimed at her, at the old white-girl myth from which he's still picking up pieces, not at you; no longer allowed to see that myth, the myth of the black man. You don't give off that myth anyway because you're looking at him and chatting with her, obviously matchmaker, salesman, or at least cashier, some menial laborer easily overlooked, but in a great position for looking. And if you are a threat, you've always got your pride to fall back on, proud of appearing threatening, the wolf in the fold. And she can feel the thrill of pitting hunter against wolf, rekindling the myth, anticipating the ritual, and can be angered that the myth, after all, sets her aside, outside; that her pleasure, while the physical issue, must never be spoken, must never be seen; that it must instead froth out of the Negro and appear strong, sturdy, ready to wield for the white hunter. Could she resent me for the nature of the strong emotion I incite in her man?

3/2

Backyard: The dog must be smelling himself, because no other animal has been inside the gate to fertilize his turf, still he goes through the timeless motions—ten, twenty minutes—before he'll squat and relieve himself. It's a charade, a bit of useless, narcissistic play acting that he trots through at least twice a day.

3/?

—Close, about to cum, he says, "should I wait for you or should I go ahead?" And there was that sense of leaving, leaving on a long journey, and no way back.

4 A.M. *Sunday, March 29, 1987*

. . . Another man, an older man who I would later give it to, gets some brief attention, gives some (with teeth) that I don't want, then I break the connection and start out of that hollowed hedge, partially anyway, but a large white man is standing there, large western sort in blue jeans and a cruel jacket, mustache, big hands (do I notice those immediately). I'm sure my rejection will be instantaneous to my touching him and I prepare to flee (inside, more calmly outside) as though it were God or electricity that had repelled me, because how can I feel any less for a man (not a sucker. I kept drawing the distinction between the real men who *just* wanted to get their rocks off—the straight sort— and those who wanted to get *me* off. They must be, I figured, less than men, those—faggots and useless to another real faggot). But he doesn't repulse, deny. His eyes warn me, but I touch his ass and chest already reassured by his delay. He is certainly unsure that it's a black man that he wants (aren't we all real men— hence the discussion today in the Af-Am library about black male and female roles in white society). My hands show my willingness to pleasure him first and foremost, I hope, and don't rub my own crotch to drive him down or away. I move up to him small and soon (I don't recall the choreography); he is sitting, lounging where the black man, Bobby, just lounged . . . Oh, my order is wrong; after Bobby I leave, don't I, to meet the other Bob, then come back to the old man briefly then to the big, hard-edged white man. He opens his pants. Are mine already open? When do I become amazed by the size of his hands? The size of his cock is pleasant (wrong word since it must necessarily choke me, this pleasure). Surprise. Do I suck him from simpler beginnings or is he already hard, already a man in my night fiction. So I'm on my knees again, before God. Tall, white, wary of me, trying to work him into a froth of masterliness. Sucking a man's cock makes him bolder, meaner, or one hopes, and even if it wasn't so in this Superman's case, his big hands, touching me anywhere were part threat. Huge warm hands twice the size of my own. I played with his nipples. His chest was larger than I'm used to, I guess, and hollowed at the center as though an organ might be missing, but I think it was more likely the mass on both sides . . . I sucked him gladly and he seemed honestly pleased with me and then with himself, which was important to me. I hope to draw out the ego, the cruel ego in the men that I suck. I sucked him and another man became involved, encouraging my sucking, playing with the big man, kissing him. I licked the big man's balls while he shanked himself some. He jerked some the first time just to add up all the pleasures around him without distraction. I made sub-missive gestures with my face and lips, both men looking down on me. I love the looking up, into their far-off heads, all dark-ness, all anonymous and dangerous. His huge hand directed my hand back to his nipple again. I was sucking him again before he was really ready and I touched the new guy's cock to keep his at-tention, I guess. I didn't want to lose either of them to jealousy. I sucked the big white man and then let him shank himself, keep-ing the head of his big penis, big rather flat and fat so it made a wide mouthful that I was afraid would scrub my teeth distracting his pleasure (so important . . .) keeping the head in my mouth or at my lips and me spitting there to lube him, wanting to optimize his self-pleasure even and knowing that he was desiring that I should swallow his manseed, feeling that in him, the desire to feed me, nurse me even as he feeds himself on my nursing him, feeds his ego, his manness, his very strength, I hope. He jerked. I squeezed his nipple and the other man did more of what he was doing, two Gods in the darkness above me. His cock was in me far enough to dominate, but not so far that I couldn't taste and *feel* the thickness of his ejaculation. Where were his hands? I felt his sensational pleasure, so thick and neutral (maybe spicy) on my tongue. I cleaned him off, but didn't stay with the big man as long as I should. Perhaps he would have held me, took me home. I just got a tender pat on the shoulder, but I was already into the soon-to-be violent fuck of the next God. A little less intimidating, he had a large cock (4 large cocks in one night, 3 of them white men, one a cruel big black man) to work with and worked fast, holding my head, squelching deep into my throat. There were three parts to his fuck, just a pause for me to catch my breath and for the man to change his grip on me. He moved to my ears, then to my shoulders. Was there a hand on the back of my head? He took control, fucked fucked fucked my throat then shoved deep into me and shot before I had air and held me so the cum and spit blew up out of my nose. I was more helpless to his pleasure than any other. I thanked him after I cleaned his cock. I told him that he had a big load in him, as if he hadn't noticed. He said he had as he put himself away. I remained on my knees, told him to get a good rest.

The old man got my cum at the end with a black man to help me during my climax, holding me.

I haven't written the paper for Sundquist and now I want to suck cock, or think about it anyway. The loads churned in my stomach, my ass is still smarting from Michel's torture. I saw him again at the I-Beam, downcast, weary. I should have invited him home but I didn't and his sadness is part of what informs the CT song.

It's after midnight. I have not started this paper. Thursday night 5 men ejaculated the semen from their hard penises into my mouth and throat. There were several other encounters but five that actually fed me and left me full and strange that evening. The first man I met was big and white and darkly bearded, but he stinked like the onions he ate for lunch and had a small dick. He was more interested in sucking me. I enjoyed rubbing his great chest and seeing his handsome dark head back in pleasure, but there was no cock for me to suck, to martyr myself to, so I moved on (after an embarrassingly long time though). The 2nd man was big, powerful and black—perhaps a little more fat than muscle. These two were on the left side of the theater. The black man wasn't into my sucking and passed me off to some white man who in turn passed me off to a dark Filipino who kept glancing at me with calculated dirty looks.

The first load came when I switched sides. I met a big black man there, uncut, rather stubby, but still a mouthful. He had a coin belt and a firm hand for me. I sucked him a good long time seeing the area around me go from full to empty to full again in the time I was sucking. I forget how he came and how it tasted to me. I think it was rather more gentle than I expected. I was on my knees licking his relaxed cock, getting him clean when a white man showed up for a threesome. The big black pulled out then and the white man utilized my mouth since I was already on my knees. He was long and choked me with full thrusts. I think he held my head. I think he came quickly and strongly. Most of the cum has tasted somewhat bitter to me. The third man, not long after, was a feminine black man, big in an army get up. He became domineering for me, I guess, and it wasn't unpleasant though I had reservations about taking drag queen cum, and the smell of him seemed to linger longer than most. He was a bit of a pain with his constant directing. "Suck me slow," but I guess it was a mouthful and I was grateful. He jerked himself, said he was going to cum on my chest, but then asked me if I wanted his cum. He put his cock back in my mouth. Every once in awhile he would hold my head hard with both hands and move it around as though he were analyzing me, forcing me to look up into that too pretty, Sylvester-like face. But there was cock and he said if I wanted his cum, I had to work for it. There was no way to bow out gracefully so I worked for it and he finally came, an ugly lump, I thought, and he pushed me away rather coldly.

The next series was most interesting. I was against the wall on the right side and a familiar white man drew up beside me, oldish, glasses, lipless, severe, still very virile-looking. That gross man in the suit was lurking near trying to get my cock, but I wouldn't give it to him and the white man could have given his cock to either one of us but he went for me. I lowered myself to his penis. Sucked him to quick hardness, then he went to work, very actively fucking me with a long, big-headed dick and fucking back into my throat so it made audible sound, my poor throat opening and closing around his attack. I think I got on my knees then and after a brief pause let him face-fuck me. He used my throat and roof and back tongue to stimulate himself, not caring about teeth. I heard him gasp (and I may have reacted for air and I felt two other dark dwellers sort of leap around me) as he came sharply into the side of my throat nearly choking me. He wasn't ungrateful, but like a man he wasn't going to stick around to help me out. He pulled up his pants and pushed his way out. The men right next to me immediately adopted me to their game. One man was sucking the huge white bulbous cock of a tall, hard-looking white man. He moved my head with his hand to receive his cock and fed it to me from the side. I heard the God-like man say yes, enjoying it, and then we split duties on that most beautiful cock. It was the largest one I've seen in SF, perhaps bigger than Roy's but not as hard or as straight and beautiful. Still the fat white smooth head felt like heaven in my mouth and I wanted him to plow me, but never got it. The two of us tongued the cock together, then somehow an Asian man got to deep-throating the God and left us two suckers out. I began sucking the man that got me involved. It was a bit anticlimactic after his friend's big big dick, and it had a flap of skin on the underside that distracted. Still, cock and he appreciated my sucking. All the white old men are groping for me, rubbing my ass and back, sexing vicariously through me. The guy I'm sucking comes and I swallow and hold and kiss him a bit while he composes. Then I go to the bathroom and meet Sig in one of the stalls. He's naked. I strip too and soon he's sucking or I am and we're playing with each other's bodies and finally shuck off to personal climaxes (anticlimax for me). Sig wore a toupee. We made a date for tonight, but he called and canceled. He's a businessman from Milwaukee and will call his next time through. So 9 tastes of male seed in two nights. I'm delirious.

Wednesday, April 8, 1987
    . . . I met the second man not too long after he came into the bushes where I was standing rather sure he would just pass me, but he went into a small veil of leaves and started pulling on a long white cock. He would be the one I worshipped this evening, I knew. Handsome, dark-haired, tall, clad in blue jeans and jeans jacket. I had to duck to get into the little cover of trees and I

was already at cock level when I met him. There was no need for preliminaries (figuring what he wanted; it seemed obvious) so I took his quickly hard and long and perfectly shaped organ into my mouth. I lipped the head and about an inch of it while we adjusted to each other in the bushes, then I was taking that god's mouthful. I can't remember how rough he was. I know he began touching me all over the face, especially around the cheek, throat and ears where his cock might create a swell or some movement. I would have died for him. I can still feel the way he clasped his hands into my hair after he had undone his pants and exposed his powerful balls and white flesh, hairy, of his belly. I ran my hands up his chest to his nipples thinking that might trigger him to use my head and throat. I got nasty with his cock, played it across my face where it felt quite big and slick and warm with my attention. I don't remember how long I sucked him, but it was all his dominance, my submission, those nice hands of his taking care that my head didn't stray. Indeed I stayed near his warm belly or leg. I licked his balls and the skin between his leg and balls sensing his pleasure. He started jamming and rocking when the cock was in my mouth again. He came a good amount, that god. I was slow to part from him. I hope he wasn't in a rush. I should have jerked off then. We stayed near a good while then he slowly pulled together, said thank you and I thanked him, touched his chest as I was leaving. He whistled as he left. We could have been friends, I'm sure.

4/17 [reading James Merrill's "The Book of Ephraim"]
—MOM, if I treated you the way Merrill treats you, I'm so sorry. I couldn't talk to you either, didn't know the words, felt suffocated by all the white space between my words, space that you seemed to read so well, that shone in your face, always the open book, Mom the mirror, and I couldn't dare look at it because I'd see that you already knew and that, to save face, I had to go ahead and tell you, had to fit words to pictures (I was so simple). But my telling you was complicated by a new poverty (or perhaps a new wealth) when I found out how close I am to dying—not a sure thing, mind you, no conveyor belt here! but, yes, I'm walking an edge. I could tip over any day now, any cough could be

the one to trigger . . . but that's what I couldn't bear to see in your face. I couldn't bear to think that I had killed you by dying first—though, I swear, I asked to take your place, I asked Him to let me run up that hill, because you didn't deserve this, you hadn't planned for it all your life, while I think I started studying it the very first time I brushed knees with Gord W. in Mr. Jackson's class. Oh, I didn't mean to flaunt my treasure that way. So, I've been all around the world this way, exploring every nub and every nook in this body. Funny, but I don't think your body ever belonged to you, and we helped Him throw you away—did we? did we put that lump of trash in you?

I've been asking some questions, Mom, questions that I don't really want to find answers to—I don't have the time—but that sounds so good, being asked. I was always afraid that only another man would be able to understand me. I think I prayed for Daddy to ask me, just once, if I had any questions. He didn't have to answer them, he just had to ask if I had any. On the way across the country, in the desert, I felt my soul being pulled out of me and dragged along behind me like a corpse on a rope. It could have been a nuclear power plant; the soul doesn't care for radiation, and I started hearing this ringing that hasn't let up to this day. So there's a line of ringing, Mom, that stretches back four years.

Monday, April 27, 1987
. . . I'm on BART and there's a man in front of me, big, white, mustached, glasses, rather cruel- and solid-looking, kind of military, and I'm turned on by him, want to be used and humiliated by him, then made love to in that odd one-sided way. "You love my cock and it'll love you, boy, boy will it love you." What is this fantasy that cuts across all of me, racial, intellectual, moral, spiritual, sexual . . . ? I hope Dale is rougher than he seems and calls me boy and etc.

Monday, May 4, 1987
. . . On telling Eve Sedgwick that I (think I) have ARC:
Well, I've told her and now I'm freed up to write, to let loose on the wonder and . . . words, words gone . . . it's horrible, just horrible that I should find enjoyment here. Where's the rock? the

stoic? I should have died. I should be the walking corpse, not this vivid dreamer. Who ever measured dreamers by their life-span? . . .

5/10

Who made this an issue for only tall, handsome (or portly, cultivated) mustachioed gentlemen with cigarette holders, pince-nez, and potential as drag queens? Who made this formula so elite, so Victorian, so pretty, when it's just as interesting down here in the gutter. Who privileged the closet—or rather, the rich, gay, white male closet—when the basement will serve the pur-pose, a hollow bush in the woods, a cave along Ocean Beach, a gutted windmill (interestingly, all female places to do male things . . . back to the womb to commit reproductive sacrilege . . . a visit to the lady to steal her son).

Thursday, May 28, 1987

Last night I went to Buena Vista, wandered about (unwanted) for two hours. I sucked and jerked off one fellow. Saw Jack (who I've yet to introduce here) and would have come home early—midnight or so, but I saw my steady suck, the punkish-looking guy. He didn't want a repeat of our scene, but I followed him back up the hill anyway. Oh, before I left there was an awkward encounter with a big, dark-haired fellow. I ended up sucking his soft dick which didn't harden till his climax. He held my head and came in me, no qualms. The second time up the hill I couldn't get the steady but I took a chance on a handsome, dark-haired, big man. I rubbed his chest and crotch and he rubbed my crotch but kind of absently, looking anywhere but in my face. This both-ered me, but in hindsight, isn't that the kind of encounter I wanted—one-sided, well-defined roles? We went in the bushes after I asked him if he liked to get sucked. He unzipped, tugged on his prick and I went down on him soft, sucking him to hard-ness. He's uncut and thick and large and once I got him hard he resigned to the pleasure. He didn't touch me. I could taste traces of his precum on my tongue, like electricity. I wish I could have sucked him all night, but when I started with the hand he started making noises. I love the loss of control, the noises that suggest loss. I need to learn how to make a guy shoot hard, not this gentleness. He shot on my tongue. I held his hard, thick, long dick for as long as he'd let me. He didn't get soft, but put himself away hard. I swallowed when he pulled away, told him what a beautiful cock he had (and a great sweatshirt from Seattle where he'd visited last weekend).

[on the next page G. F. has pasted a program from a performance of Alvin Ailey Dance, and has written across it, "I'm not in love with manness, I'm in love with blackness—as if blackness were a thing that a man could fall in love with. Women: we dance with what we have. All we have. And you with what you think you've got—what do you know?"]

It caught me off guard, The Smiths' *The Queen is Dead*. I was just crying over two of the songs, over the events in my life that co-incide, over the largeness/smallness of it all. I wish I knew or I wish I was occupied in such a way that I wouldn't care. My head is stuffed like a drum. I can't think of my mother except in hot red flashes.

8/20/87
    . . . Sex. Ed. Why do I feel so down? You're so cold to me on the phone. I can't be sure that you want me. I know you don't need me. Your world races. There's no time for me, except maybe Fri-day. Sex. It felt strained last Friday. Sophomore slump. We did it all . . . again. And I didn't come again. Perhaps I'm not surprised, but I wonder how dear Ed feels about my lack . . . Is it lack? Is it the drugs. The speed is so *new* to me. The first time left me jittery and talkative. It heightened all my senses but also preoccupied me, and climax seems to take so much "occupation." (What am I doing here? All these new catering people. I'm not into this.)
    Scenes: The ropes around my hands, the pole behind me making my head so maneuverable for him. Shit, what if he doesn't want me? What if I've had my last discipline, my last punishment? . . .

Monday, September 28, 1987
    A rush and a push and the land is ours. New Smiths album, and I took the song in my head to Buena Vista park. Ran into Michel who wanted to fuck, but I told him I was sore, asked him

to come in my mouth then to piss. It was fast, strong, unsatisfying and I had to do lots of mind work to get off. What is it? I
know it's as simple as wanting a strong master, guide, best friend.
I'm searching and destroying myself on the way. So much self-
hatred (I suppose) while I'm waiting. Is it me or is it boredom
that I loathe. When Donald didn't call (he just called a few minutes ago) the rejection pushed me out, the chance of seeing him
pushed me out. What am I doing? No sleep, dangerous sex, so
little studying! I need a strong strong daddy. Probably not Ed. Do
I really expect him to call again? Do I need his drugs? I love his
sex, admittedly, so strong, sustained. I've never had it so good,
unless we go back to some incredible moments with Roy. This is
a whole new level of emotion for me. Been reading John Preston's
S/M book. Weakly stimulating but a lesson, a thoroughly interesting one. I want to roam looking for a daddy.

Tuesday, September 29, 1987

God, Ed, I know you haven't been praying this whole time;
and you haven't been rehearsing or being good for the sake of it,
so why won't you call. October 3 is the end of these blessed holy
days and I for one will be relieved (if you call!). I don't know what
else a slave can do to get a master to remember. I suppose it's
time to send a letter to another man. I know a real master would
settle me. Not this Tom guy, really named Pete, because I don't
really like the way he looks or tastes of his slave, Art (another
slave makes me jealous). I want to understand. Ed, I'll come for
you if you want me. And this during John Coltrane.

Friday, October 16, 1987

It's looking like Ed L. is not going to call. 10:00. I'm not his
only slave, his only Friday number. When I called on Tuesday
(I should have been a little more subtle) he said he had service (church service) tonight and a date for tomorrow. I'd talk
about what we did last Friday, but I'm afraid to. Or maybe I'm
bored with it. I think I like it. I know I like parts of it. Now my
mouth hurts; a bottom wisdom-tooth is cutting and yet I still
hope (against hope) that the man will call. After 10:00 now. He's
definitely not home. Probably getting ready to relax with some
other guy.

Saturday, October 17, 1987

I went to the park last night feeling bad about Ed. I sucked off a white guy with a nice-size cock, liked the way he held my head, liked his endurance, finally liked the noise he made, the drop and swoon in his voice when he reached the point of no return, and then the salty jet of his come. He was grateful and we hugged for a bit. I could have come but held on for more encounters. Shortly after I ran into Ed G. He was on the prowl. Said he wasn't going to do anything, but obviously wanted some fresh blood. I was jealous of the things he did with a little dark-haired guy. I felt close to tears. I thought they would go home together. He cornered me later. I'd been trying to avoid him.

I went home with him. We got drunk and had intense sex. I jerked off before I serviced him, and then I serviced him for five hours. I was in a fine state of arousal most of the night and so drunk I could hardly stand up. He fucked me and pissed up my ass. He had me suck him off. By then I was exhausted, but he threw me out, and he wasn't gentle about it. I had the feeling that I'd been used and discarded. I felt like I was bothering him when I called today. This guy just wants sex from me. And I'd settle for that if we could make it steady. He's a cold man when he's not horny.

Thursday, October 22, 1987

Rain today; maybe a thunderstorm tonight. This book is so dumb (well, it doesn't talk, that's true); it's gotten lost in the past month, become all sex, all park, Strand, heavy tricking and roulette with my body. No studying, no real love, no romantic obsession.

I talked to Sam Tarrant about Ed and he told me that he's been an S and had an M fall in love with him, and that that turned him off. So the torture has to continue in public. Ed didn't call this week, won't call tomorrow or Saturday, I imagine. He seemed upset with me last weekend. I want a loving master/daddy.

Saturday, January 23, 1988

. . . I want to tell Ed that I've met Crandall. And I want to tell you about Crandall. I wish he would call so I wouldn't have to write and wouldn't/won't have to remember. Crandall calls me his nigger. He's much rougher with me than Ed and talks so genuinely I wonder if he doesn't believe what he's saying to me. It disturbs me to write what he says about carving "White Power" into my flesh and he and his friends holding me outside of an open car door (after they've stabbed me [after I've sucked them all off]) to scrub off my face . . . "The road will chew you up," he says. And White Power is our litany. He says it, he makes me say it when he's hurting me AND he really hurts me, gets big pleasure here.

3/26/88

It's too painful (is it pain?) to write. Just no desire to remember the past months, years. Too tired, too afraid. In ten years the sex entries might be a thrill. I feel my mind going, piece by piece, memory by memory, and I can't watch. To write is to watch. If I'm not dead or a vegetable in ten years I'll wish that I had kept track. And immediately, will Ed call? I hope he doesn't/I hope he does. I hope I never see Crandall again, but if he calls I'll let him in. It's not the humiliation, it's the death, the sure poison. I'm ramming myself against outstretched daggers and drinking off poisons. . . .

Sunday, May 22, 1988

Saturday, out all day, then dinner and a drink with Ed; a waste of time watching TV, then sleep around 2:00. Jorge and his hordes from hell were relatively quiet after midnight. It was a restless night but the next morning after masturbating I fell into a dream that redeemed the whole weekend for me. I dreamed that I met a man, a ruggedly handsome guy, big, thick, kind of blunt in his edges and manners; mustache, I think, and brown hair (a white man, by the way). And we fell in love. An intense "father/son" sort of thing but of a dimension I have not experienced. I remember being hugged, and taken warmly, lovingly to bed. I really don't have the words to describe the way I felt—while we were in bed, or working together. It was a love on the edge of the world; we were building some kind of vessel or shelter to save ourselves from a disaster, the end of the world perhaps, and I felt gloriously alive next to my big friend. He seemed to be everything I ever wanted—father, brother, lover, best friend, master—a no-nonsense kind of guy, he wouldn't take shit from the other workers (men and women as/if I recall) about his preference (and I don't know if their discouragement focused on our age difference, race or the homosexuality). God, he was all things, but for so brief a time. He held back the whole world and made my internal troubles get into something manageable. With him, I could get through anything, even the end of the world (there was always the assurance that we would survive, no *thrive* . . .).

Monday, July 10, 1988

Dear Gene (is that your real name),

This is Gary, the black guy you "molested" (quite wonderfully) Sunday night, and if I'm writing to thank you, it's more for the sobering reprimand and the slaps across the face than the great sex. What the hell am I doing? (and are there really other ways to do it?) Somehow I got brainwashed into thinking I had to go beyond all-the-way with Crandall to keep him. And "keeping him" is a question in itself: why do I want him? I'm not particularly attracted to him. I do enjoy the racial stuff and I don't suppose such kink is easy to find available anywhere. BUT I did find it with you (No, this is not a come-on!), a tough attractive, responsible white man, so I know it exists. Do you have a brother, Gene?

I don't know what I expect to accomplish with this note; it's a bit of self-therapy, I guess, and an honest thank-you. I hope this doesn't make you feel like an accomplice in anything, or as though you're betraying Crandall; that's not my intention. Perhaps, telling these things to myself hasn't been real or convincing enough and I'm after a sympathetic (or at least a captive) ear (eye?).

Crandall says he's loaning me to you while he's away. Well, that's okay; your sanity like your tough SOB attitude is a great turn-on; but even if I never touch you again, I would very much like (to talk to you on this subject) some advice on how to get out of this suicide pact with Crandall and into something with "growth potential." You're a lawyer; do I have a case?

Much obliged,
Gary

Tuesday, November 1, 1988

... —I have serious doubts ...

a) I'm going to test +, I know it, feel it to the depths of my being.

Well, of course! After the false measles, the candida (?) throat stuff problem, this most recent yeast infection that tore up my crotch for 2 months; after a lack of sleep, of good food, always of liquid (I can't seem to get enough and I've heard that's a classic death symptom—maybe what the Maupassant "Horla" was about), love

Love, jesus, I don't feel what I thought I'd feel writing the words. There have been some clarifying moments (usually, unfortunately, after I've drank some man's piss and died some on his come—dined, di(n)ed, died—hmmm), moments where my body actually grappled with its need. Not sex, but love, another man's proffered security and attention and concern, and humor and sex and a warm, generous world in his arms. HIS ARMS. I'm numb. ...

I can be sure 2 ways. I can test + and get it, or I can get it and test +. If I test − of course all of this changes. A year ago would I have tested − ? before I met Ed? I wonder. I may have killed myself. It sure seems like Crandall is killing me. It's his fault, the Klan's, not mine.

And still I can write this in sanity, in knowing.

My mind is a stranger to me. My body too. How will I ever write these papers? How will I pay my rent? How will I find love within my disgust. I want to stumble on love in the woods. I KNOW it's not Crandall; he really hates me (loves it—hating me). Ed was intense, wonderful, but dying and wanting someone to die with. I can't believe he wanted to come in my ass. I can't believe I let him come as close as he did (so close he might as well have!) Enough! ...

Sunday, November 27, 1988

I have a cold. I had a positive test. I still haven't finished the Chaucer paper; really haven't started writing it. But the greatest disappointment, at least as it sits with me right now, comes from an encounter at the I-Beam. That handsome, white, flat-topped man, I asked him to dance—after spending an hour looking at him (after Gurrile *told him* I was interested!)—and he said "no." How else was I supposed to break the ice?

1/12/89

Each time is like the nightmare I let happen. He'll come over (Hell, come) at midnight with what he's been saving now—ammonia death, I'm sure I'll have to say no—with what's in his bladder; and instead of going dancing I'm sitting here, or I'm cleaning up, waiting for him. This isn't love, this isn't lust, this isn't new, this isn't habit. I hate him and all of it as soon as he's gone but I can't get my hate up front. The paper smells like him. Tonight he'll come (it's been several). Why don't I call him up and say it's over; I want to live, I want to dance; drink it your damned self!

Maybe he won't come; maybe he's dead, his body sprawled bloody on the road, his car aflame, life gone gone. I wouldn't care. Maybe he's dead. I wish he were dead. Why, then, is my stomach in knots? It's midnight now. Die, bastard.

1/16/89

It's Tuesday, the 17th, somewhere after 2:00, and I'm an unhappy (vague enough?) man in an all-night diner, The Copper Penny. There's a couple of men behind me, two people at the bar and two people nearby in a booth, and that's all. So, perhaps it's safe to write in this. Delay!

I have to end things with Crandall. He came over the 12th and we did the horrible thing I'd feared (and wanted) and I was sick for two days (very sick that night), and he came over again tonight and, and, I'm sick of it. He'd wanted a threesome with Park, and that had me desiring, but ultimately he came over alone, the last time before he leaves for a week in Texas.

I'm a wimp (scared of myself more than Crandall) and won't send a final letter until he's in Texas. Give me strength (who?) to do that! Why didn't this all end a long time ago? I don't feel good about this, don't feel lust, certainly not love. Why, *why* is it still going on? Am I too lazy or too afraid to find the real thing? What is the real thing? . . . .

I hate Chihuahuas, every time you're near them they pee. They have that little shrill bark. I used to think they were cute, they're so full of action. I get dizzy looking at 'em. They advertise those little dogs on the backs of magazines that don't get no bigger than a tea cup. I'd be afraid to step back and scrunch it, or vacuum it up. I'll just have to have another cigarette. Whistle key chains. I hardly ever carry a purse anymore, reversible coat with inside pockets. Bless you, you getting a cold. There's a really ugly horrible flu going around.

Drink a gallon of three-day old piss . . .

He needs some cigarette change out of that.

And you'll shit it, you won't piss it, if it's cold, you'll cramp up first and shit it like a dam bursting.

"Rainy days and Mondays always get me . . ." "Funny, but it seems it's the only thing to do."

Do I want more coffee? "I know it sounds funny but I just can't stand the pain." "I beg, stole and I borrowed."

Do you want more coffee?

"According to your computer machine I'm stressed out."

Some man got on there and it went up to 207-something or 107-something or, well I think it malfunctioned 'cause he ought to've been dead.

Oh, why can't it be Friday?

It's medicinal, piss . . . In South America . . .

The guy that was in the bathroom scared the shit out of me. He was washing the walls. "Bless you."

Someone came in while I was away and cleaned my bathroom. The dried yellow tits on the ceiling, the drool on the wall, the horror of that exploded piss dam.

"She was like up in my face all the time."

"She's ugly."

"No, she's nice."

"The father of her baby's black. Her aunt's Russian. She goes around telling people I'm a black Russian. She's blue-eyed with this perm, beautiful."

I had a cousin who was so blonde/blue, so pretty—she married a Puerto Rican. The baby looked like something out of a horror movie—blonde kinky hair . . .

Do I have to hear this from strangers and sex partners too?

Macy's White Flowers Day Sale on MLK's birthday again this year. "You make me feel brand new." Everyone ugly trying to sing it at 4 A.M.

—I just helped another man hate himself and then I went to breakfast.

—I just passed a tar truck smothered in the fog (the smell of it trapped there and breathing like a trapped thing) and I hate you more. Three taxis in a row have slowed for me. Did I look like I might fill some early morning gap for them. The city's dead and these late walkers are like flies on a dead thing, creeping, crawling—where the world is there's art. I passed a skinny man looking to me unresistant as a vacuum pump. I could have beat him in the head, and thrown his body in the damp hedges by Kaiser Permanente's empty lot. But I felt as hollow as he looked to me and wondered how I could move past him without caving in, the repulsion was now so complete. You don't walk past that park this late by accident, but it's only accident if your plan succeeds. No one likes to hurt people on foggy nights in a dead city. No one wastes energy or flies on a garbage scow, or slaps children for laughing at old people, or crazy people for talking about the world like it's theirs too. Contempt loses face.

Happy day after MLK's birthday.

Wednesday/Thursday, December 6/7, 1989

. . . #3 was the charm, tall, 6'4" and big, 30s, maybe 40 years old, dark hair, rugged face, not a straight man, but determined and quiet about it. He'd been cruising a while. I nodded and it registered with him but I wasn't sure that he wasn't walking past me and into the acknowledgment of someone else (another big man? no, just a little larger than me, not as determined as me). He went into a cove of bushes and stood waiting for someone. I was just a step ahead of this other fellow. This giant was in heavy demand. They always are up there (5 cocksuckers to every cockman). I thought he would leave when I touched his chest, then I touched his cock. I thought he would leave when he touched my cock and found it soft and small (I always have the impression that my stuff doesn't make much of a basket . . .), but he didn't leave. I don't remember asking the question, he just did it, opened his pants and that white cock was out, not huge, but oh boy, did it become a mouthful. I felt the cock ring. I got on my knees, didn't look up at him 'less he see my blackness and change his mind for some white mouth; guilt, I'm afraid of making white men feel guilt, almost as sick and angry I am that they sometimes (most times?) feel disgust or fear manifested as contempt and disgust. I was sure he would break it off until that cock thickened in my mouth, and I think (did he?) he sighed, then I knew I had him and I guess he knew much earlier that he had me but he came to want and appreciate me then, to actually need what he was getting from me, or was he *taking* it and taking it for granted? I don't think it mattered. He could have pissed in my face like the other big white man of several months ago; could have called me a "nigger" for those other men to hear. I was also afraid those other men would horn in. That's happened too often. They didn't come any closer than curiosity alone could get them, perhaps because the big man had his hands on my shoulders. It was feeling good to him. He got hard and stayed super hard trapped in the cock ring and the warmth of my mouth. I was somewhat concerned that his cock would get too fat or as long as it (proportionately so) was fat. . . . I could feel his veins. The cock felt tough like a rock or a smooth yet knotty tree branch in my mouth. I gave him some hand action perhaps—no certainly— afraid that he would get close and stop it all. I had to show him how eager I was to take it all the way, and more than that, *all the time.* I was wanting to have telepathy, to plant the image of a nightly suck boy in his head before the man came. I wanted to show him how good it could be whenever he wanted/needed it. A rock with those veins and he had big balls and he was a big man and then he put his hands on my head and pressured me into slower throat action. He, little #1, loved it lodged there. 15–20 times then I'd pull off to swallow spit and some air, a little hand action to keep it hard hard and then another 15–20. Finally (well, after some tentative head control. I should have put his hand back on my head and swallowed that cock) he got decisive. I could feel that change but he wasn't making much noise. He didn't want bystanders to know that he was going to do the damnable—in the age of AIDS—thing and shoot semen and sperm and perhaps virus down my throat. No one would have blamed him anyway, but this way the guilt was illuminated entirely and the rape pleasure heightened 'cause he could do this dangerous thing in silence with people watching. And when he came the cock was in my throat, his hand trapping my head, gently, and sperm belched out in three thick lumps that seemed to melt away into my throat (a bystander wouldn't see me swallowing), I pulled up a little so I could taste cum the fourth time but I don't remember anything distinct. I wanted to milk it, to rest it in my warm just-fed mouth but I sensed his sensitivity or urgency so I pulled out, rubbed his chest and thanked him somehow. "That was fun" or "See you again." His urgency and he-man nonchalance—no, it was more embarrassed contempt, a smirk, a half grin, not even a thanks, a "see you" more like, "good job, faggot, nigger; I'll sleep well and won't think about you after I fasten my pants"; sealing off forever (or until we happen upon each other again) the bit of vulnerability I brought him. It felt good to get treated like his slut. I wish he had pissed in me then left in the same way. I'll always love, yes LOVE, Crandall Walters for pushing my envelope. For filling me with piss freely, without conscience. . . .

Tuesday, March 20–21, 1989

I should mention a happening (too large!) in the Castro, a moment, a situation? I was walking past the donut shop toward Market Street when two black guys, late teens, early twenties, dressed in the hyper-athletic, street-warrior garb of the day, tore past me. One of them actually asked me to excuse him so I wasn't too terribly disrupted by them, maybe a little curious, a little embarrassed to be black and yet so different from them; I was perhaps amused by it all, or pretending to be when two white men hollered after the brothers, "Did you knife someone? Did you make off with someone's wallet?" or the like. I paused a moment to find some kinship with their accusation, to find amusement and more embarrassment as I was being indicted too, indirectly at least. A 24 bus had just sped up toward Market, so it was easy to put two and two together (when I needed to, when those white bastards provoked me to), and I hollered back at the white men, "they're running for the bus," loud enough, I hope, to counter their slur. I hope the big picture fell into place for the white men. Oddly, I guess I hate these men more than Crandall and his sort, but it's only the quick and stupid vs. the deliberate and stupid. . . .

Last night I went to BUENA VISTA park and pigged out on half a dozen men (was it that many?). Three of the men came in my mouth and I drank it. That's a horrible two minutes after the climax, or rather the 2nd of the two minutes as the guilt and gorge rise in us both. Why am I jeopardizing my life for an ounce, no a teaspoon of . . . I don't even know what it is? If I described it in the glowing terms I'm tempted to or in the transcendent way so many others have used, I'd know too well, too easily. It's the essence, the reduction of another man's pleasures, desires, maybe his hopes and his dreams, and I want it more keenly when I don't know the man, when he's a big man or a man with a big cock. Loss of control in him and in me. I want some token of that kind of contact, an abandon that forgets all the bullshit that destroys daytime relations, particularly where race difference becomes involved. Yeah, we are one and at the same time so far apart, so caught up in ourselves that the danger of each other cannot intrude. That's the point when it comes. But I'm conscious at these times; I'm not coming; I'm not delirious—just possessed, possessed for him, an extension of him like a hand. . . .

Late March 23–24, 1989

Carolina lost to Michigan this time. I couldn't watch it; I was at the Park Hyatt, and it's a good thing; I only moped four hours instead of 8. Spending too much money. The Hyatt is still more money to spend. Robert Mapplethorpe is dead at 43 of AIDS. I almost knew him. I could control a world from this little room and yet I don't . . . I can't even clean off my desk, just that!

Roaches? Of course there are roaches, fool, so why do you act surprised—no, why are you surprised and indignant? and why do you forget so quickly? I can't be that clean, but I want to be. I want to be so clean and white and Western. I want to blend, to disappear and reappear as one of the current "chosen."

Thursday, May 18, 1989

Jesus, I did it again. Leslie is right: I just don't care (and maybe my not caring about myself is a consequence of not caring for anybody else). I'm not sure of the formula, but for certain everybody loses in this. To the point: I'm speeding. I let some Angelo Blanc stick a needle in my arm (four times; three times my veins tried to tell me something. Angelo says they roll). Look at me, I just wrote "says" like I'll see this man again. It was suicide the first time. What does 2 times absolute idiocy reveal? But wait, why did I call a man I just spent 24 painful, intimate, intoxicating, sexy, brutal hours with, "some." Okay, Angelo Blanc does sound like a Jane Roe generic; I didn't believe Angelo when he first said it, last night in his truck on our way to my studio.

Crazy on top of crazy. It should have ended when that strange, invigorating American Playhouse ended last night. I should have gone to bed (this pen is going to break; I'm pressing so hard and writing so fast [carelessly too]). I hope I don't have a heart attack from this. The horror strikes on the news! Worse, my T-cells will drop precipitously, I'm sure (or I'll break a tooth), and after a bit of good news from always caring, always available Dr. Colbert. My count, which had dropped to 300 last month was back up to 460 last week. All the other markers indicated improvement or stability, and my physical went well (God, Dr. C. is a comfort—big woman, no pretensions, an obvious wig). I got this good news on Tuesday and by Wednesday I was back (fun how I usually get writing and sundry shit done on this drug, but I know it's going to make me pay). Wait, where's my positive attitude. I want to live!!! That's true. Write it!

I WANT TO LIVE, but I also want to be content. I want love and money, education and fame, friends and good sex; I want a relationship that lasts more than 40 minutes (an hour and $\frac{1}{2}$ is a long-term relationship according to Gene). Actually the majority of my encounters have lasted under 15 minutes (I don't believe this), the time it takes a white man to come. Okay, so I want to live but I want to live happily and this qualification seems so foreign, abstract, obscure—nonapplicable for me, maybe anyone in this country, this world (I don't believe that) (I better keep my mouth open; my jaws keep trying to break a tooth).

. . . Already feeling ugly, defeated, desperate to suck the scum out of any old herpatetic drunk, when the handsome (in the poor moonlight, or whatever's reflected in the fog) young, 6'2" top barely slows down—how do they know? I can't even see me, not my hand, not my dick. How can they know I'm black. I usually blame it on my nose and an accidental profile between an accidental part in the leaves that got caught in accidental light. Everything conspires against a black man in the gay sex jungle (I hate this!)—the wind, the moon (white boys must smell black boys; that's the form of disgust that they register anyway) vomit, human shit, several days old (I got some on my sneakers one un-happy night in the park and before I realized it the apartment was pungent with it—it was the smell of sex and soil and night vege-tation, but I couldn't stand it. I put the sneakers in a waste basket full of water and Lysol and closed the bathroom door). The jungle itself will part to reveal a black man before a white man comes too close, close enough ("It's fine if you lay awake, don't turn on that radio; your ears want the rest"—sort of something my dad said to me one bum night in El Paso. I think it inspired "Tawny." 10:28: I should wash those few dishes, pick up these clothes, my desk, get the big junk out of the floor and prepare to lie awake 4 or 5 hours in bed) to feel embarrassment, shame, pity, some-thing, for not continuing. Oh, some get close and then turn and leave you with "hello" still on your breath; they turn gleefully contemptuous, like they'd found one of the things worse than their own miserable (drug-ridden, AIDS-infested) selves. (That was unnecessarily ugly . . . and the guys, the white ones espe-cially, don't look that way until you get home and think about where you were, what time it was, and what you wanted to do.) (James Brown to the end, to the bone, to the dust.) 10:37: and I've said nothing about Angelo and sex. (Who's this woman singing a whole song on Brown's disc . . . ? Gorgeous stuff. Rejuvenating? Healing? James Brown's music, finally, for health.)

I do feel good writing this, dying and writing this. Those color comics of healthy T-cells being attacked by the virus, becoming maternity ward and AIDS college for the buggers, and all the while looking like strength, security, hope and other positive what-not . . . the ones Dr. Colbert took an educator's pride in showing me, identifying the schematics (most all of the comic) in case I thought T-cells and AIDS looked so cheerful and neat, a disease I could handle with an eraser or a few doses of white out . . . they come to mind as I think about writing to save my life ("writing for health" more compact). . . .

When did we have to justify piss-drinking, Crandall and I? When I started to feel like the phony-T-cell baby was thicken-ing, growing in spite of AZT (or a placebo, mind you, which would nullify all the positive spite I'd invested in ridding my-self . . . exorcism or abortion?). I think it was the piss-drinking which remained a huge unexplained burden over the reasonable and productive work I was doing with Olowin. It canceled everything, every move toward defining Crandall, defining my hatred (did I say that?), attraction, fear, and eventual repulsion of the man, every move veered off into myth (slavery stuff), instant-psychology (which I find I can do as quickly as I can construct a sentence, though I didn't start this particular bowl of psychology, Crandall, I mean, with Dr. Olowin).

Friday, May 19, 1989
It's one month till my 28th birthday. What's that "it's"? Strange, it doesn't feel at all extra, as though I'm going to, or have to carry, some sexless, faceless, apolitical (who cares?), unfriendly, unconcerned and remorselessly public entity into my 28th year. Is it too late to revise the thought, too late to make new time-travel plans? "One month till my 28th birthday!" The shortened statement requires the greater emphasis, like a pre-celebration, a shock or a warning.

Wednesday, 5.31.89
. . . —Peter marries Kyung to keep his secrets (stores his secrets in her and she can't repeat them, can't decipher them).
—Child to lock her at home ("Keiko," Anna's story).
—Fathers' war relived in the desert in 1970–71.
—Vietnamese or Korean kid molested (but after he asks for it—does it for candy, for love)
—Gary wrote a story about the death (Making Movies) but didn't know the whole story; didn't understand the sexual dynamic.
—Peter and Gary do it roughly after night at punk club—thrashing, hurricane of men (Fishbone or Bad Brains). Next week Pete joins the Marines.
—Starts with a chain letter, then series of letters, "I can feel this town dying around me."
—Sharpest black man I ever met. Will change late in story to "sharpest man of any color I ever met."
—Wife growing, developing in spite of child. Peter's fear of wife uncovering his past. Has bought all 5 of Gary's books, but burns them one evening after a fight with his wife over her night classes. Wife pregnant at the time.

—Father had died and left Peter a very wealthy man. In his lifetime he'd seen the wealth transferred quickly from great-grandfather, to grandfather, to father, to himself. Wealth and responsibility rushing at him like a train. Folks had warned him about Korean wife, about damage to political aspirations (g'father saw Peter as the next congressman from Va. and had coaxed the boy back from Korea, back from the West Coast, reeled him in with great skill and care, genuine care. Didn't think father could cut it, so-so teacher after military career. Peter was a late child).

White, white, white from the father (but only to please the g'father) but g'father had grown intelligent with age.

—Pete maintains friendship to keep his own secret safe, a secret he isn't sure G knows (only intuitively).

—All white, though you kept imagining something exotic about yourself—a secret you'd come to love.

I'm going to write—rewrite "Making Movies" with Pete as the movie character and 7 years older than Tawny. The death of the Korean kid is going to take on a new dimension; the sexual anger could absolve Tawny, could seem to make Pete the primary actor and that would be unfair. That throws a wrench in Tawny's directorship. Why wouldn't Pete (7 years older) have natural priority here?

I called Crandall this afternoon. I was lying in bed, late again, with two nights of libido stored up (not to mention all that play in the park) and I called him, half-hoping his machine would take the call; but he answered and he seemed genuinely happy to hear from me. It made me feel good, sickeningly (?). I made all the moves. This is all my doing; I have no one else to blame. I wonder if I ever did! All that bitching (it was more heartfelt than that) I did with Olowin . . . seems a waste of time, of energy. So many things . . .

So many things going right and now I do this.

Too many things going wrong and now I do this.

8–23 (Wednesday) 89

. . . Dear Master Park,

Here's that letter you wanted. I'm laying here sideways in the bed with *Slavery Defended* opened to about midway, sampling the arguments and thinking about how good it felt to serve. Not that it matters, but I enjoyed Thursday immensely, particularly the sleaze and humiliation of some of it. Ultimately my service depends on the strength of my attention, hence my addiction to those things that I enjoy.

My pain is high on your list of pleasures and I do like giving in to your desires, but some of the more grueling extended tortures stick in my mind and make me hesitant to call or answer your calls. Master Crandall and others use the pain more sparingly. Crandall relied more on the various humiliations—filling one frequently and overfull with his piss (occasionally 3 or 4 times a day and twice at night). He made his relief obvious in sighs and grunts.

Honestly the pain frightens me and brings me out of the stupor I need to be in in order to be a subservient slave. I need some pain but the extended periods seem to drive the desire to serve out of me—all I can do is soberly register the craziness of what I'm doing.

The racial humiliation is a huge turn-on. I enjoy being your nigger, your property and worshipping not just you, but your whiteness (this was the thing that connected Crandall and I so completely).

I really wanted your cum and more of your piss.

9-3-89

. . . He might come back tonight (but no speed for me tonight) for a quickie, for the climax, the resolution and liquid release that we/*he* never got through our 20 hours, Sat–Sun, though his cock seeped and hardened largely, convincingly many times. I want what I let him come here for.

I want what I let him come here for.

A rhetorical and lewdly exacting contraction of my selfishness, my obsession or physical addiction to the fruit or actual product of my labors and, as pleasurable or identity-smashing as they seem to be there must be a desire or a suicidal disregard for the death (inherent, apparent, impugned, imprinted, imbued) or threat or immune-suppressing action so obviously present in his come (cum), as his body is a billboard of the misfortune he carries with him now—black cancers on his back and arm and leg and the endless horrible possibilities that I drain off each time I do this thing. Was I afraid I wouldn't see him tonight if I wrote this? Perhaps I should have jerked off and put this tired and that dying issue to rest (. . . for good would be best but if he calls in a month and I haven't found happiness as Tom Goya's suck boy or a return to the bliss that I never fully utilized or understood the operations of with Joey Edel . . .). Angelo's supposed to call at 6:00. I'm weak and fatigued but not sleepy—perhaps I should take a valium? Have to get up at 6:30 tomorrow! Well, 6:24—he said he had to go to San Jose but also could be an excuse to chill. He could be ill(er).

4-14-90
. . . A story
location: Phoenix Arizona
origin of name?
South Africa (subtitled: Red Bicycle, Ham-hands)
Climax: Jan allows Hammonds to drive her home and put her to bed. To this point she considers him a quiet, rugged, polite, self-contained, even boring, ranch hand. She thinks about shaping him into the husband that Charlie never became, thinks about how large his penis is. Wants even to be molested (Charlie rapes her the last night of sex, the last night she sees him).

Hammonds is not the innocent that Jan supposes and he picks up on the drunk woman's advances. Sex is a common thing for this man and he has a very refined, very urban approach to it, beginning with a bit of ecstasy or cocaine or speed. (Perhaps he has no memory. Acts on instincts, self-preservation, money.) Bright eyes, but bright from his stimulant not from any residual boyishness. Talks rather country, like a Texan, rather slow, deliberate, careful; but not like a hayseed. Jan could tell. (People honking their horns. Did the baseball team win? Someone lose their brakes on a busy street?) He'd been out of the country a long time. His blazer and gray slacks were as fine, good, proper as Norm's but without the Eastern, Ivy League smarminess (?). No v-neck sweater or seersuckers shirt like Erwin and Monroe, two pretty Chapel Hill transplants (they'd started for LA but broke down outside of Tempe and set up house there, the two of them together, keeping their collegiate edge, trappings, -ness intact so the neighborhood wouldn't figure, assume they were sucking each other instead of co-ed pussy [like all the mid-aged married men were boasting of]).

Ham is a sexual maverick, prides himself on the # of broncos he can bust female and male, not too particular though he does have it in mind to marry a "good woman." Sees this in Jan (though he knows her case—raped and abandoned by her husband. Word gets out in this group of friends, it's batted about like a therapy ball game).

That night: He talks her into it, and Jan (simultaneously) decides that she's going to suck this man's cock. He offers it to her very frankly figuring she'd be compelled after their conversation of sexual prudery (at party before). He offers it as a dare and Jan, thinking she would shock him, accepts. For a while she wanted him to back down, then she wanted to pull out, but his body language (blocking the bedroom door) told her not to expect an easy retreat. This was childish; this wasn't rape.

Ham has a thing about/for victims. Volunteers time at a home for battered kids. The fetishism of this becomes apparent as bedroom scene unfolds.

Jan wants to suck him, but doesn't want to be thought crude. Feels she should decline to maintain her reputation (no sex since husband left . . . tried a lesbian encounter, a tantric retreat where an older group of free radicals, men and women, touched her and encouraged her to orgasm without feeling her own genitals. She could touch others, but not her own . . .).

She is a nice girl, who doesn't like nice men.

Jan wants Ham to make the move, either 1) to zip himself up with a laugh and something said to the effect: "a nice girl wouldn't . . ." and go or 2) to take her by force.

Note he doesn't want to fuck. Jan has sort of offered this as an option. Says he doesn't like condoms. Jan finds herself helpless and daredevil in her desire and offers her cunt anyway. Ham reiterates he doesn't want to fuck her. He leaves the stress on the *her* ambiguous and thrusts Jan into further dilemma: He doesn't want to fuck *me* in particular (because I've been raped down there) or he really doesn't like to fuck. She decides on the former, even thinks she understands his manipulation but can't do anything with this knowledge. She would prefer to fuck because she can't see down there. Also she has become a verbal person. Feels a new responsibility for her actions (until it comes to sex).

Jan doesn't want any responsibility for her sexual activity. Looks for strong men that will force her and then leave. Ham is pressing her to make the decision herself.

Ham knows she won't back down from the dare, so he pushes her to the edge of capitulation. He knows if he tells her he'll still respect her she will do it, but he doesn't say it. Indeed he tries to make her feel slovenly (calls her whore and bitch—sort of a game, sort of not).

Finally: Jan sucks Ham near climax (he throat-fucks her) but as she feels the man hardening the threat to her child invades her. She digs into the sewing bag next to the bed and stabs the man even as her mouth fills with his salty fluid. She runs to the boy's room. Screams when she sees the black manboy in bed with him. The boy screams when he sees her mouth full of Ham's blood.

Description of the face-fuck. Pushing back words, words of acquiescence, certainly words of rebellion. Jack hammering words, then thoughts. A search through various rooms in her mansion, her home-chambers in her throat.

(I've got to move.)

Monday, April 23, 1990—

One of the more peculiar evenings I've had without anything really happening. Moving backward, I just called a man at 848-4300 extension 1027. Sounds like sex. Sounds like money too, money mostly—the 4300 is surely reserved for institutions and would-be institutions, and an extension—? Well, it had to be some graveyard spawn (can't you imagine a whole room of them abuzz on telephone to people they don't know, people they just as soon talk to dead as alive for a credit company). Money doesn't sleep; debt doesn't die so I would not have been surprised to get a call (he called me first around 11:30, 'cause it was after Eric's 11:00 message—Eric's good about remarking time, location, points of sexual attention—and I returned his call) from a collections agency around midnight.

But I returned his call because it could have been sex. My hours (2½–3 *minutes* actually) of sex with Ed (of the drug-sunken eyes and big—"relative"—uncut cock) still fresh in my mind, or my nose as his funk is still in my sheets, still under my bottom lip! A man calls, leaves no name, simply says "Gary, call #." No "thank you" no "goodbye" (I don't recall one). The 4300 belongs to a Mariott and the extension to a man named Paul (don't recall the last name Slavic, Jewish, Lizzarro—something). I was sure it was sex. Said "this is Gary, who is this?" or was it: "who is this/This is Gary." The pause told me it wasn't sex; indeed, I suddenly thought *I* had the wrong number (imagine that: [the wrong # of a "wrong #"] and that's [this "wrong #"] what it turned out to be).

He asked me was I from New York. I thought sex and said I'd been there. But he was looking for his cousin, Gary Fisher *from* New York. My first thought after. . . .

this was a falling one—what would it be like to make sex (love? no; I was reading Bataille) to an uncle. I hadn't misheard, I simply misconnected. Now an instant later I'd linked *uncle* to *nephew* (had to go through *niece* to get there) and *cousin* to *cousin* and felt (instantly) disheartened, even repulsed—no, disheartened by uncle/nephew; repulsed by cousin/cousin—by the incest of it. Fragment later repulsed gave way to bored since it never was so much to begin with. I laugh at my repulsions, can hardly remember them later (citrus and a greasy dish gives me the urge these days to vomit, but that's not a repulsion, is it?). Anyway, I was *not* repulsed by the thought (the mistaken thought, I remind you), I only thought I was. Honestly, and simply (if there's a distinction to be noted), simply and honestly I felt bored by the thought of two cousins doing it, unless one cousin was older as this "wrong #" sounded as though (seemed) he would be.

Wait: wasn't I the wrong #? I was the 5th, 6th (or 8th?) wrong # this Paul (can a voice with a name be a wrong #? Sure I was Gary Fisher to him but only one—and the wrong one it was clear—of the 4 Gary Fishers that had called and 3 G. Fishers [wouldn't that make me 1 of 7? ALL of them wrong!] that had called). Sure my # was right for who I am though being one of nine wrong #s might conflate and confuse a simple issue. Now I'd become one of many wrongs for poor Paul who had a singular and rather attractive (residue from the potentiated sex between us—though I'm sure he's straight) integrity to me. He was the one and only "wrong #" in my life that night. It seemed unfair that he should seem almost "right" or at least his calling seem almost providential, or at the very least his calling me should seem like a convenience (I enjoyed being that, service-oriented, a real bottom, whore, sex slave fiend, et al.)—I felt like a convenience store. Not that he had made me a convenience store, because I had done that myself, but because he would use me as one. He told me the whole uncharged tale of this cousin who he'd lived with for 12 years (too long to be a sexual interest, even chattel) like a brother (again the gorge at incest, the overwhelming monotony of it—is that why I don't do it with other black men, or is it charged, and if it's charged is it positive [+] in the direction of white men: "I find them beautiful [the bigger ones mostly], hunky charmingly awkward and dominant" and negative [−] in the direction of black men: "I don't find them [the big ones] attractive [not always true—even among these half-truths, half-baked truths and flat out lies—truly, and sometimes size wins over beauty, brains, money and history, (even true and obvious history) . . . (room for *because*) smart, charming in any way, or least (most?) of all responsive to me. Or are the charges opposite this. Don't I know what's healthy and uplifting for me and only suck the destructive or counter-productive (some would say this is redundant cubed—that is black × gay × the thing [black-and-gay]).

black × gay × (black × gay) for some kinky sexual gratification built on and fueled by self-hatred. That's not simple enough, I know, but which came first: the sex or the hatred? Indeed, I believe it was none of the above. It was FEAR. Fear of being hurt (because I am black) leads to an excitement which strangely mimics the excitement I feel when a man (particularly—[?] though I have precious little variation to contrast this with the general—especially—[?]—
(particularly a white man, although I know, have known, few black men [fewer brown (and no yellow)]
(particularly a white man—though the word, if not the idea of *particular* comes out of an imagination—or lack of it!—or out of a strategy for a sexual future that includes mainly, if not only white men—because certainly little or nothing in my past would require me to imply distinction between or to qualify or to filter out the white man from a pool

—because certainly little or nothing in my past required my distancing him from some general quantity or *quality* that included blacks or browns, yellows or reds; little or nothing required that I distinguish him, qualify him or filter him from the pool, since pool here (for him and for me) implies no variety, no turbulence, no movement, not a ripple, no nothing; pool here doesn't imply at all, it doesn't *do* anything except watch itself unwatched (?) . . . ahhh! then perhaps it does im-ply, that is M-ply like white narcissus—or like the TV serial that tests its own worth (dares the sleepy conservative eye, and the tighter corporate wallet) by dangling its own suspense week after week, foreshadow unresolved, unresolvable—like what narcissus remembered, suspended and constant, though always in ecstatic jeopardy of folding in on himself; the face in the pool threatens to imply. And if it threatens to imply something not itself then it risks breaking the silence, risks revealing me to me, know if not . . . no I don't know what a white man sees below the surface of himself, if not me, 'cause certainly I've been taught that I'm this way through and through, a dark dense star, horribly attractive, irresistible, a lodestone, the plunge at the very heart of . . . what now can only be perceived as ripples. Unresolved till unresolvable. I am a ball of twine so tight, dense, confused and unravellable that I might as well be without start or finish, might as well be of a single substance through and through or of no substance at all for all I'm worth to your curious mind; a thing of this moment and that same thing always threatening to mock you in your progress, in your urgency for results without resolution, for change without improvement, for the very next best thing.

So, particularly (especially or primarily) a white man, when he holds and protects me from others like him, brings me an excitement which strangely and uniquely parallels that which he causes me when he threatens or frightens me. Of course, if my white man goes he takes his protection and his comfort . . . Obviously, then: without him, why would I need him. Want might be another problem, but want's based on memory, on fantasy, on the way things might have been. Without these I couldn't want him, but I could have created him anyway as something to avoid, as a barrier to desire and hence its fixation.

It was the age I heard in Paul's voice, the weight too, but more the age that helped me mistake "uncle" for "cousin," that prodded me to leap a gulf between us, to scale a wall, to turn a phrase . . . "Sir." It was a "no, sir" of no particular deference, of no signal importance unless it's understood to cannibalize itself, the "sir" doing more for the "no's" emptiness than it does for Paul. It was a "no, sir" between two men who weren't cousins but between two strangers who almost found their different solace in the same pathetic and faulty situation somewhere between the time the situation (not between two men who weren't uncle and nephew, nor between two men who *were* black and white) failed and the time its frozen machinery hit the ground—at the fair, they ease it, the pressure drop, and warn heart patients. The excitement of the situation occurred sometime after it was possible but during its doom (and long after fear or protection felt credible). We talked five minutes through a cool and clinical hope, wanting to know things we didn't care about, wanting to tell things we knew wouldn't get cared about, exchanging orphans for the sake of exchange, perhaps to stifle the incestuous impulse to secularize it (3 Garys or G's had simply hung up because it was wrong) by actually allowing a bit of it. For a minute I *was* his cousin and there was some pretty sexy doubt to go with it. In the next minute when I wasn't his cousin the doubt still remained unsatisfied. And in the next, when I became who I am and he hung up unsatisfied, the doubt still remained with me. Perhaps it will take years to shake it, which is the sort of doubt that wracks some rape victims, all victims of unspeakable crimes—they eventually must find pleasure in the violation or die. If I had been his cousin and there had been no doubt about it . . . no pause, no pleasure drop.

12/11/90 Wednesday (by an hour and a few seconds)
. . . give up everything to the pursuit of cocks, to the consumption of sperm and piss for no other reason than the fact that I'm a nigger and that's what God put niggers on this earth to do. I truly love and savor the taste of sperm and of hot piss whether hot salty morning piss or piss from beer-drinkers who swell their bladders for the sole purpose of emptying their waste into my nigger body. I've thought about the philosophical foundation for my activity, my vocation and duty. The simplicity of it astounds me and yet I have no words for it, just an image, at once holy

and profane, of the nigger on his knees taking cock juices into his body, particularly piss as a kind of spiritual cleanser, an erasure of whatever else he may aspire to beyond his being a nigger. Sperm is perfect nigger food and piss perfect nigger drink and a committed nigger should be able to live, to thrive off this nourishment alone. Piss and sperm nourish the nigger body and feed his black soul. Sperm feeds the wish, the already thwarted potential for the nigger to seek more than a life as a urinal and sperm bank. It feeds the wish but only leads to more wishes, greedier hungry wishes that only sperm can fulfill. Sperm is addictive for niggers, as addictive as crack for niggers who can't see beyond the white goo and must devote their life to the massive and constant ingestion of this drug merely to stay alive. Sperm is life for all men, but for the nigger who takes it into his body, as a nigger should, sperm is a *way of life*, a purpose for being. Sperm is more important than the nigger body itself and will ultimately consume him. He must feel toward this purpose, this reward to the exclusion of all else. A nigger cocksucker is a slave to sperm, a disciple to it; he who consumes it to a point of self-obliteration is the nigger jesus, given over eternally to the sin and redemption of men who crave a nigger's full hot lips milking their (usually white) rods to creamy explosions. Their wickedness is transferred to the nigger, lost in him; he gobbles up their sin as he consumes their waste and their wasted tablespoons of life, transforming them into the cumming man's pleasure and spiritual release as the pisser fulfills, completes himself in the filling and humiliation and degradation of the nigger jesus. The nigger takes his hot sacrament from the cocks of men who know where a nigger should be, why he should be, how he should be and find pleasure in reaffirming that I AM PROUD TO BE A NIGGER

December 31, 1990

—A blue moon on New Year's Eve . . . I'm not working; I'm not partying; I may go to Alamo Square to see the full moon but I will fight off the urge to do more.

—The moon is very bright, almost oppressive. The general celebration seemed modest (esp. by comparison to that moon) — some horns, a few firecrackers, a little yelling. I don't know what I expected.

—Lee "Scratch" Perry to open the year. He's not helping my resolve, I don't think, but he's not hurting it either.

—Resolutions: simple and obvious, I hope: to stay alive (by whatever means necessary) and full of pleasure; to be honest at least to myself; to learn to enjoy my own company, my own work and my own play; to meet a complementary friend/lover.

Oh, January 1, 1991

. . . —potential in numbers! How about those spots on your leg! already names in your knowledge, not just *possible* assassins' faces in a crowd, real ones! You know these guys. You know that less than year after Crandall got spots he was gone. Six months and all the spunk and spirit—the nastiness anyway—went out of him, that is: he tried to repent.

—Note: you wouldn't let Crandall Walters repent and you may have been the only one who could have. What a strange power. Did I relish it for awhile?

January 2, 1991

—I should actually—probably—get some sleep or get started on this visualization book, but both have that save-my-life feel which frightens me back to reality (or bores me—can't figure out which and makes me flu [flee/flu . . . hmm] all but the most routine—lists and copying) —Oh,—(who do I direct this to?), will this Interferon work? will I even be offered the chance? If it doesn't and the spots come will I kill myself (physically or visually)? I want help—don't I?—but I'm unsure where to turn and how . . .

—All the little instant shocks, do they add up to life? I mean the purchases, the restaurants and loud times, the dancing, the glory hole club, Len's calls, writing in this journal, ETC.—does this somehow add up to life? or is it a reprieve from thoughts about death since surely thoughts about death are less living than a succession of singularly inconsequential, or even trivial explosions. 1:40 A.M. and these things matter, or at least they take on a life of their own. I wish reading was as easy as writing. I wish thought, I mean sustained thought or meditation, I wish it came as easy as writing. I wish I wrote with more than writing in mind (—as this is it's a gratuitous gesture at best, a reliving of those many inconsequential explosions that have filled a day—or maybe a rationalization of them, a reasoning, a definition—because they/it seems so much of nothing on its own). I wish I had a great, and great big book in me. I wish writing could save my life (the way I may believe reading can).

January 24, 1991

. . . I don't know his name, but a few years ago—6 or 7?—a black man from Oakland made a sensation with his huge, gaudy, hyper-publicized funeral and the infamous events that led up to it. He sold drugs in the East Oakland community, started as a common pusher but somehow worked his way past middlemen and suppliers to become Oakland's first drug entrepreneur. My story would cover this man's rise to prominence in the community, from his violent gang days to the more eloquent and ironically acceptable place as a key businessman.

Must deal with the *schizophrenia* in the black community over the whole drug issue—seen at once as anathema, a form of genocide in the community; and as a way out of it, a sure money-maker.

Must deal with the *business* of drugs. Taking off from Pat's remembrances of summers in NYC when the pot would suddenly become scarce and blacks and latinos in need of chemical solace would turn to always available heroin. She believed the cops, perhaps even the government regulated the drug flow, amounts and types, in an effort to control urban violence, particularly during the summers during the 60s when riots were anticipated. What are drugs as political tools (for a governor, a president trying to be reelected)? What are they as business tools? Why don't these industries show up on the stock market? Find out about the black (stock) market in drugs, the ample trade. And what about the participation and annihilation of peoples? Was it good business sense? Yeah—that can be one of the dilemmas in the story. Lead character won't sell crack because it's bad for business—too cheap and too deadly.

Deal with the *irony* of unfairness or *racism* in even this illegitimate business. How he must take business from the black community just to survive and advertises that his product is black-owned and -operated. The family nature of operations makes him a hero. Runs organization like a bake sale.

Church involvement: donates large sums to neighborhood churches which both sedates them and funds their more positive activist concerns. He puts this drug money back into the community renovating housing, hotels, funds development (including a bay front shopping and apartment complex).

—Buys up and revamps much of East Oakland with the mayor's blessing. Until the mayor begins to see (Slipped through a crack) this man as a challenge to his position.

Reference to *The Godfather* (leave drugs to the darkies, the coloreds; they're animals anyway. Let them lose their souls). Internal question of the story—what is soul in America? Isn't money more important to a community . . . ?

—Violence from rival gangs originally but he comes to absorb the gangs, turns them into a police force, an army of sorts. Note cops have been allowing the gangs to kill themselves off; if anything encouraging battles to kill off young black men. Police both isolate and insulate the community—a new strategy of genocide. San Francisco stops its media war against Oakland—stops its constant and lopsided discussion of the violence in the city in favor of a media blackout. Very little is broadcast about the black community and . . . police fail more and more frequently to respond to urban violence, so they are less and less aware of the change in the streets, the harmony and cooperation this man is promoting, fostering, organizing.

Character is to be congratulated for the strength and autonomy of his organization but must stress the corrosive element at the center of it.

Meanwhile becoming big in the white business world, the white political realm as well. Pivotal moment should be embracing American politics. Not money, not even drugs but POWER that destroys character. Trying to outscum the scum of this country.

(test out his synthetic heroin [may actually decrease violence]; trying to replace crack.)

Chapter I "I need your help" (similar to opening of *G'father*). At a party for "family," several gangs present, churches

II Origins, philosophies, politicians, TV personalities, smaller skirmishes to a battle with the mayor and police (hints of homosexuality)

III The central dilemma. Success with a corrosive center. Fucking outlaw super entrepreneur/hero

IV Internal jitters

V Power as speed (actually desires political, social legitimacy)

What we see: the graffiti artists (young Asians), the rappers, the punks, the queers

—Starts a record company, studio. Finds rapper who becomes biggest star in country. Driving motion toward legitimacy. Could have backed NWA but instead an M.C. Hammer–type figure.

Hmm. How is this going to play in the black community? . . .

2/6

3:18 A.M. No, I haven't been sleeping well, but I feel okay tonight staying up to read an old journal and listen to *Revolver* (how could I have missed this one?). Some good memories in this old journal, 1982, when I was thinking about leaving Chapel Hill and had lost my fear of sex (probably the year I contracted HIV though it does no good at all to pinpoint it). Reading this seems to empower me. I have no money; I have a killer disease; I've lost my mother six years now; I don't think I'll ever fall in love! and yet I feel empowered tonight by some old and powerful reveries ("Tomorrow Never Knows").

—Stimulating: the thought of battling something few believe they can defeat. Tomorrow I will go by the HAF office, get some info on Interferon; I'll take an aspirin in the morning in the hopes of raising my T-cells like that one lucky fellow's done and recorded in the latest Bay Times. And tomorrow I'll go to the Box with a meeting in mind. . . .

March 23, 1991

(A rainy Saturday; not much sleep after the church.)

Idea:

Two black men meet on the Buddy Line. They speak the languages well—English and the language of phone sex—so they don't recognize each other.

Mike: Hello?

Greg: Hello?

Mike: Where are you calling from? . . .

Greg: Primarily a bottom; how about you?

Mike: Primarily a top. . . .

They lie about their appearance. Not what they wished they looked like or even what they wished they had but rather common, even dull descriptions—brown and brown, good shape but not body builders.

They lie to each other and compromise their own wishes or desires; they lie to themselves by not lying enough.

Mike: You want to be my boy?

Greg: Yeah.

Mike: You want to be my slave?

Greg: Yeah.

Mike: Yeah?

Greg: I want to pretend I'm black . . .

Mike: And I'm your white master?

Greg: Yeah.

[Date missing]

What's all this? A gum wrapper? A sock? Christ, a magic marker? I hope the cap is on it. I get my toes around the marker and pull it up through the covers. Yes, it's open so there must be a large spot of orange on the sheets down there.

"Are you naked?" The man on the other end of the line asks everything in a husky desperate way like he's running out of air in a coal mine. "I'm naked," he says, "are you?"

"Yes, yes." I say still worrying more about that big, orange spot down below. How big is it? How old is it? God, is it still wet?

"Are you naked on top of the covers?" he asks me.

"Yes, I'm on top of the covers."

"How's your cock?"

"Good, how's yours?"

"Okay." Now I'm remote, uninterested. The orange spot is everything. I hope he doesn't notice it because this is a man I can get turned on with. Once he suggested that I get up early every morning to drink his sizzling morning piss. He'd drop it by on this way to work. This was the sort of sexy shock talk I wanted from him, the sort of uninhibited celebration of shock, a celebration of talk itself.

"Sizzling, orange, hot morning piss. Mmm. Full of the vitamins you want."

"What's your name? Your real name?"

My real name changes every other call. "Greg," I say, meaning it.

"What do you look like, Greg?"

Hmm. What do I look like tonight? I think about the fantasies I've created in the past. Blonde waifs with hungry mouths and eyes. Lean, sweet-faced swimmers and/or runners with marble thighs. Short, thick Irish wrestlers, gymnasts and street thugs. Thin, delicate, almost effeminate mulatto boys from the Indies.

"I want a black boy, Greg." He repeated this from deep down in the coal mine. I wondered if he'd turned his face into the pillow. I wasn't sure what he said. "I want a black boy tonight, Greg."

23 April 1991

. . . Paranoia, coffee-induced but full of specters from the sober present. Three new dots on my skin. Will I keep chasing these things till there's not a patch on me left unscarred by the chemo? Suicide doesn't seem like quite the option it was several months ago. Was I trying to threaten my body into resistance?

29 April 1991

Sex and sex complication, specifically this man Alex who I met (met?—sucked off twice and spent three hours fondling, caressing, licking and denying) at the Clementina church. How do I tell him that I am positive (that I have ARC? That I have AIDS)? The man started sucking up my cum during my climax (here in my bedroom—we came back here). If he's positive then we're a match. If he's not . . . I have to tell him. If it weren't for these fucking scars from the chemo (actually worse than the lesions they replaced) I might actually lie, risk killing this beautiful man. I need to tell him tomorrow. We have a date for Thursday.

I'm protecting myself, I guess, by not getting fixed on Alex. I finally meet a white man not twisted by the color thing but there's the disease to get over; it's got to change the complexion of everything.

30 April 1991

Got some responses to my bulletin board ads. Yesterday I sucked off this rather repulsive man named Grant. There have been other calls but no meetings. Matthew seemed really enthusiastic about a master-slave (racially tinged) thing, but I went out to the GH club and missed our date. Maybe he'll call again. Maybe he's too pissed. I was eager until he asked about my health and mentioned a probing and scrutiny of my body (as merchandise in the fantasy). I have no way to cover the scars from the chemo. What will I tell Alex. I should have been here to get his call. . . .

3 May 1991

. . . Last night I told Alex that I'm HIV-positive. He could look at my legs and see how far gone I was. I wonder if our fuck was a last hurrah. He was very kind to me, and any more would have to be considered charity because the slower-motion dead don't give of themselves freely—not to us—without a thought of charity, do they?

I will call him, like he asked me to, or he'll call me. He has to see the kids tomorrow, or was it tonight and tomorrow too? I'm a returnable bottle, just drop me back where you got me; or damaged goods—always returnable even if you use a little. When *does* truth catch up with intentions (esp. "honest" and "the best" intentions)? But how can I blame you. A businessman's dodge, a busy and busy-living man's escape.

God, he felt so good. I didn't even let myself go—I didn't even drop that force-field shell that covers every inch of my skin when I'm with a naked human body—and yet I know that he felt good. Now I am pariah and he won't call and I won't force him to charity.

He thanked me for telling him, but he didn't really want to know. I sensed a hurry in him to have-it-all before I got the chance to tell him. I was almost in love with him—now I'm free to love him at our new distance. No more body veil; my new veil is distance. . . .

January 13, 1992

. . . If I think about tomorrow, and tomorrows, I will dream and my fantasies will be wet, plumped with run-off from a hoary snow-capped world of distances (places I've been, wanted to go to, want now to go to). If I don't think about tomorrow my world gets small, claustrophobic (I don't deny some excitement there) —no big armed white thought comes home to me, takes off his clothes in the dark and defines his love just for me; no thought, no hope of it.

—Look at the excitement in the smallness of things, the fraction of things—days, minutes, particles of time—and back it with silver like you'd back glass for a mirror—back it with the silver of distances, of, say, tomorrow, reading your stories to a group of students at Duke, or of yesterday, remembering (re-membering, yes!) your legs so clear and beautiful in the air as Roy fucked you, and your perfect, perfect feet, worth kissing.

—Make a mirror, one that you don't *need* to stand in front of because it's so familiar to you, so obvious, but one that you still (and always) enjoy standing in front of because you still (and always) like what you see. And when you like yourself again offer what you like to a man who can appreciate it.

18th, 19th August

976-8080? Was that the # for much sex, much chaos? It's 5:30 and I don't know why I'm awake but I'm curious to sit in (lie in) on a session of 976. Can't *do* anything—I'd be at church if I could, but I can listen and remember and maybe stroke my own. Sex is an easy alternative to fear, but why do I have to come to these crossroads *so* late? . . .

Friday, August 28, 1992

. . . KS. I'm so thoroughly occupied (pre-, re-, and post-) with this occurrence, with these purple fingerprints all over my arms and thighs, that I feel it's dishonest to write about anything unless I include this. It's totally changed the way I live, the way I dress, the way I move, the places I go, the activities I join. On a sunny day I'd rather stay indoors: because I no longer wear t-shirts or short-sleeve tops. I've folded them all and put them on a shelf out of sight (and mind, as they used to torture me). I feel most comfortable in a long-sleeve white shirt. No one questions its appropriateness even on the hottest day. I would probably invest in more of them if I didn't maintain some small hope that this malady will end. God, then to be left alone with a closet full of long-sleeve white shirts would be the torture; or don't I invest in more of them because I'm running out of energy for this charade, I'm anticipating death before the need for more white shirts so why waste the money. My thoughts probably run the line between these positions too. "A cure for what ails us."

I keep thinking this is a game, so simple that I'm losing for thinking too much, too far ahead, too fast and too broad, for thinking while I should be sleeping—the remedy, I honestly believe (sometimes, on occasion), is in my head, in a simple compartment, within a simple room, within a simple building that I can see from here, not far along a path so broad and so bright that I've been following it without knowing all along. The single key to building, room and compartment is free and available to me like the toilet key at a filling station, a rural route where few travel and now fewer (if any two ever did) stop, and nobody, *not another soul,* has ever yet had to use the facility there, so when you ask for the key note that strange pride and juvenile delight in the station attendant's eyes and as he places it warmly in your palm, covering your hand with both his, and again he's to show you where to go, offers to check your oil and water and to do your windows while you enjoy the facilities . . . and yet again, as he asks you in utter rural-route innocence, if everything came out all right. No, he hasn't even noticed that you're black or remembered that he's white and that you two are half a continent away from the reconciliation of big cities. (After you're gone he walks into the facility, closes the door and smells the remnants of you and suddenly you are cured!)

Somehow the mesh between you two is too simple, and perhaps too big for such doubts. All those anxieties and inhibitions, restrictions and recriminations those time-honored and blood-cherished hatreds and passions, those myths, histories and great churning philosophers of difference pass right through. You leave them in the starchy water when your situation gets drained. He's made a sauce using an old family recipe. You've sprinkled conversation abundantly.

Monday, January 18, 1993

. . . Got in a mess on the bus. I brought ice cream aboard and then refused to leave when the driver got rigid in his rules and principles. Might be worth a story. We sat there in our stand-off for half an hour. A woman offered me a plastic bag (but that was unacceptable to the driver). A man offered me one/two dollars to wait for the next bus, then offered the driver money. I asked him for twenty dollars. A suited man cursed me, made the whole scene edgy instead of just absurd. He was like a little sharped-toothed dog waiting for an undefended pant leg. MUNI brass, a short, dark-haired woman, tried to get me off. I asked her to come aboard and explain but she refused. She did come on board to make disparaging third-person comments about me to the other passengers. When I refused to leave she began calling other authorities (who never came). The next 24-bus came and I got on it without incident. The sup-woman gave me her ID# and the whole event disintegrated most unsatisfyingly (I hope). Everybody was inconvenienced, busses backed up. When I finally got home I expected the ice cream to be melted but it was just as good as before. (Coconut and strawberry) — the little-dog man kept asking me if it was *that* good. He wanted to know what it cost and how much of it was left. He couldn't understand how 2 dollars wouldn't cover it. Except for him and the driver, people were either quiet or very direct in their appreciation of the absurdity of the situation. The man who offered the money and the woman who offered the bag eventually took a cab together. I wonder if they took Matthew's cab. That would be ironic and funny since I might have taken the 24-bus right before this one and spared many a lot of weirdness if I hadn't stopped to say hello to Matthew. Maybe I was hoping Matthew would offer me a ride. Maybe I was hoping to renew our short-lived cocksucking routine. (He came over twice and I offered him regular cocksucking, any hour . . .) I stopped, missed the first 24-bus, to restate that offer. I don't think he'll call tonight or even soon but some small anticipation has me still awake this evening. . . .

2:30

I'd love to stay up all night asking why — why did I lose my entire adulthood to this slow death? why didn't I realize how slow it would be and speed up the things that made 60–80 or 100 years worth living. Here I am no further along than I was ten years ago.

Now, with these spots, even if death is ten years away I don't know how to enjoy life. I can't get naked, can't get honest or open or truly nasty with anyone. It's only the spots. More than any other single piece to this nightmare. The spots keep my mind indoors, keep my ambitions under wraps. I've always been ashamed of my body (hateful, spiteful) never loving and nourishing even when it begged for it. All those chances to get buff-n-beautiful, to fulfill the gayboy dream (even in black) would not have been wasted if I'd understood the nature and purpose of immediate beauty. I think Roy tried to show me, looked me in the eye so many times and told me I was beautiful. Others told me. I felt it, but I felt ugly too, a lot and a long time ugly. Do the spots fit a pattern of self-loathing, oppression, etc., et al.? I can't believe that, not even to save my life. I didn't create this drama, this tragedy, but perhaps I'm playing the part a bit too well. . . .

Oh, we're dropping bombs on Baghdad again, still! Petty punishments. Small angers consume me. Nothing large enough to barter with, however, small sharp things like rusted nails. No one talks about it but everyone seethes with these little angers, these little hates. I can understand the strange mood on the bus when I instigated that 30 minutes of absurdity. Lots and lots of little things without direction or pull, in need of a great shiny magnet to pull it all to some dangerous point. Just scattered piles of anger and hate rusted in inactivity. I guess I was attempting to stir up my own. That bit of craziness I could control, that bit of anger directed at a system and people so married to systems that they couldn't see the humor in what happened.

It's late. Those men are not going to call. Throw off the anticipation and go to sleep. I need someone to order me around, someone to force me to take care. Beat me, tie me down if need be, but make me be good to myself.

Saturday, April 3, 1993
North Carolina just beat Kansas for a berth in the final! The thrill is mixed with the dangerous surreal situation I began this week. I'm in a hospital room at Alta Bates. I'm being treated for pneumonia, which means I probably have it. I want to probe the

thing that makes this visit exciting. Remember Park and Crandall and the creepy delight they've promised. I wonder if I should call Park and invite him to some kinky hospital games. Or is this the wake up call—the last chance. Michigan and Kentucky next.

—I need to enjoy the moment (even if the exact one is annoying with these hiccups).

I fell back in bed, surprised by the drama of exhaustion.

4.30.93

Call it, call it the death book; call it burning up, burning out, call it the no-choice-now book, or, hopefully, call it another one in a continuous series. Snuck out of Alta Bates. If my sleeve rises too high (I used the 2nd button) the white and gray ID bracelet will be noticeable to this keenly observant jewish fellow sitting next to me. Snuck out of AB, took off the throw-away smock, the ones with the 40 snaps that seem to fit any other 40 and even when they're snapped up right feels like surrealism and dadaism in an ancient cave on a French colony, an over-the-shoulder summer number in Africa. (Huh?) Took off all that stuff at Brad Lewis's urgence. He told me I'd have to sneak out, because not sneaking out would cost me my Medicaid coverage (which I don't really have anyway, yet). My last bill, by the way, was $18,000. I have to laugh whenever I look at it, all the procedures, chemicals and equipment I don't remember or understand. Just a strange concoction of symbols on 8–10 pages, two rows, the second one boasting amounts, and $5,470 for cancer drugs (in 5 days) would have to be a boast. What magnificent arrogance, almost awe-inspiring. I see why Dad sold the house without much fight.

I'm racing on decadrine or some horrid little white pill that ruins my appetite and then suspends the food that I do manage to get down in a dead flesh tank full of bile. Thank God I remembered to put the multizymes in my back pack. Snuck out of there for an Alvin Ailey show (Ailey who died 8 years ago of AIDS around the same time as my mom died of breast cancer).

District Storyville

Kickin'! Just color and phrenzy. Couldn't have lasted 15 minutes and yet I'm exhausted, bad lungs or no; Just color, Hyper color, Hyper movement, the sort that doesn't allow blinking.

Catatonic color, color in static green vase in the mind. Got you, gotcha while you weren't looking, while you weren't expecting to have to look. Just color and phrenzy. Girl pang and Boy tazz, much butt and much leg wiggle from the knee to the (?) shoe. Attitude on a Harlem scale. Bad lungs or no I could relate, I could redress, I could desire. Decadrine twitch or no, I could gas-up and renal-fail to this sort of ecstasy. Didn't try to understand. In my stupor this was as pleasant and crazy as marveling at Christmas wheels and aluminum trees on a snowy, sports-staticked afternoon in a New Jersey tenement. This was the TV show *Mom* got to watch. The after-church show before she even took off that round-feathered-sequined-plum-colored hat. This was the one that made my father move over or finally relinquish the couch, turn off his Army boot ritual and promise, for a full half hour not to fart, not even quiet ones (which should have made him stand up and study his warm underwear, I would think). This was color before color and black sass before even color TV could show it. This is the stuff relegated to postcards and an occasional video. This is peach stationery–sort of sentiments and balloon stickers and a couple of gumballs that got smashed across your words in the post. Blue-fucking-gumballs too, but such bright bright words. Warm up words because you can't get that hot in a letter. You'd have to be sneaking out of a hospital, still smelling like that foul lotion and hailing a cab because you don't have the stamina to walk one block to the bus or wait ten minutes for it, you don't have the lungs for that kind of wait. But now, on dance respirator you could (at least) watch all night. Just color dance : : green stuff on an odorless white tissue in a pastel room with a view.

I'll love this show tonight.

Shelter

I'll love this show tonight whether I remember it tomorrow or just that I saw it. 6 women in plain urban surplus-wear gave a rousing from the dead sort of thing. All over the floor, all over the beat. All over the unpredictable silence. All over the margins. All over the audience's desire (to applaud, to cherish, to misunderstand). All over the charity-thang. All over me.

Revelation

Part III. Gospel. Jesus dead but a comfort. Patron saint of comfort for the dying, the mourning. Jesus watching long naked black legs stretched out in agonies and ecstasies of dance or death. At first there were two, no eight. I don't remember, but wasn't there a triangle of brown people in brown shades, then men in mesh shirts. The spotlights in rings like the brown debris around Saturn. Prayers, a hymn of movements. I'm too angry for this sort of dance but maybe not for these bodies. I must love the long black leg in control, the tan sprite, the coy puck, the only man allowed a limpness—puckish act-up shooting out in angle to the gospel order. (am I rechoreographing? did I see this) This segment was not preachy and the gospel was not without ironies, jumping up in unexpected Caribbean moments. Then that big sunsetty yellow fan dance. The ladies with their straw scallops and their wooden stool sauntering—moseying—jumping for position. A long, hot song from them and then black men in tuxedos with the tip of dramatic mirrors add a burst of future Broadway, of whiteworld elegance, whiteworld ceremony. The sun gets pale, the sky lavender, the coolness translates out of heat and grief and God-challenge and into love and human arrangements.

5.1.93

I've been in the hospital 2 days now. Really just for peace of mind. Everything else I could have administered at home and today I will ask to do just that. I'm in a decadron (sp) fury over the slowness . . . Do I have to step up to the nurses' desk and drop before I get satisfaction. I don't know how badly I need this treatment or even how much I want it but I do want some fucking comfort at a scary time and it's not forthcoming. Beautiful room but the end of the hall, and maybe there are two other patients deader than I am. The nurse is a waste of pink-uniform with all the charm of a Stepford wife (that's mean, but she is chilly). Get me out of here before I go crazy.

ks in my lungs (still a bit of guess work on Lewis's part but). I'm trying to cough as loud and as long as I can. Abandoned down at the end of the hall in the room with the beautiful view. Remember when some old woman in an older volunteers uniform (gray-green with volunteer badges) came through to Carol-Merrill this so-so waterscape, to tell me the volunteers were responsible for filling up at least that one dead pink wall. κs in my lungs—nails on the coffin even in Lewis's book. He's talking in months ("as a last resort we can radiate your chest but it burns your esophagus!" Undoubtedly uncomfortable and it only buys a month). I'm moving like a worm now (not digesting as efficiently, not already cool in the dirt)—slow, slow, slow. I cough when I walk, when I bend over, when I do nothing but think about coughing. In the lungs where I can't see it but . . . The lesions are flaking away on my calves, my nails are overcoming the fungus, my desire to live is strong. And if I die I don't want it to be while I'm waiting for some tech to find me on his schedule. I hate speeding and waiting, waiting and writing on speed. I will nap to make up for the sleep I've lost waiting upright (often standing). Forget it.

Try to imagine a gargoyle sitting on your chest. 4:30 A.M. He's laughing and you can't make any noise. . . .

5.18.93

. . . I thought I was dying when Doug, dear Doug, brought me to Alta Bates last night but I may have been in better shape than I thought, at least better shape than Dr. Lewis thought—he *said* so. . . .

I haven't been able to talk much about suffering, not real, not immediate (only in fantasy and memory), so I won't start right here even if this and all those other open journals are just the place for it. How many? Can't include the seven or eight closed journals: a proud number—body of evidence to destroy or send to Eve—can't decide—don't have to decide until the will. But there exist six or seven pieces of journal that I call "open"—two big ones, two medium ones, three or four notebooks that add up to something, marginalia in composition books, other books, and a smattering of unbound stuff. I might even include sketches and pastels that relate to what I've written. Yes, some of these start in on that issue of misery, or seem flavored with it, as hard as I've tried to avoid it. They dwell on the dark hours spent staring at a candle trying to forget my pain, on the particulars of the pain itself, on the draining revelation that my medicines are killing me too.

Some suffering (A) might be useful; it might pay off in the

future. Suffering is an exercise and this journal is a gym (the YMCA, I think). So when I come back to a piece of suffering, a moment of it, again and again, and add to it a name or a fantasy or a good scene, I'm working muscles. If it develops into a story . . .

Suffering (B) abstractly, generally, and even in all that great, deep, minute detail—why that's okay. It's suffering specific pain specifically. Every day, day to day, a single pain remembered, singularly. Or pain to pain, each so clear it seems like a visual experience, particularly in the dark, particularly at night. And the collection of them act like rare jewelry in a box. I'm only hopeful that I will live to see the party where I can wear them strongly and honestly and not be driven home by the talk, never mind the pain itself.

Or suffering (C) a hybrid that I describe as the number of runs to the toilet, strung together on any sleepless, mindless night between the 1st and the 15th of May, 1993. Lying on the cool floor, head by the toilet trying to recreate a feeling of release, or the urgent sensations that made you run in the first place.

And if it happens: the bowels stir, the muscles twitch, ache, threaten knots. And the shockjuice mixes explosively with the acid already burning a new hole in your stomach. You gleefully, yes almost that, jump onto the stool and unload a half gallon of brown water, then you thank your body sincerely like you've only just met it. But this is once in 36–48 hours, or in 24–36 runs to the toilet. So I find it hard to go further, to wallow deeper, if that wasn't already deep enough.

> Pain in the abstract
> Pain in fiction
> Pain overseas . . .

> 36/36=1 run per hour=
> no sleep=delirium by the third night,
> death (by suicide or homicide) by the fourth night

> Gayle Winston @ Shanti 777 2273
> a therapist who makes housecalls
> Am I that sick?—that kind of sick?

Wish I lived in the hills. Not those hills. These big fat American hills! Near that white house—the Clairmont? the Fairmont?

—parked on that green lot with such stretch-limo nonchalance. Four tiers of real estate away, and I'm still in pretty good territory myself—1000 dollars a night *without* a fucking San Francisco skyline or the Golden Gate Bridge view. Black as I am I made it this far, and with any little ambition I can make those four tiers seem like decorator steps.

Just as soon as I get over this asthma. Doc says I'm fragile there, but surprisingly healthy everywhere else. What he sees and what I feel are two. I call up to him wanting to be thorough in my self-diagnosis. "I seem to remember"—I actually say that— I seem to remember having asthma as a kid, seven or eight. Or maybe I'm just struggling for continuity—I do that. Could have been just a long string of colds, a bronchitis, an adenoidal thing. And they say about HIV it haunts your childhood for little nightmares to give you.

But it's not just the asthma; it's also, and mostly, the crazy course it took. It started three years ago with a cough, congestion, a chest cold that came and went uninvited, but hardly worth bothering about, like crashers at our catered parties—who cared as long as they were dressed well and didn't eat too much? Then it was bronchitis, with a big ugly cough, like a big ugly coat, or like too many late nights in the windy, foggy woods. Then boom!— it's stomach pain, ulcers and KS in the bowel, and no enzymes left to make good shit, so I force out little pellets like a rabbit, or I fail to hold back a tepid cascade of fluid that was all the meager but vital stuff I could eat and drink that hour, or I wait in bed crosslegged against the sourwater, weak from depletion, thinking about the days of discomfort ahead, while something horrible from my childhood, like an REO Speedwagon album spins on in infinite-repeat mode.

5. 19. 93

Dear Eve,

I sit in front of my old Smith Corona with the opening lines of "Proud Blood" (another hammerhorror story) in head and on newsprint, in that swirl, that valley of swirls where revisions get revisions in the same nanosecond they were created (and I'm talking about *within* the nanosecond, not on the non-funky fringe, the suburban ridges, but inner-innersecond revisions, in immediate and constant danger of [4] deadly carjacking, [8] child abandonment, [9] teller-machine hold-ups, [15] police brutality, [17] child-on-child brutality, [20] rat bites & mouse droppings, [21] buildings collapsing, [34] bus killings, [35] bus births, [37] dull graffiti, [40] drive-by shootings, [45] deadly aggressive pan-handling, [49] lynchings [50] anti-abortion violence [67] sexual harrassment, [70] war [73] greedy, genocidal civic leadership— in danger of collapse, like an old star. There are no white sub- urbs or designer malls around the dusky coronas of black holes, not anymore—just shitloads of nothing, nada, nix—welcome to nowheresville). Indeed, I was already blasting away at those first lines, fast as thoughts could take shape, when I looked up into a mighty absence of D's and d's, and n's and 3's. My computer's gone, the typewriter's going and I'm relating this days later (wor- ried about tense) from a hospital bed with a wonderful, guiling view of the Clairmont hotel. [. . . .] Scars to the left of it, scars to the right, an eyesore above it like hell itself had been turvied or some sad, sore ghetto clinging to its ghettoness through the city's rigorous gentrification and scourge plans, had crawled out from God-knows-where to sleep even here at the summit of wealth and comfort. No, it didn't trickle up; it didn't even look up in fear, so petty and innocuous is poverty on the hill, so comedic, so topsy- turvy.

I'm in a hospital bed recovering (I'm told) from drug rav- aged intestines and joints and head and nerve endings. Hating my doctor, or at least blaming him at this point. Later I will pin my suffering on a strange new virus, an upscale, designer sort of bug with an expensive cure. CMV (I'm told) is rare but seems to be taking a toehold in more developed countries, and most particularly in those sanctuaries of wealth and whiteness within that never knew such distemper, so the victims wait months, years perhaps, harrassed by the persistence but perplexed by the subtleness of their problem, popping Tums or Tagamet until they can't swallow even these, and running to their doctors emaci- ated . . . Right now, I hate my doctor for my crazy symptoms. I imagine coming down off crack might feel better. And yet I've accumulated so much love and respect (maybe a little lust too) for this man that I will take his next prescription unquestioned—same way I used to have sex. I love the doctor for trying the outrageous. The outrageous is harder for me to question—something in my mix of pessimissism (that spelling must be wrong, but I'm a black man in a hospital bed without a dictionary. Let's try *pessimississippism* in partial celebration of the flag flying over the white limousine) and sense of wonder (also read: non-, dis-, or unbelief) call for the outrageous, the unorthodox and unacceptable—the same way I had sex, I guess.

Two nights ago I was going to die. I hadn't eaten—couldn't for days—and the nebulizer—I mean the NEBULIZER, that robot from "The Day The Earth Stood Still" which makes a klatuklatu-klatuklatuklatu noise as it pumps Albuterol (Proventil if you're rich) vapors into your lungs and blood and brain and toenails (—in just three puffs! but my instructions were to take the mist deeply and nonstop for fifteen minutes four times a day!) sends me into a delirium of flashbacks and prayer and pressure drops and diarrhea (much of it in my bed!) and dry heaves and waking nightmares and creeping skin and suicidal tendencies and unexpected euphoria and Poe-ish exponentials of hate and fear and fright, fantasy and fascination (I actually regret that I couldn't write at the time); I was shivering so and yet too hot for blankets or even clothes which I'd removed much before the start of the ordeal anticipating, I think, a ritual of healing for which I'd lit a half dozen blue candles placing them at even intervals around the room and rubbed my body with a fragrant blue tincture (of Jupiter, I believe)—"boy power and boy healing" according to the dark-haired no-nonsense woman at the occult store—and fanned the room with a smoulder of sage leaves and mhyrr (myrrh myhrr myrhr mhyrr murmur?) chunks. I regret not writing because I believe the product might have rivalled Poe's for depth of search if not breadth of wind, and it certainly would have raised more than a few neck hairs. If my life was not in immediate danger, which I believe it was, then surely my sanity was, in which case, I accept, my beliefs, or lack of them, cd be called into question, but hell—what's a body without sanity! Flannery O'Connor's lupus, the disease that crippled her but also drove her like a fast car, is related to contemporary immuno-deficient diseases like AIDS. I was pleased to stumble on this tidbit, pissed to remember how much more driven, how much quicker was her car.

Eve, I would take opium (not tincture of opium which they're giving me here at the hospital for diarrhea—black in a hospital with bed with a 300,000 dollar view of a white limousine and no dictionary) to drive that fast and that sporty, that loving and that armaggedon-bent. I wouldn't mind dying like her if I'd already lived with a conviction that strong.

So, like I was saying, I started to copy this story "Proud Blood" about a family of fundamentalist hurricane survivors invited to a morning news show to tell their inspirational story and I ran out of D's and m's and n's and 3's and who knows what else. I want to enroll in summer school to keep my insurance, to get money for a new computer, and perhaps to work more toward my degree. It's still important to keep busy, to keep an identity, and I am first a student, I think.

Love, Gary

Monday, May 24, 1993

The view from the inn, the beautiful Alta Bates Inn . . . Really not so bad if you're six hours into your next day and no one knows you're here so no one has visited you. This Bates Inn is a hospital. Top floor, top drawer but a hospital room just the same. To be sure, I lay listening to an old man (I hope he was old) agonize and groan for hours last night. What happened to him?

How did things get so ugly so fast? I have CMV in my gut, maybe in my eyes. I still have the KS all over and in my lungs where it seems to trigger my asthma. But this latest thing just seems like too much, too expensive, too burdensome. They (the doctors) are giving me Foscarnet (in heavy doses!) because it doesn't hurt my bone marrow but I have to take so much fluid with it I'm literally drowning. Bad bad, but even worse is the three months of treatment after the hospital. All this IV at home? And what—where is home? I don't have the strength to move. I don't have the strength to *move*. Depending on friends is a source of comfort and embarrassment. I'll have to get a nurse. I wish I had managed a lover. I should call John and ask him how he is coping. Trouble, trouble, trouble. You can't stay in the hospital forever, can you?

Stomach so full. Nothing moving. Body's not moving so why should food. Why should food even consider. I wonder if they have a room where I can walk off my food. And what is this crust? this scaling like a fish? Happened to my mom too. (Must be a side effect of hospitalization.) I remember one of my sisters rubbing lotion on my mother. Don't remember which part of her. Honestly I don't remember much about my mother's hospitalization. I came near the end, full of suitable concern and drama but not very well informed. I knew lotion couldn't save her. We couldn't save her. We didn't even know how to try. Can I save me? I feel like living today; I haven't felt quite this way for awhile. Gary Z. called. He made me feel good, but not this good. Hell, it could be simple drug euphoria—so far the side effects from these drugs have proved more predictible than the intended ones. I wish my asthma would lift so I could talk back. I lay there listening to Z-man like a piece of plantlife, afraid of a coughing fit or a full blown asthma attack should I speak. Talking is the biggest challenge now, my lungs the biggest obstacle. In the future I should try not to dissect myself . . . In the near future I'll have to worry about blindness. Blindness later. Talking now.

"I am not a man. I am not a beast. I am about as shapeless as the man in the moon." The hunchback of Notre Dame said it for both—all—of us! Could I feel any uglier? Could I feel any more wonder?

> Red gloves
> Cinnamon
>
> breathless white iv intern
> Dressed to the elbows
> she must use them
> to free the sterile sticks
>
> I hold very still
> Afraid to lose
> six inches of catheter
>
> Dup, dup, dup
> in cinnamon swirls

alcohol then iodine
dup, dup, dup
We breathe

5.24.93

I'm sure it's too soon to write about this incident, this weird piece of wires-crossed and cool inhumanness. After a warm, comforting morning with Kathy (with her koala bear on her stethescope and a lingering odor of sour milk) Stephany comes bursting in, hyper-punctual with drugs. She says hello while handing me a container shaped like an anti-freeze I'd seen, the white CAT-scan fluid. "Drink this."

White, lemon-tinged, it tastes already digested and gets nauseating after the second gulp. Nothing therapeutic, just a latex lump. Better to view your innards with. Now I have to wonder what they don't know from all the other x-rays, bronchoscopies, endoscopies, pokings, scrapings, sputum inductions and various unremembered (I'm amazed how spaced out I've been during most of this) invasions into my body. Seems I know they're trying to help me but the snowball effect tends to be cold and painfully circular. . . . And to this point I've seen nothing but.

I was whisked down to radiology full of CAT-scan fluid, afraid my bowels would open up, but also excited. How often do you get to stick your body through a great white donut, get your image rolled and sliced like sushi, then get your mess interpreted by the best doctors in the area? But, for all the rush, I got nothing. I sat uncomfortably in my wheelchair while the large black woman in charge made numerous calls to find a doctor's order for my scan. She had in front of her an order for a head and spine scan. She insisted that I was having headaches and offered me Tylenol. "If you aren't having headaches you wouldn't be here." I thought about how people had defined me over the last 10–12 days and I wasn't pleased; my ailment and hence a large part of my current identity were lost to me. Remedy seemed a crapshoot and a long shot because I couldn't prepare myself, couldn't ask the body to accept. So I refused, sometimes wholesale. They couldn't stick or poke or scan me in any way without my permission. I knew someone had fucked up this time too. I said I wasn't having headaches. She said my doctors thought so. I said they were wrong. She looked at me like I'd farted. I was afraid to touch my brow in exasperation for fear she'd . . .

Well, nothing continued to happen, not even the head scan. She wanted to wait for a return call from Dr. Lewis. Then it crossed her mind that I might be the wrong patient, still she couldn't be sure—and "errors in this profession" she explained to me "could be costly." Lewis never returned the call. After a half hour of bickering I offered what I thought was a practical solution. I told the nurse what was ailing me and where she should scan. "Why don't we just change that order?" Again she gave me her look. "We can't change anything without a doctor's consent. My god, what if I made a mistake?" "You're making a mistake now," I countered, but all irony was lost in a sudden flurry of activity. Someone from transportation called. Someone from transportation arrived moments later and I was whisked back to where I belonged.

I returned to the most profuse apologies (and a solemn offer of flagile and carafate . . .). Let me give Stephany a break— she's nice, attentive and very competent. She's no Kathy, but then Kathy is the occasional miracle that repositions all of us. No one had been so kind to me, so intuitive about my fears.

5.29.93

I'm not sure of the date: I'm not sure of anything. Eve reminded me of something I'd told a doctor whose question seemed too specific for any patient . . . I told him: "Doctor, I'm sorry, I'm not all here. Maybe it's a defense mechanism, I don't know, but part of me has gone away." It took him a moment to understand. I don't think I understand yet.

Eve experienced the same defensive removal. There's a need here to just leave. I'm going to get lost in the gray (silver) distances of the bay, Mt. Tam, a pine tree. . . .

Don't know if I'm allowed bar-BQ chips yet. I'm asking the esophagus, the first sphincter, the upper/lower pillows of ulcerated belly—fierce response before the question's even out! Chase it with cold water. Shut up! Sit there! Don't ask things for ten minutes! Twenty! Lunch lasts 2 hours, dinner 3, breakfast, usually bland and soft-spoken, falls unnoticed, unremembered through the most anxious (and gossipy) chambers, without a fart. 6 minutes. . . .

5.31.93

. . . Leslie was just here. Felt like she'd always been here (and she stayed a good long while). I'm feeling very loved. We talked about growing up. About Nick, about abuse, about me coming out of the AIDS closet. . . .

6-3-93

Chris Sugiyama's birthday. She came by the hospital with pictures of my new place, if and when I get out of the hospital. I had nothing to give her but I don't think she wanted anything. Especially not to play witness to the information that came down just as she was leaving. Remember that sputum sample I forced up about a week ago. That goddamn bit of yellow stuff that I personally forced up after many medical-types had tried and failed . . . Well, my sample cultured positive for some, for one, indicator of exposure to TB. I could be a carrier of TB! Sure, it's only one indicator and this TB skin test might be more accurate and might easily overrule the sputum (they're going to read it tomorrow, a little graph, a piece of hopscotch with three reddish dots in it. I'm watching them *so* carefully now!). But for now I'm a leper! The nurses closed my door and when they appear they have on masks and a new sense of urgency and I don't feel healthy or on the road to healthy anymore, and this is what Chris had to witness on her way out of here on her birthday!

I just asked for a glass of milk. Surreal from this cage. It's become a cage. I'm sure I'm not allowed out. I wouldn't want to go out. They're going to move me two rooms down, out of this choice room into a room that doesn't ventilate into the hospital, that spits it outside. (I have to contact everyone with this change, this trauma!) I don't feel it but what if I do have TB? How soon can I know? How soon can this gnawing be over? The staff will never treat me the same even if the indicator is false. Belinda (is that her name? — pretty Asian woman. Chris doesn't like her hair) seems to think there are no false indicators. They'll (doctors) will treat me for TB anyway and then culture and then treat and then culture . . . until the cultures are clear. They will begin with the assumption that the sputum is correct. What about the hopscotch graph? Please be negative. Please be obvious and countermanding. Please make them take that sign away.

The milk. The woman I originally asked to bring me the milk slipped outside my door on something wet and forgot to bring it. Milk and an accident outside the new leper's room. Revelations. Pure jinx. I apologized for jinxing her. Only 30% joking. What if I am infected? There goes *all* of Doug's plans. There goes all of that hope and legwork, all of that love.

And now it's starting to rain, the long rain, all weekend while friends are trying to move me to safety, trying to save me, but who can save me if TB is in my cards, who's got time to postpone while I get one more cure, one more reprieve. My right eye is blurry with an image like a light bulb or a skull, has been for weeks and I've felt sicker because of it, now I feel utterly spooked by it. What's it been asking, telling. Shut up! Just the facts: I'm closed up in a room that was, an hour ago, a haven, a womb, an incubator. Now it's a cage, a hole (hold), a big question mark for all who enter. All that rapport gone! All those friends and would-be mothers gone. I'm in doubt. I feel in-doubt. A lot of this is drug-talk I'm sure. . . .

— Nothing's smooth. Not the persistent gas, not this blockage in my right eye's vision, not this TB indication, not this rainy day, not this swelling in my legs and the related pain, discomfort, not this onslaught of pills and powders and infusions, not this sudden pariah handling, not this sleep deprivation, not this jittering asthma treatment, not the steroid which may be retaining the water, not the distant way I have to organize my life (even though that's the easiest since Doug is so intricately, almost lovingly involved — that doesn't belong in this list of bumps).

— Mark Bauer came over yesterday. He got my letter overnight, it seems, and was here in such loving, caring capacity . . . He held me before he left. I cried on his chest. He got into bed with me (mask and all) and let me cry on his chest. He's got a chest to cry on and I cried on it and I wonder now what might have been, even with HIV I wonder what might have been. . . .

6/3/93

. . . I'm afraid to talk to Eve. I fear that I've run out of things to say.

—On the other hand: these calls keep me alive, motivated, inspired, soothed, pampered, secure, wanted, needed, believed-in, smiling, happy. I love it when she says "lots of love to you" into my machine. I should answer immediately.

—No, I've never finished one of Eve's books and I don't see it happening in the near future. Academic talk could prove my loyalty. I've never offered this sort of talk. She's on my case too. It's time to get busy and I'm still putzing.

This cough scares me. Late night.

6.7.93

. . . I was in so much pain I thought I might ask Robert to let me cry on him. I don't think he's gay, but he's a nurse (or almost) and he's a big sturdy, caring sort of guy who might put a shoulder out. I was going to draw him in with last-days remorse and just lay my head on his shoulder or his chest or stomach and have a good cry. Steroids will do that too. Looking at Robert I think he would understand.

6.8.93

I have a blood clot where they made the incision for the Hickman line. It means a day or two of blood thinning with Heperin. Blood thinning! As if life itself isn't thin enough. I don't even know where the little bit of energy to write this entry comes from. My heart seems to pound so viciously from behind the Hickman mess. I eat and my heart pounds. I walk and it pounds. Right now I'm feeling good enough to leave here but it's chemicals. "Better living through chemicals" has been phrase of the week. I really love Doc Lewis. He comes into my quarantine without a mask and gets frank . . . He's part miracle, part walking mistake but beautiful for being so driven and on my behalf. He says he's really come to like me. That I'm the best patient he's ever had, etc. And I can see the sincerity in his tired, young, driven eyes. There's genuine affection between us, or is it a doc/pat thing that goes on all the time. I need to ask Rafael Campo. We need to collaborate on the doc/pat thing before I'm consumed.

—I'll need Eve's help buying hats. Can't wait to tell her tomorrow. . . .

6.14.93

Eating a white fleshy peach that Dina brought to me, and thinking about a letter I wrote to my dad. Trying not to be coerced (to one side) by the asthma inhalers I just used (one medicine for each of the nerves that might cause your lungs to spasm — each?). Trying not to be discouraged by the thick ankles and the yellowed scales of dead flesh and fungus that web heels and toes. Trying to stave off the need to sleep because I don't know for sure where life begins and ends—not like I need to—and I don't want to miss anything. Trying not to be excited, frightened, concerned, happy, thrilled (or any combination, variation, gradation of these) about my new apartment which I may see tomorrow. Will it be too small, or just right, or will I die and leave it all for naught? Still feel so fragile. Still feel so hopeful. Mitchell has been in and out of the hospital every day (excepting two months) for more than a year. I've puzzled that. He's been in a lot, feels fortunate to be alive. I still feel odd to think about death. Remembering Ton's crazy half hug half repulsion while she entreated me to get well, get well. I hope she doesn't think she can catch it, or was she afraid for my catheter?

—Henry Threadgill trying to make me forget my bloated leg. M. S. Contin, morphine. What kind of name it that for the most legendary of painkillers? M. S. Contin, is it a boat or a woman, a secretary? Why doesn't W. T. return my call and G. L. too. Gone at the mention of AIDS. I thought G. was a sympathizer/empathizer. Marveling at the strength and love and friendship of the bunch that moved me into a new apartment (sight unseen) and then brought over a Zachary's pizza to celebrate. "Try some Ammonia" that incredible tuba! Friends, think tuba—forget you G. and W. and McCall and my fair-weather friends. Dad?

So many things (that could blow up into deadly ones) to overcome.

"Long-ago Child/Fallen Star" 10:15 of balm? healing? escape? Tried to meditate to it in that room at 1492. Thought I would die with it on, thought I would disappear. Brought it to the hospital.

So old. This music is as old as I am. As old as I will ever be, and I'm not being a mystic or even spiritual. I picked this up when I first knew what music was. This informed me, and so maybe I expected magic. What I got was all I ever got, the first and oldest thing . . . a parent and that used to be comfort enough. Did this 10:15 ever metamorphose into a lover? God, I wanted the music to be my lover, so clean, so available, and on occasion it *must* have been because I slept *so* easily, the spooned sleep of lovers, the first-lovers sleep of me and Tony K. (not Roy even though he was real and T.K. was only what I wanted).

6.17.93

An old woman just came into my room (on my last day, during my last Foscarnet treatment at Alta Bates) to tell me about the rather awful impressionist print on the wall. So bad it detracts from the incredible view of the city that has sustained me for 3 weeks now. She explained that she picked up the print when she was in Europe (as she is wont to do) because she thought it would be relaxing. It's not. The composition slants nervously and the grain of the print suggests the cheapest of materials, the most minimal of thought and care. It all looks like bad Seurat. The old woman went on to detail the obvious—a woman is walking what looks like a goat, taking him to be tethered she thinks. "Many patients in this room," she says, "have found this very relaxing." I'm sure she meant the picture in toto and not just walking the goat. She moved along so quickly in her remarks that I wasn't sure I was supposed to speak but I finally commented that I liked the hedge and the grass because they remind me of home. They do not. Indeed the way they obscure the houses of the street beyond them has bothered me (but not to the point of real interest, perhaps until now as I analyze this whole strange event). She then said, without looking at me (I don't believe she ever looked at me, not even during her mundane greeting—the whole of it was so rote as to be completely unmemorable and worth writing about only as a trophy to the hollowness of so much of the effort, action, and concern, care—many, if not all, things medical! *and* so many of the caretakers. Hollow!)—she then said: "I thank you for sharing that with me," and then she left. I said thank you with a stinging sincerity, I hope. Were those last words of hers dismissal or did she intend to pile my observation on top of the others who'd said, collectively at least, the picture relaxed them? . . .

7.2.93

    . . . I'm in considerable pain after my operations. The Hickman was stuck, mired with blood clots I imagine, so Dr. Pearl had to open up the old incision and cut away at the tube from both ends. I hope he got it all out. One hole got local anesthesia, the other got none. Installing the passport or port-a-cath seemed like major surgery to me. I turned my head to look into an inch-long incision, hole really, that was the inside of my arm joint. Cut away, red, and invaded by a white tube. I actually felt some little bit of cutting and just knew things would go badly, but they didn't. Pearl talked an assistant (with a ridiculously long involved last name; he didn't offer his first) through so I knew what was happening at each step. After they pushed the tube up my arm (some part of which I felt) Pearl produced a hand-sized beige box that might have been a vibrator or a stun gun; it actually tracks the tube—green at the origin, yellow as the tube proceeds and red where it ends. The first try of this clever wand made a fool of my doctors: the tube ended in my neck. I had to turn my head toward the doctor (toward the gruesome site) as far as it would go, pressed into the pillow, then take a deep breath. Somewhere in the deep breath Pearl pulled the tube out of my neck. I'm assuming the next tunnel was the right one.

    Most memorable was the washing the nurses gave me on and around the sites of my operations. They used something cool and sudsy and implored me not to touch myself. They stretched out first one arm, laying it on a platform and later the other so that I formed a crucifix (and the crucified). The second arm got a thorough washing, even under the arm. It felt delightful. Even between the fingers. I asked if she had a nail brush, but she thought I meant a nail polish brush. Did Pearl note even one of my jokes? They were all actually for him. The nurses were incidental. I wanted him to know I was clever, not just sick.

    After the x-ray I met up with Chris Sugiyama. I was sent up to the infusion room where three men sat with little pleasure. They regarded my noise (or didn't regard it at all) with indifference. Lunch, or the remnants, sat in front of an old man in a recliner. He slept, or pretended to. Another old, emaciated man had hardly touched his tray. His young hippy-ish partner or care-taker tried to feed him, chicken, I would discover, but the skinny man looked like he hadn't eaten a piece of a good meal in months. Chris and I sat closest to the sleeping man. Oh, I'd been sent for a temporary port because my passport won't be healed up for use until Monday. (Shit.) With three holes already in me I was dread-ing the fourth. Was it dread, the shock of chocolate on an empty stomach (Chris's gift), mixed with anesthetic and trauma of even light surgery that made my heart do a funny dance? Or perhaps it was the inhalers on an empty stomach. I remember the horrors of Albuterol and Ensure. The nurse said I was probably hypogly-cemic and she brought orange juice and graham crackers. After Becky took my vitals and the numbers verified my continued health, I relaxed. It may have been the comfort of a nurse's at-tention. The strange heart dance stopped when her care started. Chris sat with concern. (She's been a gem of great effect today and I bought her lunch but can't really repay the kindnesses. My god, she offered to dust, to wash dishes! Together we took out the trash. She took most of it.) In Chris's truck—indeed from the time we left the infusion room I felt very fragile and held my arms still, unnatural. Oh, during the heart dance the nurse asked if I wanted lunch. Sure I did but I didn't want to inconve-nience Chris so I declined, but I did ask the old skinny man how it was. I got more than I wanted. He touched his sunken cheek and told me about the chicken and told us how he hadn't eaten in 3 months (weeks? I don't remember, but to look at him . . .) and how he vomited everything and would probably vomit this. He worked his mouth silently for a few seconds and I thought he might vomit right then. I asked him not to think about it while I finished the first pack of crackers. My urgent need to cram went unfazed but I felt the poignancy of the moment. It bounced off Chris perhaps. It bounced off my own fiction. This moment I still feel as fragile as that old man. I say "old" but he might have been forty inside that frail shell . . .

So here I am after one those gorgeous purple M. S. Contin pills. 30 mg.'s of warmth and rosy edges. The pain's not gone but it's not important either. . . .

8.25.93

Time is moving deliciously slow tonight (this morning. I've napped, watched some TV, ate a sample of all the leftovers in the fridge, wrote, took pills. [Boy, tense still scares me—the most basic tool of my trade and I can't be sure]). Nick (the GG park trick) called and I acted much asleep. He hung up . . .

How did I defile things so quickly, let such dopey scum into my house, drink its seed. Call the only two remaining tentacles of that sex monster that possessed, depressed, eviscerated all that was left of me before the physical breakdown that put me on this rollercoaster. Now I'm dodging the phone again, dodging the N-word, dodging the urge to kill myself in another man's misery (also his excitement, pleasure, satisfaction, revenge—and vicariously [or single-handedly, anyway,] mine). I should be glad to get a boner. I'm not dead down there but I'm afraid of the distance, the heights and depths . . . Dan, my VNH attendant, played with me until I got hard. Seemed innocent enough but I like Dan a little less, trust him a lot less.

8.27.93

. . . —The landlord has reprimanded apt #11 and I hope the weekend will be quieter.

—My digestion is up and down, so are my legs, like a balloon and I can't imagine/remember the old days.

—My lungs click like a clock when I breathe. Doesn't bother me unless I think about it, but, think about it, my every breath is numbered and I could count them if I wanted to. Sometimes I get violent with the breath so I can shake up that strange clock but it always returns to . . .

—Kate, PGE might be able to get me a new refrigerator. I do like the pink thing but let's be realistic.

9.1.93

. . . I feel like I'll never get organized. Perhaps I should be worried, interested, in things more organic. Disease, sex, walks in the park, the water in my legs. This apartment houses a tremendous amount of energy, a tremendous amount of emotion and yet its principal dweller is an invalid with little energy and two-dimensional emotion. I'm missing the sex . . .

Not the loathing, the humiliation. I'll no longer describe that as sex. Lie. I've had two encounters that I *know* as sex. Don't remember either very well. Just that the first man was speeding away and smelled, tasted dusty (and foul) like a speed freak. And the second man stayed much too long but satisfied all my oral needs, all my strange tastes. He didn't want to but eventually he had to give me his water because I wouldn't take my mouth away from his cock. He wanted to be sucked off twice and I obliged him, over a four–five hour period I obliged/indulged him. Promised him pleasure . . . Older man (did he say he was 38?), 60 possibly, but hard as a rock the whole time.

Andrew Young describes the night MLK was shot. Pictures of burning cities. The riots after the Rodney King verdict was my most exciting experience short of a sex encounter. . . .

9.19.93

. . . I want to write about KS. I haven't really written about what I look like now. I have a new skin. I have a new identity. They are not the same, but they do on occasion converge, even eclipse one another. First it's odd to be writing so specifically about things so specific when the largeness of my situation is what impresses me. I want to write large. Don't I want to write large? Can I get to the large through an analysis of these many small things? So I want to talk about KS. This film ("And the Band Played On") keeps using KS as the telltale sign, the first indication, the marker, the scarlet letter. I thought KS was rare, even among AIDS survivors.

The spots, the lesions, patches — they are so random (Even the name is slippery. What should I call these things, individually, I mean. One KS. Look, there's a KS. I have a KS on my hand, under my thumb). They refuse a common shape or texture or size and they sprout-spring-develop-appear unpredictably, time and location. (Backtrack: even the action of the disease is slippery.) Some are clustered; some are island-like. Some are small — just dots. Some are large, sprawling, giraffe-like.

I'm looking at my arm and I don't trust what I just said. There is a geometry to this, a poetry too. If I didn't know it was cancer and AIDS I'd say my arm — my right arm — is interesting, attractive.

The spots are grayish, purplish, a light eggplant, mauve —

a combination. (Yes, it's hard to write and watch movies at the same time.)

I'm that sick.

I could die that soon.

Why does my hope seem so long and so broad, a great big room full of possibilities, future light, and death is a broken bulb there in the center of it. A conundrum! Does the dark of the bulb matter to the room? Are there windows and is it daylight? Can a room full of this light rejuvenate the bulb, fix it, change it? How much light does it take to change a light bulb.

40 million people will have it by the end of the decade.

I'm in good company. I'm in plenty of company. I'm less afraid. It's a big big room and it's full of everybody's hope I'm sure.

Afterword

by Eve Kosofsky Sedgwick

Gary Cornell Fisher III (he dropped the middle name and roman numeral in his 20s) was born in Bristol, Pennsylvania, 19 June 1961, to Cornell and Virginia Fisher. The first child in an army family that relocated frequently, he lived in Phoenix, El Paso, Düsseldorf, Virginia, and North Carolina before graduating from Pine Forest Senior High School in Fayetteville, N.C., in 1979. He grew up with three younger sisters, Leslie, Luchina, and Crystal. The family never had much money, and Fisher supported himself—mainly by working in restaurants and, later, catering—from the age of 18, when he entered college at the University of North Carolina at Chapel Hill.

As an undergraduate at Chapel Hill from 1979–83, Fisher majored in English and took several creative writing classes. In his early career fantasies he was a multimedia superstar (or, briefly, a lawyer). While he remained passionate about a vast range of popular music, he seems in college to have come to a settled understanding of himself as a writer. From that time on, his notebooks show an incessant and profuse activity of drafting and redrafting stories and (especially in college) poems. Discovering Southern literature, especially the fiction of Faulkner and O'Connor, seems to have given him decisive access to the development of his own style.

It was also in college that Fisher began to describe himself as gay and sought out his first sexual experiences, all with men. Judging from his journals, the issue of being gay, in itself, seems not to have been an especially fraught one for him, though he did suffer in these years from unrequited erotic obsessions, discouragement, loneliness. Although he wasn't out in his daily life of classes, work, and straight friends, he danced avidly at nearby gay bars and felt comfortable there. He had his first experiences of anonymous sex in two men's rooms at the UNC library, and a relationship with a somewhat older man living nearby who remained an important figure for him throughout his life. His college years coincided with the beginning of the AIDS epidemic, and it was probably as a college undergraduate that he became infected with the virus.

In 1983 Fisher moved to San Francisco without any particular plan for the future; after a discouraging series of temporary jobs, in 1984 he entered the graduate program in English at Berkeley. Continuing to live in San Francisco and commute across the bay, he did well in graduate school, was admitted to the Ph.D. program after three semesters, became a gifted teacher of composition and of American and African-American literature, and developed strong friendships with a few other graduate students. Several of the faculty who taught him recognized their encounter with an unusual talent. But despite the support and flexibility of a few of his professors, the mesh between the graduate program and Fisher's real aptitudes and ambitions was strained. At the time of his death, ten years into the program, he was still enrolled but hadn't yet taken his orals and didn't have a realistic plan for doing so. His identity as a graduate student and teacher was important to him—and not only because of things like insurance, though increasingly for such reasons—but the reading and writing that meant most to him were hardly oriented toward that career path.

One aspect of being a graduate student that seems to have been transformative for Fisher was the access, in classes and especially among his friends, to a sustained and speculative conversation about race. His journals suggest that Fisher's willingness to be reflective about race had always before encountered a withering wall of static: the realization that, brought up surrounded by white families, attending predominantly white schools, and sharing values that he didn't readily associate with African-American culture, his own identification as black could hardly be a settled or simple thing. To see that unsettled and unsimple were constitutive conditions—rather than prohibitive ones—for thinking about race and racism was probably the single event that most galvanized the writing and perception of his last decade. Along with interpretive and artistic power, however, this development also opened him to new experiences of anger and pain.

The realization that he might have HIV infection came early to Fisher and deepened gradually. Over many years he shared the knowledge with very few of even his close friends, until less than a year before his death when an acute health breakdown necessitated a long, frightening hospitalization. At that point Doug Sebesta, the one nearby friend in whom he had confided and who had assumed virtually single-handed responsibility for his care, made him start letting other friends and family members know what was going on. Once the secrecy about his illness was over he acutely savored the company and care of many people who loved him. Leslie, the oldest of his sisters—"Bug" in his stories—moved to San Francisco to be near him, while his middle sister, Luchina, living and working in Chicago, would nonetheless manage to be with him for weeks at a time. Other cherished friends and caring associates on the scene included Eric Peterson, Chris Sugiyama, AnnMarie Caesman, Mark Bauer, Dina Alkassim, Gina Margillo, Nick Johnson, Brad Lewis, Thierry Jahan, and Don Northfelt. Despite the identification with death and the dead that he had been exploring in his journals, Fisher maintained from that point on an extraordinarily aggressive fight against the deterioration of his health. He demanded heroic measures from his doctors and himself through several crises; and until only a few days before his death it was clear that to die was the very last thing he had in mind. His father, from whom he had been estranged since his mother's death, was in touch with him toward the end and was about to visit when Gary Fisher died on 22 February 1994, in the company of his sister Luchina, at the age of 32.

In the spring of 1987, as a visiting professor at the University of California-Berkeley, I taught a graduate class in gay/lesbian literature—I think I called it "Across Genders, Across Sexualities"—in which Gary Fisher was a student. There were too many students enrolled to fit around the seminar table, and I can still picture Gary habitually sitting on the floor, almost always silent, just by the door. I noticed him early because he was the only African-American student in a class where issues of race were going to be fairly salient, and I worried that he would feel pressured to speak or to withdraw—scrutinized, resentful, or claimed, or just lonely. I also worried about the pressure of his actual or imagined judgments of the substance of these discussions—and how those might impinge on my teaching. (And I had assigned my students to keep journals for the semester, so I knew even a silent judgment would impinge eventually, for better or worse.)

Gary's demeanor during the first few weeks of class neither alarmed nor reassured me. His was a light and sweet, but oddly formidable presence: his station by the door and his silence seemed to make him a kind of allegory for the liminal. Several times he missed classes. I didn't know then, though now that I've been immersed in his papers I do, that his note-taking when he did attend classes was meticulous verging on mechanical, maybe in proportion to how alienated he felt from a given course: mercifully, his detailed record of this one sports some lapses and relaxations. It was an edgy seminar in general—I think it was the first explicitly gay one offered in that department—and because of his silence and his absences I couldn't be sure whether Gary was quite *in* it. I knew he had a beautiful smile, infrequently used in this setting, and a reserve whose specific gravity might not have been as palpable to himself as it was to those around him. Really I wasn't sure whether he was a serious student or a flake, or fake.

The seminar began in January, and things continued in this way until a day in March when Gary turned up for the first time at my office hours. I can't remember much about our conversation except the stark double twist of it. He handed me his class journal. And apologized for missing so many classes, but—he hadn't told this to other people, so would I please not do so either?—he was dealing with a lot of ill health; in fact with ARC.

It wasn't commonplace back then, at least it hadn't happened to me before, to hear from young people that the futures they look forward to are so modest in duration.

I think it was as soon as he left my office that I opened his journal and started to read the entries and, it turned out, stories ("Tawny" and "Red Cream Soda"), and notes, and photocopied collages gathered in it. If the news of grave illness in our students sat strangely, at least "back then," in any teacher's ear, the news of genius is something else. Now in front of me again are my dippy handwritten sentences from the bottom of the last page of the first half of Gary's journal, beginning, "Generally, what I most get from this journal is that you're a pretty sensational writer. Are you doing anything about this, intensively? Are you taking it seriously, in terms of your time & plans? There are so many sentences in here that are just right. The journal form seems not a bad one for you, but some of the dialogic/operatic effects of "Tawny" go, in *their* way, much beyond it . . . ."

It wasn't that Gary's journal was especially forgiving about the aspects of the seminar that had been worrying me. He'd written, for instance, "2/2 Not thrilled by the class discussion Friday. Race is up front in both stories and yet . . . and yet race like homosexuality has sort of a hyperpresence in the graduate student mind and needn't be talked about. [. . .] Did we even get close to the line of absence that not mentioning it creates? I couldn't find any shape, any form of where it might have been, not even a discussion on victim/victimizer or martyrdom; it just wasn't there, and I didn't say anything because I thought this was charity, and talking to it would have been as crude as flinging coins back at a sidewalk philanthropist."

I identified with, as I was envious of, the excitement of realizing one could put a sting like that in a paragraph's tail—which didn't, either, soothe the hurt of being at the other end of it. Of course, I wasn't sure what response I was supposed to make, or had it in me to, to the claims of either real vocation or encroaching fatality (let alone both). I could tell that Gary was shy—at least with me—and I, shy with almost anyone, was only more so with him.

It didn't help a bit that I was already an old hand at the same strategy he'd adopted for dealing with the rage that concomited with his talent and identity. He put the rage naked on paper, then half-shielded the paper from sight with the smoke screen of a deprecating or even puppyishly ingratiating persona. I recognized the strategy too well—and knew the dimensions of his luminous sweetness too little—to find his rather beatific manner at all relaxing in those days.

As for his writing talent, I understood it through the image of, say, two creative people let loose in an art studio, only one of whom, maybe not even the one more visibly gifted, would find the place more absorbing on the fifth day or the fiftieth than on the first. To say that someone has found an art: doesn't it mean that they have learned, not just to solve problems in the medium, but to formulate new problems in it—whether soluble or not—that would be worth solving? This ability, this generative autotelic habit, was so unmistakably established in Gary's writing that the leaps that didn't work were almost more thrillingly instructive than the ones that did. The wild formal surmise behind even a rather unrealized story like "Second Virginity" gives one a taste of being Flaubert, or Proust, or the moviemaking little boys in "Games." "What if I could just — ?" is the formal question the author seems, all but rejoicing, always to blurt out; in this way readers experience how powerful new desires are born and shared.

And because this deepest kind of talent resides in the learning process more than in the writing process of a given moment, Gary's mutilated career offers no such consoling possibility as that he had already accomplished the best writing he would be capable of. It is certain that he had not.

After that seminar was over, I returned to the East Coast and it got harder to stay in touch with Gary. We'd had some nice, feather-light and feather-soft talks in Berkeley, but neither in conversation nor writing had we developed much of an idiom for friendship. And since there was nothing remotely apprentice-like about Gary's writing, I couldn't tender teacherly observations on the bottoms of those stories forever. (For that matter, Gary quickly reverted to his maddening habit of promising for months to put stories in the mail *that very day*.) I had it in mind—and I think he did too—to make sure we wouldn't lose each other. But I'm not sure we could have avoided it without the wonderful fortune of having, in Eric Peterson, a mutual friend so affectionate and patient that the thread of contact, however finely spun, was never irremediably distant from our fingers.

Even so, it wasn't until after I was diagnosed with breast cancer in 1991 that we began to get real. A note from Gary a few months later, when I was in the middle of chemotherapy:

Can't figure out exactly why I haven't called; unless it's fear of your pain, fear of my own and fear that I'll fumble-up in talking about it. I've been able to write about it with real depth of feeling, I think. (The last sentence is no indication of this.) So, I'll exercise some pain/fear on paper here and then I'll be able to call. Make sense?

x

There it is, exorcised. You didn't think I really wanted to waste a nice card on all that, did you? I've met a nice guy — Sherman's his name and he reads. He describes himself this way so I'll respect it now. He works at a bookstore because he can read vast amounts at a discount. He has a beard and a dab of hair beneath his lip (what's that called?), all of it dark. This is all I know about him — though, surprisingly, we met at a sex club. I'm anticipating something physical after we've accomplished all three meals (breakfast on Friday) and talked about dying-too-soon. I'm not sure but I suspect he's positive too. He talks about various illnesses, depressions, lethargies and odd humours with too much ease. And I suspect a great many men at the sex clubs. . . .

I'm living with two straight people — I mean really straight. I wonder if they'd recognize human anatomy when they see two men fucking. They know I'm gay, but I think they deal on a conceptual level — so of course I've said nothing about my condition. I've said nothing to Eric as well though he might suspect. Sympathy is difficult, sorrow impossible to handle right now so I don't tell Eric though he's probably my dearest friend. I might regret this later; there must be a richness in battling an illness with friends (seems so obvious I must be looking at it wrong, must have misspelled something, must have). I'm saving Eric, I guess, for when I need . . . I'm still too healthy. . . .

I had a small battle with ks recently. The kimo made me ill, even at such low dosages. I can't imagine. . . . I guess I need to talk to you.

—Fucking flags everywhere!

—I have a batch of stories for you.

—Haven't started your book but I *love* having it . . . want to wallow in it.

> Absolute love
>
> . . . G

How abruptly this note restructured, for me, the space of Gary's and my relationship. I'd been aware of not knowing much about his life, but assumed it was because, simply, I didn't *know* him—I'd assumed there were circles of companionship and intimacy far interior to the loose, light holding of our attenuated contact. It was true Gary had said to me, four years earlier, that he wasn't telling people about his illness. But I'd assumed, especially as time went on, that he meant authority figures and strangers, not friends. I'd assumed that being an active, out gay man in San Francisco meant belonging to a community of people dealing with HIV.[1] And I'd assumed, the several times Eric had set up dates for the three of us and Gary had missed them because of measles, upset stomach, or fatigue—and Eric never seemed surprised—I'd certainly assumed Eric was interpreting them through the same grid of HIV-related anxiety that I was.

In a way, then, I was learning that I was much closer to Gary than I'd thought. But by the same stroke I was learning that to be close to Gary must be a strange, perhaps a fractured or fracturing thing. Waiting behind the revelation that he hadn't told Eric about his illness was the realization that his closest friend must know him as someone who just naturally didn't show up half the time; who naturally dropped out of one's life for long periods. Aspects of Gary that I had before imagined in terms of a more or less concentric, consolidating selfhood and privacy—his passion as a writer, his sexual life, his complex understanding of racism, for example, along with his friendships and his relation to illness—I now saw might coexist as far sharper, less intergrated shards of personality, history, and desire.

Gary and I saw each other next in December of 1991. We revelled in a long exchange of war stories at a bar in the Castro, and I finally felt we were finding our feet with each other, and some ground to put them on. At least, the particular awe or shyness that can separate the healthy from the ill no longer kept us apart.

I remember describing to Gary what I'd experienced as the overwhelming trauma of half a year of chemotherapy-induced baldness—a narcissistic insult, of no medical significance whatever, that had so completely flooded my psychic defenses that, for the whole duration of the treatment, almost every hour of consciousness had remained an exhausting task.

Gary said, yes, this was what it felt like for him to have KS lesions on his arms. Nobody else ever saw them: he always wore long-sleeved shirts. But alone, he said, in his apartment, he would spend hours, sometimes whole days of months, paralyzed in front of his mirror, incredulous, unable—also unable to stop trying—to constitute there a recognizable self. Impaled by the stigma.

After Gary's death I recounted this conversation to one of his sisters. She said: I think that's how Gary experienced being black, too.

> Dear Sir, I am a fit, intelligent black slave with a keen desire to please. I'm 5'8", 145 lbs, 28 years old, strong, trim, naturally muscular, yet small enough to pose no real threat to you, which I expect you will demonstrate right away. I enjoy being overpowered by a big horny man, made to submit to all of his desires (though I'd be willing to do so without force). I'm a good cocksucker, well-trained by two overendowed masters, and find tremendous contentment and satisfaction in having my mouth and throat full of cock, like a child. I would gladly suck your cock all night long or anytime and anywhere you see fit.

"What is this fantasy that cuts across all of me, racial, intellectual, moral, spiritual, sexual . . . ?" Gary asked his journal in 1987, and continued—"I hope Dale is rougher than he seems and calls me boy and etc." A lot of things were happening at once for Gary Fisher in the few years after he moved to San Francisco, and there's no easy way of tracing the feedback loops by which the transformations of his sexual practice, political consciousness, literary vocation, theoretical interests, and relation to illness and death were making one another happen. What seems clear is that exposure to the varied sexual vernaculars of San Francisco catalyzed for him a project of sexual representation that—visionary, mundane, ungraceful, and sublime—was frightening even to him in its ambition and intensity. It was a project, not in the first place of *representing sex*, but of stretching every boundary of *what sex can represent*.

"Representation" is no straightforward matter, especially in the vicinity of sex; witness the starkness of Gary's metamorphoses between the supersubtle exegete of a hermeneutic of antiracist suspicion, on the one hand, and on the other—in the sexualized space of Buena Vista Park in the small hours—the black man whose pleasure in offering service is incomplete unless he can induce some white man to call him "nigger" and seem to mean it. The sexuality in these journals is prismatic, analytic. Under the pressure of a stringent demand of *sexual* relevance, *sexual* excitation or pleasure, it bends and differentiates the elements of its culture.

In doing so, it is partly responding to a long, speculative tradition of sadomasochistic exploration in which the representational limits of sexuality are never presumed, always experimental. Over the past fifteen years, there has been a need—and an opportunity—to defend S/M as a sexual minority movement within the context of American intolerance of all sexual variety. Both mainstream and feminist anti-S/M propaganda have refused to perceive any complexity at all in what they see as the completely continuous relation between S/M violence and violence *tout court*. This has resulted, reactively, in a public self-presentation of S/M that emphasizes the *dis*linkages between the social realities of power and violence, on the one hand, and the sexualized representation of power and violence, on the other; that emphasizes, too, the crisp way in which S/M play can explicitate and therefore manage issues of power, consent, and safety that often remain dangerously obscured in more conventional sexual relations.

It is true that these hygienic dislinkages are among the representational possibilities put into play by sadomasochism. For many people, they may be the most important, exciting, or enabling ones, and their articulation is by now a staple of what might be called "official" S/M culture. What remains underarticulated outside of fiction, though, is the richness of experimental and experiential meaning in these scenes when they are understood as neither simply continuous with, nor simply dislinked from the relations and histories that surround and embed them. Which also means that, as in Gary Fisher's stories and journals, the ontologies of power, consent, and safety may be anything but simplified in the representational field of such a sexuality. If not simplified, however, the issues are treated in another way: they are powerfully dramatized, embodied, and borne witness to.

For instance, there is a sturdy anecdotal tradition that many people who do S/M are survivors of sexual trauma or abuse. The anti-S/M movement has a victim-discrediting use for this lore: it makes sense to them that people too abject or damaged to stay out of harmful situations would seek out abusive treatment in this realm as well. In their view, the mimetic aspect of S/M guarantees that no new meanings, feelings, or selves may ever emerge through its practice. One can view both trauma and mimesis less rigidly, though; there are people—Gary Fisher was one—for whom the only way out is through. Suppose, as Gary seems to suppose, the sadomasochistic scene to occur on a performative axis that extends from political theater to religious ritual; an axis that spans, as well, the scenes of psychotherapy and other dramaturgically abreactive healing traditions. According to this understanding, the S/M scene might offer a self-propelled, demotic way—independent of experts and institutions—to perform some of the representational functions that, for instance, in *Trauma and Recovery* Judith Lewis Herman assigns to the trauma therapist: the detailed, phenomenologically rich reconstruction of the fragments of traumatic memory; claiming and exercise of the power to reexperience and transform that memory, and to take control of the time and rhythm of entering, exploring, and leaving the space of it; and having its power, and one's experience of it, acknowledged and witnessed by others.[2] (I don't offer this comparison with the anaphrodisiac intent of making sex sound as respectable as therapy; both are potent, body-implicating, and time-bending representational projects.)

The fierce beam of history that propelled Gary Fisher's sexual imagination was evidently less that of individual trauma than of a more collective violence and loss. All the more was it a trauma that he couldn't otherwise make present to himself, a violence that his culture offered him the most impoverished means for realizing and hence for mourning. Like others gone before him, he forged a concrete, robust bodily desire in the image of historical dispossession, humiliation, compulsion, and denegation, among other things. Probably any sexuality is a matter of sorting, displacing, reassigning singleness or plurality, literality or figurativeness to a very limited number of sites and signifiers. Tenderness (here brief, contingent, illuminating); a small repertoire of organs, orifices, and bodily products; holding, guiding, forcing; "your" pleasure and "my," different and often nonsynchronous, pleasure; infinite specificities of flavor, shape, and smell; the galvanized, the paralyzed; the hungry, impartial, desiring regard in which ugliness may be held as intimately as beauty, and age as youth: these are among the elements here splayed through the crystal of anonymity. And while for another person, or at another place or time, it might have been true that fatality played no very necessary role among these elements of a sexuality, for this person at this time and place it too was central, the need to give a face—or many faces—to a fate.

Some other contexts for reading *Gary in Your Pocket:*

Joseph Beam, ed., *In the Life: A Black Gay Anthology* (Boston: Alyson, 1986).

Melvin Dixon, *Vanishing Rooms* (New York: Dutton, 1991).

Essex Hemphill, *Ceremonies* (New York: Plume, 1992).

Essex Hemphill, ed., *Brother to Brother* (Boston: Alyson, 1991).

Marie Howe and Michael Klein, eds., *In the Company of My Solitude: American Writing from the AIDS Pandemic* (New York: Persea, 1995).

Isaac Julien, *Looking for Langston.*

Walt Odets, *In the Shadow of the Epidemic: Being HIV-Negative in the Age of AIDS* (Durham, N.C.: Duke University Press, 1995).

John Rechy, *The Sexual Outlaw: A Documentary* (New York: Grove Press, 1977).

Marlon Riggs, *Tongues Untied.*

Amy Scholder and Ira Silverberg, eds., *High Risk: an Anthology of Forbidden Writings* (New York: Plume, 1991).

Darieck Scott, "Jungle Fever? Black Gay Identity Politics,

White Dick, and the Utopian Bedroom," *GLQ* 1:3 (1994), pp. 299–321.

Mark Thompson, ed., *Leatherfolk: Radical Sex, People, Politics, and Practice* (Boston: Alyson, 1991).

David Wojnarowicz, *Memories that Smell Like Gasoline* (San Francisco: Artspace Books, 1992).

In April of 1993, Gary wrote me, "I want to compile my book this spring (this fucking month!). Would you, could you, might you write an introduction—any peculiarly related thing you want to say—oh, and no rush, I can attach it later. I just really want to be attached to you on this."

Of course I said yes—not because I thought mine would be the perfect aegis for his stories to appear under; not for that matter because I thought they needed any aegis but their own—but because I wanted to do anything that would encourage Gary to get them published and out there and read, ideally during his life.

I was always underestimating the diffidence that kept Gary from circulating his work, though, and after his health gave out that spring and summer, it slowly came to be understood between us that the book would probably be posthumous; that I would take responsibility for getting it published; that it might include journals, notebooks, even letters as well as stories. We both liked the idea of offering people who hadn't known him or his writing, as well as the few who had, a sort of "portable Gary"—hence the title we agreed on. We also agreed on the cover art.

Since Gary's death, I along with other people have had a lot of second thoughts about calling the book *Gary in Your Pocket*. After much consultation, I even chose an alternate title, *Soul Releasing*, from one of his poems. As one of the manuscript's readers put it, *Gary in Your Pocket* risks sounding "in some ways trivializing." In metaphor, it seems to make Gary small, appropriable; and it may be all too resonant in the context of the posthumous publication of an African American writer, mediated by an older, Euro-American editor and friend, from the press of a mostly white, Southern university. Gary and I were both very conscious of a history of white patronage and patronization of African American writers, the tonalities of which neither of us had any wish to reproduce. Sexuality was a place where Gary was interested in dramatizing the historical violences and expropriations of racism; friendship, authorship, and publication, by contrast, were not.

Yet, whether well- or ill-advisedly, *Gary in Your Pocket* has insisted on remaining the title of this volume. Its Whitmanian intimacy has, perhaps unexpectedly, come to feel more powerful rather than more dubious since Gary's death. The indignity, the promiscuity of book publication—of an individual spirit held often mute in a closed box that anyone can buy and put in their pocket—answers eerily to the indignity of death; but also to the survivors' yearning for a potent, condensed, sometimes cryptic form of access to the person who would otherwise be lost. But, as in Whitman, it is also publication that allows the dead to continue to resist, differ, and turn away from the living.

> Or if you will, thrusting me beneath your clothing,
> Where I may feel the throbs of your heart or rest upon
>   your hip,
> Carry me when you go forth over land or sea;
> For thus merely touching you is enough, is best,
> And thus touching you would I silently sleep and be
>   carried eternally.

> But these leaves conning you con at peril,
> For these leaves and me you will not understand,
> They will elude you at first and still more afterward, I will
>   certainly elude you,
> Even while you should think you had unquestionably
>   caught me, behold!
> Already you see I have escaped from you.[3]

Gary often sent me revisions of his stories, though he never expressed confidence that his revisions should stand; he asked me to choose among the versions, and I have done so here. The closest thing I could find to Gary's own notion of a canon is the envelope of his stories addressed (but never sent) to Marilyn Hacker at the *Kenyon Review* a few weeks before he died. The stories in that packet were "After the Box," "Mo-day," "Corner-store," "Tawny," "Arabesque," and "Red Cream Soda," and the versions of them in this volume are the ones he chose. "Picaro" may have been unfinished, but the version of it here is the one that was on Gary's computer; "Several Lies about Mom" was clearly unfinished—there were overlapping drafts of the last section on the computer—so I've edited it substantively. The only story I had to assemble from parts of different versions was "Games," for which there was no complete recent version—it is the most palimpsestic of these stories. The poems presented few textual problems.

The other material in this volume was chosen from the thousands of pages of notebooks and journals that Gary kept in longhand from high school on. Reading through this material, I felt grateful to whoever taught him the handsome, legible cursive that fills the eleven massive, consecutively dated bound volumes, the couple of dozen nonconsecutive bound or spiral notebooks, the hundreds of loose pages. I wanted to assemble a characteristic, followable selection of this writing within a reasonable compass; necessarily, the editorial hand here has been a good deal more active. In particular, while gaps within a paragraph are marked with bracketed ellipses, I have also freely omitted any amount of material that occurs between paragraphs marked here with introductory dashes or ellipses. I've also changed all the names that occur in a sexual context. There are dozens of them, and virtually all are of people unknown to me; I'm not struck with the desirability of maintaining a precise documentary dossier on anyone's sexual activity, and in particular, can't know which of the people named here would experience such interpellation as extremely intrusive. No doubt some would not, but surely many would.

The people I want to thank for help in conceptualizing and preparing the book include all of Gary's intimates named above, and especially Doug Sebesta, the executor of his will, who made sure I had access to every page of his writing; Don Belton; Michele Wallace; Randall Kenan; Rafael Campo; Gayle Rubin; Ken Wissoker; Denise Fulbrook; and Katie Kent, also a friend of Gary's, who not only collated versions of the stories and painstakingly transcribed most of the journal and notebook material, but helped me think about useful ways of framing it all.

It's no surprise that there is vastly more rich stuff in Gary's notebooks than I've had room to present in this volume. Each journal entry included here has had to stand for many, many re-

lated ones; unfinished narratives of Kitchie, Tawny, and Bug fill
many manuscript pages; most haunting are the laundry lists of
genius:

—Tea set/shadow
Matty and Suzy rag dolls
A loose weave
An ancient Indian breeze
   blowing off the desert
Note use of hot/cold wet/dry
The asphalt hot right through her tennies
A Batman-and-Robin attack
small sparkling world
Holding a moth
Bippy, Cheshire cat
—incompetent teacher

things trapped and stirring,
and it scared him to know
it was his
—Birds twirling in the sand

Soda cracker

She got rid of the bad stuff,
but then the good stuff went bad

   —They were piss ants. Kitchie had taught Bug and Luchina to call them baby sweet ants, but no one was going
to change what they stank like when you smashed them or
when a whole line of them bit up your leg.

—Bertha
pull out the stops
kick out the jams

   —At night sometimes when the house stood still between air-conditionings, he could hear his own heart against
the bed. It would well up and ring in his pillow like some

—"She don't never get mad, do she?" bus
"When God goes shopping" United Presbyterian Church
"Cyclops titties"

Asked this woman [. . .] what she was looking at, woman said calmly—coquettishly "you." Friend says "busted," woman says "don't you like to be looked at?"

Friend says "busted!" (embarrassed)

(Ass, fuck) After she leaves trying to make her out to be crazy "eyes rolling all funny."

I need to get the overt religiosity out of "RC Soda." There's no real ground for it—broad use of a stale archetype. I can make it subtler and better.

—Just watched a man flicking the ash off his cigarette. It really occupied him. He flicked, turned the cig in his fingers, flicked again, turned 2 more turns as if he would clean the cigarette thoroughly of needless ash. He was sculpting the head of it. His mouth worked diligently at something which he flicked. He looked content if a little nervous (on the bus)

. . . . Victor on spit:

My dad (TK look-alike) used to spit (before he left us). I spit now, but not very well. I get it on my shoe or my collar or my pants leg but hardly ever in a uniform glot on the sidewalk. I spit on my mother's dress once, but she understood and just took her talk away for awhile. I spit on a girl's dress walking by it in a hurry, and into the wind so it was hardly my fault.

Spit was a novelty to me, nasty, older than my britches. It was my contribution to the great city outdoors, like a dog's shit or gum wrappers and cigarette butts, my mark, moments of grammar (in a situation/text) on a thing I hardly understood.

—Waking up, it's funny. I feel like I left that world of my dreams still going on, like a movie I'd felt uncomfortable with and left. It didn't stop when I left it and I immediately thought—I can't go back to sleep yet or I'll end up right back in this dream. Are there different levels, sliding in and out? A dream dimension?

The few times when I saw Gary delirious in the hospital, the things he said wouldn't make much sense, but no fever or confusion could burn out the princeliness of that sentence structure. Once when he wanted us to leave the room so he could (as he fantasied) get up and walk to the bathroom in his short hospital gown, he murmured, "I am about to ask you to perform a task as delicate in conception as it is arduous in execution." Nor did he cease conferring the beatific smile. The hours we spent in this fragmentary fellowship, holding and being held, always reminded me of the gentle, imperious deathbed dictations of Henry James, sometimes in the person of Napoleon, sometimes in his own:

> You can believe anything of the Queen of Naples or of the Princess Caroline Murat. There have been great families of tricksters and conjurors; so why not this one, and so pleasant withal? Our admirable father keeps up the pitch. He is the dearest of men. I should have liked above all things seeing our sister pulling her head through the crown . . . .

> Invoke more than one kind presence, several could help, and many would—but it is all better too much left than too much done. I never dreamed of such duties as laid upon me. This sore throaty condition is the last I ever invoked for the purpose.[4]

Perseveration of a voice worn to the very warp and woof of its syntax: experiencing this, I recognized the good sense of the psychoanalyst Christopher Bollas, when he decided in his writing to render "id" as *idiom,* and to describe a self as "a kind of 'spirit' of place, unique to the strange aesthetic of an idiom":[5]

> The idiom that gives form to any human character is not a latent content of meaning but an aesthetic in personality, seeking not to print out unconscious meaning but to discover objects that conjugate into meaning-laden experience. (pp. 64–65)

> Being a character, then, means bringing along with one's articulating idiom those inner presences—or spirits—that we all contain, now and then transferring them to a receptive place in the other. . . . [I]n the ordinary to-and-fro of life, as

we pass back and forth the spirits of life, we hardly know quite whom we are holding for the other, however briefly, although we will know that we are being inhabited. (p. 62)

Although it is difficult to witness how one person "moves through" the other, like a ghost moving through the internal objects in the room of the other's mind, we know it is of profound significance, even though exceptionally difficult to describe. (p. 56)

If an idiom is like a syntax—at least, if it is for some people—then to be inhabited like this will be familiar to those who sometimes fall asleep reading, and then dream their own mental semantics into the sentence structure of the author. The time of immersion in this volume has brought me many such experiences. Almost every night of it I have dreamed, not *of* Gary, but *as* him—have moved through one and another world clothed in the restless, elastic skin of his beautiful idiom. I don't know whether this has been more a way of mourning or of failing to mourn; of growing steeped in, or of refusing the news of his death. One thing I couldn't doubt: for all its imposing reserve and however truncated, Gary's is an idiom that longs to traverse and be held in the minds of many people who never knew him in another form.

August 1994

Notes

1. I think I was underestimating the redoubled silencing effect that the stigma of HIV may have for, specifically, African-American men. Marlon Riggs discussed this eloquently in "Letter to the Dead" (*Thing*, Fall 1992, pp. 40–44).
2. Judith Lewis Herman, M.D., *Trauma and Recovery* (New York: Basic Books, 1992).
3. Walt Whitman, "Whoever You Are Holding Me Now in Hand," *Leaves of Grass*, ed. Sculley Bradley and Harold W. Blodgett (New York: Norton, 1973), p. 116.
4. Leon Edel, ed., *Henry James Letters* (Cambridge, Mass.: Harvard Univ. Press [Belknap Press], 1984), 4 vols., 4:811–12.
5. Christopher Bollas, *Being a Character: Psychoanalysis and Self Experience* (New York: Hill and Wang, 1992).

Eve Kosofsky Sedgwick is Newman Ivey White Professor of
English at Duke University. She is the author of *Fat Art, Thin
Art* (Duke, 1994), *Tendencies* (Duke, 1993), *Epistemology of
the Closet*, and other books.

Don Belton is the editor of *Speak My Name: Black Men on
Masculinity and the American Dream* and author of *Almost
Midnight*. A former reporter for *Newsweek*, he has taught at
Macalester College and the University of Michigan,
Ann Arbor.

Library of Congress Cataloging-in-Publication Data
Fisher, Gary, 1962?–1994.
Gary in your pocket : stories and notebooks of Gary Fisher /
edited with an afterword by Eve Kosofsky Sedgwick ; intro.
by Don Belton.
(Series Q)
ISBN: 0-8223-1804-0 (cl: alk paper). — ISBN 0-8223-1799-0
(pa: alk. paper)
1. Fisher, Gary, 1962?–1994—Notebooks, sketchbooks, etc.
2. AIDS (Disease)—Patients—Literary collections.   3. Gay
men—United States—Literary collections.   4. Afro-
American gays—Literary collections.   I. Sedgwick, Eve
Kosofsky.   II. Title.   III. Series.
PS3556.I8135A6   1996
818'.5409—dc20   96-80 CIP